The
GOLDEN HOUSE

BY SALMAN RUSHDIE

FICTION

Grimus

Midnight's Children

Shame

The Satanic Verses

Haroun and the Sea of Stories

East, West

The Moor's Last Sigh

The Ground Beneath Her Feet

Fury

Shalimar the Clown

The Enchantress of Florence

Luka and the Fire of Life

Two Years Eight Months and Twenty-Eight Nights

The Golden House

NONFICTION

Joseph Anton: A Memoir

The Jaguar Smile: A Nicaraguan Journey

Imaginary Homelands: Essays and Criticism 1981–1991

Step Across This Line: Collected Nonfiction 1992–2002

PLAYS

Haroun and the Sea of Stories (with Tim Supple and David Tushingham)

Midnight's Children (with Tim Supple and Simon Reade)

SCREENPLAY

Midnight's Children

ANTHOLOGIES

Mirrorwork: 50 Years of Indian Writing, 1947–1997 (co-editor)

Best American Short Stories 2008 (co-editor)

The GOLDEN HOUSE

A NOVEL

SALMAN RUSHDIE

PENGUIN
HAMISH
HAMILTON
An imprint of Penguin Random House

HAMISH HAMILTON

USA | Canada | UK | Ireland | Australia
New Zealand | India | South Africa | China

Hamish Hamilton is part of the Penguin Random House group of companies
whose addresses can be found at global.penguinrandomhouse.com

Published by Penguin Random House India Pvt. Ltd
7th Floor, Infinity Tower C, DLF Cyber City,
Gurgaon 122 002, Haryana, India

Penguin
Random House
India

First published in the United Kingdom by Jonathan Cape 2017
Published in India in Hamish Hamilton by Penguin Random House India 2017

10 9 8 7 6 5 4 3 2 1

ISBN 9780670090297

For sale in the Indian Subcontinent only

Book design by Caroline Cunningham

Printed at Thomson Press India Ltd, New Delhi

www.penguin.co.in

To Alba and Francesco Clemente

through whose friendship and hospitality

I came to know the Gardens

Give me a copper penny and I'll tell you a golden story.

– The cry of street-corner storytellers in ancient Rome, quoted by Pliny

Ours is essentially a tragic age, so we refuse to take it tragically. The cataclysm has happened, we are among the ruins, we start to build up new little habitats, to have new little hopes. It is rather hard work: there is now no smooth road to the future: but we go round, or scramble over the obstacles. We've got to live, no matter how many skies have fallen.

– D. H. Lawrence, *Lady Chatterley's Lover*

La vie a beaucoup plus d'imagination que nous.

– François Truffaut

PART I

1

On the day of the new president's inauguration, when we worried that he might be murdered as he walked hand in hand with his exceptional wife among the cheering crowds, and when so many of us were close to economic ruin in the aftermath of the bursting of the mortgage bubble, and when Isis was still an Egyptian mother-goddess, an uncrowned seventy-something king from a faraway country arrived in New York City with his three motherless sons to take possession of the palace of his exile, behaving as if nothing was wrong with the country or the world or his own story. He began to rule over his neighbourhood like a benevolent emperor, although in spite of his charming smile and his skill at playing his 1745 Guadagnini violin he exuded a heavy, cheap odour, the unmistakable smell of crass, despotic danger, the kind of scent that warned us, look out for this guy, because he could order your execution at any moment, if you're wearing a displeasing shirt, for example, or if he wants to sleep with your wife. The next eight years, the years of the forty-fourth president, were also the years of the increasingly erratic and alarming reign over us of the man who called himself Nero Golden, who wasn't really a king, and at the end of whose time there was a large – and, metaphorically speaking, apocalyptic – fire.

The old man was short, one might even say squat, and wore his hair, which was still mostly dark in spite of his advanced years, slicked back to accentuate his devil's peak. His eyes were black and piercing, but what people noticed first – he often rolled his shirtsleeves up to make sure they did notice – were his forearms, as thick and strong as a wrestler's, ending in large, dangerous hands bearing chunky gold rings studded with emeralds. Few people ever heard him raise his voice, yet we were in no doubt that there lurked in him a great vocal force which one would do well not to provoke. He dressed expensively but there was a loud, animal quality to him which made one think of the Beast of folk tale, uneasy in human finery. All of us who were his neighbours were more than a little scared of him, though he made huge, clumsy efforts to be sociable and neighbourly, waving his cane at us wildly, and insisting at inconvenient times that people come over for cocktails. He leaned forward when standing or walking, as if struggling constantly against a strong wind only he could feel, bent a little from the waist, but not too much. This was a powerful man; no, more than that – a man deeply in love with the idea of himself as powerful. The purpose of the cane seemed more decorative and expressive than functional. When he walked in the Gardens he gave every impression of trying to be our friend. Frequently he stretched out a hand to pat our dogs or ruffle our children's hair. But children and dogs recoiled from his touch. Sometimes, watching him, I thought of Dr Frankenstein's monster, a simulacrum of the human that entirely failed to express any true humanity. His skin was brown leather and his smile glittered with golden fillings. His was a raucous and not entirely civil presence, but he was immensely rich and so, of course, he was accepted; but, in our downtown community of artists, musicians and writers, not, on the whole, popular.

We should have guessed that a man who took the name of the last of the Julio-Claudian monarchs of Rome and then installed himself in a *domus aurea* was publicly acknowledging his own madness, wrongdoing, megalomania and forthcoming doom, and also laughing in the face of all that; that such a man was flinging down a glove at the feet of destiny and snapping his fingers under Death's approaching nose, crying, 'Yes! Compare me, if you will, to that monster who doused Christians in oil and set them alight to provide illumination in his garden at night! Who played the lyre while Rome burned (there actually weren't any fiddles back then)! Yes: I christen myself Nero, of Caesar's house, last of that bloody line, and make of it what you will. Me, I just like the name.' He was dangling his wickedness under our noses, revelling in it, challenging us to see it, contemptuous of our powers of comprehension, convinced of his ability easily to defeat anyone who rose against him.

He came to the city like one of those fallen European monarchs, heads of discontinued houses who still used as last names the grand honorifics, *of-Greece* or *of-Yugoslavia* or *of-Italy*, and who treated the mournful prefix, *ex-*, as if it didn't exist. He wasn't ex-anything, his manner said; he was majestic in all things, in his stiff-collared shirts, his cufflinks, his bespoke English shoes, his way of walking toward closed doors without slowing down, knowing they would open for him; also in his suspicious nature, owing to which he held daily separate meetings with his sons to ask them what their brothers were saying about him; and in his cars, his liking for gaming tables, his unreturnable ping-pong serve, his fondness for prostitutes, whiskey and devilled eggs, and his often repeated dictum – one favoured by absolute rulers from Caesar to Haile Selassie – that the only virtue worth caring about was loyalty. He changed his cellphone frequently, gave the number to almost no one, and didn't answer it when it rang. He refused to allow journalists or photographers into his home but there were two men in his regular poker circle who were often there, silver-haired lotharios usually seen wearing tan leather jackets and brightly striped cravats, who were widely suspected of having murdered their rich wives, although in one case no charges had been made and in the other, they hadn't stuck.

Regarding his own missing wife he was silent. In his house of many photographs, whose walls and mantelpieces were populated by rock stars, Nobel laureates and aristocrats, there was no image of Mrs Golden, or whatever she had called herself. Clearly some disgrace was being implied, and we gossiped, to our shame, about what that might have been, imagining the scale and brazenness of her infidelities, conjuring her up as some sort of most high-born nymphomaniac, her sex life more flagrant than any movie star's, her divagations known to one and all except to her husband, whose eyes, blinded by love, continued to gaze adoringly upon her as he believed her to be, the loving and chaste wife of his dreams, until the terrible day when his friends told him the truth, they came in numbers to tell him, and how he raged!, how he abused them!, calling them liars and traitors, it took seven men to hold him and prevent him from doing harm to those who had forced him to face reality, and then finally he did face it, he accepted it, he banished her from his life and forbade her ever again to look upon her sons. Wicked woman, we said to one another, thinking ourselves worldly-wise, and the tale satisfied us, and we left it there, being in truth more preoccupied by our own stuff, and only interested in the affairs of N. J. Golden up to a certain point. We turned away, and got on with our lives.

How wrong we were.

2

What is a good life? What is its opposite? These are questions to which no two men will give the same answers. In these our cowardly times, we deny the grandeur of the Universal, and assert and glorify our local Bigotries, and so we cannot agree on much. In these our degenerate times, men bent on nothing but vainglory and personal gain – hollow, bombastic men for whom nothing is off-limits if it advances their petty cause – will claim to be great leaders and benefactors, acting in the common good, and calling all who oppose them liars, envious, little people, stupid people, *stiffs,* and, in a precise reversal of the truth, dishonest and corrupt. We are so divided, so hostile to one another, so driven by sanctimony and scorn, so lost in cynicism, that we call our pomposity idealism, so disenchanted with our rulers, so willing to jeer at the institutions of our state, that the very word *goodness* has been emptied of meaning and needs, perhaps, to be set aside for a time, like all the other poisoned words, *spirituality,* for example, *final solution,* for example, and (at least when applied to skyscrapers and fried potatoes) *freedom.*

But on that cold January day in 2009 when the enigmatic septuagenarian we came to know as Nero Julius Golden arrived in Greenwich Village in a Daimler limousine with three male children and no visible sign of a wife, he at least was firm about how virtue was to be valued, and right action distinguished from wrong. 'In my American house,' he told his attentive sons in the limousine as it drove them from the airport to their new residence, 'morality will go by the golden standard.' Whether he meant that morality was supremely precious, or that wealth determined morality, or that he personally, with his glittering new name, would be the only judge of right and wrong, he did not say, and the younger Julii, from long filial habit, did not ask for clarification. (*Julii,* the imperial plural they all preferred to *Goldens:* these were not modest men!) The youngest of the three, an indolent twenty-two-year-old with hair falling in beautiful cadences to his shoulders and a face like an angry angel, did, however, ask one question. 'What will we say,' he asked his father, 'when they enquire, where did you come from?' The old man's face entered a condition of scarlet vehemence. 'This, I've answered before,' he cried. 'Tell them, screw the identity parade. Tell them, we are snakes who shed our skin. Tell them we just moved downtown from Carnegie Hill. Tell them we were born yesterday. Tell them we materialised by magic, or arrived from the neighbourhood of Alpha Centauri in a spaceship hidden in a comet's tail. Say we are from nowhere or anywhere or somewhere, we are make-believe people, frauds, reinventions, shapeshifters, which is to say, Americans. Do not tell them the name of the place we left. Never speak it. Not the street, not the city, not the country. I do not want to hear those names again.'

They emerged from the car in the old heart of the Village, on Macdougal Street a little below Bleecker, near the Italian coffee place from the old days that was still somehow struggling on; and ignoring the honking cars behind them and the outstretched supplicant palm of at least one grubby panhandler, they allowed the limousine to idle in mid-street while they took their time lifting their bags from the trunk – even the old man insisted on carrying his own valise – and carried them to the grand Beaux-Arts building on the east side of the street, the former Murray mansion, thereafter to be known as the Golden house. (Only the eldest son, the one who didn't like being out of doors, who was wearing very dark dark glasses and an anxious expression, appeared to be in a hurry.)

So they arrived as they intended to remain, independently, with a shrugging indifference to the objections of others.

The Murray mansion, grandest of all the buildings on the Gardens, had lain largely unoccupied for many years, except for a notably snippy fifty-something Italian-American house manager and her equally haughty, though much younger, female assistant and live-in lover. We had often speculated on the owner's identity, but the fierce lady guardians of the building refused to satisfy our curiosity. However, these were years in which many of the world's super-rich bought property for no reason other than to own it, and left empty homes lying around the planet like discarded shoes, so we assumed that some Russian oligarch or oil sheikh must be involved, and, shrugging our shoulders, we got used to treating the empty house as if it wasn't there. There was one other person attached to the house, a sweet-natured Hispanic handyman named Gonzalo who was employed by the two guardian dragons to look after the place, and sometimes, when he had a bit of spare time, we would ask him over to our houses to fix our wiring and plumbing problems and help us clear our roofs and entrances of snow in the depths of winter. These services, in return for small sums of cash money folded discreetly into his hand, he smilingly performed.

The Macdougal–Sullivan Gardens Historic District – to give the Gardens their full, overly sonorous name – was the enchanted, fearless space in which we lived and raised our children, a place of happy retreat from the disenchanted, fearful world beyond its borders, and we made no apology for loving it dearly. The original Greek Revival-style homes on Macdougal and Sullivan, built in the 1840s, were remodelled in Colonial Revival style in the 1920s by architects working for a certain Mr William Sloane Coffin, who sold furniture and rugs, and it was at that time that the rear yards were combined to form the communal Gardens, bounded to the north by Bleecker Street, to the south by Houston, and reserved for the private use of residents in the houses backing onto them. The Murray mansion was an oddity, in many ways too grand for the Gardens, a gracious landmark structure originally built for the prominent banker Franklin Murray and his wife Harriet Lanier Murray between 1901 and 1903 by the architectural firm of Hoppin & Koen, who, to make room for it, had demolished two of the original houses put up in 1844 by the estate of the merchant Nicholas Low. It had been designed in the French Renaissance manner to be both fancy and fashionable, a style in which Hoppin & Koen had considerable experience, gained both at the École des Beaux-Arts and, afterwards, during their time working for McKim, Mead & White. As we later learned, Nero Golden had owned it since the early 1980s. It had long been whispered around the Gardens that the owner came and went, spending perhaps two days a year in the house, but none of us ever saw him, though sometimes there were lights on in more windows than usual at night, and, very rarely, a shadow against a blind, so that the local children decided the place was haunted, and kept their distance.

This was the place whose ample front doors stood open that January day as the Daimler limousine disgorged the Golden men, father and sons. Standing on the threshold was the welcoming committee, the two dragon ladies, who had prepared everything for their master's arrival. Nero and his sons passed inside and found the world of lies they would from now on inhabit: not a spanking-new, ultra-modern residence for a wealthy foreign family to make their own gradually, as their new lives unfolded, their connections to the new city deepened, their experiences multiplied – no! – but rather a place in which Time had been standing still for twenty years or more, Time gazing in its indifferent fashion upon scuffed Biedermeier chairs, slowly fading rugs and sixties-revival lava lamps, and looking with mild amusement at the portraits by all the right people of Nero Golden's younger self with downtown figures, René Ricard, William Burroughs, Deborah Harry, as well as leaders of Wall Street and old families of the Social Register, bearers of hallowed names such as Luce, Beekman and Auchincloss. Before he bought this place the old man had owned a large high-ceilinged bohemian loft, three thousand square feet on the corner of Broadway and Great Jones Street, and in his far-off youth had been allowed to hang around the edges of the Factory, sitting ignored and grateful in the rich boys' corner with Si Newhouse and Carlo De Benedetti, but that was a long time ago. The house contained memorabilia of those days and of his later visits in the 1980s as well. Much of the furniture had been in storage, and the reappearance of these objects from an earlier life had the air of an exhumation, implying a continuity which the residents' histories did not possess. So the house always felt to us like a sort of beautiful fake. We murmured to one another some words of Primo Levi's: 'This is the most immediate fruit of exile, of uprooting: the prevalence of the unreal over the real.'

There was nothing in the house that hinted at their origins, and the four men remained obstinately unwilling to open up about the past. Things leak out, inevitably, and we found out their story in time, but before that we all had our own hypotheses about their secret history, wrapping our fictions around theirs. Even though they were all fairish of complexion, from the milky-pale youngest son to leathery old Nero, it was clear to everyone that they were not conventionally 'white'. Their English was immaculate, British-accented, they had almost certainly had Oxbridge educations, and so at first we incorrectly assumed, most of us, that multicultural England was the country that could not be named, and London the multiracial town. They might have been Lebanese, or Armenian, or South Asian Londoners, we hypothesised, or even of Mediterranean European origin, which would explain their Roman fantasies. What dreadful wrong had been done to them there, what awful slights had they endured, that they went to such lengths to disown their origins? Well, well, for most of us that was their private affair, and we were willing to leave it at that, until it was no longer possible to do so. And when that time came, we understood that we had been asking ourselves the wrong questions.

That the charade of their newly adopted names worked at all, let alone for two entire presidential terms, that these invented American personae living in their palace of illusions were so unquestioningly accepted by us, their new neighbours and acquaintances, tells us much about America itself, and more about the strength of will with which they inhabited their chameleon identities, becoming, in all our eyes, whatever they said they were. In retrospect one can only wonder at the vastness of the plan, the intricacy of the details that would have had to be attended to, the passports, the state ID cards, the drivers' licences, the SSNs, the health insurance, the forgeries, the deals, the pay-offs, the sheer difficulty of it all, and the fury or perhaps fear that drove the whole magnificent, elaborate, cockeyed scheme. As we afterwards learned, the old man had worked on this metamorphosis for perhaps a decade and a half before he put the plan into action. If we had known that, we would have understood that something very large was being concealed. But we did not know. They were simply the self-styled king and his *soi-disant* princes, living in the architectural jewel of the neighbourhood.

The truth is that they didn't seem so odd to us. People in America were called all sorts of things – throughout the phonebook, in the days when there were phonebooks, nomenclatural exoticism ruled. Huckleberry! Dimmesdale! Ichabod! Ahab! Fenimore! Portnoy! Drudge! To say nothing of dozens, hundreds, thousands of Golds, Goldwaters, Goldsteins, Finegolds, Goldberrys. Americans also constantly decided what they wanted to be called and who they wanted to be, shedding their Gatz origins to become shirt-owning Gatsbys and pursue dreams called Daisy or perhaps simply America. Samuel Goldfish (another golden boy) became Samuel Goldwyn, the Aertzoons became the Vanderbilts, Clemens became Twain. And many of us, as immigrants – or our parents or our grandparents – had chosen to leave our pasts behind just as the Goldens were now choosing, encouraging our children to speak English, not the old language from the old country: to speak, dress, act, *be* American. The old stuff we tucked away in a cellar, or discarded, or lost. And in our movies and comic books – in the comic books our movies have become – do we not celebrate every day, do we not *honour*, the idea of the Secret Identity? Clark Kent, Bruce Wayne, Diana Prince, Bruce Banner, Raven Darkhölme, we love you. The secret identity may once have been a French notion – Fantômas the thief, and also *le fantôme de l'Opéra* – but it has by now put down deep roots in American culture. If our new friends wanted to be Caesars, we were down with that. They had excellent taste, excellent clothes, excellent English, and they were no more eccentric than, say, Bob Dylan, or any other sometime local resident. So the Goldens were accepted because they were acceptable. They were Americans now.

But at last things began to unravel. These were the causes of their fall: a sibling quarrel, an unexpected metamorphosis, the arrival in the old man's life of a beautiful and determined young woman, a murder. (More than one murder.) And, far away, in the country that had no name, finally, some decent intelligence work.

3

This was their untold story, their exploding planet Krypton: a sob story, as things kept secret often are.

The grand hotel by the harbour was loved by everyone, even by those too poor ever to pass through its doors. Everyone had seen the interior in the movies, the movie magazines, and their dreams: the famous staircase, the swimming pool surrounded by lounging bathing beauties, the glittering corridors of stores including bespoke tailors who could imitate your favourite suit in an afternoon once you had picked out your preferred worsted or gaberdine. Everyone knew about the fabulously capable, endlessly hospitable and deeply dedicated staff for whom the hotel was like their family, who gave to the hotel the respect due to a patriarch, and who made all who entered its hallways feel like queens and kings. It was a place to welcome foreigners, yes, of course, from its windows the foreigners looked out at the harbour, the beautiful bay that had given the unnameable city its name, and marvelled at the great array of seagoing vessels bobbing before them, motorboats and sailboats and cruise craft of every size, shape and hue. Everyone knew the story of the birth of the city, how the British had wanted it precisely because of this beautiful harbour, how they had negotiated with the Portuguese to marry the princess Catherine to King Charles II, and because poor Catherine was not a beauty the dowry had to be pretty damn good, especially because Charles II had an eye for a beautiful girl, and so the city was part of the dowry, and Charles married Catherine and then ignored her for the rest of his life, but the British put their navy in the harbour and embarked on a great land reclamation scheme to join up the Seven Isles and built a fort there and then a city and the British Empire followed. It was a city built by foreigners and so it was right that foreigners should be welcomed in that grand palace of a hotel looking out on the harbour which was the whole reason for the city's existence. But it was not only for foreigners, it was too romantic a building for that, stone-walled, red-domed, enchanted, with Belgian chandeliers shining down upon you, and on the walls and on the floors the art and furniture and carpeting from every part of that giant country, the country that could not be named, and so, if you were a young man wanting to impress your love you would somehow find the money to take her to the lounge facing the sea and as the sea breeze caressed your faces you would drink tea or lime juice and eat cucumber sandwiches and cake and she would love you because you had brought her into the city's magic heart. And maybe on your second date you would bring her back for Chinese food downstairs and that would seal the deal.

The grandees of the city, and the country, and the world made the grand old hotel their own after the British left – princes, politicians, movie stars, religious leaders, the most famous and most beautiful faces in the city, the country and the world jostled for position in its corridors – and it became as much a symbol of the city that could not be named as the Eiffel Tower, or the Colosseum, or the statue in New York harbour whose name was *Liberty Enlightens the World.*

There was an origin myth about the grand old hotel which almost everyone in the city that could not be named believed even though it wasn't true, a myth about liberty, about overthrowing the British imperialists just as the Americans had. The story went that in the first years of the twentieth century a grand old gentleman in a fez, who just happened to be the richest man in the country that could not be named, once tried to visit a different, older grand hotel in the same neighbourhood and was refused entry on account of his race. The grand old gentleman nodded his head slowly, walked away, bought a substantial piece of land down the road, and built upon it the finest and grandest hotel ever seen in the city that could not be named in the country that could not be identified, and in a short period of time put out of business the hotel which had refused him entry. So the hotel became, in people's minds, a symbol of rebellion, of beating the colonisers at their own game and driving them into the sea, and even when it was conclusively established that nothing of the sort had really happened it changed nothing, because a symbol of freedom and victory is more powerful than the facts.

One hundred and five years passed. Then, on November 23, 2008, ten gunmen armed with automatic weapons and hand grenades left by boat from the hostile neighbouring country to the west of the country that could not be named. In their backpacks they carried ammunition and strong narcotics: cocaine, steroids, LSD and syringes. On their journey to the city that could not be named they hijacked a fishing boat, abandoned their original vessel, brought two dinghies aboard the fishing boat and told the captain where to go. When they were near the shore they killed the captain and got into the dinghies. Afterwards many people wondered why the coastguard had not seen them or tried to intercept them. The coast was supposed to be well guarded but on this night there had been a failure of some sort. When the dinghies landed, on November 26, the gunmen split up into small groups and made their way to their chosen targets, a railway station, a hospital, a movie theatre, a Jewish centre, a popular cafe and two five-star hotels. One of these was the hotel described above.

The attack on the railway station began at 9.21 p.m., and lasted for an hour and a half. The two gunmen fired indiscriminately, and fifty-eight people died. They left the station and were eventually cornered near a city beach, where one was killed and the other captured. Meanwhile, at 9.30 p.m., another team of killers blew up a gas station and then started shooting at the people in the Jewish centre when they came to the windows. Then they attacked the centre itself and seven people died. Ten people died at the cafe. Over the next forty-eight hours perhaps thirty people died in the other hotel.

The hotel that was loved by everyone was attacked around 9.45 p.m. Guests in the swimming pool area were shot first, and then the gunmen went toward the restaurants. A young woman working in the Sea Lounge where young men took their girlfriends to impress them helped many guests escape through a staff door, but when the gunmen burst into the lounge she herself was killed. Grenades were set off and a murder spree followed during what became a three-day siege. Outside there were TV crews and crowds and someone shouted, 'The hotel is on fire!' Flames leapt from the windows of the topmost floor and the famous staircase too was ablaze. Among those trapped by the flames and burned to death were the wife and children of the manager of the hotel. The gunmen had blueprints of the hotel's floor plan and their blueprints were more accurate than those held by the security forces. They used the drugs to stay awake and the LSD – which is not a psychostimulant – combined with the other drugs (which were) to create in the killers a manic hallucinogenic frenzy and they laughed aloud as they killed. Outside, the TV crews reported on escaping hotel guests and the killers watched TV to find out where the guests were escaping from. By the end of the siege over thirty people had died, many of them members of the hotel staff.

The Goldens, under their abandoned original name, lived in the city's most exclusive neighbourhood, in a gated community on the most exclusive hill, in a large modern house overlooking the art deco mansions lining the Back Bay into which the red sun dove head first every night. We can imagine them there, the old man, not so old then, and the sons, also younger, the big brilliant clumsy agoraphobic firstborn lummox, the middle one with his night-running ways and his society portraits, the youngest boy with the darkness and confusion in him, and it seems that the game of giving themselves classical names was one the old man had encouraged them to play for many years, just as he taught them from their earliest days that they were not ordinary people, they were Caesars, they were gods. The Roman emperors, and afterwards the Byzantine monarchs, were known by Arabs and Persians as *Qaisar-e-Rúm*, Caesars of Rome. And if Rome was Rúm, then they, the kings of this eastern Rome, were Rumi. That led them to the study of the mystic and sage Rumi, aka Jalaluddin Balkhi, whose quotes the father and his sons batted around like tennis balls, *what you seek is seeking you, you are the universe in ecstatic motion, be notorious, unfold your own myth, sell your cleverness and buy bewilderment, set your life on fire, seek those who fan your flames,* and *if you desire healing, let yourself fall ill,* until they grew weary of his nostrums and started making them up to make one another laugh, *if you want to be rich, make yourself poor, if someone is looking for you, that's who you're looking for, if you want to be right side up, stand upon your head.*

After that they were no longer Rumi and became Latinate Julii, the sons of Caesar who were or would be Caesars in their own right. They were an old family claiming to be able to trace their ancestry all the way back to Alexander the Great – alleged by Plutarch to be the son of Zeus himself – so they were at least the equal of the Julio-Claudians who claimed descent from Iulus, the son of pious Aeneas, prince of Troy, and therefore from Aeneas's mother, the goddess Venus. As for the word *Caesar*, it had at least four possible origins. Did the first Caesar kill a *caesai* – the Moorish word for elephant? Did he have thick hair on his head – *caesaries*? Did he have grey eyes, *oculis caesiis*? Or did his name come from the verb *caedere*, to cut, because he was born by *Caesarean section*? 'I don't have grey eyes, and my mother gave birth to me in the usual way,' said the old man. 'And my hair, though still present, has thinned; nor have I killed any elephants. To hell with the first Caesar. I choose to be Nero, the last one.'

'Who are we, then?' the middle son asked. 'You are my sons,' the patriarch said with a shrug. 'Choose your own names.' Afterwards, when it was time to leave, they discovered that he had had travel documents made up for them in the new names, and they weren't surprised. He was a man who got things done.

And here as if in an old photograph is the old man's wife, a small sad woman with her greying hair up in an untidy bun and the memory of self-harm in her eyes. Caesar's wife: required to be above suspicion, yes, but also stuck with the worst job in the world.

In the evening of November 26 something happened in the big

house, an argument of some sort between Caesar and his wife, and she sent for the Mercedes and the driver and left the house in distress, on her way to seek the consolation of her friends, and that was how she came to be sitting in the Sea Lounge of the hotel that everyone loved, eating cucumber sandwiches and drinking heavily sweetened fresh lime juice, when the hallucinating gunmen burst in giggling with joy, with spiralling eyeballs and psychedelic imaginary birds fluttering around their heads, and began shooting to kill.

And yes, the country was India, of course, the city was Bombay, of course, the house was a part of the luxurious Walkeshwar colony on Malabar Hill, and yes, of course, these were the Muslim terrorist attacks launched from Pakistan by Lashkar-e-Taiba, the 'Army of the Righteous', first on the railway station formerly known as Victoria Terminus or VT and presently, like everything else in Bombay/Mumbai, renamed after the Mahratta hero-prince Shivaji – and then on Leopold Cafe in Colaba, the Oberoi Trident Hotel, the Metro Cinema, the Cama and Albless Hospital, the Jewish Chabad House, and the Taj Mahal Palace and Tower Hotel. And yes, after the three-day sieges and battles were done, the mother of the two older Golden boys (of the youngest son's mother we will have more to say hereafter) was numbered among the dead.

When the old man heard that his wife was trapped inside the Taj his knees gave way and he would have fallen down the marble steps of his marble house, from his marble living room to the marble terrace below, if there had not been a servant close enough to catch him, but then there was always a servant. He remained on his knees and buried his face in his hands and his body was racked by sobs so loud and convulsive that it seemed as if a creature hidden deep within himself was trying to escape. For the entire duration of the attacks he stayed in the position of prayer at the top of the marble steps, refusing to eat or sleep, pounding his chest with a fist like a professional mourner at a funeral, and blaming himself. I didn't know she was going there, he cried, I should have known, why did I let her go. In those days the air in the city felt dark as blood even at high noon, dark as a mirror, and the old man saw himself reflected in it and didn't like what he saw; and such was the force of his vision that his boys saw it too, and after the bad news came, the news that ended their whole life up to that point, the weekend walks around the racecourse with representatives of the great old families of Bombay and the new-money people too, squash and bridge and swimming and badminton and golf at the Willingdon Club, movie starlets, hot jazz, all of it gone forever because drowned beneath a sea of death, they went along with what their father said he wanted now, which was to leave this marble place forever, and the broken quarrelling city in which it stood, and the whole dirty corrupt vulnerable country as well, their everything which their father now suddenly or perhaps not so suddenly detested, they agreed to obliterate every detail of what it had been to them and who they had been in it and what they had lost: the woman whose husband had shouted at her and so drove her to her doom, whose two sons had loved her, and who had once been so badly humiliated by her stepson that she tried to kill herself. They would wipe the slate clean, take on new identities, cross the world and be other than what they were. They would escape from the historical into the personal, and in the New World the personal would be all they sought and all they expected, to be detached and individual and alone, each of them to make his own agreement with the everyday, outside history, outside time, in private. It did not occur to any of them that their decision was born of a colossal sense of entitlement, this notion that they could just step away from yesterday and start tomorrow as if it wasn't a part of the same week, to move beyond memory and roots and language and race into the land of the self-made self, which is another way of saying, America.

How we wronged her, the dead lady, when in our gossiping we ascribed her absence from New York to her infidelity. It was her absence, her tragedy, that made sense of her family's presence among us. She was the meaning of this tale.

When the emperor Nero's wife Poppaea Sabina died he burned ten years' supply of Arabian incense at her funeral. But in the case of Nero Golden all the incense in the world couldn't finally cover up the bad smell.

*

The legal term *benami* looks almost French, *ben-ami,* fooling the unwary into believing it might mean 'good friend', *bon ami*, or 'well-liked', *bien-aimé*, or something of the sort. But the word is actually of Persian origin, and its root is not *ben-ami* but *bé-námi. Bé* is a prefix meaning 'without' and *nám* means 'name'; thus *benami,* 'without a name', or anonymous. In India, benami transactions are purchases of property in which the ostensible buyer, in whose name the property is acquired, is just a front man, used to conceal the property's real owner. In old American slang, the benami would be called the beard.

In 1988 the government of India passed the Benami Transactions (Prohibitions) Act, which both outlawed such purchases and made it possible for the state to recover property 'held benami'. Many loopholes, however, remained. One of the ways in which the authorities have sought to close these loopholes is the institution of the *Aadhaar* system. *Aadhaar* is a twelve-digit social security ID number allocated to each Indian citizen for his or her lifetime and its use is mandatory in all property and financial transactions, allowing the citizen's involvement in such transactions to be electronically traced. However, the man we knew as Nero Golden, an American citizen for over twenty years and the father of American citizens, was clearly ahead of the game. When what happened happened and everything came to light we learned that the Golden house was owned outright by a lady of a certain age, the same lady who served as the senior of Nero's two trusted confidantes, and no other legal document could be shown to exist. But what happened did happen, and after that even the walls Nero had so carefully erected came tumbling down, and the full, appalling extent of his criminality stood before us, naked in the daylight of the truth. That was in the future. For now, he was simply N. J. Golden, our rich and – as we discovered – vulgar neighbour.

4

In the secret, grassy quadrangle of the Gardens, I crawled before I could walk, I walked before I could run, I ran before I could dance, I danced before I could sing, and I danced and sang until I learned stillness and silence and stood motionless and listening at the Gardens' heart, on summer evenings sparkling with fireflies, and became, at least in my own opinion, an artist. To be precise, a would-be writer of films. And, in my dreams, a film-maker, even, in the grand old formulation, an auteur.

I've been hiding behind the first-person plural, and may do so again, but I'm getting around to introducing myself. I am. But in a way I'm not so different from my subjects, who were self-concealers also – the family whose arrival in my neck of the woods provided me with the big project for which I had, with growing desperation, been searching. If the Goldens were heavily invested in the erasure of their past, then I, who have taken it upon myself to be their chronicler – and perhaps their *imagineer,* a term invented for the devisers of rides in Disney theme parks – am by nature self-effacing. What was it that Isherwood said at the outset of *Goodbye to Berlin*? 'I am a camera with its shutter open, quite passive, recording, not thinking.' But that was then, and this is the age of smart cameras that do all one's thinking for one. Maybe I'm a smart camera. I record, but I'm not exactly passive. I think. I alter. Possibly I even invent. To be an imagineer, after all, is very different from being a literalist. Van Gogh's picture of a starry night doesn't look like a photograph of a starry night, but it's a great depiction of a starry night nonetheless. Let's just agree that I prefer the painting to the photograph. I am a camera that paints.

Call me René. I have always liked it that the narrator of *Moby-Dick* doesn't actually tell us his name. Call-me-Ishmael might in 'reality', which is to say in the petty Actual that lay outside the grand Real of the novel, he might have been called, oh, anything. He might have been Brad, or Trig, or Ornette, or Schuyler, or Zeke. He might even have been called Ishmael. We don't know, and so, like my great forebear, I forbear to say unto you plainly, my name's René. Call me René: that's the best I can do for you.

We proceed. Both my parents were college professors (do you note, in their son, an inherited note of the professorial?) who bought our house near the corner of Sullivan and Houston back in the Jurassic era when things were cheap. I present them to you: Gabe and Darcey Unterlinden, long-time married couple, not only respected scholars but beloved teachers, and, like the great Poirot (he's fictional, but you can't have everything, as Mia Farrow said in *The Purple Rose of Cairo*) . . . Belgians. Belgians long ago, I hastily clarify, Americans since forever, Gabe oddly persevering with a curious, heavy and largely invented pan-European accent, Darcey comfortably Yankee. The professors were players of ping-pong (they challenged Nero Golden when they heard of his fondness for the game, and he beat them both soundly, though they were both pretty good). They were quoters of poetry to each other. They were baseball fans, oh, and giggling addicts of reality television, lovers of opera, jointly and constantly planning their never-to-be-written monograph on the form, to be called *The Chick Always Dies*.

They loved their city for its unlikeness to the rest of the country. 'Rome iss not Italy,' my father taught me, 'and London iss not England and Paris iss not France, and dis, where we are right now, dis is not de United States of America. Dis iss New York.'

'Between the metropolis and the hinterland,' my mother added her footnote, 'always resentment, always alienation.'

'After 9/11, America tries to pretend it loves us,' said my dad. 'How long does dat last?'

'Not so fucking long,' my mother completed his thought. (She was a user of swear words. She claimed she didn't know she was doing it. They just slipped out.)

'Iss a bubble, like everyone says now,' my father said. 'Iss like in de Jim Carrey movie, only expanded to big-city size.'

'*The Truman Show*,' my mother helpfully clarified. 'And not even the whole city is in the bubble, because the bubble is made of money and the money isn't evenly spread.'

In this they differed from the common opinion that the bubble was composed of progressive attitudes, or rather they held, like good post-Marxists, that liberalism was economically generated.

'De Bronx, Queens, maybe not so much in de bubble,' my father said.

'Staten Island, *definitely* not in the bubble.'

'Brooklyn?'

'Brooklyn. Yeah, maybe in the bubble. Parts of Brooklyn.'

'Brooklyn's great . . .' my father said, and then in unison they finished their favourite and much-repeated old joke, '. . . but iss in Brooklyn.'

'De point is, we like de bubble, and so do you,' my father said. 'We don't want to live in a red state, and you – you'd be done for in for example Kansas, where dey don't believe in *evolution*.'

'In a way, Kansas does disprove Darwin's theory,' my mother mused. 'It proves the fittest are not always the ones who survive. Sometimes the unfittest survive instead.'

'But iss not just crazy cowboys,' my father said, and my mother jumped in.

'We don't want to live in *California*.'

(At this point their bubble got confusing, becoming cultural as well as economic, right coast versus left coast, Biggie-not-Tupac. They didn't seem to care about the contradictoriness of their position.)

'So dis iss who you are,' my father wanted me to know. 'The boy in the bubble.'

'These are days of miracle and wonder,' my mother said. 'And don't cry, baby, don't cry, don't fucking cry.'

I had a happy childhood with the professors. At the heart of the bubble were the Gardens and the Gardens gave the bubble a heart. I was raised in enchantment, safe from harm, cocooned in liberal downtown silk, and it gave me an innocent courage even though I knew that outside the magic spell the world's dark windmills awaited the quixotic fool. (Still, 'the only excuse for privilege', my father taught me, 'is to do something useful with it'.) I went to school at Little Red and to college on Washington Square. A whole life contained in a dozen blocks. My parents had been more adventurous. My father went to Oxford on a Fulbright, and after he finished, with a British friend in a Mini Traveller, he crossed Europe and Asia – Turkey, Iran, Afghanistan, Pakistan, India – back in that earlier-mentioned Jurassic era when dinosaurs roamed the earth and it was possible to make such journeys without losing your head. When he came home he had had his fill of the wide world and became, along with Burrows and Wallace, one of the three great historians of New York City, co-author, with those two gentlemen, of the multi-volume classic *Metropolis*, the definitive history of Superman's home town where we all lived and where the *Daily Planet* arrived on the doorstep every morning and where, many years after old Supe, Spider-Man took up residence, in Queens. When I walked with him in the Village he pointed out where Aaron Burr's place once stood, and once outside the movie multiplex on Second Avenue and Thirty-Second Street he told me the story of the Battle of Kip's Bay, and how Mary Lindley Murray saved Israel Putnam's fleeing American soldiers by inviting the British general William Howe to stop his pursuit and come to tea at her grand home, Inclenberg, on top of what would come to be known as Murray Hill.

My mother too had been intrepid in her fashion. When she was young she worked in public health with drug addicts and subsistence farmers in Africa. After I was born she narrowed her horizons and became first an expert in early-childhood education and eventually a psychology professor. Our house on Sullivan Street, at the far end of the Gardens from the Golden mansion, was filled with the pleasing accumulated clutter of their lives, threadbare Persian rugs, carved wooden African statuary, photographs, maps and etchings of the early 'New' cities on Manhattan Island, both Amsterdam and York. There was a corner dedicated to famous Belgians, an original Tintin drawing hanging next to a Warhol screen print of Diane von Furstenberg and the famous Hollywood production still of the beautiful star of *Breakfast at Tiffany's* with her long cigarette holder, once known as Miss Edda van Heemstra, afterwards much beloved as Audrey Hepburn; and below these, a first edition of *Mémoires d'Hadrien* by Marguerite Yourcenar on a small table next to photographs of my namesake Magritte in his studio, the cyclist Eddy Merckx and the Singing Nun. (Jean-Claude Van Damme didn't make the cut.)

In spite of this little nook of Belgiana they did not hesitate to criticise their country of origin when asked. 'King Leopold II and the Congo Free State,' my mother said. 'Worst colonialist ever, most rapacious set-up in colonial history.' 'And nowadays,' my father added, 'Molenbeek. European centre of fanatical Islam.'

In pride of place on the living-room mantelpiece sat a decades-old, never-used block of hashish still wrapped in its original cheap cellophane packaging and stamped with an official Afghan government seal of quality bearing the likeness of the moon. In Afghanistan in the time of the king the hashish was legal and came in three price- and quality-controlled packages, Afghan Gold, Silver and Bronze. But what my father, who never indulged in the weed, kept in pride of place on the mantel was something rarer, something legendary, almost occult. 'Afghan Moon,' my father said. 'If you use that it opens de third eye in your pineal gland in de centre of your forehead and you become clairvoyant and few secrets can be kept from you.'

'Then why have you never used it,' I asked.

'Because a world vissout mystery iss like a picture vith no shadows,' he said. 'By seeing too much it shows you nossing.'

'What he means is,' my mother added, 'that, (a), we believe in using our minds and not blowing them, and, (b), it's probably adulterated, or *cut,* as the hippies used to say, with some dreadful hallucinogen, and, (c), it's possible that I would object strongly. I don't know. He has never put me to the test.' *The hippies,* as if she had no memory of the 1970s, as if she had never worn a sheepskin jacket or a bandanna or dreamed of being Grace Slick.

There was no Afghan Sun, FYI. The sun of Afghanistan was the king, Zahir Shah. And then the Russians came, and then the fanatics, and the world changed.

But Afghan Moon . . . that helped me in the darkest moment of my life, and my mother was no longer able to object.

And there were books, inevitably, books like a disease, infesting every corner of our shabby, happy home. I became a writer because of course I did with those forebears, and maybe I chose movies instead of novels or biographies because I knew I couldn't compete with the old folks. But until the Goldens moved into the big house on Macdougal, diagonally across the Gardens from ours, my post-graduation creativity had been stalled. With the boundless egotism of youth I had begun to imagine a mighty film, or a *Dekalog*-style sequence of films, dealing with migration, transformation, fear, danger, rationalism, romanticism, sexual change, the city, cowardice and courage; nothing less than a panoramic portrait of my times. My preferred manner would be something I privately called Operatic Realism, my subject the conflict between the Self and the Other. I was trying to make a fictional portrait of my neighbourhood but it was a story without a driving force. My parents didn't have the doomed heroism of properly Operatic-Realist leads; nor did our other neighbours. (Bob Dylan was long gone.) My celebrated superstar-African-American-movie-director-in-a-red-baseball-cap film studies professor haughtily said after reading my early screenplays, 'Very prettily done, kid, but where's the blood? It's too quiet. Where's the engine? Maybe you should allow a flying saucer to land in the goddamn Gardens. Maybe you should blow up a building. Just make something happen. Make some noise.'

I didn't know how. And then the Goldens arrived and they were my flying saucer, my engine, my bomb. I felt the excitement of the young artist whose subject has arrived like a gift in the holiday mail. I felt grateful.

It was the age of non-fiction, my father told me. 'Maybe stop trying to make sings up. Ask in any bookstore,' he said, 'iss de books on de nonfiction tables dat move while de made-up stories languish.' But that was the world of books. In the movies it was the age of superheroes. For non-fiction we had Michael Moore's polemics, Werner Herzog's *Woodcarver Steiner*, Wim Wenders's *Pina*, some others. But the big bucks were in fantasy. My father admired and commended to me the work and ideas of Dziga Vertov, the Soviet documentarist who detested drama and literature. His film style, Kino-Eye or Ciné-Eye, aimed at nothing less than the evolution of mankind into a higher, fiction-free form of life, 'from a bumbling citizen through the poetry of the machine to the perfect electric man'. Whitman would have liked him. Maybe I-am-a-camera Isherwood too. I, however, resisted. I left the higher forms to my parents and Michael Moore. I wanted to make the world up.

A bubble is a fragile thing, and often in the evening the professors talked worriedly about its bursting. They worried about political correctness, about their colleague on TV with a twenty-year-old female student screaming abuse into her face from a distance of three inches because of a disagreement over campus journalism, their colleague in another TV news story abused for not wanting to ban Pocahontas costumes on Halloween, their colleague forced to take at least one seminar's sabbatical because he had not sufficiently defended a student's 'safe space' from the intrusion of ideas that student deemed too 'unsafe' for her young mind to encounter, their colleague defying a student petition to remove a statue of President Jefferson from his college campus in spite of the repressible fact that Jefferson had owned slaves, their colleague excoriated by students with evangelical Christian family histories for asking them to read a graphic novel by a lesbian cartoonist, their colleague forced to cancel a production of Eve Ensler's *The Vagina Monologues* because by defining women as persons with vaginas it discriminated against persons identifying as female who did not possess vaginas, their colleagues resisting student efforts to 'de-platform' apostate Muslims because their views were offensive to non-apostate Muslims. They worried that young people were becoming pro-censorship, pro-banning-things, pro-restrictions, how did that happen, they asked me, the narrowing of the youthful American mind, we're beginning to fear the young. 'Not you, of course, darling, who could be scared of you,' my mother reassured me, to which my father countered, 'Scared *for* you, yes. Vith this Trotskyist beard you insist on wearing you look like an ice-pick target to me. Avoid Mexico City, especially de Coyoacán neighbourhood. This iss my advice.'

In the evenings they sat in pools of yellow light, books on their laps, lost in words. They looked like figures in a Rembrandt painting, *Two Philosophers Deep in Meditation,* and they were more valuable than any canvas; maybe members of the last generation of their kind, and we, we who are post-, who come after, will regret we did not learn more at their feet.

I miss them more than I can say.

5

Time passed. I acquired a girlfriend, lost her, acquired another, lost her as well. My secret movie script, my most demanding lover, disliked my attempts at these misconceived relationships with human beings, and sulked, and refused to yield up its secrets. My Late Twenties were steaming toward me, and I like a swooning nickelodeon hero lay helpless across the tracks. (My literary parents would no doubt have preferred that I refer, instead, to the climactic railway-tracks scene in Forster's *The Longest Journey*.) The Gardens were my microcosm, and every day I saw the creatures of my imagination staring back at me from the windows of houses on both Macdougal and Sullivan, hollow-eyed, pleading to be born. I had pieces of them all but the shape of the work eluded me. At #XX Sullivan Street, on the first floor, with garden access, I had placed my Burmese – I should say Myanmaran – diplomat, U Lnu Fnu of the United Nations, his professional heart broken by his defeat in the longest-ever battle for the post of Secretary General, twenty-nine consecutive rounds of voting without a winner, and in the thirtieth round he lost to the South Korean. Through him I planned to explore geopolitics, to dramatise the push by some of the most authoritarian regimes in the world toward the outlawing by the UN of the giving of religious offence, to bring to a head the vexed question of the use of the American veto in defence of Israel, and to arrange a visit to the Macdougal–Sullivan Gardens by Aung San Suu Kyi herself. I knew, too, the story of U Lnu Fnu's personal heartbreak, the loss of his wife to cancer, and I suspected that, derailed by the double defeat of his upright life, he might fall away from probity and finally be undone by financial scandal. When I thought of this the hollow-eyed man at the window of #XX Sullivan shook his head in disappointment and retreated into the shadows. Nobody wants to be the bad guy.

My imagined community was an international bunch. At #00 Macdougal Street there lived another solitary individual, an Argentine-American to whom I had given the temporary, working name of 'Mr Arribista', the arriviste. About him, whatever his name finally became, Mario Florída, maybe, or Carlos Hurlingham, I had this treatment:

Arribista, the new citizen, plunges into the great country – 'his' country, he marvels – as a man does who reaches a promised ocean after a long journey across a desert, even though he has never learned how to swim. He trusts the ocean to bear his weight; and it does. He does not drown, or not immediately.

Also this, which needed to be expanded:

Arribista has been, all his life, a square peg pushing sweatily against a round hole. Is this, at long last, a square hole for him to fit squarely within, or has he, during his long journeyings, become rounded? (If the latter, then the journey would be meaningless, or at least at its end he would have fitted in well where he began. He prefers the image of the square hole, and the grid system of the city streets seems to confirm that reality.)

And perhaps it was because of my own romantic failures that Arribista, like the gentleman from the UN, had been abandoned by the woman he loved:

His wife is also a fiction. Or, she crossed over many years ago from fact into fantasy, when she left him for another man, younger, more handsome, in all respects an improvement on poor Arribista, who is, as he well knows, in all ways that women like – looks, conversation, attentiveness, warmth, honesty – only averagely equipped. *L'homme moyen sensible*, who reaches for inexact hand-me-down phrases like that one to describe himself. A man clad in old familiar words, as if they were tweeds. A man without qualities. No, that isn't true, Arribista corrects himself. He has qualities, he reminds himself. For one thing, he has this tendency when lost in the stream of consciousness to denigrate himself, and in this respect he is unfair to himself. As a matter of fact he is something very like an excellent person, excellent in the way of his new country, which celebrates excellence, which rejects the 'tall poppy syndrome'. Arribista is excellent because he has excelled. He has done well; very well. He is rich. His story is a success story, the story of his very considerable success. It is an American story.

And so on. The imaginary Sicilian aristocrats in the house directly across the Gardens from the Golden place – provisionally, Vito and Blanca Tagliabue, Baron and Baroness of Selinunte – were still mysterious to me, but I was in love with their ancestry. When I pictured them stepping out of an evening, always in the height of fashion, to attend a ball at the Metropolitan Museum or a film premiere at the Ziegfeld or to see the new show by the new young artist in the newest gallery on the West Side, I thought of Vito's father Biaggio, who

> on a hot day near the south coast of Sicily, lightly tanned and in the prime of life, strides out across the wide expanse of his family estate, which went by the name of Castelbiaggio, holding his best shotgun by the barrel while resting the weapon on his right shoulder. He is wearing a broad-brimmed sun hat above an old burgundy smock, well-worn khaki jodhpurs and walking boots polished until they shone like the noonday sun. He has excellent cause to believe that life is good. The war in Europe is over, Mussolini and his moll Clara Petacci are hanging from their meathooks, and the natural order of life is coming back into being. The Barone surveys the marshalled ranks of his grape-heavy vines like a commanding officer taking the salute of his troops, then moves forward rapidly through wood and stream, up hill and down dale and then up again, heading for his favourite place, a little promontory high above his lands where he can sit cross-legged like a Tibetan lama and meditate on the goodness of life while looking out to the far horizon

across the glinting sea. It is the last day of his life as a free man, because a moment later he spots a poacher with a full sack over his shoulder crossing his territory and without hesitation he raises his shotgun and shoots the fellow dead.

And after this it would be revealed that the dead youth was a relative of the local Mafia don, and the Mafia don would declare that Biaggio too must die to pay for his crime, and then there would be agitations and protestations, and delegations from the political authority and also from the Church, arguing that for the Mafia don to kill the local milord would be, well, extremely visible, extremely hard to ignore, it would make more trouble for the Mafia don than would be comfortable for him, so for the sake of his own ease perhaps he could forgo this murder. And in the end the Mafia don relents,

I know all about this Barone Biaggio, hmm, about his suite in the Grand Hotel et Des Palmes in Palermo – what is it? Suite 202 or 204 or maybe both? – he goes there to party and to whore, hmm?, which is fine, it is our place, we go there for the same reasons, and so, if he goes there today and stays there for the rest of his fucking life we will not kill the little fucker but if he tries to set foot outside the hotel he should remember that the corridors are crawling with our guys and the whores work for us as well and before his foot touches the ground of the square outside the building he will be dead, his bloodied head with the bullet in his forehead will hit the ground before his fucking shoe. Hmm? Hmm? Tell him that.

In the screenplays and treatments for screenplays that I carried around in my head the way Peter Kien in Canetti's *Auto-da-Fé* carried whole libraries, the 'baron in the suite' remained imprisoned in the Grand Hotel et Des Palmes, Palermo, Sicily, until his dying day, forty-four years later, he went on partying and whoring in there, food and drink was brought to him every day from his family's kitchen and wine cellar, his son Vito was conceived there on one of his long-suffering wife's infrequent visits (but born where his long-suffering wife preferred, in her bedroom at Castelbiaggio), and when he died his coffin left by the front door, feet first, surrounded by an honour guard composed of most of the staff of the hotel, and several of the whores. – And Vito, disillusioned by Palermo, by the Mafia and by his father too, grew up to make his home in New York, and became determined to lead the opposite life to his father's, utterly faithful to his wife Blanca, but refusing to spend a single evening stuck alone with her and the children at home.

I fear I may have given the reader an unnecessarily poor impression of my character. I would not wish you to think of me as an indolent fellow, a ne'er-do-well and a burden on my parents, still in need of a real job after getting on for three decades of life on earth. The truth is that, then as now, I was and am rarely out on the town at night, and I rose and rise early in the morning in spite of being a lifelong insomniac. I was also (and remain) an active member of a group of young film-makers – we had all been to graduate school together – who, under the leadership of a dynamic young Indian-American producer-writer-director called Suchitra Roy, had already made a host of music videos, embedded Internet content for Condé Nast and *Wired*, documentaries that appeared on PBS and HBO, and three well-regarded theatrically released, independently financed feature films (all three had been selections at Sundance and SXSW and two had won Audience Awards) in which we had persuaded A-list performers to work for scale: Jessica Chastain, Keanu Reeves, James Franco, Olivia Wilde. I offer this brief CV now so that the reader may feel in good hands, the hands of a credible and not inexperienced storyteller, as my narrative acquires what will be increasingly lurid characteristics. I also introduce my work colleagues because their running critique of this, my personal project, was and continues to be valuable to me.

All that long hot summer we would meet for lunch at our favourite Italian restaurant on Sixth Avenue just below Bleecker Street, sitting out at a sidewalk table wearing substantial sun hats and Factor 50, and I would tell Suchitra what I was doing and she would ask the tough questions. 'I understand that you want your "Nero Golden" to be something of a mystery man, that's fine, I see that that's right,' she told me. 'But what is the question his character asks us, which the story must finally address?' At once I knew the answer, though I hadn't ever quite admitted it even to myself until that moment.

'The question,' I told her, 'is the question of evil.'

'In that case,' she said, 'sooner or later, and the sooner the better, the mask must begin to slip.'

The Goldens were my story, and others could steal it. Muckrakers could purloin what was mine by the divine right of I-was-here-first, the squatter's rights of this-is-my-turf. I was the one who dug in this dirt for longest, seeing myself, almost, as a latter-day A. J. Weberman – Weberman the *soi-disant* Village 'garbologer' of the 1970s, who rooted around in Bob Dylan's trash to discover the secret meanings of his lyrics and the details of his private life, and although I never went that far, I thought about it, I confess, I thought about attacking the Golden garbage like a cat in search of a fishbone.

These are the times we live in, in which men hide their truths, perhaps even from themselves, and live in lies, until the lies reveal those truths in ways impossible to foretell. And now that so much is hidden, now that we live in surfaces, in presentations and falsifications of ourselves, the seeker after truth must pick up his shovel, break the surface and look for the blood beneath. Espionage isn't easy, however. Once they were settled in their lavish home, the old man grew obsessed by the fear of being spied on by truth-seekers; he called in security personnel to sweep the property for listening devices, and when he discussed family matters with his sons, he did it in their 'secret languages', the tongues of the ancient world. He was sure we were all snooping into his business; and of course we were, in an innocent village-gossip way, according to the natural instincts of ordinary people by the parish pump or water cooler, trying to fit new pieces into the jigsaw puzzle of our lives. I was the most inquisitive of all of us, but with the blindness of the foolishly obsessed Nero

Golden didn't see that, thinking of me – quite inaccurately – as a no-account ne'er-do-well who had not found a way of making his fortune and could therefore be discounted, who could be erased from his field of vision and ignored; which suited my purposes excellently.

There was one possibility that I confess didn't occur to me, or to any of us, even in our edgy, paranoid era. Because of their open and generous alcohol consumption, their comfort in the presence of unveiled women, and their evident failure to practise any of the major world religions, we never suspected that they might be . . . oh, my . . . Muslims. Or of Muslim origin, at least. It was my parents who worked that out. 'In the age of information, my dear,' my mother said with justifiable pride when they had done their work at their computers, 'everyone's garbage is on display for all to see, and all you need to know is how to look.'

It may seem generationally upside down but in our house I was the Internet-illiterate one while my parents were the super-techies. I stayed away from social media and bought 'hard copies' of the *Times* and *Post* every morning at the corner bodega. My parents, however, lived inside their desktops, had had Second Life avatars ever since that other world went online, and could find the 'proverbial eedle in the e-stack', as my mother liked to say.

They were the ones who began to unlock the Goldens' past for me, the Bombay tragedy that had driven them across the world. 'It wasn't so difficult,' my father explained, as if to a simpleton. 'These are not low-key people. If a person iss vell known, a straightforward image search vill probably vork.'

'All we had to do,' my mother said, with a grin, 'was to go right in the front door.' She handed me a folder. 'Here's the skinny, sugar,' she said, in her best hard-boiled gumshoe accent. 'Heartbreaking material. Stinks worse than a plumber's handkerchief. No wonder they wanted to leave it behind them. It's like their world got broken like Humpty Dumpty. Couldn't put it together again, so they took off and came here, where broken people are a dime a dozen. I get it. Sad stuff. We'll be sending in our expense sheet for your early attention.'

There were people, that year, claiming that the new president was a Muslim, there was all that trumped-up birth certificate crap, and we weren't going to fall into the elephant trap of bigotry. We knew about Muhammad Ali and Kareem Abdul-Jabbar and in the days after the planes hit the buildings we had agreed, all of us in the Gardens, not to blame the innocent for the crimes of the guilty. We remembered the fearfulness that made taxi drivers put little flags on their dashboards and stick God Bless America decals on the partition screen, and attacks on Sikhs in turbans embarrassed us because of our countrymen's ignorance. We saw the young men in their Don't Blame Me I'm Hindu T-shirts and we didn't blame them and were embarrassed that they felt the need to wear sectarian messages to ensure their safety. When the city calmed down and got its groove back we felt proud of our fellow New Yorkers for their sanity and so, no, we weren't going to get hysterical about that word now. We had read the books about the prophet and the Taliban and so on and we didn't pretend to understand everything but I made it my business to inform myself about the city from which the Goldens had come and which they did not wish to name. For a long time its citizens had prided themselves on intercommunal harmony and many Hindus were non-vegetarians there and many Muslims ate pork and it was a sophisticated place, its upper echelons were secular, not religious, and even now as that golden age faded into the past it was really Hindu extremists who were oppressing the Muslim minority, so the minority was to be sympathised with, not feared. I looked at the Goldens and I saw cosmopolitans, not bigots, and so did my parents, and we left it there, and felt good about doing it. We kept what we had learned to ourselves. The Goldens were fleeing from a terrorist tragedy and a grievous loss. They were to be welcomed, not feared.

But I couldn't deny the words that had tumbled out of my mouth in reply to Suchitra's challenge. *The question is the question of evil.*

I didn't know where the words had come from, or what they meant. I did know that I would pursue the answer in my Tintinish, Poiroty, post-Belgian way, and that when I found it, I would have the story that I had decided was mine and mine alone to tell.

6

There was once a wicked king who made his three sons leave their home and then kept them bottled up in a house of gold, sealing the windows with golden shutters and blocking the doors with stacks of American ingots and sacks of Spanish doubloons and racks of French louis d'or and buckets of Venetian ducats. But in the end the children turned themselves into birds resembling feathered snakes and flew up the chimney and were free. Once they were out in the open air, however, they found they could no longer fly, and tumbled painfully into the street to lie wounded and bewildered in the gutter. A crowd gathered, uncertain whether to worship or fear the fallen snake-birds, until someone threw the first stone. After that the hail of stones quickly killed all three of the changelings, and the king, alone in the golden house, saw all his gold in all his pockets all his stacks all his sacks all his buckets begin to glow more and more brightly until it caught fire, and burned. The disloyalty of my children has killed me, he said as the flames rose high all around him. But that is not the only version of the story. In another, the sons did not escape, but died with the king in the blaze. In a third variation, they murdered one another. In a fourth, they killed their father, simultaneously becoming both parricides and regicides. It is even possible that the king was not entirely wicked, or had some noble qualities as well as many appalling ones. In our age of bitterly contested realities it is not easy to agree upon what is actually happening or has happened, on *what is the case,* let alone upon the moral or meaning of this or any other tale.

The man calling himself Nero Golden veiled himself, in the first place, behind dead languages. He was fluent in Greek and Latin and had obliged his sons to learn them too. They conversed sometimes in the speech of Rome or Athens, as if these were everyday tongues, just a couple of the myriad vocabularies of New York. Earlier, in Bombay, he had told them, 'Choose your classical names,' and in their choices we can see that the sons' pretensions were more literary, more mythological, than the father's imperial longings. They did not want to be kings, though the youngest, it will be noted, cloaked himself in divinity. They became Petronius, Lucius Apuleius and Dionysus. After they made their choices their father used their chosen names for them always. Brooding, damaged Petronius became, in Nero's mouth, either Petro or Petrón, making him sound like a brand of gasoline or tequila, or, finally and enduringly, Petya, which dispatched him from ancient Rome toward the worlds of Dostoevsky and Chekhov. The second son, lively, worldly, an artist and a man about town, insisted on choosing his own nickname. 'Call me Apu,' he demanded, defying his father's objection ('We are not Bengalis!') and answering to nothing else, until the diminutive stuck. And the youngest, whose fate would be the strangest of all, became simply 'D'.

It is to the three sons of Nero Golden that we must now turn our attention, pausing only to state what all four Goldens, at one time or another, emphatically insisted upon – that their relocation to New York was not an exile, not a flight, but a choice. Which may well have been true of the sons, but, as we will see, in the case of the father, personal tragedy and private needs may not have been his only motives. There may have been people beyond whose reach he needed to place himself. Patience: I will not reveal all my secrets at once.

Dandyish Petya – conservatively attired but invariably smart – had some words of his namesake Gaius Petronius, described by Pliny the

Elder, Tacitus and Plutarch as the *arbiter elegantiarum* or *elegantiae arbiter*, the judge of stylishness in Nero's court, engraved on a bronze plaque above his bedroom door: 'Leave thy home, O youth, and seek out alien shores. The far-off Danube shall know thee, the cold North-wind, the untroubled kingdom of Canopus and the men who gaze on the new birth of Phoebus or upon his setting.' It was a strange choice of quotation, since the outside world was frightening to him. But a man may dream, and in his dreams be other than he is.

I saw them in the Gardens several times a week. I grew closer to some of them than others. But to know the actual people was not the same as bringing them to life. By now I had begun to think, just write it down however it comes. Close your eyes and run the movie in your head, open your eyes and write it down. But first they had to stop being my neighbours, who lived in the Actual, and become my characters, alive in the Real. I decided to begin where they began, with their classical names. To get some clues to Petronius Golden I read *The Satyricon* and studied Menippean satire. 'Criticise mental attitudes,' was one of my notes to myself. 'Better than lampooning individuals.' I read the few extant satyr plays, *Cyclops* by Euripides, and the surviving fragments of *The Net Fishers* by Aeschylus, and Sophocles' *The Trackers*, as well as Tony Harrison's modern 'remake' of Sophocles, *The Trackers of Oxyrhynchus*. Did this ancient-world material help? Yes, in that it guided me toward the burlesque and the bawdy and away from the high-mindedness of tragedy. I liked the clog-dancing satyrs in the Harrison play and made a note, 'Petya – bad dancer, so absurdly uncoordinated that people find him funny.' There was also a possible plot device here, because in both *Fishers* and *Trackers* the satyrs stumble upon magic babies – Perseus in the former play, Hermes in the latter. 'Reserve possibility of introducing supernaturally powerful infants,' I wrote in my notebook, and beside it, in the margin, '??? or – *NO*.' So I was unclear not only about the story, and about the mystery at its heart, but also about the form. Would the surreal, the fantastic, play a part? At that moment, I was unsure. And the classical sources were as confusing as they were helpful. The satyr plays, to state the obvious, were Dionysiac, their origins probably lying in rustic homages to the god. Drink, sex, music, dance. So upon whom, in my story, should they shed most light? Petya 'was' Petronius, but Dionysus was his brother . . . in whose story the question of sex – or gender, to avoid the word his lover, the remarkable Riya, so disliked – would be central . . . . made a note. 'The characters of the brothers, to some extent, will overlap.'

And for Apu I went back to *The Golden Ass*, but, in my story, metamorphosis was to be a different brother's fate. (The sibling overlap again.) I made, however, this valuable note. 'A "golden story", in the time of Lucius Apuleius, was a figure of speech that denoted a tall tale, a wild conceit, something that was obviously untrue. A fairy tale. A lie.'

And as for the magic baby: instead of my earlier '??? or – *NO*', I have to say that, without the help of Aeschylus or Sophocles, the answer turned out to be *YES*. There would be a baby in the story. Magic or cursed? Reader: you decide.

The sad, brilliant strangeness of the man we called Petya Golden was clear to everyone from the first day, when in the failing winter-afternoon light he planted himself alone on a bench in the Gardens, a big man, like an enlargement of his father, large and heavy-bodied with his father's sharp, dark eyes that seemed to interrogate the horizon. He wore a cream suit under a heavy herringbone tweed greatcoat, gloves and orange muffler, and there was an outsize cocktail mixer and a jar of olives beside him on the bench and a martini glass in his right hand, and while he sat there in his monologic solitude and his breath hung ghostly in the January air he just started talking aloud, explained to nobody in particular the theory, which he ascribed to the surrealist film-maker Luis Buñuel, of why the perfect dry martini was like the Immaculate Conception of Christ. He was perhaps forty-two years old then and I, seventeen years his junior, approached him gingerly across the grass, ready to listen, instantly in love, as iron filings are drawn to the magnet, as the moth loves the fatal flame. As I approached I saw in the twilight that three of the Gardens' children had paused in their play, abandoning their swings and jungle gym to stare at this strange, big man talking to himself. They had no idea what the crazy newcomer was talking about but were enjoying his performance anyway. 'To make the perfect dry martini,' he was saying, 'you must take a martini glass, drop an olive into it, and then fill it to the brim with gin, or, according to the new fashion, vodka.' The children giggled at the wickedness of this alcohol talk. 'Then,' he said, jabbing the air with his left forefinger, 'you must place a bottle of vermouth close to the glass in such a position that a single shaft of sunlight passes through the bottle and strikes the martini glass. Then you drink the martini.' He took a flamboyant gulp from his glass. 'Here's one I prepared earlier,' he said, clarifying for the benefit of the children, who now ran away, laughing with delighted guilt.

The Gardens were a safe space for all the children whose homes had access to them, and so they ran about unguarded. There was a moment, after the martini lecture, when some of the neighbourhood mothers grew concerned about Petya, but there was no need for them to worry about him; children were not his vice of choice. That honour was reserved for the booze. And his mental condition was a danger to nobody but himself, though it could be disconcerting to the easily offended. The first time he met my mother he said, 'You must have been a beautiful young woman but you're old and wrinkly now.' We Unterlindens were strolling in the morning Gardens when Petya in his greatcoat, muffler and gloves came up to introduce himself to my parents, and this was what he said? This was his first sentence after 'Hello'? I bridled and opened my mouth to scold, but my mother put a hand on my arm and shook her head, kindly. 'Yes,' she replied. 'I see that you are a man who tells the truth.'

'On the spectrum': I hadn't heard the term before. I think that in many ways I have been a kind of innocent, and autism for me was not much more than Dustin Hoffman in *Rain Man* and other cruelly named 'idiot savants' reciting lists of prime numbers and drawing incredibly detailed maps of Manhattan from memory. Petya, my mother said, was certainly high on the autism spectrum. She wasn't certain if what afflicted him was HFA, high-functioning autism, or AS, which was Asperger's. Nowadays, Asperger's is no longer considered a separate diagnosis, having been folded into the spectrum on a 'severity scale'. Back then, just a few years ago, most people were as ignorant as I, and Asperger's sufferers were often put into the dismissive box marked 'mad'. Petya Golden may have been tormented, but he was by no means mad, not even close to it. He was an extraordinary, vulnerable, gifted, incompetent human being.

He was physically clumsy, and sometimes, when agitated, clumsy too in the mouth, stammering and stuttering and being infuriated by his own ineptitude. He also had the most retentive memory of anyone I ever met. You could say a poet's name, 'Byron', for example, and he would do twenty minutes of *Don Juan* with his eyes closed. 'I want a hero: an uncommon want, / When every year and month sends forth a new one, / Till, after cloying the gazettes with cant, / The age discovers he is not the true one.' In search of heroism, he said, he had tried to be a revolutionary Communist at university (Cambridge, which he left without his architecture degree because of his affliction), but admitted he didn't try hard enough to be a good one, and besides there was the disadvantage of his wealth. Also, his condition was scarcely conducive to good organisation and dependability, so he would not make a good cadre, and anyway his greatest pleasure lay not in revolt but in argument. He liked nothing better than to contradict everyone who offered him an opinion, and then to bludgeon that individual into submission by using his apparently inexhaustible storehouse of arcane, detailed knowledge. He would have argued with a king over his crown, or a sparrow over a crust of bread. He also drank far too much. When I sat down to drink with him in the Gardens one morning – his drinking began at breakfast – I had to pour the booze into a plant while his attention was distracted. It was impossible to keep up with him. But the industrial quantities of vodka he put away appeared to have no effect whatsoever on that faultily wired but still prodigious brain. In his room on an upper floor of the Golden house he was bathed in blue light and surrounded by computers and it was as if those electronic brains were his real equals, his truest friends, and the gaming world he entered through those screens was his real world, while ours was the virtual reality.

Human beings were creatures he had to put up with, with whom he would never feel at home.

What was hardest for him – in those early months before we found out the answers for ourselves, which eventually I told him we had done, to put him at his ease, which it failed to do – was to avoid spilling the family beans, their real names, their origins, the story of his mother's death. Ask him a direct question and he would answer honestly because his brain made it impossible for him to lie. Yet out of loyalty to his father's wishes he managed to find a way. He trained himself in locutions of avoidance, 'I will not answer that question', or, 'Maybe you should ask someone else', statements his nature could accept as true and therefore allow himself to make. Sometimes, it's true, he skated perilously close to treason. 'As to my family,' he said one day, apropos of nothing, as was his wont (his conversation was a series of random bombs falling out of the blue sky of his thought), 'consider the non-stop insanity that went on in the palace during the time of the twelve Caesars, the incest, the matricide, the poisonings, the epilepsy, the dead babies, the stench of evil, and of course there's Caligula's horse to consider. Mayhem, dear boy, but when the Roman in the street looked up at the palace what did he see?' Here an arch, dramatic pause, and then, 'He saw the palace, dear boy. He saw the bloody palace, immovable, unchanging, *there.* Indoors, the powerful were fucking their aunties and cutting off each other's dicks. Outside, it was clear that the power structure remained unchanged. We're like that, Papa Nero and my brothers. Behind the closed doors of the family, I freely admit, it's hell in there. Remember Edmund Leach in his Reith lectures. "The family with its narrow privacy and tawdry secrets is the source of all our discontents." Too bloody true in our case, old sport. But as far as the Roman in the street is concerned, we close ranks. We form the bloody *testudo* and forward march.'

Whatever else there is to say about Nero Golden – and by the time I'm done, much will be said, much of it horrifying – there was no questioning his devotion to his firstborn child. Plainly in some sense Petya would always remain part child, lurching unpredictably into crazy mishaps. As if AS wasn't enough, by the time he came to live among us his agoraphobia was pretty bad. The communal Gardens, interestingly, didn't scare him. Sealed off from the city on all four sides, they qualified, somehow, in that strange broken-mirror mind, as being 'indoors'. But he rarely went into the streets. Then one day he took it upon himself to tilt at his mental windmills. Defying his hatred of the undefended world, challenging himself to overcome his demons, he plunged meaninglessly into the subway. The household panicked at his disappearance and a few hours later there was a call from the police precinct at Coney Island which had him in a holding cell because, growing afraid in a tunnel, he began to create a considerable disturbance, and when a security officer came on board at the next station Petya began to abuse him as a Bolshevik apparatchik, a political commissar, an agent of the secret state; and was handcuffed. Only Nero's arrival in a large, grave, apologetic limousine saved the day. He explained his son's condition and, unusually, was listened to, and Petya was released into his father's custody. That happened, and, afterwards, worse things as well. But Nero Golden never wavered, looked constantly for cutting-edge medical help, and did his best for his firstborn son. When the final tally is made, that must weigh heavily in the scales of justice, on his side.

What is heroism in our time? What is villainy? How much we have forgotten, if we don't know the answer to such questions any more. A cloud of ignorance has blinded us, and in that fog the strange, broken mind of Petya Golden fitfully shone like a manic guiding light. What a presence he might have been! For he was born to be a star; but there was a flaw in the programme. He was a brilliant talker, yes; but he was like a whole cable box full of talk-show networks that jumped channels frequently and without warning. He was often frenziedly cheerful but his condition caused a deep pain in him, because he was ashamed of himself for malfunctioning, for failing to get better, for obliging his father and a posse of doctors to keep him functional and put him back together when he broke.

So much suffering, so nobly borne. I thought of Raskolnikov. 'Pain and suffering are always inevitable for a large intelligence and a deep heart. The really great men must, I think, have great sadness on earth.'

One summer evening – this was during the Goldens' first summer among us – they threw a glittering soirée, spilling out from their mansion onto the lawns we all shared. They had employed the city's finest publicists and party planners, so a sizeable selection of 'everybody' showed up, a goodly proportion of the boldface menagerie as well as us, the neighbours, and that night Petya was on fire, glittering-eyed and babbling like a brook. I watched him twirl and pirouette in his Savile Row finery among and around the starlet and the singer and the playwright and the whore, and the money guys discussing the Asian financial crisis, who were impressed by his mastery of such terms as 'Tom Yum Goong', the Thai term for the crisis, and his ability to discuss the fate of exotic currencies, the collapse of the baht, the devaluation of the renminbi, and to have an opinion on whether or not the financier George Soros had caused the collapse of the Malaysian economy by selling the ringgit short. Perhaps only I – or his father and I – noted the desperation behind his performance, the desperation of a mind unable to discipline itself and descending, therefore, into the carnivalesque. A mind imprisoned by itself, serving a life sentence.

That night he talked and drank without stopping, and all of us who were there would carry fragments of that talk in our memories for the rest of our lives. What crazy, extraordinary talk it was! No limit to the subjects he reached for and used as punching bags: the British royal family, in particular the sex lives of Princess Margaret, who used a Caribbean island as her private boudoir, and Prince Charles, who wanted to be his lover's tampon; the philosophy of Spinoza (he liked it); the lyrics of Bob Dylan (he recited the whole of 'Sad-Eyed Lady of the Lowlands', as reverently as if it were a companion piece to 'La Belle Dame sans Merci'); the Spassky–Fischer chess match (Fischer had died the year before); Islamic radicalism (he was against it) and wishy-washy liberalism (which appeased Islam, he said, so he was against it, too); the Pope, whom he called 'Ex-Benedict'; the novels of G. K. Chesterton (he was a fan of *The Man Who Was Thursday*); the unpleasantness of male chest hair; the 'unjust treatment' of Pluto, recently demoted to the status of 'dwarf planet' after a larger body, Eris, was discovered in the Kuiper

Belt; the flaws in Hawking's theory of black holes; the anachronistic weakness of the American electoral college; the stupidity of non-electoral college students; the sexiness of Margaret Thatcher; and the 'twenty-five per cent of Americans' – on the far right of the political spectrum – 'who are certifiably insane'.

Oh, but there was also his adoration of *Monty Python's Flying Circus*! And all of a sudden he was flustered and stumbling to find the right words, because one of the dinner guests, a member of a prominent Broadway family of theatre owners, had brought along, as his plus-one, the Python Eric Idle, who was then enjoying a revival of fame thanks to the Broadway success of *Spamalot,* and who arrived just as Petya was expounding, to the serenely elegant sculptor Ubah Tuur (of whom there will be much more to say in a moment), upon his hatred of musicals in general; he exempted only *Oklahoma!* and *West Side Story,* and had been offering us idiosyncratic snatches of 'I Cain't Say No' and 'Gee, Officer Krupke' while explaining that 'all other musicals were shit'. When he saw the Python standing there listening he blushed brightly and then rescued himself by including Mr Idle's musical among the blessed, and led the company in a rousing chorus of 'Always Look on the Bright Side of Life'.

However, his near-gaffe had ruined his mood. He mopped perspiration from his brow, rushed indoors and disappeared. He did not rejoin the party; and then well after midnight, when most guests had left and only a few of the locals were taking the warm night air, the windows of Petya's room on the upper floor of the Golden house were flung open and the big man climbed out onto the ledge, swaying drunkenly and dressed in a long black greatcoat that made him look like a Soviet-era student revolutionary. In his agitated condition he sat down heavily on the windowsill with his legs dangling, and cried out to the skies, *'I am here by myself! I am here because of myself! I am here because of nobody! I am here all by myself!'*

Time froze. We, in the garden, stood paralysed, looking upward. His brothers, who were in the Gardens among us, seemed as incapable of movement as we. And it was his father, Nero Golden, who came silently up behind him and, grabbing him from behind in a great embrace, fell backwards with his son into the room behind. It was Nero who came to the window and, before he closed it, waved at us in furious dismissal.

'Nothing to see here. Ladies and gentlemen, nothing to see. Goodnight.'

For a period after the something-like-suicide-attempt Petya Golden found it hard to emerge from his curtained room, which was illuminated by the lights of a dozen screens and a host of lamps with pale blue light bulbs, and in which he remained day and night, hardly sleeping, busily engaged in his electronic mysteries, including playing chess against anonymous e-opponents in Korea and Japan, and, as we afterwards discovered, rushing himself through a crash course in the history and development of video games, understanding the war-gaming programs devised in the 1940s to run on the earliest digital computers, Colossus and ENIAC, then rushing contemptuously through *Tennis for Two, Spacewar!,* and the early arcade games, through the age of *Hunt the Wumpus* and *Dungeons & Dragons,* skipping past the banalities of *Pac-Man* and *Donkey Kong, Street Fighter* and *Mortal Kombat,* and on and on through *SimCity, World of Warcraft,* and the more sophisticated subjectivities of *Assassin's Creed* and *Red Dead Redemption* and then into levels of sophistication at which none of us could guess; and watching the vulgar fictions of reality television; and subsisting on grilled Double Gloucester cheese sandwiches prepared by himself on a small electric stove; feeling, all this while, profoundly sickened by himself and the burden he had to bear. Then his internal weather changed and he moved from self-hatred to hatred of the world, and, in particular, as the world's nearest representative authority figure, of his father. One night that summer, insomnia, my constant friend, forced me to get out of bed around 3 a.m., pull on some clothes and wander into the communal Gardens to take the warm night air. The houses were all asleep; all but one. In the Golden residence the lights were on in a single second-floor window, in the room Nero Golden used as an office. I couldn't see the old man but Petya's silhouette, with the broad shoulders and the flat-top haircut, was easily recognisable. What was startling was the extreme animation of that silhouetted figure, the arms waving, the weight shifting from leg to leg. He turned slightly, and looking at him in near-profile I understood that he was screaming with rage.

I couldn't hear anything. The study windows were well soundproofed. Some of us suspected them of actually being inch-thick bulletproof glass, a hypothesis to which the silent image of Petya shouting lent much credence. Why did Nero Golden feel the need to bulletproof his windows? No answer to that one; the rich in New York feel the need to protect themselves in unpredictable ways. In my family of academics we adopted an air of interested amusement when faced with our neighbours' eccentricities, the painter permanently attired in silk pyjamas, the magazine editor who never removed her sunglasses no matter what the hour, and so on. So, bulletproof glass, no biggie. In a way the dumbshow accentuated the power of Petya Golden's hysterical performance. I am an admirer of German expressionist cinema in general and of the work of Fritz Lang in particular, and all of a sudden the words 'Dr Mabuse' popped unbidden into my head. At the time I brushed the thought aside, because I was more preoccupied by another consideration: perhaps Petya really was going off his rocker, not just metaphorically, but actually. Perhaps behind the autism and agoraphobia lay an actual derangement, an insanity. I resolved to watch him more carefully from then on.

What was the argument about? There was no way to know; but to my mind it seemed like an expression of Petya's savage complaint against life itself, which had dealt him such a poor hand. The next day the old man was to be seen pensive on a bench in the Gardens, sitting there like stone, silent, immovable, unapproachable, with a darkness on his face. Many years later, when we knew everything, I remembered thinking about Lang's great film *Dr. Mabuse the Gambler* that summer night in the Gardens under Nero Golden's illuminated, silenced window. The film, of course, is about the career of a criminal mastermind.

No hint of the dramatic events at the Goldens' party ever reached the newspapers (or the gossip websites, or any of the other digital megaphones birthed by the new technology). In spite of the high celebrity content of the guest list, in spite of the hovering team of waitstaff who might have been tempted by the easy money on offer for a salacious phone call, the code of silence under which the Goldens lived appeared to wrap itself around all who entered their presence, so that not a whisper of scandal ever escaped their powerful, almost Sicilian force field of *omertà.* Nero had hired the most powerful members of the city's tribe of publicists, whose most important task was not to get, but to suppress, publicity; and so what happened in the Golden house very largely stayed in the Golden house.

I believe now that Nero Golden knew in his heart that his performance as a New Yorker without a past was short-lived. I think he knew that in the end the past would not be denied, that it would come for him, and have its way. I think that he was using his immense capacity for bravado to stave off the inevitable. 'I'm a man of reason,' he informed his dinner guests on the night of Petya's meltdown. (He had a weakness for self-praising orations.) 'A man of affairs. If I may say so, a great man of affairs. Believe me. Nobody knows affairs better than I do, let me tell you that. Now, America is too God-bothered for my liking, too wrapped up in superstitions, but I'm not that kind of man. That kind of thing gets in the way of commerce. Two plus two is four, that's me. The rest is mumbo-jumbo and gobbledegook. Four plus four is eight. If America wants to be what America is capable of being, what she dreams of being, she needs to turn away from God and toward the dollar bill. The business of America is business. That is what I believe.' Such was his bold (and often repeated) assertion of pragmatic capitalism, which reassured me, incidentally, that we Unterlindens had been right about his irreligious nature; and yet he was, they all were, in the grip of a huge fantasy: the idea that men would not be judged by who they once were and what they had once done, if they only decided to be different. They wanted to step away from the responsibilities of history and be free. But history is the court before which all men, even emperors and princes, finally must stand. I think of Longfellow's paraphrase of the Roman Sextus Empiricus: The mills of God grind slowly, but they grind exceeding small.

7

Lucius Apuleius Golden, aka Apu, the second pseudonymous Golden boy – for some reason, even though he was already forty-one, the word *boy* fitted better than *man* – was only a year younger than his brother Petya, their birthdays less than twelve months apart, their horoscope sign (Gemini) the same. He was a handsome, childish man, with a wicked goatish mischief in his smile, a gleeful giggle irresistibly combined with a pretence of constant melancholy, and an ever-changing monologue of lamentation in which he catalogued his failures with young women outside the toilets of late-night hot spots (his way of disguising a long string of successes in that area). He wore his hair shaved close to his skull – a concession to encroaching baldness – and wrapped himself in a voluminous pashmina shawl and didn't get on with his older brother any more. They both stated, in separate conversations with me, that they had been close as young children, but their relationship had eroded as they grew older, because of their irreconcilable temperaments. Apu, a wanderer in the city, an explorer of everything it had to offer, was unsympathetic to Petya's 'issues'. 'That stupid brother of mine,' he told me when, as sometimes happened, we went out drinking, 'he's such a scaredy-cat.' And he went on to say, 'He should be careful. Our father despises weakness and doesn't want it near him. Once he decides you're a weakling you're dead to him. You're fucking dead.' Then, as if he had just heard what he had said, heard the sound of the armour cracking, he drew back and corrected himself. 'Don't pay any attention. I've had too many drinks and anyway it's just the way we talk. We talk a lot of nonsense. It doesn't mean anything.'

I heard that speech as envy. Nero Golden was, as we could all see, deeply caring for and solicitous of his psychologically wounded firstborn son. Perhaps Apu didn't get the attention from the patriarch he so openly craved. (I wondered often why the four Goldens all continued to live under the same roof, especially when it became plain that they weren't getting along, but when I found the courage to ask Apu why that was I got nothing but cryptic, allegorical answers, owing more to *One Thousand and One Nights* or *The Diamond as Big as the Ritz* than to anything that might be called the truth. 'Our father,' he might reply, 'is the one who knows where the treasure cave is hidden, the one that responds to the words *open, sesame.* So we stay because we're trying to find the map.' Or, 'The house, you know, is literally built on an underground mass of pure gold. Every time we need to pay for things we just go into the cellar and scrape off a tiny piece.' It was as if the house exercised some power over them all – the genealogical house or the actual house, it was sometimes hard to separate them. For whatever thicker-than-water reason, they felt bound to one another, even if their actual feelings for one another deteriorated over time toward open hostility. The Caesars in their palace, their whole lives a great gamble, performing their dance of death.)

Apu's greed for America was omnivorous. I reminded myself that of course he and Petya would have been here before, as much younger men, living with their parents in the Broadway loft during college vacations, in all probability knowing nothing about the benami house just a short walk away which their father was readying for the distant future. How Apu must have prospered sexually in that much younger, grittier city! No wonder he was glad to be back.

Soon after his arrival he asked me to tell him about the November night when Barack Obama was elected president. On that night I had been in a Midtown sports bar where a well-known doyenne of Upper East Side society, a Republican, was jointly hosting an election night party with a distinctly downtown Democrat film producer. At 11 p.m., when California declared and pushed Obama over the finish line, the room exploded with emotion, and I realised that I, like everyone else, had been unable to believe that what was happening would really happen, even though the numbers had clearly indicated an Obama victory a couple of hours earlier. The possibility of another stolen election was not far from our thoughts and so relief mingled with elation when the majority was definite; *they can't steal this now,* I reassured myself, and felt tears on my face. When I looked at Apu after I told him this I saw that he was crying too.

After the big moment in the sports bar, I told him, I walked the streets half the night, going to Rockefeller Center and Union Square, watching the crowds of young people like myself shining with the knowledge that, perhaps for the first time ever, they had by their own direct actions changed their country's course. I was drinking in the optimism that was flowing all around us, and, like a properly jaundiced literary person, I formulated this thought: 'And now, of course, he will disappoint us.' I wasn't proud of it, I said, but these were the words that came to mind.

'You're already so disenchanted, while I'm a dreamer,' Apu asked, still weeping. 'But awful things have happened to me and my family. Nothing terrible has ever happened to you or yours.'

Thanks to my parents, I knew something by then about Apu's 'awful things' – but I wondered about his tears. Could this relatively recent arrival in America already be so invested in his new country that an election result could make him cry? Had he already bonded with the country in his youth and was now feeling the rebirth of that long-lost love? Were they the tears of a sentimentalist or a crocodile? I put that question away and thought, when you get to know him better you'll have the answer. And so I took another step toward becoming an occasional spy; I was absolutely clear, by now, that these were people worth spying on. As for what he said about me, it was not entirely accurate, because I was, on the whole, caught up in the early fervour of the Obama presidency, but it was prescient, because as the years passed my alienation from the system grew, and eight years later when people younger than myself (most of them young, white and college-educated) expressed their desire to rip that system up and throw it away, I didn't agree, because that kind of grand gesture seemed like an expression of the same spoiled luxuriousness that its proponents claimed to hate, and when such gestures were made they invariably led to something worse than what had been discarded. But I got it, I understood the alienation and anger, because much of it was mine as well, even if I ended up at a different, more cautious, gradualist, and, in the eyes of the generation following mine, contemptible point on the (political) spectrum.

He was mystically inclined, drawn to all things spiritual, but, as I say, mostly concealed his passion from us, although there was no reason to conceal it, because New Yorkers were just as much in love with weird belief systems as he was. He found a witch, a *mãe-de-santo* in Greenpoint, and in her cramped *terreiro* he followed her in the worship of her favoured Orisha (a minor deity) and of course of the Supreme Creator Oludumaré as well. But he was unfaithful to her even though she instructed him in sorcery, and followed with equal enthusiasm a Canal Street Kabbalist named Idel, who was an adept in the ways of the forbidden Practical Kabbalah, which sought through the use of white magic to affect and change the sphere of the divine itself, and the world as well. He also went eagerly, led by friends who found his eagerness seductive, into the world of Buddhist Judaism, and meditated along with the city's growing cohorts of 'BuJus' – classical composers, movie stars, yogis. He practised Mysore yoga and became a master of the Tarot and studied numerology and books bought in antiquarian bookstores that explored the black arts and gave instructions concerning the construction of pentacles and magic circles within which the amateur wizard could be safe while casting his spells.

It was soon clear that he was an exceptionally gifted painter, of a technical facility as great as Dalí's (though put to better use), figurative in an age of conceptualism, his male and female figures, often nude, contained within, or containing, or surrounded by, or surrounding, the symbolist icons of his arcane studies, flowers, eyes, swords, cups, suns, stars, pentagrams, and male and female sexual organs. Before long he had a studio space off Union Square and was making vivid portraits of *le tout* New York, the elite ladies (yes, mostly ladies, though some striking young men as well) who were overjoyed to strip off for him and to be painted into a lush world of high spiritual meaning, wrapped in tulips or swimming in the rivers of Paradise or Hell, before returning to the temples of Mammon where they lived. Because of his remarkable technical control he developed a rapid fluency of style which meant he could usually complete a portrait in a day and that, too, endeared him to the fast-lane crowd. His first solo show was in 2010, curated by the Bruce High Quality Foundation in a Chelsea pop-up space, and took its title from Nietzsche, *The Privilege of Owning Yourself.* He began to be a famous artist, or, as he put it with a kind of cynical comic modesty, 'famous on twenty blocks'.

America changed them both, Petya and Apu – America, that divided self – polarising them as America was polarised, the wars of America, external and internal, becoming their wars as well; but in the beginning, if Petya arrived in New York as the heavy-drinking polymath who was afraid of the world and found living in it a constant hardship, then Apu came as the sober romantic artist and promiscuous metropolitan, flirting with everything that was visionary yet with a clarity of vision that allowed him to see people plain, as his portraits showed: the panic in the eyes of the fading dowager, the vulnerable ignorance in the stance of the ungloved boxing champion, the courage of the ballerina with blood in her slippers like the Ugly Sister who cut off her toes to squeeze her foot into Cinderella's glass shoe. His portraits were anything but sycophantic; they could be very harsh. Yet people hastened to his door with fat cheques in their hands. To be done by Apu Golden, nailed to his canvas, became desirable, valuable. It became a thing. Meanwhile, away from his studio, he ran voraciously through the city, embracing it all like a young Whitman, the undergrounds, the clubs, the power stations, the prisons, the subcultures, the catastrophes, the flaming comets, the gamblers, the dying factories, the dancing queens. He was his brother's antithesis, a gluttonous agoraphile, and came to be thought of as a magic creature, an escapee from a fairy tale, though nobody could say for certain whether he was charmed or doomed.

He was a far more flamboyant dresser than his older brother, and his look altered frequently. He wore contact lenses in many colours, sometimes different colours for each eye, and until the very end I did not know what his natural eye colour was. His clothing embraced all the fashions of the planet. On a whim he would abandon the pashmina shawl and put on, instead, the Arab dishdasha, the African dashiki, the South Indian veshti, the bright shirts of Latin America or, sometimes, in a Petya-low-key mood, the buttoned-up gravity of the bespoke English three-piece tweed suit. He might be seen on Sixth Avenue in a maxiskirt or a kilt. This mutability confused many of us about his orientation, but as far as I know he was conventionally heterosexual; though it is true that he was a sort of genius of compartmentalisation, he kept different groups of friends in sealed-off boxes and nobody in one box was even aware of the existence of other, different containers. So it's possible that he had a secret life beyond the frontiers of heterosex, maybe even a promiscuous one. But in my opinion that is unlikely. As we shall see, he was not the Golden brother for whom gender identity was an issue. In his mystical explorations, however, he certainly did develop a number of peculiar, occultist affiliations which he didn't care to discuss. But now that everything is known I can begin to reconstruct that life he kept concealed.

We had the movies in common, and liked to spend weekend afternoons at the IFC Center or Film Forum watching *Tokyo Monogatari* or *Orfeu negro* or *Le charme discret de la bourgeoisie.* It was because of the movies that he shortened his name to echo Ray's immortal Apu. His father objected, he confessed to me. 'He says we are Romans, not Bengalis. But that is his preoccupation, not mine.' Nero Golden found our movie dates amusing. When I came by to pick up Apu he was sometimes waiting in the small backyard that gave out onto the communal Gardens and, turning to face the house, he'd roar, 'Apuleius! Your girlfriend's here!'

One last note regarding his name: he spoke with admiration about the second-century author of *The Golden Ass*. 'The guy inherited one million sesterces from his father in Algeria and still wrote a masterpiece.' And regarding his older brother's name as well as his own: 'If Petya's the satyr, or even the satyr-icon, then I'm definitely the fucking donkey.' (Then, a dismissive shrug.) But late at night, when he'd had a few drinks, he inverted the thought. Which felt like a better fit; because, to tell the truth, of the pair, he was the priapically satyric one, while poor Petya was very often the long-eared ass.

On the night of the Goldens' party in the Gardens, Petya and Apu met the Somali woman, and the ties that held the clan together began to break.

She had been brought to the gathering by her gallerist, who was now also, though not exclusively, Apu's: a twinkling silver-haired rogue named Frankie Sottovoce who had gained notoriety in his youth by spray-painting the twelve-inch-high letters NLF on one of the three monumental Claude Monet paintings of water lilies at the Museum of Modern Art, to protest the war in Vietnam, echoing the act of the unknown vandal who, in the same year, 1974, had scratched the two-foot-high letters IRA into the lower right-hand corner of Peter Paul Rubens's *Adoration of the Magi* in King's College Chapel, Cambridge, an act for which Sottovoce, when feeling boastful about his radical-left activist younger self, would also improbably claim responsibility. The paintings were easily restored, the IRA lost its war, the Vietcong won theirs, and the gallerist went on to have a distinguished career, and discovered and successfully promoted, among many others, the metal-cutting sculptor Ubah Tuur.

Ubah means 'flower' or 'blossom' in Somali, and is sometimes written as *Ubax*, the 'x' in Somali being a throaty sound that Anglophone throats struggle to make, a voiceless pharyngeal fricative. Hence 'Ubah', a simplified concession to non-Somali pharyngeal incompetence. She was beautiful in the way the women of the Horn are beautiful, long-necked and graceful in the arms, and in the long summer evening she seemed to Petya a flowering tree beneath whose boughs he could rest, healed by her cooling shade, for the rest of his life. At a certain point in the evening she sang: not the ululating Somali song he had expected to emerge from those rich lips but Patti Smith's famous ode to love itself, full of darkness and desire, with its comforting, treacherous repetitions, *can't hurt you now, can't hurt you now* . . . and by the time she was done he was lost. He rushed in her direction and stopped dead in front of her, at a loss. Overcome by his sudden rush of impossible, unspeakable love, he began to babble at his just-discovered dream girl about this and that, poetry and subatomic physics and the private lives of movie stars, and she listened gravely, accepting all his short-circuit non sequiturs as if they were entirely natural, and he felt, for once in his life, understood. Then she began to speak and he listened mesmerised, mongoose to her cobra. Afterwards he was able to repeat verbatim every single word that came out of her flawless mouth.

Her early work, she said, was inspired by the primitive artists she had met on a visit to Haiti, who cut oil drums in half, flattened the two halves, and then, using the simplest of tools – hammers and screwdrivers – cut and beat them into intricate latticework images of branches, foliage and birds. She talked to Petya for a long time about using a blowtorch to cut steel and iron into lace-like intricacies and showed him images of her work on her phone: the remains of wrecked (bombed?) cars and tanks, transformed into the most delicate filigree forms, the metal penetrated by shapely patterned air and acquiring an airiness of its own. She spoke in the language of the art world, *war of symbols, desirable oppositions,* the high-abstract insider jargon, describing her quest for *empathetic images creating a balance as well as a clash by contrasting ideas and materials,* and she examined, too, *the absurdity of having opposing extremist stances, like a wrestler in a tutu.* She was a brilliant speaker, charismatic and almost incomprehensibly fast, pushing a hand through her hair and clutching at her head as she spoke; but in the end he burst out (his autism forcing him to speak the truth), 'I'm sorry, but I don't understand anything you're saying.'

Immediately he hated himself. What kind of a fool, with the words 'I love you' stuck in his throat, offered his brilliant beloved scorn instead of adoration? Now she would hate him and would be justified in doing so and his life would be meaningless and damned.

She stared at him for a long moment and then burst into healing laughter. 'It's a defence mechanism,' she said. 'One worries one will not be taken seriously if one lacks a sufficiency of theory, especially if one is female. Actually, my work speaks pretty clearly for itself. I push beauty into horror and I want it to disturb you and make you think. Come up to Rhinebeck and take a look.'

I'm now sure – as I piece together the puzzle of the Golden house, and try to reconstruct my memory of the exact sequence of events of that important night, setting them down as they come back to me – that this was the point of the evening at which things started to go wrong for Petya, as his desire to accept Ubah's invitation did battle with the demons that obliged him to fear the outside world. He made a strange gesture with both arms, half helpless, half angry, and at once began to soliloquise in a rapid series of non sequiturs about whatever crossed his anguished mind. His mood grew darker as he expostulated on various topics, coming at last to the question of Broadway musicals and his dislike of most of them. Then came the awkward Python episode and his disappearance indoors and then his anguish on the windowsill. Love, in Petya, was never far from despair.

All that summer he was sad, locked in his room bathed in blue light, playing and (as we afterwards discovered) creating computer games of immense complexity and beauty, and dreaming of that haunting face behind a protective face mask and of the steel-cutting flame moving in her hand as she created fantasy and delicacy out of brute metal. He thought of her as a kind of superhero, his blowtorch goddess, and wanted above all things to be with her but he feared the journey, a Prince too full of troubles to be able to pursue his vanished Cinderella. Nor could he call her and tell her how he felt. He was like a continent of erratic garrulity containing a no-go zone of oral paralysis. And finally it was Apu who took pity on him and offered to help. 'I'll rent a car with blacked-out windows,' he declared. 'We're going to get you *access*.'

Apu swore, afterwards, that that had been his only motive: to get Petya across the frontier of his fear and give him a shot at the girl. But maybe he wasn't telling the truth.

And so Petya screwed up his courage and made the call, and Ubah Tuur invited the brothers up for the weekend, and was understanding enough to tell him, 'There's a good solid fence all the way around the property, so maybe you can think of it as interior space, like your communal Gardens. If you can get your head around that I can show you the work that's standing on the land as well as what's in the studio.'

In the last light of day, wearing her soiled work dungarees, her hair loosely piled up under a back-to-front Yankees baseball cap, the protective mask, just removed, dangling from the crook of her elbow: without even trying, she was a knockout. 'Here, I want you to see this,' she said, and took Petya's hand in hers, and led him through the crepuscular land littered with her giant intricate forms, like the lacy armour of immense gods, like battlefield detritus reworked by light-fingered elves, and he uncomplaining, believing in the existence of the fence he could not see in the failing light, not even by the light of the full bright moon above; she rounded the long low farmhouse where she lived, led him between the farmhouse and the barn where she worked, and said, 'Look.' And there at the foot of the land, where it fell sharply away, was the rolling river, the wide and silver Hudson, taking his breath away. For a long moment he didn't even think about the fence, didn't ask if he was safely enclosed or dangerously exposed to the frightening everything of the world, and when he did begin to ask, 'Is there . . .' and as his hand fell to trembling she held it firmly and said, 'The river is the wall. This is a safe place for us all.' And he accepted what she said and was not afraid, and stood there watching the water until she led the brothers indoors to dinner.

He became his loquacious self again in the warm yellow light of her kitchen, eating her mango curry chicken, its sweetness doing battle on his palate with the berbere spices mixed into it. But while he talked on and on about his enthusiasm for the video-gaming world, interspersing accounts of the latest games with recitals of river poetry under the influence of the shining river, her attention wandered. The night lengthened and the script of the visit was thrown away and Ubah Tuur felt an unexpectedness rise in her; a treachery. How is it you're not married? she asked Petya. A man like you, you're a catch. But while she said it her eyes slid across to Apu. Who was *sitting perfectly still,* he told me, *doing nothing,* but afterwards Petya accused him of *mumbling, you were muttering something, you bastard, you used black magic on her,* while he, Petya, tried to answer Ubah, the words stumbling, a long time ago, yes, someone, but since then the waiting, the waiting for an emotional imperative, and she, talking to him but looking at his brother, And so now, have you found the emotional imperative, flirtatious, but her eyes on Apu, and he, mumbling, according to Petya, though he himself always denied to me that he mumbled.

I know what you did, you rat, Petya would shriek later, maybe you put something in her food also, the spices would have disguised it, some evil chicken entrail powder you got from your Greenpoint witch, and the mumbling, what were you saying, a hex, a hex.

And Apu straight-faced, making matters worse, Where is my father's pet son now? What about two plus two is four? Four plus four is eight? I did nothing. Nothing.

You fucked her, Petya wailed.

Well, yes. I did that. I'm sorry.

It may have gone somewhat differently. I wasn't there. It may well have been that the usually loquacious Petya was tongue-tied all night, silenced by love, and lively worldly Apu monopolised the talk, and the woman. It may be that she, Ubah, universally held to be a graceful courteous woman, not usually reckless, surprised herself on this occasion by yielding to sudden lust for the wrong brother, her fellow artist, the rising star, the ladies' man, the charmer. The motivations of desire are obscure even to the desirous, the desiring and the desired. *I do betray / My nobler part to my gross body's treason,* Bard of Avon, Sonnet 151. And so without full knowledge of the why and wherefore, we inflict mortal wounds on those we love.

A dark house. Creaking floorboards. Movements. There is no need to rehearse the banal melodrama of the act. In the morning the guilt on the faces of both the guilty, as easy to read as a headline. Large, heavy Petya, lithe, shaven-headed Apu, the woman between them like a storm cloud. There's nothing to explain, she said. It's what happened. I think you both should go.

And then Petya imprisoned by his fear of the world in his brother's rented car with darkened windows trembled with humiliated, unmanned fury in the back seat, three hours of silent horror as they drove back to the city. At such moments a man's thoughts may begin to turn to murder.

8

Eighteen years after Apu was born the old man had an extramarital involvement and was not careful and a pregnancy resulted which he chose not to have aborted, because, in his opinion, it was always his business to do the choosing. The mother was a poor woman whose identity did not become known (a secretary? a whore?) and in return for a certain financial consideration she gave the child up to be raised as his father's son, left town, and disappeared from her baby's story. So like the god Dionysus the child was twice born, once of his mother and then again into his father's world. Dionysus the god was always an outsider, a god of resurrection and arrival, 'the god that comes'. He was also androgynous, 'man-womanish'. That this was the pseudonym the youngest child of Nero Golden chose for himself in the classical-renaming game reveals that he knew something about himself before he knew it, so to speak. Though at the time the reasons he gave for his choice were, in the first place, that Dionysus adventured far and wide in India, and indeed the mythical Mount Nysa where he was born might have been located on the subcontinent; and, in the second place, that he was the deity of sensual delight, not only Dionysus but, in his Roman incarnation, also Bacchus, god of wine, disorderliness and ecstasy, all of which – Dionysus Golden said – sounded like fun. However, he soon announced that he preferred not to be known by the divine name in full, and went by the plain, near-anonymous single-letter nickname, 'D'.

His integration into the family had been no easy matter. With his half-brothers, from the beginning, he had poor relations. All his childhood he had felt excluded. They called him Mowgli and howled comically at the moon. His wolf-mother was some jungle whore; theirs was the mother wolf of Rome. (At this point it seems they had decided to be Romulus and Remus, though Apu later denied this to me, or rather suggested that it had been an idea in D's head, not his own.) They had already mastered Latin and Greek when D was still learning to talk, and they used these secret languages to banish him from their conversations. They both afterwards denied this, too, but admitted that the way he entered the family, and also the age gap, had created serious difficulties, questions of loyalty and natural affection. Now, as a young man, D Golden when in his brothers' company alternated between ingratiation and rage. It was plain that he needed to love and be loved; there was a tide of emotion in him that needed to wash over people and he hoped for a returning tide to wash over him. When this kind of passionate reciprocity didn't happen he snapped and ranted and withdrew. He was twenty-two years old when the family took possession of the Golden house. Sometimes he seemed wise beyond his years. At other times he behaved like a four-year-old child.

When, as a child, he plucked up his courage and asked his father and stepmother about the woman who gave him birth, his father would simply throw up his hands and leave the room. His stepmother would grow angry. 'Leave it!' she cried one fateful day. 'That was a woman of no consequence. She went away, got sick and died.'

What was it like, to be Mowgli, born of a woman of no consequence, who had been so cruelly cast off by his father and then in the outer darkness had died one of the myriad deaths of the forgotten poor? I heard a shocking story later, from Apu, after the code of silence was broken. There had been a time when the old man's relationship with their mother was in difficulties. He raged at her and she shouted back. I sat up and paid attention because this was the first time in my conversations with the Goldens that the faceless, nameless woman, Nero's wife – since ancient times an unlucky thing to be – had walked out onto the stage and opened her mouth; and because, according to the story, Nero had shouted and screamed, and she had screamed and shouted back at him. This was not the Nero I knew, in whom the force of his rage was kept under control, emerging only in the form of self-glorifying bombast.

At any rate: after the explosion the family split into two camps. The older boys took their mother's side but Dionysus Golden stood firmly by his father and persuaded the patriarch that his wife, Petya and Apu's mother, was not fit to run the household. Nero summoned his wife and ordered her to surrender the keys; and after that for a time it was D who gave instructions and ordered groceries and decided what food would be cooked in the kitchens. It was a public humiliation, a dishonouring. Her sense of her own honour was profoundly linked to that iron ring, a majestic *O* three inches in diameter, from which hung maybe twenty keys, large and small, keys to the larder, to cellar strongboxes packed with gold ingots and other arcana of the rich, and to various secret crevices all over the mansion where she concealed only she knew what: old love letters, wedding jewellery, antique shawls. It was the symbol of her domestic authority, and her pride and self-respect hung there along with the keys. She was the mistress of the locks, and without that role she was nothing. Two weeks after she was commanded by her husband to give up the key ring, the deposed lady of the house attempted to take her own life. Pills were swallowed, she was found by Apu and Petya slumped at the foot of the marble stairs, an ambulance came. She was clutching Apu by the wrist and the ambulance men said, please come with us, her holding on to you is important, she's holding on to life.

In the ambulance the two paramedics played good cop, bad cop. — Stupid bitch scaring your family, you think we have nothing better to do, we have serious things to deal with, real injuries, emergencies that are not self-inflicted, we should just leave you to die. — No the poor thing, don't be so hard on her, she must be so sad, it's all right, darling, we will look after you, things will get better, every cloud has a silver lining. — To hell with the silver lining, she doesn't even have a cloud, look at her house, her money, these people think they own us. — Don't mind him darling, it's just his way, we are here to take care of you, you're in good hands now. She was trying to mutter something but Apu couldn't make out the words. He knew what they were doing, they were trying to keep her from slipping into unconsciousness, and afterwards, after the stomach pump which he had had to watch because of her claw-hand clutching at his wrist, when she was conscious again in a hospital bed, she told him, The only thing I was trying to say in the ambulance was, my child, will you please punch that rude bastard on the nose.

She returned home in a kind of triumph, because of course she was restored to her position as head of the household and the traitor child who was not her child begged for her forgiveness, and she told him she forgave him, but actually she never did, and barely spoke to him again for the rest of her life. Nor did he truly want her forgiveness. She had called his mother a woman of no consequence and deserved everything he had inflicted upon her. After that his brothers slammed emotional doors in his face and told him he was lucky they were not violent men. He swallowed his pride and pleaded for their forgiveness also. It did not come quickly. But as the years passed a reserved cordiality slowly grew up between them, a brevity of interaction that outsiders mistook for inarticulate brotherly love, but was no more than mutual toleration.

Unasked questions hung in the air, unsolved mysteries: Why did the young boy who grew up to be D Golden want so desperately to run the household that he would humiliate his stepmother to fulfil his desire? Was it to prove he belonged? Or was it, as it could so easily have been, to avenge the dead woman who gave him birth?

'I don't know,' Apu said dismissively when I asked him. 'He can be an extraordinary little shit when he wants.'

From his acute sense of difference rooted in his illegitimacy, D Golden constructed a form of Nietzschean elitism to justify his isolation. (Always when considering the Golden men, one encounters the shadow of the *Übermensch.*) 'How should there be a "common good",' he quoted the philosopher in the Gardens. 'The term contradicts itself: whatever can be common always has little value. In the end it must be as it is and always has been: great things remain for the great, abysses for the profound, nuances and shudders for the refined and, in brief, all that is rare for the rare.' This struck me as no more than youthful posing; just a few months older than he, I recognised in him my own weakness for philosophising. D was in fact quite the striker of poses, a Dorian Gray type, slender, lissom, bordering on the effeminate. His self-image – that only he of all his tribe had the capacity for greatness, only he had the depth of character to plunge deeply into sorrow, that only he was rare – sounded pretty straightforwardly defensive in origin. But I had much compassion for him; he had been dealt a tough hand, and we all build our walls, do we not, and maybe we don't even know what we are building them against, what force will finally storm them and destroy our little dreams.

I went with him sometimes to listen to music. There was a red-headed singer he liked called Ivy Manuel who did a weekly late-night set in a place on Orchard Street, sometimes wearing a tiara on her head to prove she was a queen. She sang cover versions of 'Wild Is the Wind' and 'Famous Blue Raincoat' and 'Under the Bridge' before moving on to a few of her own, and D sitting in front of her at a little round black iron table closed his eyes and swayed to Bowie and Cohen and put his own words to the Chili Peppers under his breath. Sometimes I feel like I haven't been born yet, sometimes I feel I don't want to be born. Ivy Manuel was his friend because, he said – not joking – all the straight girls he met wanted to hit on him but Ivy was lesbian so they could actually have a friendship. He was the most beautiful of all those Goldens, as any magic mirror would readily have confirmed, and he could be the most beguiling of them too. All of us in the houses on the Gardens were victims of his wounded openness and in the larger neighbourhood too he quickly became a figure. He professed to be disturbed by the attention. Everywhere I go people look at me, he said, there's always someone looking, like I'm someone, like they expect something from me. Get over yourself, Ivy told him, nobody wants shit from you. He grinned and bowed his head in mock-apology. Charm was his disguise as it was Apu's; beneath the surface he was brooding and often sad. From the beginning he was the one with the darkest darkness in him, even though he came into the world like sunshine, with a full head of white-blond hair. The hair darkened toward chestnut, and the skies of his character grew overcast also, there were frequent downward spirals into gloom.

Ivy didn't make a big deal out of her sexuality, as a musician she didn't like to hang labels on herself. 'I have no problem being out, but I don't think it has anything to do with my music,' she said. 'I like who I like. I don't want people to not listen to my music because of that and I don't want people to listen to my music because of that.' But her audience was skewed heavily female, a lot of women plus the charming young man who didn't want people to look at him, and me.

The Goldens all told stories about themselves, stories in which essential information about origins was either omitted or falsified. I listened to them not as 'true' but as indications of character. The yarns a man told about himself revealed him in ways that the record could not. I thought of these anecdotes as card players' 'tells', the involuntary gestures that give away a hand – the rubbing of the nose when the hand is strong, the fingering of an earlobe when it's weak. The master player watches everyone at the table to discover their tells. This was how I tried to watch and listen to the Golden men. Yet one night when I went with D to the place on Orchard Street to hear Ivy Manuel sing Bowie's ch-ch-ch-ch and Mitchell's don't-it-always-seem-to-go and an odd funny science-fiction song of her own called 'The Terminator', regarding the usefulness of time travel to potential saviours of the human race, and afterwards I sat drinking beers with the two of them in the empty venue, I missed the most obvious tell of all. I think it was Ivy who raised the increasingly complex subject of gendering, and D responded with a story from Greek mythology. Hermaphroditus was the child of Hermes and Aphrodite with whom a nymph named Salmacis fell so deeply in love that she begged Zeus to unite them forever, and so they became one, the two of them in a single body in which both sexes remained manifest. At the time I thought it was a way of saying how close he felt to Ivy Manuel, how they were joined forever as friends. But he was telling me stranger things and I didn't know how to listen; things about himself.

The point about metamorphosis is that it's not random. Philomela, assaulted by her brother-in-law Tereus, raped and with her tongue cut out, flew away from him as a nightingale, free, and with the sweetest singing voice. As in the story of Salmacis and Hermaphroditus, the gods permit that bodies be transformed into other bodies under the pressure of desperate needs – love, fear, liberation, or the existence within one body of a secret truth which can only be revealed by its mutation.

He carried three silver dollars in his pockets at all times so that he could cast the ancient Chinese hexagrams of divination. He cast one that night in the place on Orchard Street. Five unchanging broken lines and an unchanging unbroken one at the top. 'Twenty-three,' he said, 'it figures,' and put the coins away. I knew nothing about the *I Ching*, but later that night I googled the hexagrams. In the age of the search engine all knowledge is just a motion away. Hexagram 23 is named 'Stripping', and is described as the hexagram of splitting apart. Its inner trigram means 'shake' and 'thunder'.

'Let's go home,' he said, and walked out on us without looking back.

I let him go. I don't chase after people who indicate that they have had enough of my company. And maybe my own sensitivities got in the way of my understanding; because it was a long time before I thought, maybe there are reasons other than vanity, narcissism and shyness for his fear of being watched.

Always in the beginning some pain to assuage, some wound to heal, some hole to fill. And always at the end failure – the pain incurable, the wound not healed, the remnant, melancholy void.

To the question about the nature of goodness I asked at the very beginning of this narrative, I can at least give a partial answer: the life of the young woman who fell in love with Dionysus Golden one afternoon on a Bowery sidewalk and who stood by him and enfolded him in that unshakable love through everything that followed – that is, for me, one of the best definitions of a good life I have found in my own relatively brief, relatively parochial existence. *'Le bonheur écrit à l'encre blanche sur des pages blanches*,' Montherlant told us – happiness writes in white ink on a white page – and goodness, I'd add, is as elusive to pin down in words as joy. Yet I must try; for what these two found, and held on to, was nothing less than that – happiness created by goodness, and sustained by it, too, against extraordinary odds. Until unhappiness destroyed it.

From the day he first met her – she was wearing a white shirt and a black pencil skirt and smoking an unfiltered French cigarette on the sidewalk outside the Museum of Identity – he understood that there was no point trying to keep secrets from her, because she could read his mind as clearly as if there had been an illuminated series of news stories crawling across his forehead.

'Ivy said we should meet,' he said. 'I thought it was a stupid idea.'

'Why did you come, in that case?' she said, turning her head away, looking bored.

'I wanted to see you, to see if I'd want to see you,' he told her. This interested her, but only vaguely, it seemed.

'Ivy told me your family is exiled in some way you don't care to discuss,' she said. Her eyes as wide as the sea. 'But now that you are standing here I see that you personally are probably in exile from yourself, maybe ever since the day you were born.' He frowned, evidently annoyed. 'And you know this how?' he asked, sharply. 'Are you a museum curator or a shaman?'

'There is a particular kind of sadness,' she replied, dragging on her Gauloises, looking like Anna Karina in *Pierrot le fou*, 'that reveals a man's alienation from his own identity.'

'This modern obsession with identity revolts me,' he said, perhaps too emphatically. 'It is a way of narrowing us until we are like aliens to one another. Have you read Arthur Schlesinger? He opposes perpetuating marginalisation through affirmations of difference.' He was wearing a trench coat and a snap-brim fedora because summer was coming but had not yet arrived, like a woman making false promises of love.

'But that is what we are, aliens, all of us.' A faint shrug of the shoulders and the suggestion of a moue. 'The point is to become more precise about the types of aliens we choose to be. And yes I have read that old dead straight white man. You should look at Spivak's work on strategic essentialism.'

'Do you want to go somewhere for a whiskey,' he asked, still sounding irritated as he asked it, and she continued to regard him as someone a little simple who was in need of intelligent assistance. Her stockings had black seams running up the backs of her calves. 'Not now,' she said. 'Now, you should come inside and learn about the new world.'

'How about after that?'

'After that, still no.'

They spent that night together in her Second Avenue apartment. There was so much to talk about that they did not have sex, which was overrated, he said. She didn't argue but made a mental note. In the morning he went downstairs to get her croissants, coffee, whiskey, cigarettes and the Sunday papers. The keys were on top of a little mahogany table in the hall, a sort of box on legs, not an antique but a good reproduction. He lifted the lid and saw the gun lying on the small red velvet cushion, a pearl-handled Colt revolver, also a good reproduction, probably. He picked it up, spun the revolving cylinder, put the business end against his temple. Afterwards he said he did not pull the trigger, but she was watching him through the open bedroom door and heard the click as the hammer hit an empty chamber. 'Found the keys,' he said. 'I'll get breakfast.'

'Don't spill anything,' she called after him. 'I don't want a mess on the hall carpet.'

Riya, that was her name. Quite a girl. Just three or four years older than he was but already holding down a senior position at the Museum, as well as crooning love songs some nights on Orchard Street, and making her own indie fashion line from old lace and black silk, often with floral brocade motifs, Oriental-themed, Chinese- and Indian-style. She was half Indian and half Swedish-American, her long Scandinavian surname, Zachariassen, too much of a mouthful for American mouths, so just as he was D Golden she went by Riya Z.

The alphabet is where all our secrets begin.

'Come inside and learn about the new world.' There was a museum for Native Americans on Bowling Green and there was the Italian

American Museum on Mulberry Street and the Polish American Museum in Port Washington and there were two museums for the Jews, uptown and downtown, and those were identity museums too obviously, but the MoI – the Museum of Identity – was after bigger game, its charismatic curator Orlando Wolf was after identity itself, the mighty new force in the world, already as powerful as any theology or ideology, cultural identity and religious identity and nation and tribe and sect and family, it was a rapidly growing multidisciplinary field, and at the heart of the Identity Museum was the question of the identity of the self, starting with the biological self and moving far beyond that. Gender identity, splitting as never before in human history, spawning whole new vocabularies that tried to grasp the new mutabilities.

'God is dead and identity fills the vacuum,' she said to him at the doorway to the gender zone, her eyes filled with the bright zeal of the true believer, 'but it turns out gods were gender benders from the start.'

Her black hair was cut short and close to the head. 'Great haircut,' he said.

They were standing amid pots and seals and stone statuary from Akkad, Assyria and Babylonia. 'The Great Mother, Plutarch says, was an intersex deity – the two sexes both present in her, not yet split apart.'

Maybe if he rented an old convertible, red and white with fins, they could go for a drive, maybe all the way across America. 'Have you seen the Pacific Ocean?' he asked her. 'It's probably a disappointment like everything else.'

They went on walking. The Museum was dark, punctuated by brightly illuminated objects, like exclamations in a monastery. 'These Stone Age objects could be transgender priestesses,' she said. 'You should really pay attention. It's as important for cis people as for the MTF community.'

The word took him back to childhood; suddenly he was studying Latin again, with fierce attention, to destroy his brothers' power to exclude him by using the secret language of Rome. 'Prepositions that take the accusative,' he said. '*Ante, apud, ad, adversus / circum, circa, citra, cis. / Contra, erga, extra, infra.* Never mind. Cisalpine and Transalpine Gaul. I get it. The Alps now divide the sexes.'

'I don't like that word,' she said.

'What word?'

'Sex.'

Oh.

'Anyway, God is not dead,' he said. 'Not in America, anyway.'

MTF was male to female, *FTM* was vice versa. Now she was pouring words over him, *gender fluid, bigender, agender, trans* with an asterisk: *trans**, the difference between *woman* and *female, gender nonconforming, genderqueer, non-binary,* and, from Native American culture, *two-spirit.* The Phrygian goddess Cybele had MTF servitors called gallae. In the African room the MTF okule and the FTM agule of the Lugbara tribe, the transsexual Amazons of Abomey, Queen Hatshepsut in male clothing and false beard. In the Asia room he stopped in front of the stone figure of Ardhanarishvara, the half-woman god. 'From Elephanta Island,' he said, and clapped his hand to his mouth. 'You didn't hear me say that,' he said to her with genuine ferocity.

'I was going to show you the *fanchuan* costumes from cross-dressing Chinese operas,' she said, 'but maybe you've had enough for today.'

'I should go,' he said.

'I'll take that whiskey now,' she replied.

And at breakfast the next morning, sitting up in white sheets eating a croissant, smoking a cigarette and with another glass of whiskey in her hand, she murmured softly, 'I know the name of the country you won't name,' she said, 'and I also know the name of the city you won't talk about.' She whispered the words into his ear.

'I think I'm in love with you,' he said. 'But I want to know why you have a gun in the little table in the hall.'

'To shoot men who think they are in love with me,' she answered. 'And maybe myself as well, but I haven't made my mind up about that.'

'Don't tell my father what you know,' he said, 'or you probably won't need to make that decision.'

I close my eyes and run the movie in my head. I open my eyes and write it down. Then, again, I close my eyes.

9

Here is Vasilisa, the Russian girl. She is striking. One might say she is astonishing. She has long dark hair. Her body is also long, and exceptional; she runs marathons, and is a fine gymnast, specialising in the ribbon element of rhythmic gymnastics. She says that in her youth she came close to the Russian Olympics team. She is twenty-eight years old. Her youth was when she was fifteen. Vasilisa Arsenyeva is her full name. Her region of origin is Siberia and she claims descent from the great explorer Vladimir Arsenyev himself, who wrote many books about the region, including the one that became a Kurosawa film, *Dersu Uzala*, but this line of descent is not confirmed because Vasilisa, as we will see, is a brilliant liar, accomplished in the arts of deceit. She says she was raised in the heart of the forest, the immense *taiga* forest that covers much of Siberia, and that her family was of the tribe Nanai, whose menfolk worked as hunters, trappers and guides. She was born in the year of the Moscow Summer Olympics and her heroine, as she grew up, was the great gymnast Nelli Kim, half Korean, half Tatar. Sixty-five countries, including the United States, boycotted those Moscow games but in the depths of the forest she was far away from politics, though she did hear about the fall of the Berlin Wall when she was nine years old. She was happy because she had begun to look at a few magazines and wanted to go to America and be adored and send US dollars back to her family at home.

This is what she has done. She has flown the coop. Here she is in America, in New York City and also, now and often, in Florida, and she is much admired, and making money doing the work the beautiful do. Many men desire her but she is not looking for a mere man. She wants a protector. A tsar.

Here is Vasilisa. She owns a magic doll. When, as a child, an earlier Vasilisa was sent by her wicked stepmother to the house of Baba Yaga, the witch who ate children, who lived in the heart of the heart of the forest, it was the magic doll who helped her escape so that she could begin her search for her tsar. So the story goes. But there are those who tell it differently, saying that Baba Yaga did eat Vasilisa, gobbled her up the way she gobbled up everyone, and when she did, the ugly old witch acquired all the young girl's beauty – that she became, outwardly, the spitting image of Vasilisa the Fair, though she remained sharp-toothed Baba Yaga on the inside.

This is Vasilisa in Miami. She is blonde now. She is about to meet her tsar.

In the winter of 2010, a few days before Christmas, the four Golden men, alerted by menacing weather forecasts and accompanied by Fuss and Blather, Nero's two trusted assistants, and me, flew south from Teterboro Airport aboard what I did not know until Apu told me was known to regular users of such aircraft as a PJ, and so we escaped the great blizzard. In the city we left behind, everyone would soon be complaining about the slowness of the snowploughs and there would be allegations of a deliberate slowdown to protest Mayor Bloomberg's budget cuts. Twenty inches of snow fell in Central Park, thirty-six inches in parts of New Jersey, and even in Miami it was the coldest December ever recorded, but that only meant it was sixty-one degrees, mean temperature, which wasn't really that cold. The old man had rented a group of apartments in a large mansion on a private island off the tip of Miami Beach, and we were warm enough most of the time. Petya liked the island; its only point of contact with the mainland was a single ferry port and no outsiders were allowed to set foot on the charmed soil unless spoken for by residents. Peacocks, both bird and human, strutted here without fear of being observed by inappropriate eyes. The wealthy exposed their knees and their secrets and nobody ever told. So Petya was able to persuade himself that the island was an enclosed space and his fear of the outdoors retreated growling into the shadows.

— Oh, you don't know what a PJ is either? Private Jet, darling. You're welcome.

Apu – sociable Apu, not my dark-clouded contemporary, D – had invited me to come with them, and 'Go,' my mother told me, even though I'd be away from home for the holidays, 'enjoy this, why not?' I didn't then know that I would not be able to welcome the fictional baby Jesus or the actual new year with my parents ever again. I couldn't have guessed what would happen, but I feel bitter regret.

Apu was in his element, schmoozing with the island's rich salad of Russian billionaires and seducing their wives into having their portraits painted, preferably scantily clad. I padded along after him like his faithful dog. The billionaires' wives did not notice my presence. That was fine; invisibility was a condition to which I was accustomed, and which, most of the time, I preferred.

And D Golden: he had brought Riya with him and the two of them were wrapped up in each other and kept themselves largely to themselves. And the servitors served – the entourage entouraged – Ms Fuss fussed and her younger sidekick Ms Blather blathered – and the Goldens' stay went smoothly enough. I, their tame Tintin, was happy enough also. And on New Year's Eve the island threw a well-heeled party for its well-heeled residents, the usual expensive fireworks, top-of-the-line lobsters and high-maintenance dancing, and Nero Golden announced his intention to take the floor.

The old man was quite the dancer, I discovered. 'You should have seen him a few years back on his seventieth birthday,' Apu told me. 'All the pretty girls lining up to take their turns, and he waltzing, tangoing, polka-ing, jiving, dipping and twirling them all. Joined-up dancing, not the disco-jigging, strap-hanging and pogoing of our degraded time.' Now that I know the family secrets, I can in my mind's eye set him down on the great terrace above the sea of the family home in Walkeshwar Colony, and envision the elite beauties of Bombay society happy in his arms. While his put-upon wallflower wife – 'Poppaea Sabina' I'll continue to call her, going along with the family's Julio-Claudian preferences – watched disapproving but silent from the sidelines. He was older now, past seventy-four, but he had lost neither his balance nor his skill. Once again there were young women waiting to be twirled and dipped. One of them was Vasilisa Arsenyeva, whose motto in life was taken from Jesus Christ, the gospel according to Saint Matthew, chapter four, verse nineteen. 'Follow me, and I will make you fishers of men.' She had excellent timing. As the new year struck, in the midnight or witching hour, she cast her fateful hook. And once she started dancing with him, nobody else could do so. She was the end of the line.

This is Vasilisa. She is dancing with her tsar. She has her arm around him and this is what her face is saying: I'm never letting go. Taller than he is, she bends down slightly so that her mouth is close to his ear. His ear leans into her mouth, to understand what it is telling him. This is Vasilisa. She puts her tongue in his ear. It speaks a wordless language all men can understand.

The Vanderbilt House is the heart of the island. Rewind: here is William Kissam Vanderbilt II on his two-hundred-and-fifty-foot yacht, making a swap deal with the developer Carl Fisher. The yacht in exchange for the island. Shake hands on that. Here is Bebe Rebozo, accused at the time of Watergate of being 'Nixon's bagman', joining a group that bought the island from the guy who bought the island from the guy who bought the island from Vanderbilt. The island has a history. It has an observatory. It has, as previously stated, peacocks. It has discretion. It has golf. It has class.

And this cold holiday season at the Vanderbilt House, after the New Year's Eve dance on the fine parquet outdoor dance floor laid down amid trees festooned with strings of lights, and burning braziers, and live music, and women in their jewels and security guards guarding the jewels and the men who bought the jewels admiring their property, the island also has a much-talked-about winter-and-spring, November-and-April love affair. My money for your beauty. Shake hands on that.

New Year's is for dancing and when the music stops she commands Nero, go home and sleep, I want you rested for me when we really begin. And he obediently walks back to his bed like a good boy, with his sons looking on in astonishment. This is not really happening, their looks say. He's not really falling for this. But such is his authority that not one of them speaks. The next night he empties the apartment he has rented for himself and his two assistants, banishing employees and family to the other three rented accommodations, where there are plenty of spare bedrooms. He is alone on the seventh floor looking down at the tops of the palm trees, the small half-moon of beach, and the bright water beyond. Dinner – shrimp cocktails, cold cuts, avocado and kale salads, a fruit basket, tiramisu for dessert – has been delivered by motor launch from a fine dining establishment on the south side of the Miami River and has been set out on the dining table. There is ice and caviar and vodka and wine. At precisely the appointed time, not a minute earlier or later, she comes to his door, gift-wrapped in gold, with a bow at the back of her dress so that he can easily unwrap her.

They agree that they do not want to eat.

Here is Vasilisa the Fair giving herself to her tsar.

The first night and the second night, the first two nights of the new year, she demonstrates her wares, lets him see the quality of what's on offer, not only physically but emotionally. She . . . and here I rear back and halt myself, ashamed, prufrocked into a sudden *pudeur*, for, after all, how should I presume? Shall I say, I have known them all, I have seen her like a yellow fog rubbing her back against, rubbing her muzzle upon, shall I say, licking her tongue into the corners of his evening? Do I dare, and do I dare? And who am I, after all? I am not the prince. An attendant lord, deferential, glad to be of use. Almost, at times, the Fool . . . But, setting aside poetry, I'm too deeply in to stop now. I am imagining her already. Perhaps kneeling beside him on the bed. Yes, kneeling, I think. Asking, is this what you meant? Or this? Is this what you meant at all?

He is the king. He knows what he wants. And: everything you want, she says, when you want it, it's yours. And on the third night she discusses business. This is not a shock to him. This makes things easier. Business is his comfort zone. She produces a printed card, the size of a postcard, with boxes to tick. Let's go through the details, she says.

Obviously I should not stay in the house on Macdougal. That is your family home, for yourself and your sons. And I am not your wife, so I am not your family. So you can choose (a) a residence in the West Village, for convenience, for ease of access, or (b) on the Upper East Side, for a little distance, a little more discretion. Very well, (b), this is also my preference. So, the size of the apartment, two bedrooms minimum, no?, and maybe one more as art studio space?, good! And will I own it or is it a rental, and if so for how many years? OK, think about it. We proceed to the car, and I leave this to you completely, (a) Mercedes convertible, (b) BMW 6 series, (c) Lexus SUV. Oh, (a), so nice, I love you. The question arises of where I will have accounts, (a) Bergdorf, (b) Barneys, (c) both of the above. Fendigucciprada, this goes without saying. Equinox, Soho House Every House, you see the checklist. The subject of a monthly allowance. I must comport myself in a manner that befits you. You see the categories are ten, fifteen, twenty. I recommend generosity. Yes, in thousands of dollars, darling. Perfect. You will not regret. I will be perfect for you. I speak English, French, German, Italian, Japanese, Mandarin and Russian. I ski, water-ski, surf, run and swim. The flexibility of my gymnastic youth, this I retain. In the coming days I will know better how to satisfy you than you know yourself and if equipment is needed to assist this, if a room must be constructed, a room for us, let us call it a playroom, I will make sure it is done immaculately and with the greatest discretion. I will never look at another man. No other man will touch me nor will I tolerate any inappropriate advances or remarks. You deserve and must have exclusivity and it is yours, I swear to you. This is all for now, but there is one more matter for later.

This is the matter of marriage, she says, lowering her voice to its huskiest and most alluring level. As your wife I will have honour and standing. Only as your wife will I truly and fully have this. Until then, yes, I am happy, I am the most loyal of women, but my honour is important to me. You understand. Of course. You are the most understanding man I have ever met.

10

repeat: in too deep to stop now. I must go on imagining, must continue the peep show, put another nickel in / in the nickelodeon. Yes: in my imagination it's now a movie. Wide screen, black and white.

The three sons of Nero Golden, PETYA, APU and D, two of them considerably older than their father's new love and the third just four years younger, are collectively at a loss. In spite of all their differences, this is a vital family matter, and they come together to discuss it, but do not find it easy to formulate a strategy. They meet away from the rented apartments, standing in a tight group on the island's small beach, which is empty on account of the unseasonal cold weather, the low temperature, the high wind, the racing clouds, the threat, soon realised, of driving, freezing rain. They wear hats, coats and mufflers and look like a conspiracy of Czech intellectuals standing on a sea coast in Bohemia, closely observed, like trains. In spite of the frowns of the two older men, RIYA Z is there with D, clinging to him tightly as if she thought she might otherwise blow away. RIYA is the same age as Vasilisa. D has worked this out but does not mention it.

The camera watches them in extreme close-ups until they speak, but cuts to wide shots when we hear their voices.

PETYA

(he expresses his concerns theoretically, as is his awkward, inexorable way)

The crux of a great person's life is the choice between doing what is right and what he wants to do. Abraham Lincoln, who was a proficient wrestler and enjoyed a good bout, probably would have preferred spending his time on the mat to starting a war in which approximately two per cent of the population died, roughly six hundred and twenty thousand people, but it was the right thing to do. No doubt Marie Curie would have preferred to spend time with her daughter instead of being killed by X-ray radiation, but guess what activity she chose. Or take the case of Mahatma Gandhi, who when young showed himself to be a sharp dresser in a British bespoke suit which was a whole lot nicer than some loincloth. However, the loincloth, politically speaking—

APU

(interrupts what might otherwise turn into a long catalogue)

So obviously our father should know better than to run after some Russian, let me avoid a word here, some Russian gymnast.

Circling, tight shot, around and around them on the blowing sand, slightly higher than their heads, looking down like a surveillance drone.

D

He's going to marry her. That's her plan. She won't let up and he can't resist.

PETYA

In the event of a marriage a number of legal issues arise. Next-of-kin status will be problematised, also executorship of a living will, and the broader subject of inheritance. There is also the uncertainty about where they may marry to discuss, the variations between the laws of Florida and the State of New York.

APU

Our father is not a fool. He may be, at present, a fool for her, but in all essentials he is not a fool. He has been a deal-maker all his life. He will see the good sense of a cast-iron prenuptial agreement.

PETYA

(his voice rises to a wail, mirroring the rising sound of the wind)

Who will talk to him about it?

(pause)

I can't.

(pause)

He won't like it.

APU

We should all do it together.

D

(shrugs, gets ready to walk away)

I don't give a damn about the money. Let the old man do what he wants.

He and RIYA turn to leave.

RIYA

(in ECU, to APU *and* PETYA*)*

Have you considered that she may make him happy, and actually find it in her heart to love him? But even if she is faking it, this can still be good. Things are good which reduce the amount of global misery, or the quantity of injustice, or both. So if she reduces his unhappiness even for a brief time, even fraudulently, then that counts as good.

I see the life he has made for you all. He is like a great roof and you shelter beneath it. Step away from him you are caught in the storm, all of you, but right now he is there. He is there until he won't be there. But he is not only a house in which you live. He is a man and has the needs of a man, to desire and to be desired. Why do you want to deny him? Do you imagine that just because of the calendar it stops? Let me tell you. It doesn't matter how old you are. It never stops.

PETYA

(repeats, shamefaced, skipping sadly as the rain comes down)

It never stops, it never stops, it never stops, it never stops, it never stops, it never stops, it never stops, it never stops, it never stops, it never stops, it never stops, it never stops, it never stops, it never stops, it never stops, it never stops . . .

The downpour begins in earnest. Water on the camera lens. Fade to white.

11

This is Vasilisa's best friend, and her personal fitness trainer, and her name is, let's say, Masha. Masha is petite, smaller than Vasilisa, but very strong, lesbian, and also, inevitably, blonde. Masha wants to be a movie actress. When Nero Golden hears this he says, 'Darling, with that ambition, you're the right size, but you're on the wrong coast.'

The old man has extended his stay on the island and the family and entourage are staying too but there has been a rearrangement of accommodations. Vasilisa is moving into the Nero apartment with her friend and personal fitness trainer and all other persons are to be relocated in the other spaces. Nobody is very pleased except for Nero, Vasilisa and Masha. Then on the night the ladies move in Nero takes them out for a meal. There are good places to eat on the island but Nero wants the best, and the best involves getting into his Bentley sports car with Vasilisa by his side and Masha curled up in the back and taking a ride over on the ferry to the famous Italian place from which he had ordered the uneaten food on the night of the first tryst. At the famous Italian place the ladies in their excitement drink too many vodka shots; Nero, the designated driver, restrains himself. By the time the three of them are back on the island the ladies are laughing loudly and behaving flirtatiously, which is just fine with Nero. Back in the apartment he does a couple of vodka shots himself. But then, a strange turn of events. The personal trainer leans in to Vasilisa the Fair and kisses her on the mouth. And Vasilisa responds. And then a silence in the room as the two ladies embrace and Nero Golden sits in his armchair, watching, not remotely aroused, shocked, feeling like a fool, even more so when the two ladies get up without acknowledging him, turn out the lights in the living room as if he wasn't there, and go into his bedroom – his bedroom! – and shut the door behind them.

In their absence it is the carelessness about the extinguishing of the lights that first enrages him. In his house! While he is present! As if he were nothing and no one! His anger reveals to him his dreadful error. He sees himself as a deluded old man and now his pride rears up and demands that he come back into his true self, the man of power, the financial titan, the quondam construction and steel magnate, head of his family, the colossus standing in the great courtyard of the golden house, the once and future king. He stands up and leaves the two women in the bedroom to do as they please and walks steadily toward the apartment's front door.

There is a small closet by the door in which, on a shelf above the hanging coats, there stands a small leather valise. The old man has always believed in the mutability of things; has known that no matter how solid the ground beneath your feet may seem, it can, at any moment, turn into quicksand and suck you down. Always be prepared. He was prepared for the great move from Bombay to New York, and he is prepared for this smaller departure now. He takes down the overnight bag, makes sure the keys to the other apartments are in his trouser pocket where they should be, and quietly leaves. He does not slam the door. He knows that in the apartment next door, where Petya sleeps along with the little cloud of helpers, there is a small maid's room that is unoccupied. Nero does not need luxury right now. He needs a door to close and a bed behind it and that is enough. In the morning he will deal with what must be dealt with and he will have all his strength then. His head will once more be in control of his heart. He enters the maid's room, removes his jacket and tie and shoes, doesn't bother with the rest of it, and is quickly asleep.

He has underestimated her. He has made an incorrect assessment both of his own vulnerability and of her determination. Beneath all his strength there is loneliness and she can smell that as a hunting dog smells its wounded quarry. Loneliness is weakness, and this is Baba Yaga in the skin of Vasilisa the Fair. If she wishes, she can eat him up. She can eat him up right now.

Are you awake? Oh my darling, I'm so sorry. I am so ashamed of myself. I was drunk, I'm sorry. I have a poor head for alcohol. I'm so sorry. I always knew she kind of had a thing for me but I never expected. I have sent her away, we will never see her again, I swear to you, she is out of my life, she doesn't exist any more. Please forgive me. I love you, please forgive me this one time and you will never have to forgive me again. I will make it up to you in one hundred ways, you will see, it will be my daily business to make you forget this and forgive. I was drunk so I became a little curious, I don't even like women, I'm not that way, I didn't even like it, actually I just passed out and went to sleep and when I woke up of course I was horrified, my God, what have I done, that man who has only been good to me, I apologise from the bottom of my heart, I kiss your feet, I wash your feet with my tears and dry them with my hair, I even thought for five seconds that maybe it will excite you, this was stupidity, stupidity caused by drink, I'm so sorry, when I'm drunk I can become a little irresponsible, a little wild, this is why I will never get drunk again except if you want me to, only if you want me a little wild and irresponsible in your arms, then it will be my complete pleasure to please you in that way, forgive me, accept my shame and my humble apology, where are you, let me come to you. Let me just come for one moment and apologise to your face, and then if you tell me to go, I will go, I will have deserved it, I know this, but do not make me go without one chance to tell you to your face that excuse me, I did a wrong thing, a very wrong thing, but I was drunk, and I ask you to see me standing before you in shame, and maybe you can find it in your heart to excuse me, to see in me all the love all the gratitude all the love standing before you and for the sake of that you may let me in, you may not shut the door in my face, you may see the truth in my eyes and forgive me, and if you do not then I have no rights, I will bow my head and go and you will never see me again, never see again my naked shame, never see my body trembling and sobbing before you for my shame, you will never see me, I will never be able to touch you again, so many things, never again, so many things that will never happen again, if you send me away, I will go, but maybe, for you are a great man, you will let me stay, it takes a great man to forgive, and this was a nothing, a mistake, a stupidity, and you may see that and let me stay, but let me come to you, I will come to you now, just as I am, wherever you are, if you want me to kneel naked at your door I will do it, I will do anything, everything, only let me come, where are you, only let me come.

So this is the moment. He can hang up on her, cut his losses, be free. He has seen who she is, the mask slipped and she revealed herself, and all her words can't make him unsee what he saw or unfeel what he felt when they turned the lights out and went into his bedroom – his bedroom! – and closed the door. He can walk away.

She has bet everything on the one shot she has: that he will want to make himself unsee that sight, unfeel that feeling. That he will want to turn on the light, open the bedroom door, and find her there, alone, and waiting. That he will tell himself that story, the story of true love, and step into that tale.

He doesn't hang up, but listens. He goes back to the apartment where she is waiting. And of course she offers up her apology in many ways, and many of those ways are pleasing to him, but that is only the surface. Below that veneer is the truth, which is that she knows her power now, knows that in their relationship she is and always will be the stronger one, and that there isn't much he can do about it.

La Belle Dame sans Merci hath thee in thrall.

*

Monologue of V. Arsenyeva Concerning Love and Need

Please. I require no sympathy regarding the poverty of my origin. Only those who have never been poor think there is anything sympathetic about poverty, and for this point of view the only proper response is contempt. I will not pause long to describe the hardships of my family though they were various. There was the question of food, and the question of clothing, and the question of warmth, but somewhere there was never any question about a sufficiency of drink for my father, I might say an over-sufficiency. In my young years we moved to the town of Norilsk near the former gulag Norillag which of course shut down like sixty years ago but left behind the town, which the prisoners had originally built. At age twelve I learned that the town was forbidden to all non-Russians and so also not so easy to leave. So I understand the Communist oppression and also the afterwards not-Communist oppression but I have no interest in discussing. Also my father's drunkenness. Poverty is a disgusting condition and to fail to emerge from it is also disgusting. Fortunately I excelled at all things both physical and mental and so I have been able to come to America and I am grateful for it but also I know my presence here is the fruit of my own labour so there is nobody actually to thank. I leave the past behind and I am myself in this place, wearing these clothes, now. The past is a broken cardboard suitcase full of photographs of things I no longer wish to see. Of sexual abuse also I will not speak though this also occurred. There was an uncle and after my parents' divorce there was a mother's boyfriend. I close the suitcase. If I send money home to my mother it is to say, please, keep the suitcase closed. Also for my father now are hospital bills for the cancer. I send money but I have no relationship. Case closed. I thank God I am beautiful because it allows me to leave ugliness out of my life. I am focused forward, one hundred per cent. I am focused on love.

What people call love, cynics say, it is really need. What people call forever, according to the cynical loveless, is really rental. I rise above such considerations, which are base. I believe in my good heart and its capacity for a great love. Need exists, that is clear, but must be satisfied, that is a precondition without which love cannot be born. One must water the soil so that the plant may grow. With a great man one must accommodate his greatness and he in turn will be great in his kindness and to come to an agreement, and this is normal, it is, one may say, the watering of the soil. I am a matter-of-fact person, so I know a house must be built before one can live in it. First build a solid house, then have a happy life therein, forever. This is my way. I know his sons are afraid of me. Maybe afraid for their father, maybe for themselves, but they are thinking only of the house and not of the life within it. They do not think about love. The house I am building is the house of love. They should understand this but if they do not I will go on with the construction work nevertheless. Yes, they call it the golden house, but what is that if there is not love in every room, in every corner of every room? It is love that is golden, not money. They have never needed, those sons, what did they ever need? They live inside a magic spell. Their self-deception is very great. They say they love their father but they are confusing need with love. They need him. Do they love him? I will have to see more evidence before I can reply. He should have love in his life while he can.

That one with his witch, he should understand: his father is the wizard of his life. That one with his strange girl, he should understand: his father is his identity. That one with his broken head, he should understand: his father is his angel.

Their worry is about inheritance. They should understand three things. In the first place, is it right that after I give this man my love, that I should be put out in the street? Of course not, and so provision must be made, that is matter of fact. In the second place, I have signed the agreement regarding our relationship he gave me to sign, just as he wanted it, without argument, this is my trust, this is my loving confidence. So they are all protected and need not fear me. In the third place, what they fear most of all is the coming of a brother or a sister. They fear my womb. They fear my womb's desire to be filled. They don't even know if their father is capable any more of fathering but they are afraid. To this, I shrug. They should understand that I am a person of great self-discipline. I am the general of myself and my body is the foot soldier that obeys what the general commands. In this case I understand what he has said, the man I love. He has been clear. At his age he is not prepared to go back to the beginning of being a parent, to have a baby, its squealing, its shit, to have a child whose adulthood he will not see. This he has said. This clause is in the agreement I have signed. I have signed the baby away. I have so instructed my body, my womb. There will be no baby with this man I love. Our love is the baby and that baby is already born and we are nurturing it. This, he wishes to do, and I also, his wish is also mine. This is love. This is how love triumphs over need. Those sons with all their need, let them learn love from their father, and from me.

Monologue of Baba Yaga Inside Arsenyeva's Skin

I await my time. I sit, I cook, I spin, with downcast eyes I am silent and let him speak. This is fine. I await my time.

Everything is a strategy. This is the wisdom of the spider. Silently, silently spin. Let the fly buzz. Before I ate her and put on her skin I lay across the stove in my hut, the hut standing on a chicken leg, and I waited, and they came to me, and became my food, and in the end she came too, the one I wanted, and instead of swallowing her I dived inside and let her swallow me. It doesn't matter what it looks like! I ate her even as I allowed her to eat me. It's a special digestive trick: a reverse takeover of the feeder by the fed. And so farewell, chicken-legged hut in the forest! Goodbye forever, foul Russian smell! Now am I perfumed and clothed in beauty, my eyes behind her eyes, my teeth behind her teeth.

Everything she does is false, every word a lie, because here I am inside her, pulling her strings, casting the web of her words and deeds around the little fly, the old fool. He believes she loves him! Ha ha ha ha ha! Cackle, cackle! That's a good one, that is.

See how I will live now! The automobiles, the cuisine, the furs. No more flying commercial! I hate flying commercial almost as much as flying on chicken legs or broomsticks. I spit on commercial flights. See me pass through General Aviation like a queen! I enter my PJ and all around me grovel and seek my approval and my comfort, my joy, my ease. Feel the softness of my bed and the quality of my work-out gear. I have a new personal trainer. No sex with him! Be careful! That was close.

In the traditional world, it is known that for the female of the species metamorphosis is easier than for the male. A woman leaves her father's house, sheds his name like old skin and puts on her husband's name like a wedding dress. Her body changes and becomes capable of containing and then expelling other bodies. We are used to having people inside us, dictating our futures. Maybe a woman's life gains its meaning through such metamorphoses, such swallowing and expulsions, but for a man it is the opposite. The abandonment of the past makes a man meaningless. What are these Golden men doing then, fleeing into meaninglessness, into the absurd? What force is so powerful that it drives these men away from the significance of their lives? They are ridiculous now. An exile is a hollow man trying to fill up with manhood once again, a phantom in search of lost flesh and bone, a ship in search of an anchor. Such men are easy prey.

— What? What does that stupid one say? The youngest son? 'This is a time of many metamorphoses, many genders, and the world is more complex than you believe, Chicken-Leg, Spider-Woman!' Is that what he's trying to tell me, glaring at me while he clings to his *Nouvelle Vague* lover's arm? We will see, sweetie-pie. Let's see how things work out and who's standing up laughing at the end, smoking a cigarette at the end of the world. You are Dionysus, and, I admit, a little bit weird, but I am Baba Yaga, the weirdest sister of them all. I am Baba Yaga the Witch—

I conceal this voice deep inside myself, so deep that she, myself, can convince herself she cannot hear it, that it is not her truest voice. At the level of the skin, of the tongue, a different voice speaks, and she tells herself a different story, in which she is virtuous and her deeds are justified, both absolutely, by moral standards, and empirically, by the events around her. By him, the old one, the king in the golden house, who he is, how he treats her, what his faults are. But there it is, the deep voice speaking, commanding her at the deepest level, the level of the molecules of instruction, twined into the four helical amino acids of her being, which is also mine. It is who I is. It is who she am.

12

It was hard for the youngest of the Goldens to give up the habit of loneliness. He had felt lonely from his earliest days as the odd-one-out child of an illicit liaison, partly accepted, partly resented in the grand houses he was obliged to call his home, first in Bombay, then in New York. Even in large crowds, he had felt alone, and yet now, with only Riya for company, he was visited by feelings he at first found hard to name. Eventually he found the words. Togetherness, companionship. He was becoming one half of a joint entity. The word *love* felt alien on his lips and tongue, like a parasitic visitor from another planet, but, occupying Martian or not, the word had certainly landed in his mouth, and taken root. *I am in love,* he said to himself in the bathroom mirror. It seemed to him that the mirror-face speaking in sync with his own actually belonged to someone else, a person he did not know. He was becoming this person, he thought, a self unknown to himself. Love had begun to stir forces in him that would soon transform him completely and irreversibly. This information had lodged itself in his thoughts and the idea of *imminent transformation* had begun to alter things in his brain, just as the word *love* had started to affect his speech. But it was knowledge which, for a time, he repressed.

He was the first one to move out of the Macdougal Street house. 'Let the old man do what he wants,' he had told his brothers in Florida, but that didn't mean he had to stick around to watch. One day Vasilisa Arsenyeva arrived followed by quantities of expensive luggage which hinted that Nero Golden might not have been her first benefactor. Clearly she had already moved beyond the initial agreement, which was non-cohabitational. Very soon afterwards Nero's youngest son packed his own bags and left for Chinatown, where Riya had found them a small, clean third-floor walk-up in a salmon-pink building with the window frames picked out in bright yellow paint. Below them on the second floor was Madame George Tarot Crystal Ball Horoscope Tell Ur Future, and, at street level, Run Run Trading Inc. with its hanging ducks, its striped-blue-and-pink parasols shading its trays of produce, and its ferocious lady proprietor, Mrs Run, who also owned the building and refused all requests to change light bulbs in the hall or turn up the heating when the weather got cold. Riya was immediately at loggerheads with Mrs Run but she didn't want to give up on the place because outside the sitting-room window was the flat roof of the neighbouring building and on sunny days they could slide open the sash window and climb through and it was like having a backyard in the sky.

They had begun to dress alike, in the winter in motorcycle leather, aviator shades and Brando caps, and sometimes behind the shades he added smudged eyeshadow like hers, so that people thought them twins, both pale, both physically frail-looking, both escapees from the same art-house movie. And in the spring she, and so also he, affected spiky black hair and she like a goth Moreau sat out on the roof with a large acoustic guitar and sang the song of their love, *'Elle avait des yeux, des yeux d'opale / qui me fascinaient, qui me fascinaient,'* with a cigarette hanging from the corner of her mouth, *'Chacun pour soi est reparti / Dans le tourbillon de la vie . . .'*

For this was how their relationship had developed: into something loving, yes, but also scratchy, fractious, and that was his fault, she said, for she was all in, had been from the beginning, she was an all-or-nothing person, but he was somewhere in between.

'Yes, I love you, this is why we are living together, but you don't own me, your family knows a lot about owning things, but I'm not property, and you need to understand my freedom. And besides, there are important things you aren't telling me about yourself, and I need to know those things.'

When she spoke like this a dizziness came over him, as if the whole world was flying apart into fragments, and he was very afraid of the fragmented world and what it meant for him, the song was right, life was a whirlwind, *un tourbillon.* But he had told her everything, he pleaded, he had spilled the family secrets to her like a child at his first confession. 'I don't even know why I went along with what the old man wanted,' he said. 'Leaving there, coming here, changing identities, all of it. It wasn't my mother who died at the hotel. It wasn't even anyone I liked. I don't even know who my mother was, she vanished, so it's like he killed her long ago. Or like a Z-Company boss had her killed.'

'That's what, Z-Company?'

'It's the mafia,' he said. 'Z is for the godfather, Zamzama Alankar. Not his real name.'

She shrugged. 'You want to know why I have the gun in the drawer? I'll tell you. It's like a bad TV show. My father Zachariassen got drunk and murdered my mother when I was home for Thanksgiving and I ran out into the street yelling help police and he fired at me as I was running and shouted I'll find you, I'll hunt you down. By then he was a full-blown psycho. He used to be an airline pilot for Northwest but after the Delta merger the carrier was looking to downsize and his up-and-down moods got him fired and then he started drinking and they got worse and he became a scary person. He was living with my mother in Mendota Heights, Minnesota, which is a pretty well-off first-ring suburb of the Twin Cities, above his pay grade. My mom was an orphan, her parents had died and left her money, so she had bought the house and car and I grew up there and went to a good school but after he lost his job they were struggling. By that time I was done with college, I put myself through Tufts on a scholarship and different jobs, and I was working here in the city, and after the murder I left Mendota Heights fast and closed that chapter forever. Except that I keep the gun. He's gone to jail for like a million years without possibility of commutation or remission but I'm not getting rid of the weapon.'

She played the song on the guitar some more, but didn't sing.

'So my sob story is better than yours,' she finally said. 'And I'll tell you why you agreed to your father's crazy plan. You agreed because there, where you came from, you weren't free to be who you need to be, to become who you need to become.'

'And what is that?'

'That is what I'm waiting for you to tell me.'

It's the thing she keeps coming back to ever since he told her about it, what he did to his stepmother, her humiliation, her near-suicide. You are a loving person, I see that, she says, but this I don't understand, how you could stoop so low.

I think, he says, that hatred can be as strong a family tie as blood, or love. And when I was younger I was full of hate and it was the bond joining me to the family and that's why I did what I did.

It's not enough, she says. There is more.

The limo arrives at a warehouse in Bushwick where she needs to inspect some South Asian artefacts that the Museum of Identity has been offered. Come, she had urged him, at least two of them concern the visit of Dionysus to India, so you'll be interested. She doesn't trust the dealer. She has been sent paperwork certifying that the items were legally exported from India but these documents can be illicitly obtained. In the old days before the Indian Antiquities and Art Treasures Act, she says, it was actually harder to smuggle stuff out, because people were not sure whom to bribe. But since 1976 the exporters know which inspectors to deal with, so it's more straightforward. Acquisitions are complicated by such questions of provenance. Still, worth a look.

There is a painting of Dionysus surrounded by panthers and tigers and she has no interest in it. The other piece is a marble bowl around which a triumphal procession has been carved and it is exquisite, a riotous crowd of satyrs, nymphs, animals and at their heart the god. See how feminine he is, she says. He's right on the gender borderline, you almost don't know whether to call him goddess or god. She's looking penetratingly at D as she speaks, an unasked question in her eyes, and he shies away.

What, he says. What is this. What do you want.

This is almost certainly an unauthorised export, she says to the dealer, handing back the bowl. The documentation is unconvincing. We can't acquire.

They are in the car on the way home. Construction work on the approach to the Manhattan Bridge, slowing the traffic to a crawl. Come on, she says, you didn't come to me by accident, you didn't just show up at the MoI because you had zero interest in what we explore there. And your stepmother, maybe there's something in you that wants to die, some part of you that doesn't want to be alive any more, and that's why you pushed her to the edge of death. Here's what you need to tell me about. Why did you want to step into her shoes? What part of you wanted to be her, the mother, the housewife, with the household keys, in charge of domestic duties? Why was that need so imperative that you did such an extreme thing? Yeah, I need to know about all that. But before me, you need to know about it yourself.

Let me out of the car, he says. Stop the fucking car.

Really, she answers without raising her voice, you're going to get out of the car?

Stop the goddamn motherfucking car.

Afterwards he found it hard to remember the fight, he just remembered the sensations her words provoked, the explosion in his brain, the fogged vision, the pounding heart, the shaking caused by the obvious absurdity of her accusations, the insulting wrongness of her attack. He wanted to call upon an almighty judge to declare her guilty, but there was no eye of heaven watching them, no recording angel to be summoned. He wanted her to apologise. Damn it. She had to apologise. *Profusely.*

He returned in a fury to the house on Macdougal Street, saying nothing to anyone, wrapped in a storm that warned everyone to leave him alone. Riya and he didn't speak for four days. On the fifth day she called, sounding like the composed adult she was. *Come home. I want company in bed. I want . . . Zzzzzz Company.*

He began to laugh, couldn't help it, and then it was easy to say sorry, sorry, sorry.

We'll talk about that, she said.

She was sitting on the floor reading a book. On a small bookshelf in the Chinatown apartment she kept seven books, some famous works – by Juan Rulfo, Elsa Morante and Anna Akhmatova – others less lofty, *Green Eggs and Ham, Twilight, The Silence of the Lambs* and *The Hunt for Red October*. It was Akhmatova she had chosen to read.

You will hear thunder and remember me,
And think: she wanted storms. The rim
Of the sky will be the colour of hard crimson,
And your heart, as it was then, will be on fire.

'When I'm done with a book,' she said, 'it is also done with me and moves on. I leave it on a bench in Columbus Park. Maybe the Chinese people playing cards or Go won't want my book, the nostalgic Chinese bowing mournfully at the statue of Sun Yat-sen, but there are the couples coming out of City Hall with their wedding licences and stars in their eyes, wandering for a minute among the cyclists and the kids, smiling with the knowledge of their newly licensed love, and I imagine they might like to discover the book, as a gift from the city to mark their special day, or the book may like to discover them. In the beginning I was just giving books away. I got a new book, I gave away an old one. I always keep just seven. But then I began to find that others were leaving books where I had left mine and I thought, these are for me. So now I replenish my library with the random gifts of unknown strangers and I never know what I will read next, I wait for the homeless books to call out: you, reader, you are for me. I do not choose what I read any more. I am wandering through the discarded stories of the city.'

He stood in the doorway, contrite, awkward. She spoke without looking up from the page. He sat down beside her, his back against the wall. She leaned toward him, just a little, so that their shoulders touched. Her arms were crossed, her hands hugging her shoulders. She stretched out one finger and touched his arm.

'If you smoked cigarettes,' she said, 'we would have something in common.'

Cut.

'The following day,' he says. It is the following day, a day in the present tense. 'Here we are on the following day,' he says. 'Tomorrow, one of the two impossible days. Here we are and it is tomorrow.'

'I am a free spirit,' she says, twisting her mouth dismissively, *nothing special,* her mouth says. 'But you are everywhere in chains. You have inner voices to which you don't listen, emotions boiling up in you which you suppress, and disturbing dreams you ignore.'

'I never dream,' he says, 'except sometimes in another language, in Technicolor, but they are always peaceful dreams. The rolling sea, the grandeur of the Himalayas, my mother smiling down at me, and green-eyed tigers.'

'I hear you,' she says. 'When you are not snoring, often you howl, but it is more like an owl than a wolf. Who . . . who . . . who . . . that's how you are. This is the question you can't answer.'

They are walking on the Bowery and the pavement and sidewalk around them are ripped apart by construction work. A jackhammer starts pounding and it is impossible to hear anyone speak. He turns to her and mouths silently, really not saying anything, just opening and shutting his face. The jackhammer stops for a minute.

'That's my answer,' he says.

Cut.

They are making love. It is still tomorrow, still the afternoon, but they are both in the mood and see no reason to wait until dark. However, they both close their eyes. Sex has many solitary aspects even when there is another person present, whom you love and wish to please. And seeing the other is no longer required once the lovers are well practised in their favourite ways. Their bodies by now are educated in each other, each learning to move in ways that accommodate the other's natural movement. Their mouths know how to find each other. Their hands know what to do. There are no rough edges; their lovemaking has been smoothed.

There is a way it most often goes, a difficulty that usually presents itself. He has a problem achieving and maintaining an erection. He finds her immensely attractive, he protests as much at the moment of each failure, each softening, and she accepts it and embraces him. Sometimes he does succeed for a moment and attempts to enter her but then at the moment of penetration softens again and his flaccid sex squashes up against hers. It does not matter because they have found many other ways to succeed. Her attraction to him is so great that at his first touch she approaches climax and so by touching and kissing, by the use of the secondary organs (hands, lips, tongue), he brings her to orgasm until she is laughing in spent delight. Her pleasure becomes his and often it isn't even necessary for him to ejaculate. He is satisfied by satisfying her. They become more adventurous with each other as things progress, a little rougher, and this too is very pleasurable to them both. She thinks, but does not say, that the usual difficulty with young men is that they become hard at once and repeatedly but, lacking patience, self-control or courtesy, they are done two minutes later. These long hours of lovemaking are infinitely more pleasurable. What she says is, and she has thought a long time before saying it: It's as if we are two women. It feels so safe, so abandoned, both. The second because of the first.

There. She has said it. It's out in the open. He is lying on his back staring at the ceiling. For a long moment he does not reply. Then:

Yeah, he says.

Another long silence.

Yeah what, she asks quietly, her hand on his chest, her fingers caressing him.

Yeah, he said. I think about that. I think about it a lot.

Flashback. Circular wipe.

It's the year Michael Jackson played Bombay. Mumbai. *Bombay.* On the TV news men in pink and saffron turbans are at the airport, jigging frantically to the music of *dhols.* A large fabric sign hanging in the arrivals hall crying out NAMASTE MICHAEL NAMASTE FROM AIRPORTS AUTHORITY OF INDIA. And MJ in black hat and red blazer with gold buttons applauding the dancers. *You are my special love, India,* he says. *May God always bless you.* The boy D twelve years old in his bedroom, watching the news, teaching himself to moonwalk, mouthing the words of the famous songs, he has all the lyrics down, one hundred per cent. Great day! And then the next morning sitting in the car with the driver on his way to school. They come down off the hill onto Marine Drive and there's a traffic jam by Chowpatty Beach. And suddenly there he is, MJ himself, walking among the stationary cars! Omigod omigod omigod omigod omigod. But no, of course it's not Michael Jackson. It's a hijra. A hijra like a giant Michael wearing Michael's black hat and red coat with gold buttons. Cheap imitations of. How dare you. Take those off. Those don't belong to you. The hijra with right hand touching hat brim doing pencil turns amid the jammed traffic, clutching at his her its groin. The hijra has a battered boombox, it's playing 'Bad', the hijra with white face-paint and red lipstick mouthing along. It's disgusting. It's irresistible. It's terrifying. How can it be allowed? The hijra is right up against his car window now, the young milord on his way to Cathedral School, dance with me, young master, dance with me. Shouting against the rolled-up window, pressing red lips against the glass. *Hato, hato,* the driver shouts, waving an arm, *get away,* and the hijra laughs, a high contemptuous falsetto laugh, and walks away into the sun.

Circular wipe.

When you showed me the statue of Ardhanarishvara I blurted out, from Elephanta Island, and then I shut my mouth. But yes, I know him-her from long ago. It is the coming together of Shiva and Shakti, the Being and Doing forces of the Hindu godhead, the fire and the heat, in the body of this single double-gendered deity. *Ardha,* half, *nari,* woman, *ishvara,* god. Male one side, female the other. I have been thinking about her-him since boyhood. But after I saw the hijra I was afraid.

Everybody was a little afraid of hijras, a little revolted, and so I was too. I was fascinated as well, that is true, but I was also afraid of the fact that I was fascinated. What did they have to do with me, these women-men? Whatever I heard about them made me shudder. Especially *Operation.* They call it that, *Operation,* in English. They take alcohol or opium but no anaesthetic. The deed is done by other hijras, not a doctor, a string tied around the genitals to get a clean cut, and then a long curved knife slashing down. The raw area allowed to bleed, then cauterised with hot oil. In the days afterwards, as the wound heals, the urethra is kept open by repeated probing. In the end, a puckered scar, resembling, and usable as, a vagina. What did that have to do with me, nothing, I had no fondness for my genitals but this, this, ugh.

What did you say just then, she interrupted. No fondness for your genitals.

I didn't say that. That is not a thing I said.

Cut.

Riya is sitting on the floor, reading from a book. 'According to the poet-saints of Shaivism, Shiva is *Ammai-Appar,* Mother and Father combined. It is said of Brahma that he created humankind by converting himself into two persons: the first male, Manu Svayambhuva, and the first female, Satarupa. India has always understood androgyny, the man in the woman's body, the woman in the man's.'

D is in a state of high agitation, walking from white wall to white wall, slapping at the wall when he reaches it, turning around to walk the other way, reaching the wall, slapping, turning, walking, reaching, slapping.

I don't know what you're trying to do to me. That job at the Museum is fucking with your head. This is who I am. I'm not some other individual. This is me.

Riya doesn't look up, goes on reading aloud. 'Few hijras settle in their places of origin. Family rejection and disapproval probably accounts for the uprooting. Having recreated themselves as beings whom their original families often reject, hijras usually take those new identities to new places, where new families form around them and take them in.'

Stop, he shouts. I'm not prepared to hear this. You want to drag me into the gutter? I am the youngest son of Nero Golden. Did you hear me? The youngest son. I'm not ready.

'"As a child I followed girlish ways and was laughed at and scolded for my girlishness." "I often thought I should live like a boy and I tried hard but I couldn't do it." "We also are part of creation."' She looks up from the book, snaps it shut, gets to her feet and goes to stand right in front of him, their faces very close together, his angry, hers absolutely expressionless and neutral.

You know what? she says. Many of them don't have *Operation.* They never have it. It's not necessary. What's important is who they know they are.

Is that a book you found on a park bench? he asks. Really?

She shakes her head, slowly, sadly, *No, of course not.*

I'm leaving, he says.

He leaves. Outside in the hot afternoon street, it's noisy, garish, crowded. It's Chinatown.

13

A *gigantic insect*. A *monstrous vermin*. A *verminous bug*. Gregor Samsa woke up one morning from troubled dreams to discover that he had been transformed in his own bed into an *ungeheuren Ungeziefer.* People disagreed on the best translation. The exact nature of the creature is not precisely specified in the Kafka story. Maybe a giant cockroach. The cleaning woman says he's a dung beetle. He himself doesn't seem too sure. Something horrible, anyway, with an armoured back and little waving legs. 'Into an *ungeheuren Ungeziefer*.' Not a thing anyone would want to be. A thing from which everyone finally turned away in horror, his employer, his family, even his beloved and formerly loving sister. A dead thing, in the end, to be taken out with the trash and disposed of by the cleaner. This was what he was becoming, D told himself, a monstrosity, even to himself.

He was walking uptown, lost in such morbid thoughts, and though the sunshine was bright he had the sense of being enclosed in darkness – of being, to be precise, brightly illuminated by a spotlight exposing him to the scrutiny and judgement of all, but surrounded by a black miasma that made it impossible for him to make out the faces of his judges. Only when he arrived at the door of his father's house did he realise that his feet had brought him back to Macdougal Street. He fumbled in his pocket for the key and went indoors, hoping not to have to face his family. He wasn't ready. He was not himself. If they saw him maybe they would see his metamorphosis written all over his body and cry out in horror, *Ungeziefer!* He wasn't ready for that.

How strange the interior of the house seemed to him now! This was not only for the obvious reason, namely that his father's mistress Vasilisa Arsenyeva had embarked upon a radical 'modernising' scheme of redecorations as soon as she moved in, thus stepping up a rung on the ladder of intimacy to the status of 'live-in lover'. The fourth finger of her left hand was still bare, but, all the Golden sons agreed, it would probably not be long until a diamond sparkled there, and after the diamond, a band of gold would surely also appear. Certainly she had begun to behave proprietorially. The whole mansion had been repainted in a chic oyster-grey colour and everything old had been or was being replaced by everything new and 'high-end' – the furniture, the rugs, the art, the lighting fixtures, the table lamps, the ashtrays, the picture frames. D had asked that his room be left untouched and she had respected that, so something, at least, was familiar. But he knew that his feeling of strangeness did not have its origins in the redecoration, but in himself. If, as he moved through the hallway and up the stairs, a mood of foreboding came over him, a sense that everything was about to change and that the change would be a kind of calamity, then the reason for his premonition was not to be found in oyster paint or silver velour sectional settees, it was not hanging in the new living-room drapes or glowing in the new dining-room chandelier or flickering in the new gas fireplaces whose flames in winter would heat up a bed of pebbles which would glitter with fashionable delight. It was true that this renewed environment was no longer the old-school, lived-in world Nero Golden had created for them to inhabit when they first arrived. It was possessed of a disturbing, ersatz otherness which the earlier version, also a kind of imitation of life, had somehow avoided. But no! It wasn't the house. The change was in himself. He himself was the darkness he felt around him, he was the force pulling the walls closer, the ceilings lower, like a house in a horror movie, and creating an air of oppression and claustrophobia. The house, to tell the truth, was much brighter than before. It was he who had grown dark.

He was running from the thing he also knew he was moving toward. He knew it was coming, but that didn't mean he liked it. He hated it, there was no escaping the fact, and that created the storm that surrounded him now. He wanted to go into his room and shut the door. He wanted to disappear.

When I think about D at this critical juncture I am reminded of Theodor W. Adorno: 'The highest form of morality is not to feel at home in your own home.' Yes, to be uncomfortable with comfort, uneasy about the easy, to question the assumptions of what is usually, and happily, taken for granted, to make of oneself a challenge to what for most people is the space in which they feel free from challenges; yes! That is morality raised to a pitch at which it could almost be called heroism. In this instance D Golden's 'home' was an even more intimate space than the family house; it was nothing less than his own body. He was a misfit in his own skin, experiencing, in intense form, this newly important variation of the mind/body problem. His non-physical self, the mind, was beginning to insist on being what the body, his physical self, denied, and the result was physical and mental agony.

The Golden house was silent. He stood for a moment on the second-floor landing outside his father's master suite. That door was closed, but the door of the room next to it, formerly a spare bedroom, now Vasilisa Arsenyeva's dressing room, stood open, revealing in the late-afternoon sunlight rack upon rack of shimmering gowns, shelf upon shelf of aggressively high heels. That's going to be a problem for me, the words dropping into his consciousness from some unknown mother ship hovering just outside the atmosphere beyond the Kármán line, your pedal extremities are colossal, can't use you 'cause your feet's too big, I really hate you 'cause your feet's too big. Yeah, Fats Waller, what you said. And now those big feet have walked him, of their own volition, right into the middle of that room where the scent of patchouli is stronger than anywhere else in the house, the scent she brought here to overpower all the scents that were here before, Vasilisa Arsenyeva, silent and haughty as cats are, leaving her spoor wherever she walks. And his hands are reaching out for those gowns, he's burying his face in the odorous sequins, breathing in, breathing out, breathing in. The darkness around him receded; the room glowed with a light that might even have been happiness.

How long was he in there? Five minutes or five hours? He had no idea, so many emotions crowding in, his whole self a swirl of confusion, but how good it felt, how fine the fabric against his cheek, how astonishing the sensation of, of *glamour,* how could he deny that, and what followed from it, what was the right next step.

Then Vasilisa was standing in the doorway, watching him. 'Can I help you?' she said.

Can I help you, really?, as if this was a department store and she was accusing him of shoplifting, so passive-aggressive, standing there so calm and even smiling slightly, don't condescend to me, lady, *can I help you,* no, probably not. OK, he's in her closet, he's nuzzling her frocks, this is true, but still, it's not right. Or maybe this is just a language problem, maybe it's a question she learned from a phrasebook, she doesn't understand about inflections, either, ask the question that way and it sounds hostile when maybe, can it be, she meant it literally, she literally wants to help me and is asking how, she's not judging me or angry and is actually holding out a hand to help, I don't want to misread her here, the situation is embarrassing enough already, but yes, she's coming right up to me and now she's hugging me, and here's another phrasebook phrase, 'Let's see what we can do for you.'

Vasilisa began pulling out stuff and holding it up against him, *this one? this one?,* she asked, and reassuringly, 'You and I we are similar,' she said, 'in the shape. Willowy, is that a word?' Yes, he nodded, it was a word. 'Willowy like the willow tree,' she went on, herself reassured by the confirmation. 'Your mother must have been tall and slim, like a fashion model.'

He stiffened. 'My mother was a whore,' he said. He had begun to tremble. 'She sold me to my father and vanished into Whoreistan.'

'Shh, shh,' she said. 'Shh now. That is for another day. Just now it is a moment for you. Try this one.'

'I can't. I don't want to spoil your clothes.'

'It doesn't matter. I have so many. Here, take off your shirt, slip this over your head. You see, only a little tight. What do you think?'

'Can I try that one?'

'Yes. Of course.'

(I want to leave them there for a minute, to give the two of them their privacy, averting my eyes discreetly and turning off my I-am-a-cellphone-camera, or perhaps turning it around, here is the landing, here are the stairs leading down to the entrance lobby where now, after the redecoration, the balloon dog keeps watch, the pickled piranha snarls from a wall, and neon words of love shine in lurid pink and green above the doorway, and here is the front door, opening. Enter Nero Golden. The king is back in his palace. I watch his face. He looks around, annoyed. He wants her standing here to greet him, where is she, didn't she read his text? He hangs his hat and cane on the stand in the entrance hall and calls out.)

'Vasilisa!'

(Imagine my I-am-a-Steadicam racing upstairs now, up and into the room where she and the young fellow in her clothes stand transfixed by his voice, and she, Vasilisa, looks at D and understands that he still fears his father.)

'He'll kill me. He's going to kill me. Oh my God.'

'No, he absolutely will not kill you.'

She hands him back his street clothes.

'Put them back on. I'm going to distract him.'

'How?'

'I will bring him upstairs . . .'

'No!'

'. . . into the bedroom and close the door. When you hear me beginning to make a lot of noise you will know it's safe to leave.'

'What sort of noise?'

'You can certainly guess what sort of noise. I don't have to be explicit here.'

'Oh.'

She pauses in the doorway before going down to Nero.

'And D?'

'*What!* I mean, sorry, yes, what?'

'Maybe I am not a completely, thousand per cent evil bitch.'

'Yeah. Yeah. Obviously. I mean no. Obviously not.'

'You're welcome.'

'Thank you.'

She smiles conspiratorially. I should end the scene there, a tight close-up of that sphinx-like Mona Lisa smile.

Later.

He has made his peace with patient, understanding Riya, and here they are with Ivy Manuel in the Jamaican place on Houston and Sullivan drinking dangerous cocktails late at night. Or, to reimagine it: the three people are seated around a simple round table in a completely black studio, drinking their drinks (dangerous cocktails are acceptable, even in Limbo), the world doesn't exist except for them as they discuss profound questions of language and philosophy. (Deliberate reference: Jean-Luc Godard movie, *Le gai savoir*, 1969, starring Jean-Pierre Léaud and Juliet Berto. Considered too didactic by many, but sometimes didacticism is required.) At first D is in low spirits, quoting Nietzsche (author of *Die fröhliche Wissenschaft*) asking 'the Schopenhauerian question: Has existence then a significance at all? – the question which will require a couple of centuries even to be completely heard in all its profundity.' But gradually the two women cheer him up, encouraging him, supporting him, cajoling him, and then, after he gives a small nod of acceptance and smiles cautiously, introducing him little by little to the vocabulary of his future, a future in which the pronoun *his* will stop being his. The first and most important word is *transition*. In music, a momentary modulation from one key to another. In physics, a change of an atom, nucleus, electron, etc., from one quantum state to another, with emission or absorption of radiation. In literature, a passage in a piece of writing that smoothly connects two topics or sections to each other. In the present case . . . in the present case, the process by which a person permanently adopts the outward or physical characteristics of the gender with which they identify, as opposed to those of the gender they were assigned at birth. The process may or may not involve measures such as hormone therapy and gender reassignment surgery.

'Don't think about surgery,' the women say. 'Don't even let it cross your mind. We are nowhere near that point yet.' (*When this scene is filmed the women actors can decide who says which line. But for now let's say this is Riya speaking, and then Ivy, and so on.*)

'You need to work out who you are. For this, there is professional help.'

'Right now you could be TG, TS, TV, CD. Whatever feels right to you.' Transgender, transsexual, transvestite, cross-dresser. 'No need to go one step further than what feels right.'

'For this there is professional help.'

'It used to be, people got labels in front of their names. Like, TS Ivy, or CD Riya. Also there was Sex Change. "Look, here comes Sex Change Sally." The whole trans world has grown up now. Now she's just Sally or whoever. No compartmentalisation.'

'You should think about pronouns, however. Words are important. If you're giving up *he*, who steps in? You could choose *they*. If you decide you don't identify as either female or male. *They* equals unknown gender identity. Very private.'

'There's also *ze*.'

'There's also *ey*.'

'There's also *hir, xe, hen, ve, ne, per, thon* and *Mx*.'

'You see. There's a lot.'

'*Thon* for example is a mixture of *that* and *one*.'

'*Mx* is instead of *Ms* and is pronounced *mix*. This is one I personally like.'

'It's more than pronouns, naturally. Some of this I told you at the Museum that first time. Words are important. You need to be certain of your identity unless your certainty is that you're uncertain in which case maybe you're genderfluid.'

'Or maybe transfeminine, because you're born male, identify with many aspects of femaleness but you don't feel you actually *are* a woman.'

'The word *woman* is being detached from biology. Also the word *man*.'

'Or if you don't identify with woman-ness or man-ness maybe you're *non-binary*.'

'So, there's no rush. There's a lot to think about.'

'A lot to learn.'

'Transition is like translation. You're moving across from one language into another.'

'Some people pick up languages easily. For others, it's hard. But for this, there is professional help.'

'Think about the Navajo. They recognise four genders. As well as male and female there are the Nádleehi, the two-spirits, born as a male, but functioning in the role of a woman, or vice versa, obviously.'

'You can be what you choose to be.'

'Sexual identity is not a given. It's a choice.'

D has remained silent up to now. Finally he speaks. 'Didn't the argument used to be the other way around? Being gay wasn't a choice, it was a biological necessity? So now we're saying it's a choice after all?'

'Choosing an identity,' Ivy Manuel says, 'is not like choosing cereal at the supermarket.'

'To say "choosing" can also be a way of saying "being chosen."'

'But it's a choice now?'

'For this there is professional help. With help, your choice will become clear to you.'

'It will become necessary.'

'So then it won't be a choice?'

'This is just a word. Why are you getting so hung up on this? It's just a word.'

Blackout.

14

At 7 a.m. on the morning of his wedding, one of the hottest days of the summer, with hurricane warnings on the weather reports, Nero Golden went, as usual, to play tennis at Fourth and Lafayette with three members of his close-knit group of friends-slash-business-partners-slash-clients. These mysterious men, there were five of them in all, I think, all looked alike: tough, walnut brown from prolonged exposure to expensive sunshine in expensive locations, with thinning hair worn close to the head, clean-shaven, strong-jawed, barrel-chested, hairy-legged. In their sporting whites they looked like a team of retired Marines, except that Marines could never have afforded the watches they wore; I counted two Rolexes, a Vacheron Constantin, a Piaget, an Audemars Piguet. Rich, powerful alpha males. He never introduced them to us or invited them to the Gardens to engage in social chat. They were his guys. He kept them to himself.

When I asked his sons how the old man had made his fortune I got a different answer every time. 'Construction.' 'Real estate.' 'Safes and strongboxes.' 'Online betting business.' 'Yarn trading.' 'Shipping.' 'Venture capitalism.' 'Textiles.' 'Film production.' 'Mind your own business.' 'Steel.' After my parents the professors had identified him for me I began, to the best of my ability, quietly to investigate the truth or otherwise of these extremely various assertions. I found that the man we knew as N. J. Golden had formed habits of secrecy long before he arrived among us, and the web of false fronts, proxies and ghost corporations he had set up to protect his dealings from public scrutiny was far too complex for me – just a young man dreaming of the movies – to penetrate from a distance. He had his fingers in many pies, with a reputation as a fearsome raider. He cloaked himself in benami anonymity but when he made his move, everyone knew who the player was. He had had a nickname back in the country that could not be named. 'The Cobra.' If I ever succeeded in making a movie about him, I thought, maybe that should be its title. Or maybe *King Cobra.* But after due consideration I set those titles aside. I already had my title.

The Golden House.

My investigations led me to the notorious 2G Spectrum scam, which had recently hit the headlines in the country that could not be named. It appeared that in that no-name country members of the no-name government had corruptly sold cellphone frequency licences to favoured corporations for startlingly low prices, and something like $26 billion had accrued in illicit profits to the companies so favoured. According to *Time* magazine, which a few people still read in those days, it ranked second on their Top Ten Abuses of Power list, right behind the Watergate affair. I read the names and stories of the companies that had been granted the licences and found the same kind of web favoured by Nero, an intricate system of companies owned by other companies in which yet other companies bought significant shares. My best guess was that Nero was the force behind the biggest of these companies, Eagle Telecom, which had merged with a German business, Verbunden Extratech, and then sold forty-five per cent of its stock to Abu Dhabi's Murtasín, who renamed it Murtasín-EV Telecom. Legal proceedings were being initiated against many of the new licence-holders in a series of special courts set up by the Central Bureau of Investigation, or CBI. This was my 'aha' moment. I had never believed that Nero would have made such elaborate plans to leave his country for no reason – he could not have foreseen the death of his wife in the terrorist attack on the iconic old hotel – and his possible involvement in this immense scandal provided a much more convincing reason for him to make preparations in case he needed to fly the coop. Naturally I did not dare to confront him with my suspicions. But my imaginary film, or my dreamed-of series of films, was becoming much more attractive; a financial and political thriller, or a series of such thrillers, with my neighbours at the very heart of it. This was exciting.

Weddings always make me think of the movies. (Everything makes me think of the movies.) Dustin Hoffman in *The Graduate* hammering on a glass wall in a church in Santa Barbara to steal Katharine Ross away from the altar. Grannies dancing in New Delhi in the rainy season in *Monsoon Wedding*. The ominous spilling of wine on the wedding gown in *The Deer Hunter*. The Bride shot in the head on her wedding day in *Kill Bill: Vol. 2*. Peter Cook performing the mawiage cewemony in *The Pwincess Bwide*. The unforgettable wedding banquet in Chen Kaige's *Yellow Earth*, at which the guests at a rural Chinese marriage in impoverished Shaanxi province are served wooden fish instead of real food, because there are no actual fish to be had, but at a wedding it is important to have fish on the table. But when Nero Golden married Vasilisa Arsenyeva in the Macdougal–Sullivan Historic Gardens at four o'clock in the afternoon, what inescapably came to mind was the most celebrated of all the wedding scenes ever filmed, except that this time it wasn't Connie Corleone dancing with her father, this time the patriarch danced with his own young bride, as I imagined the rich Italian-American melody written for the movie scene by the director's father Carmine Coppola welling up and drowning out the actual music of that moment in the Gardens, which with lamentable banality was a recording of the Beatles singing 'In My Life'.

Rewind a few hours: after Nero came home from his tennis game, sweating heavily as he always did, he was a big perspirer, as he freely admitted, 'I just have to run up the stairs and my shirt is soaked,' after he pulled off his shirt and wrapped himself in his heavy black towelling bathrobe, he summoned his three sons to a meeting in his study. 'There are questions in your heads I want to address,' he told them. 'In the first place, nothing is changing. I am still your father, that is number one, and with regard to you two, I will always love your late mother just as before, that is number two, and as to you, my youngest child, I continue to be sorry about the circumstances, but you know this, and you are my son as much as these other two, that is number three; and so, status quo, you understand this. Also, to get down to brass tacks: you are all aware that there exists a pretty ferocious prenuptial agreement which Vasilisa has signed without demur. Relax: your inheritance is safe. Status quo is maintained. Also, for me, after so many decades of being the father of all of you the idea of one more is not to be considered. Baby, I have said to her, to me *baby* is a four-letter word. This, also, she does not object to. There will not be a fourth brother. There will not be a first sister. Status quo. This promise I give to you on this, my wedding day. From you, I want only acceptance of my wife. No gold is being dug here, no inheritance-stealing babies are being made. I was not obliged to inform you of these matters but I have chosen to do so. At my age I ask you for your blessing. It is not necessary, but I request it. I ask, please, permit your father to have his happy day.'

In the garden after the judge had come and done his work and gone and Nero and Vasilisa were man and wife I watched them dance again as they had danced in Florida, the years dropping away from the old man as he moved, so erect, so agile, so light on his feet, so attentive to his partner, the language of the dance whispering its magic words and making him seem young again. And she in his arms, releasing the power of her beauty, coming in close with her lips against his ear, then arching her bare back and leaning away from him, and again and again in toward him and out away from him, rhythmically, overpowering him by the most powerful spell of all, the come-here-go-away seduction; Vasilisa letting him hold her and move her, telling us without needing to tell us: I am fearless, I have him, with all the witching power of my body I have commanded him to hold me so tightly in his arms that even if he wanted to he could not let me fall.

This is not a dance, I thought, it's a coronation.

The sons of Nero Golden watched and learned. Petya watching from an almost hidden place behind the children's climbing frame and slide, holding the rods of the frame as if they were prison bars. At one point I was standing beside him and he said, 'The quantity of love in our father is finite. It does not expand or contract. Now that it will be spread more thinly there will be less for us.' But whenever Vasilisa looked in his direction he smiled broadly. 'It's best not to antagonise the new queen,' he said solemnly, as if confiding a state secret. 'She could decide at any moment to have us killed.'

His brother Apu stood under a tree surrounded by his customary group of downtown arty types, painters, club-goers and Italians, and, beside him, chain-smoking, in his usual velvet smoking jacket with white wing-collared shirt, Andy Drescher, the famous professional curmudgeon for whom he unaccountably had a soft spot. Andy was a New York icon who had not published anything since his two volumes of poetry back in the eighties but somehow lived well at the highest echelons of the city with no obvious source of income or other means of support. I imagined him in a small cold-water walk-up eating cat food from the can and then dusting off his velvet finery and heading out to the smartest soirées to smile with desirous resignation at pretty young men and sourly to bark his celebrated complaints. His list of things and people to complain about grew constantly longer and included, at the moment, going to the movies, Mayor Bloomberg, the concept of marriage, both gay and straight, the concept of watching television when one could be having sex, machinery (all types, but especially smartphones), the East Village, mood boards in fashion designers' studios (which he called organised stealing), tourists, and writers who published books. He offended poor Riya that day (but then, he offended *everybody*) by mocking the Museum of Identity where Riya worked, and the idea that one could be whatever gender one chose if that was the way one felt. 'I'm going to buy a ten-million-dollar apartment next week,' he told Riya. 'Ask me how I can afford it.' Riya fell into the trap and asked. 'Oh, I'm now a transbillionaire,' came the reply. 'I identify as rich and so consequently I am.'

After that Riya stayed close to D, and together they watched the dancing queen in her moment of triumph, Beauty spinning around and around in the arms of the loving Beast, and all around her the Gardens, and all of us, invited and uninvited, real and fictional, as evening drew in and the strings of fairy lights in the trees heightened the enchanted Disney mood; my parents the professors happily dancing with each other, with eyes for nobody else, and sad U Lnu Fnu of the United Nations, and Mr Arribista of Argentina, and the true aristocrats of the Gardens community, Vito and Blanca Tagliabue, Baron and Baroness of Selinunte, and me, all of us happily joining with one another, lubricated by plentiful champagne, eating the excellent food provided by the finest catering service in the city, and feeling, for the short blissful time-out-of-time that a wedding can sometimes create, happy, together, and one. Even the five tennis players with the expensive wristwatches painted grins onto faces that were not built for smiling and nodded in an approximation of fellow feeling at the others in the Gardens, and applauded the monarchs' dance.

But there was a group that held itself apart and as the music played and darkness fell and gaiety grew they seemed to bunch closer and closer together as if to say, stay away from us, keep your distance, we aren't a part of you. These were men with slicked-down hair worn slightly too long at the back, and beards of the designer-stubble variety, and uncomfortable body language, wearing ill-fitting tuxedoes with white shirt cuffs protruding much too far out of the jacket sleeves, men without women, drinking water or soda or nothing, shuffling their feet, smoking heavily, and all of a sudden I thought, my *Godfather* intuition maybe wasn't just born from seeing the trilogy too many times, maybe I was onto something, because these people looked like they could be supplicants, people who had come to the don's big day so that they could kiss his ring. Or (now the gangster-movie trope really was getting me carried away) they looked like they could be packing heat. I ran the movie in my head, the sudden appearances of handguns from the bulging inside pockets of those badly tailored suits, blood spattering the wedding day with tragedy.

None of that happened. These gentlemen were in the hotel trade, we were informed, they were Mr Golden's business associates. It felt like being told that they dealt in olive oil: true, perhaps, but maybe also not the whole truth.

The oldest of the bridegroom's sons was standing by the serving table with the gold tablecloth where trays of finger food awaited the hungry, methodically working his way through a sequence of pigs in blankets. A thought occurred to me. 'Hey, Petya,' I went over to say, sounding as casual as I could, 'what do you know about 2G Spectrum?' A ripple of confusion passed over his face, maybe because the word *spectrum* had a different immediate resonance for him, and maybe because his extraordinary memory and instinct for truth-telling was doing battle with the pledge of secrecy the Goldens had taken. Finally he decided the answer wasn't covered by the pledge and therefore was not under embargo. 'Telecommunications kerfuffle,' he said. 'Shall I recite the list of companies involved? Adonis, Nahan, Aska, Volga, Azure, Hudson, Unitech, Loop, Datacom, Telelink, Swan, Allianz, Idea, Spice, S Tel, Tata. It should be added that in 2008 Telenor bought a majority share in the Unitech group's telecommunications company and currently operates twenty-two licences as Uninor. Datacom operates as Videocon. The Russian-based company Sistema owns a majority share in Telelink and is changing the operating name to MTS. Swan was originally a subsidiary of the Reliance group. Idea has bought Spice. Bahrain Telecommunications and Sahara Group both hold substantial stakes in S Tel. A PIL which is to say Public Interest Litigation is under way and will reach the Supreme Court soon. It is expected that at least one minister and several corporation executives may be faced with serious jail time. The five megahertz 2G Spectrum is valued per megahertz . . .'

'I notice,' I said, 'that you didn't mention Eagle, or Verbunden Extratech, or Murtasín.'

'I was simply listing those companies named in the scam,' he said. 'The corporations you mention have not been accused of any irregularity, nor are any actions pending against them. Are you thinking of writing a film about the admittedly amazing and inevitably in part corruption-tainted proliferation of mobile phones in that faraway country? If so, you should absolutely play the lead. Because you are so good-looking, you know, René, you really should be a movie star.'

This was a new thing with him that summer. Petya had recently decided, against the evidence of everyone's eyes but his own, that I was the most handsome man in the world. At first he declared that I was 'more handsome than Tom Cruise', then I became '*much* better looking than Brad Pitt', and these days I was '*a hundred times* as gorgeous as that George Clooney'. *Sic transit gloria,* Tom, Brad, George, I thought. Petya was not expressing homosexual longings. He was telling it the way he saw it, as he always did, and all I could do was say thanks.

'Something like that,' I answered him. 'But I don't think there's a role for me.'

'That's ridiculous,' he said. 'Write one in immediately. A big role. The romantic lead. You're so sexy, René. I'm serious. You're a sexpot.'

Maybe weddings bring out the romance in us all.

And at a certain point in the gaiety of the night, I did not fail to notice, Nero Golden was absent, and there was a light in his office window, and the men in the bad tuxedoes were absent also. Petya was on the dance floor. He was a bad dancer, so absurdly uncoordinated that people found him funny, the five tennis players half tried to stifle their alpha-male sniggers, but fortunately Petya, transported by music, did not seem to notice. And then Vasilisa was dancing with her girlfriends, all glamorous, all real estate brokers, doing their New York versions of Cossack dances involving candles and shawls and hand-clapping and high kicks and boots. Instead of fur hats and military uniforms there were gossamer dresses and female skin but nobody was complaining, we danced in a circle around the dancing girls and clapped in unison and shouted 'Hey! Hey!' when we were told to and drank the vodka shots we were given to drink and yes, Russia was good, Russian culture was fine, what a good Russian time we were having, one and all, and then Nero Golden reappeared in full Cossack costume, so there was at least one fur hat and one blue military coat with golden braid and buttons, and the girls danced around him like their captain, their king, which he was, and he waved his special *shashka* sabre in the air above their heads, and we danced around them, and drank, and shouted 'Hey! Hey!' some more, and so Nero and his beauty were wed.

The hotel-trade gentlemen in the bad tuxedoes, however, did not return.

A strange summer mist crept into the Gardens that night after midnight and made them look like the setting for a Japanese ghost story, *Ugetsu,* perhaps, or *Kwaidan.* The guests had all gone home and the debris of the celebration had been cleared away by the diligent staff of the catering company, to whom generous tips had been handed out by Nero Golden himself. A single lantern still hung from the branch of a tree, its candle sputtering to its end. I heard one single hoot of what might have been an owl, but it is possible I might have been mistaken. In the sky a pale moon glowing faintly through gathering rain clouds. A hurricane was coming. All was still before the storm.

As once before, my insomnia drove me out of my bed. I pulled on a sweatshirt and blue jeans and stepped out into the misty air and all at once it thickened and I was all alone in the swirl, as if the universe had vanished and there was only me. Then from far away I heard a sound, which was repeated, growing louder with each repetition. It was the sound of a man caught up in a wretched misery, sobbing uncontrollably. A cry to touch the heart.

I approached on tiptoe, my curiosity struggling against my more civilised instinct to give the weeping man his privacy. Not trusting the mist to conceal me, I did my best to lurk in the shrubbery, feeling a little ashamed (but only, I have to say, a little) of the victory of my voyeuristic desires. Finally I saw him, and was, I confess, astonished to recognise the night's star player, around whom everything had revolved, the bridegroom himself, kneeling on the damp grass in expensive pyjamas and beating his breast with his fists, ululating like a professional mourner at a funeral. What could have driven him out here in the small hours, abandoning his marital bed to howl at the vanishing moon? I crept as close as I dared and heard, or so I believe, these words: 'Forgive me! I killed you both.'

Let me say now that I am not a believer in the claims of the mystically or supernaturally inclined. I have no time for heaven, hell, limbo, or any other posthumous vacation destinations. I do not believe that I will be reincarnated, neither as a dung beetle nor as George Clooney or his successor in cuteness. In spite of the enthusiasms of Joyce, Nietzsche and Schopenhauer, I turn my back on metempsychosis, the transmigration of souls. The Thai film-maker Apichatpong Weerasethakul's *Uncle Boonmee Who Can Recall His Past Lives* was probably my favourite movie that year but I do not believe that Uncle Boonmee, or I, had any previous tours of duty here on Earth. I am uninterested in demon seeds; Damien, Carrie, Rosemary's Baby, you can keep right on sitting there on the pulp-fiction shelf. I have no time for angels or devils or creatures from blue lagoons. All of which is why I am at a loss to explain what I saw that night, and why I try to tell myself that it was a hallucination caused by taking too heavy a dose of Ambien (which had failed to knock me out) and then wandering woozily into the fog: some sort of waking nightmare. But the figure of the penitent Nero was real enough, and what I saw, what I know I saw, what I think I know I saw even though my rational mind rejects the idea, was the fog around him gathering, like some kind of ectoplasm, into two human shapes, the shapes of women, standing in front of the kneeling man to hear his bitter regret. The shapes did not speak, nor did they fully achieve solid form, remaining blurred and indistinct, but the thought came into my head, as clearly as if someone had said the words aloud, that these were the two mothers of his sons, the wife who died at the Taj and the poor abandoned woman who gave up her child and who, according to Mrs Golden, had died a lonely anonymous death in one of the places where the destitute go to die.

Forgive me. I killed you both. How should such a plea, made on a man's wedding night, be understood? As his expression of his guilt at finding new happiness while the unhappy dead lay at his feet? Or as his discovery that the haunting past had a far stronger hold on his emotions than the shallow, if young and beautiful, present? And where, right now, was the new Mrs Golden, and what was her opinion of her husband blubbering to ghosts in the garden? An unpropitious beginning, it had to be said. I stepped away into the fog and made my way back to my bed, where, strange to say, I immediately fell asleep and slept the sleep of the just.

The next morning Vasilisa announced the next phase of her scheme to cleanse and renew the house from top to bottom, out with the old!, in with the new! New lamps for old! And he, the old man, acquiesced. But hers was no mere act of interior redecoration. 'In Russia,' she said, 'we are not so stupid as to think that demons do not exist.' This, while I was listening (I was by then a frequent and welcome visitor). 'Excuse me, René, I understand that you are a sceptic, but reality is not a matter of choice. It does not care about your opinion on the matter. The world is as it has always been. Go to Orthodox church in Russia and you see the people brought by their families with the Devil sitting in their eyes, persons filled with hatred, also profane individuals, obscene individuals, individuals with much coldness of heart. Then, it starts. First the priest comes with the holy water and throws it and he is reciting also the passages from Holy Gospels in which Jesus, he drives the demons out, and my God, they come out, man's voice comes out of woman, there is shaking of the body and hissing and shrieks of revenge against the priest, and the holy water burns them, you see, and many persons sound like animal, like cow, like bear, like pig. There is vomiting and falling down. It is terrible but good. In this house it is different. Maybe it is not persons who are possessed but the house itself. You have brought the evil with you from the old country and now it is in the walls, the rugs, in the dark corners and the toilets also. There are phantoms residing here, maybe these ones of yours, maybe also older things, who must be driven out. If you want to watch when priest comes, I will permit, I know you are a creative young man in search of materials, but stand there near Holy Mary and speak when it begins only the words of the Jesus prayer. *Lord Jesus Christ, Son of God, have mercy on me a sinner.* Doesn't matter if you don't believe but just say this and the words will keep you safe from harm.'

Newly installed in pride of place in the spacious first-floor 'great room' of the Golden house, her face kissed by a strengthening wind blowing in through the French windows opening onto the Gardens, a wind moist with the promise of rain: an immaculate early copy of the Feodorovskaya icon of the Mother of God, the original of which hung at the Alexander Palace in the small chapel on the left side of the bedroom of the last Romanov tsarina, Alexandra, who would pray to the Virgin for hours every day. This was surprising. The sons of Nero Golden made no secret of their lack of religious belief and although I had not heard him speak on the subject I had assumed that their father felt the same way, and was indeed the fountainhead, so to speak, of their shoulder-shrugging irreligion. Yet this sacred image was Nero's wedding gift to his young wife, and now, without argument, he stood beside her before the Mother of God with clasped hands and bowed head and indicated that it was time for the exorcism to commence, and all three of the younger Goldens had been marshalled by him and were present and serious-faced, as instructed. And here right on cue was the Russian Orthodox priest, a beard in a tent, beginning to chant and to toss holy water over us all, and just at that moment Hurricane Irene showed up, the sky blackened, the heavens opened, and blazing lightning filled the room. The priest cried out in Russian and Vasilisa translated his words.

Praise God, for it is done.

Whereupon Nero Golden also exclaimed loudly, 'Shut the doors,' and his sons rushed to the French windows, and whereas I understood this to be a practical response to the wind and the driving rain, Vasilisa and the priest understood it differently. The beard shook, the tent surrounding it trembled, excited Russian words emerged, and the new Mrs Golden triumphantly translated and paraphrased them, 'Shut the doors against the rain, but there is no need to close them against the demons, for they have been driven out of my husband, and they will never return.'

Whatever took place that morning – and I was deeply sceptical about the exorcism's authenticity – it is certainly true that there were no more nocturnal walks for Nero, no more weeping on summer lawns. As far as I know, the phantoms of the two women did not appear to him again. Or if they did he controlled his feelings, turned his back on them, and did not mention their visits to his wife.

From his sanctum, that evening, came the sounds of his Guadagnini violin, playing – only adequately – Bach's powerfully emotional Chaconne.

On the Monday evening when the trouble began Nero Golden accompanied his wife Vasilisa to her preferred Russian restaurant in the Flatiron district for a dinner in honour of Mikhail Gorbachev, who was visiting the city to raise funds for his cancer charity. They were placed at the table of honour alongside the émigré billionaire with the artistically inclined wife, and the émigré billionaire who had bought his way into the newspaper business just when the newspaper business was going out of business but who fortunately owned a baseball team as well, and the émigré billionaire with a big stake in Silicon Valley and a wife with a big stake in silicon as well, and at other nearby tables were lesser billionaires with smaller boats and soccer teams and cable TV networks and wives who were not quite as impressive. For Vasilisa Arsenyeva, the girl from Siberia, her presence among this elite group was proof that her life was finally worthwhile and she insisted on taking photographs of herself with each of the Russian grandees (and of course their wives also) to text to her mother at once.

Before they left home, when she was fully dressed and looking almost criminally attractive, she knelt at her husband's feet, unzipped his pants and serviced him slowly and expertly, 'because', she told him, 'when a man like you takes a woman like me into a room like this one he should know where he stands with her'. This was an unusual miscalculation – and she was usually good at sexual calculation – because it had the effect of making Nero Golden more suspicious, not less, so that at the restaurant he watched her every movement like an increasingly bad-tempered hawk, and as the food circulated, the herrings in red coats, the beef-stuffed cabbage golubtsy, the vareniki, vushka and halushky Ukrainian dumplings, the veal pelmeni, the stroganoff, the vodka infused with gooseberries and figs, the blinchiki pancakes, the caviar, his jealousy increased, it was as if she were serving little pieces of herself up to all the men present, on little red-paper napkins, to be eaten with a little two-pronged cocktail fork, like a yummy little canapé. Of course, at this top table all the men were with wives, so everyone behaved with discretion, the billionaire with the artistically inclined wife told him he was a lucky man to have captured 'our Vasilisa', the billionaire with the unsuccessful newspapers and the successful baseball team said, 'She is like our daughter.' The Silicon Valley billionaire with the silicon wife said, 'God knows how you got her,' and made a lewd gesture with his hands suggesting something big inside the pants, but everyone had had plenty of vodka, so no offence was intended or taken, it was just man talk. But after a while he noticed that she was waving at people across the room, and they were waving back, and all of these people were men, in particular one man, a youngish man, tall, muscular, maybe forty, with hair oddly, prematurely white, wearing aviator shades even though it was night, a person who could be a tennis coach or – this was, for obvious reasons, Nero Golden's ultimate term of disapproval – a personal trainer. Or maybe a hairdresser, a homosexual, which would be fine. Or, yeah, maybe another billionaire, younger than these other guys, one with, for example, a large red yacht built at the Benetti shipyard in Viareggio, Italy, and a fondness for one-and-a-half-million-dollar hypercars named after Quechua wind gods, and fast girls to go with them. That was a possibility that could not be ignored. 'Excuse me,' she said, 'I'm just going to salute my friends.' Then she was gone, and he was watching her, the hugs, the air kisses, nothing improper but something smelled bad over there, maybe he should go and inspect these friends, these so-called friends. Maybe he should take a closer look at that blonde he couldn't see properly, that guy's date, that petite blonde with her back to him, he could see the musculature of her arms, yes, he remembered her, the bitch. Maybe he should just rip her fucking head off.

But then Gorbachev was making conversation, 'So now, Mr Golden, with your lovely Russian wife you are one of us, almost, I would say, and I can see you are a man of consequence, so allow me to ask you . . .' Except that this wasn't Gorbachev talking, it was his interpreter who was called maybe Pavel, peering over Gorbachev's shoulder from behind like a second head, and speaking so soon after the former president that he was almost in lip sync, which meant either that he was the greatest, fastest interpreter ever, or that he was making the English up, or that Gorbachev always said the same kind of thing. In any case Nero Golden in his immense and mounting irritation at Vasilisa's behaviour wasn't going to allow himself to be interrogated by the guest of honour and interrupted him to ask a question of his own.

'I have business associates in the city of Leipzig, formerly in GDR,' he said. 'They told me an interesting story and I would be pleased to hear your comment.'

Gorbachev's face became grave. 'What is the story?' his second-head Pavel asked.

'During the unrest of 1989,' Nero Golden said, 'when the protesters took refuge in the Thomaskirche, the church of Bach, the chief of the East German Communist party, Herr Honecker, wanted to send in troops with machine guns and kill everyone, and so much for the revolution, it would be gone. But because of the proposal to use the army against civilians he had to call you for permission, and you refused it, and after that it was only a matter of days until the fall of the Wall.'

Neither Gorbachev nor his second head said a word.

'So my question is this,' Nero Golden said. 'When you received that phone call and were asked that question, was your refusal instinctive and automatic . . . or did you have to think about it?'

'What is the purpose of this enquiry?' Gorbachev–Pavel said with grim faces.

'It is to raise the question of the value of human life,' Nero Golden said.

'And what is your view on the subject?' the two Gorbachevs asked.

'Russians have always taught us,' Nero said, and now there was no mistaking his deliberate hostility, 'that the individual life is expendable when set against reasons of state. This we know from Stalin, and also the poison-tipped umbrella murder in London of Georgi Markov and polonium poisoning of KGB refugee Alexander Litvinenko. Also, this journalist hit by a car, that journalist also accidentally deceased, though these are of secondary concern. Regarding human value, the Russians show us the road to the future. In this year events in the Arab world confirm, and will soon further confirm this. Osama is dead, I have no problem. Gaddafi is gone, poof, let him go. But now we will see that the revolutionaries, their end too will come soon. Life itself goes on, unkind to many. The living are of small importance to the business of the world.'

The table was silent. Then Gorbachev's second head spoke even though Gorbachev himself said nothing. 'Georgi Markov,' the second head said, 'was Bulgarian.'

Gorbachev answered very slowly, in English. 'It is not an appropriate forum for this conversation,' he said.

'I will take my leave,' Nero answered, nodding. He raised an arm and his wife at once rose from her friends' table and followed him to the door. 'Magnificent evening,' he said to the room at large. 'Our thanks.'

WIDE SHOT. MANHATTAN STREET. NIGHT.

A YOUNGISH MAN, tall, muscular, maybe forty, with hair oddly, prematurely white, wearing aviator shades even though it is night, a person who could be a tennis coach or a personal trainer, walks with his date, a petite BLONDE WOMAN with a resemblance to another personal trainer, down Broadway toward Union Square, past the AMC Loews at Nineteenth Street, past ABC Carpet, past the third, penultimate location of the Andy Warhol Factory at 860 Broadway and then the second location, in the Decker Building at Sixteenth Street. Considering their solitude, the absence of security, he is probably not a billionaire, and does not own a large red yacht or a one-and-a-half-million-dollar hypercar. He is just a guy alone with a girl in the city after dark.

Music is playing. Unexpectedly it is a Bollywood song, '*Tuhi Meri Shab Hai*', and the lyrics are subtitled. You alone are my night. You only are my day. The song comes from a film released in 2006, starring Kangana Ranaut. The name of the film is *Gangster*.

NARRATOR (V/O)

According to *The New York Times*, homicides in America reached an alarming peak in the 1990s but are now near historic lows.

There are fears that the heroin epidemic and a resurgence of gang violence may push the numbers up again in some cities: Chicago, Las Vegas, Los Angeles, Dallas, Memphis. However, more optimistically, in New York City there has been a twenty-five per cent year-on-year decrease.

The man in the aviator shades and the woman with the highly toned arms are crossing the park now, walking between the statue of George Washington and the entrance to the subway station.

The song continues, growing louder, with no need for subtitles:

SONG

Oh oh oh oh oh oh oh oh
Oh oh oh oh oh oh oh
Oh oh oh oh oh oh oh oh
Oh oh oh oh oh oh oh

As the YOUNGISH MAN and the BLONDE WOMAN pass the subway entrance, a SECOND MAN comes out of it, moving fast, wearing a motorcycle helmet, pulls out a handgun with a silencer, shoots the YOUNGISH MAN, once, in the back of the head; and as he falls and the BLONDE WOMAN opens her mouth to scream he shoots her, too, very fast, once, between the eyes. She falls straight down onto her knees and remains like that, head bowed, kneeling, dead. The YOUNGISH MAN lies face down in front of her. The SECOND MAN walks away quickly, but not running, to the corner of Fourteenth and University, past the chess players' zone, still holding the weapon. There are no chess players, it's too late at night. There is, however, a MOTORCYCLIST waiting for him. He drops the gun in the trash bin on the corner, gets on the man's motorbike and they leave. Only now, when the motorbike has gone, do POLICE OFFICERS emerge from the squad cars stationed around the square and move quickly to the kneeling woman and the fallen man.

Cut.

INTERIOR. NERO GOLDEN'S BEDROOM. NIGHT.

VASILISA is fast asleep in their large bed with its ornate, gilded rococo headboard. NERO's eyes, too, are closed. Then, in an EFFECT SHOT, he 'steps out of his body' and walks to the window. This ghost-self is transparent. The camera, behind him, sees through him to the heavy drapes, which he slightly parts, to look down at the Gardens. The 'real' NERO continues to sleep in his bed.

NERO (V/O)

I say this while I am still in full possession of all my mental faculties. I know that at a later point in my story the soundness of my mind will be called into question, and perhaps rightly so. But that is not now, that is not just yet. There is still time to admit my foolishness, and to accept also that it reflects poorly on me. To have my head turned so easily by a pretty face. I understand now the depths of her self-interest, the coldness of her calculations and therefore of her heart.

The ghost-NERO walks calmly back to the bed, and 'sits down' into the 'real' NERO, and then there is just one NERO, with his eyes closed, beside his sleeping wife.

Her cellphone begins to ring, on 'vibrate'. She doesn't wake up to answer it.

It vibrates a second time and this time NERO, without moving, opens his eyes.

The third time, VASILISA wakes up, groans, reaches for the phone.

She comes fully awake, sits straight up in bed, and with her free hand clasps her cheek in horror. She speaks rapidly in Russian into the phone, asking questions. Then she becomes silent and puts the phone down.

For a long moment they remain as they are, she sitting up with horror on her face, he lying back calmly with his eyes open, looking up at the ceiling.

Then, slowly, she turns to look at him, and her expression changes. Now the only emotion on her face is fear.

They do not speak.

Cut.

PART II

15

Regarding Mice and Giants, Percentages and Art

Apu Golden heard about the large gathering of protesters against the arrogance of the banks which had begun occupying an open space in the Financial District and when he went down to look, wearing a panama hat, khaki shorts and a Hawaiian shirt so as not to stand out too much, he found himself enchanted by the carnivalesque character of the crowd, the beards, the shaven heads, the lending library, the kisses, the odours, the passionate activists, the crazy old coots, the cooks, the young, the old. 'Even the policemen seemed to be smiling,' he told me, 'well, some of them, let's be truthful, some of the others were the usual Cro-Magnon you-cross-the-road-to-avoid-contact-with-them types.' He liked the visual and also literary aspects of the event, the recitals of poetry, the placards made from old cardboard boxes, the cut-out fists and V-signs, and he was impressed most of all by the support being given to the protesters by the mighty dead. 'So wonderful,' he told me, 'to see Goethe lying down among the sleeping bags, G. K. Chesterton standing in line for soup, Gandhi wiggling his fingers in the form of silent applause called up-twinkles – or actually of course it's Ghandi because nobody can spell any more, spelling is so boozhwa. Even Henry Ford is there, his words rippling through the crowd via the technique of the human microphone.' I went down there with him because his giggling enthusiasm was infectious and watched with admiration the speed and accuracy of his pencil as it captured the thronging scene, and yes, sure enough, there in his drawings were the immortal ghosts among the crowd, Goethe pompously pontificating, 'None are more hopelessly enslaved than those who falsely believe they are free,' and 'Ghandi' reciting his old chestnut, 'First they ignore you, then they blah blah blah, then you win.' 'He never said that,' Apu pointed out. 'It's just an Internet meme, but what to do, nobody knows anything, like I said, knowing things is boozhwa too.' Chesterton and Henry Ford in their tailcoats seemed incongruous here but they too were given respectful audience, their sentiments being right on the money, so to speak, 'An enormous amount of modern ingenuity is expended,' old G.K. opined, 'on finding defences for the indefensible conduct of the powerful,' and H. Ford standing by his assembly line cried out, 'If the people of this nation understood our banking and monetary system, I believe there would be a revolution tomorrow morning.' 'It's impressive,' Apu said, 'how the Internet has made philosophers of us all.' I personally preferred the cardboard declamations of an anonymous thinker who seemed motivated primarily by hunger. 'One day the poor will have nothing left to eat except the rich,' he admonished us, and on another cardboard speech bubble he expressed the same thought more pithily. 'Eat a banker.' This thinker wore an Anonymous mask, the mustachioed smiling white-faced Guy Fawkes face popularised by the Wachowskis in *V for Vendetta,* but when I asked him about the man whose face he was wearing he admitted he had never heard of the Gunpowder Plot and did not remember, remember the fifth of November. Such was this would-be revolution. Apu sketched it all.

He showed this work in a space run by Frankie Sottovoce on the Bowery, a 'grittier' environment than Sottovoce's Chelsea galleries. It was a joint show with Jennifer Caban, the most prominent artist-activist of that argumentative instant, who, at one point during the opening, lay full-length in a bathtub full of fake money; and they were soon both acclaimed and derided for their partisanship. Apu resisted the bathtub photos and also the partisan label. 'For me the aesthetic aspect is always primary,' he tried to argue, but the zeitgeist wasn't listening, and in the end he surrendered to the descriptions that were imposed on him and the measure of political celebrity they conferred. 'Maybe now I am famous on more than twenty blocks,' he mused to me. 'Maybe now it's more like thirty-five or forty.'

In the house on Macdougal Street Apu's new agitprop notoriety was accorded scant respect. Nero Golden himself said nothing, neither praise nor damnation, but the thin line of his lips said as much as speech would have. He left it to his wife to let rip. Vasilisa on the living-room floor surrounded by glossy home-decoration magazines paused in her work to give Apu a Russian earful. 'Those beggars in the street, making noise and filth and for what? Do they think the power they are attacking is so weak, it will quail before the rabble? They are like a mouse that stamps on the foot of a giant. The giant feels nothing and doesn't even care to squash the mouse. Who cares, really? The mouse will run away soon. What will they do when winter comes? The weather will crush them. No need for anyone else to waste effort. Also, they have no leaders, this peasants' army you love. They have no programme. Therefore, they are nothing. They are a mouse without a head. They are a dead mouse that does not know it is dead.'

Only half in jest she threw a glossy magazine at him. 'Who do you think you are, excuse me? You think when their revolution comes they will put you among their holy ninety-nine per cent because you drew some pictures? In my country we know something about what happens when the revolution comes. You should kneel with me before the Feodorovskaya Madonna and we will pray to the Blessed Virgin for our salvation, so we are not murdered in a windowless cellar by the army of the headless mouse.'

There was a change in Vasilisa Golden now. At some moments, when the light fell on her face in a certain way, she reminded me of Diane Keaton in her *Godfather* role, her face, mind and heart frozen by her daily need not to believe what was staring her in the face. But 'Kay Adams' had married 'Michael Corleone' believing him to be a good man. Vasilisa had married, so to speak, the Marlon Brando character himself, so she was under no illusion about the ruthlessness, amorality and dark secrets that are the inevitable consiglieri of men of power, and when the light fell on her face in another way it was clear that she wasn't Diane Keaton after all. She was complicit. She suspected him of a terrible crime and she agreed with herself to set the suspicion aside because of the life she had chosen for herself, the life she deemed worthy of her beauty. And, perhaps, because she was now afraid. She still believed in her power over him, but she now also believed in his power, and knew that if she tried to pit her force against his, the consequences for her could be . . . extreme. She had not come into this house to face extreme consequences and so her strategy had to be altered. She had never been an innocent abroad. But in the aftermath of the shootings in Union Square she had grown tougher. She was clearer about the man with whom she was in bed and she knew that certain silences might be required of her if she was to survive.

Regarding the Family: An Interrogation

— Again, sir: why does a man abandon his homeland, change his name, and start his life afresh halfway across the world? — Why, because of grief, sir, the death of a beloved wife, which propelled him out of himself. Because of grief, and the need to leave it behind, and the leaving behind of it achieved by the shedding of the self. — Plausible. And yet one is not wholly convinced. And yet it remains to ask again: what of the preparations for departure, which predated the tragedy? An explanation for that must be given, surely? — You search for a subtext, then? You suspect shenanigans, skulduggery, jiggery-pokery? — Innocent until proven guilty. No charges against this patriarch in the 2G Spectrum scam. This, one concedes. And surely a fellow on the run from the law would, having rendered himself pseudonymous, affect a low profile? Surely such a fellow would not bruit himself abroad in his newfound land? Whereas this fellow, increasingly, and persistently, and with ever increasing brio, does he not, bruits. — Sir, he does. Which may, as you say, denote innocence. But one thinks, also, of the parable of the scorpion and the frog. The scorpion acts according to its nature even when it is suicidal to do so. Additionally, or by way of confirmation, he is of brazen character, this fellow. He is sure, one feels, of his own invincibility, secure in the certainty of his own invulnerability. If indeed there are laws he has broken, or, how should one put this, people he has alienated – for one's most dangerous adversaries are not necessarily law-abiding themselves – then he is certain he is beyond their reach. The reach of dangerous adversaries is not limitless. They may be dangerous on their own turf, but it is not easy for them to stretch beyond it, and they do not try to do so. — Or so I speculate. This is not my area of expertise. — But it is clear that Nero feels increasingly secure, and armoured by this growing self-belief he goes forth a-scorpioning, blaring and foghorning, establishing, as they say nowadays, his brand. — A word with many meanings, sir, including these: an identifying mark formerly burned on criminals or slaves. A habit, trait, or quality that causes someone public shame or disgrace. A torch. A sword. — We shall see which of those, in this case, applies.

To continue: It had become clear by the election year of 2012 that Nero Golden did not intend to lead a quiet life. Of all the four-and-twenty-blackbird dainty-dishes into which he had stuck a finger during the course of his previous life it was the construction and development business that came most naturally to him and remained strongest in him, and so it was that the word GOLDEN, a golden word, coloured gold, in brightly illuminated gold neon, and all in capital letters of gold, began to be seen on hard-hat sites around town, and out of town also, and the name's owner began to be spoken of as a new power player in that most closed of elites, the small number of families and corporations who controlled the building of this golden city, New York.

— Families, sir? When you say families are you meaning to say, if I may put this delicately, *famiglie*? — No, sir, or not entirely. The industry in 2012 was much cleaner than previously. In the 1990s the construction companies all belonged to the mob and their bids were absurdly inflated.

Now the Five Families' influence was diminished. On some of Nero Golden's sites the workers included non-union. Twenty years earlier these workers would have been killed. — So you speak now of reputable persons: Doronin, Sumaida, Khurana, Silverstein, Stern, Feldman, the aristocrats of real estate. — Not entirely, sir, as I said. The mob abides. Now that it's all over and all is out in the open we can point to Nero Golden's covert dealings with such associates as the Philadelphia descendants of Petruchio 'Chicken Little' Leone, and Atlantic City's Arcimboldo 'Little Archie' Antonioni, and in Miami Federico 'Crazy Fred' Bertolucci. We may also mention that in New York City, several of the Golden towers were built by Ponti & Quasimodo Concrete Co. – 'P&Q' – an operation in which there was a strong interest taken by Francesco 'Fat Frankie' Palermo, an allegedly senior figure in the Genovese crime family. — This is known? — Now, at the end of *l'affaire Golden*, it is known. What is more, Nero Golden was clearly quite comfortable in his dealings with these individuals and the families behind them. — Comfortable. — Sir: revealingly at ease.

Two last questions: Did Chicken Little, Little Archie, Crazy Fred and Fat Frankie wear, upon their ample chins, designer stubble? And did they own, and in the evening sometimes wear, bad tuxedoes? — Sir: they did.

Here is Nero Golden, lifting his ban on the media, showing a photographer from a glossy free magazine around his beautiful home. (No more secrecy now; instead, everything on display.) Here is Nero Golden, showing another such magazine around his beautiful wife. He speaks of his wife as his inspiration, as his lodestar, as the source of his 'renewal'. I am an old man, he says, and maybe for men such as myself it's time to wind down, go on the boat, pick up the golf clubs, winter in Florida, pass the baton. This until recently I was ready to do, even though my sons, God knows, show little interest in the family business. My youngest, can you believe it, he works now for a girls' youth club on the LES, he's doing good works, and this is fine, but maybe I need him too, a little attention, please. And then, an artist, and then Petya. So it is. But such concerns do not worry me any longer because I am as a man reborn. A woman will do this for you. A woman like Mrs Golden, she is the elixir of life, she turns a man's hair black again, she tightens his abdomen, she puts miles back into his legs, and his mind, yes, his business mind also, she sharpens it like a knife. Look at her! Can you doubt me? Did you see her *Playboy* photos? Of course not ashamed, why would one be ashamed? To own one's body, to care for it and make it excellent, to see no disgrace in beauty, that is liberation. She is the ideal of the liberated woman and also the ideal of the wife. Both sides of the coin. Yes: a lucky man. For sure. She's the jackpot, no doubt.

16

Regarding Love: A Tragedy

On the day my parents died I wasn't in the car. It was Memorial Day weekend and they were heading out of town but I changed my mind at the last moment and stayed in the city because Suchitra Roy wanted me to help her cut a video for an Italian fashion house. Of course I was in love with Suchitra, everyone who ever crossed the path of that human dynamo fell at least a little bit in love with her, and for a long time I had been too scared of her sheer energy, the scale of the woman, her black hair flying behind her in the wind on Sixth Avenue, her blue-and-gold skirt glowing above the latest sneakers, her arms spreading in a dozen different directions like a Hindu goddess managing to enfold the whole city in her embrace . . . too scared to admit to myself that I'd fallen for her, but by now there was no doubt about it, and the only question was, when was I going to tell her, or would I tell her at all. There was a voice in my head saying *do it now, you fool,* but a second, often louder voice, the voice of my cowardice, arguing that we had been friends for too long, that after a certain point it became impossible to transmute friendship into romantic love, that if one attempted to do so and failed one could be left without the friendship or the love, and here was Eliot's Prufrock in my head again, agonising in my own inner voice, *Do I dare,* and regarding the terrible and terrifying question of a declaration of love, *Would it have been worth while / If one, settling a pillow or throwing off a shawl, / And turning toward the window, should say: / 'That is not it at all, / That is not what I meant, at all.'*

I decided to stay and work with her, and at the end of the edit we would go out for a beer and I would declare myself. Yes. I would. So I did not get into my parents' car, and because of that I am alive today. Life and death are both meaningless. They happen or don't happen for reasons that have no weight, from which you learn nothing. There is no wisdom in the world. We are all fortune's fools. Here is the earth and it is so beautiful and we are so lucky to be here with one another and we are so stupid and what happens to us is so stupid and we don't deserve our stupid luck.

I'm making no sense. Let me tell you about the road.

The Long Island Expressway was a road full of family stories and when in the summer we drove out to our borrowed place on Old Stone Highway in The Springs – owned by a Columbia University grandee who, having once developed full-blown Lyme disease and suffered from it for several years, no longer wished to travel to the kingdom of the tick – we checked off all the familiar landmarks. Mineola, the cemetery there, I had a great-aunt and -uncle in whose posthumous direction to nod a respectful head. Great Neck, Little Neck, raised thoughts of Gatsby in us all, and though we did not drive by Remsenburg, where P. G. Wodehouse had lived for so many years during his post-war exile from England, we often imagined, as we drove, a fictional universe in which Fitzgerald's and Wodehouse's creations might visit one another. Bertie Wooster and Jeeves might have intruded on the rarefied world of the Eggs, silly-ass Bertie stepping into sensible Nick Carraway's shoes, and Reginald Jeeves the fish-eating, Spinoza-loving gentleman's gentleman and genius finding a way to give Jay Gatsby the happy-ever-after ending with Daisy Buchanan for which he so profoundly longed. Dix Hills, my father in a creaky Belgian dad-joke effort invariably pronounced with a French accent. *Dee Heels.* And I said, I always said, that it sounded to me like a daytime soap star. And Wyandanch; as we passed that exit one parent or the other would inevitably tell the story of the

Montaukett chief or *sachem* of that name who sold most of the East End of Long Island to an Englishman named Lion Gardiner, and later died of the plague. Wyandanch often cropped up again when we had reached the East End and my parents reminisced about the story of Stephen Talkhouse, Wyandanch's descendant, who walked fifty miles a day every day between Montauk, Sag Harbor and East Hampton. And in between Wyandanch and Talkhouse we passed a sign directing us toward an entirely fictitious Native American lady, Shirley Wading River. In reality this road sign led to two distinct communities, one called Wading River and the other Shirley, but Shirley Wading River grew large in our family lore. As sci-fi buffs we sometimes put her together with the post-apocalyptic Chiefs, Three Hydrogen Bombs and Makes Much Radiation, from William Tenn's 1958 classic *Eastward Ho!,* and at other times we imagined her gigantic, like Grendel's mother, or a sort of giant Australian-style *wandjina* or ancestor, shaping the landscape as she walked.

They listened to the radio as they drove. The oldies channel, 101.1, for music, WNYC for words, until the signal faded and then they waited until East Hampton Music showed up on the dial, the sign that the weekend was about to begin, nights of soft rock and lobster roll, that was another dad-joke. In between the New York stations and WEHM there were audiobooks and that year their plan was to listen to Homer. I think – I can't be sure, but I think – that by the time they set off for their Memorial Day weekend they had reached Book Four of the *Odyssey,* Telemachus visiting the palace of Menelaus on the day his daughter, the daughter of recaptured Helen of Troy, married Achilles' son.

So maybe they were listening to the passage in which Menelaus recounts the day that Helen came to the great wooden horse, suspecting that there were Greek warriors within, and with immense and seductive deception imitated the voices of all their wives (I imagine her reaching up and caressing the wooden belly of the beast erotically as she spoke), so sensually that Diomed, Menelaus himself and Ulysses too wanted to spring out of the horse then and there; but Ulysses restrained himself and his fellows, save only Anticlus, who was about to cry out, and would have done so, had Ulysses not *clapped two brawny hands over his mouth and kept them there,* and, according to some versions of the tale, strangled the life out of him to protect the hidden Greeks. Yes, maybe that immortal moment rang in their ears, when the metal pipe lying in the road just lying there metal fucking pipe fell off some fucking truck did the truck driver stop no he didn't did he even know no he probably didn't did he secure his load properly no he absolutely fucking didn't because there in the road

the metal pipe

in the HOV lane because these were my parents my beloved my only and they weren't speedsters no sir they preferred to trundle along safely in the no entry no exit multiple occupancy sensible road use lane marked with a diamond because why who cares why but on this occasion not so fucking safe because the metal pipe

rolling

I'm approaching the horror and must take a break to compose myself and maybe write more later.

No.

There is no later.

Now.

The pipe was seven feet long. It rolled into the path of another car which gave it what the reports called a *glancing blow.* The pipe spun about, somehow got itself up so that it bounced end over end, and smashed through the windshield of my parents' car and hit my father in the head, killing him instantly. Their car, out of control, veered out of the HOV lane into the path of the fast traffic and in the multiple collision that followed my mother was also killed. To get them out of the vehicle, the emergency services had to send for the Jaws of Life, but they were both gone. Their bodies were taken to North Shore University Hospital at Plainview, in Nassau County, where they were both pronounced dead on arrival. At midnight, just after I had fearfully declared my love to Suchitra Roy in the British-style pub on the corner of Bleecker and LaGuardia and been given the almost entirely unexpected news that she also had deep feelings for me, I received the call.

For a good deal of that year I stopped thinking almost completely. All I heard was the thunderous beating of the death angel's gigantic wings. Two people saved me. One was my new beloved, brilliant, loving Suchitra.

The other was Mr Nero Golden.

With their characteristic carefulness – WHICH DIDN'T SAVE THEIR LIVES DID IT, THE CARELESSNESS OF OTHERS ERASES OUR OWN CARE, THE CARELESSNESS OF A PIPE REARING UP, SMASHING INTO MY FATHER'S FACE, OF WHICH MINE IS A POOR ECHO, WE WHO COME AFTER ARE THE COUNTERFEITS OF THE REAL ONES WHO PRECEDED US AND ARE GONE FOREVER, STUPIDLY, MEANINGLESSLY, SLAUGHTERED BY A RANDOM PIPE, OR A BOMB IN A NIGHTCLUB, OR A DRONE – my parents had left their affairs in good order. There were all the necessary, careful legal documents, carefully composed, which ensured that my status as sole heir was protected, and there was insurance to pay what the state required of that heir, and there would be a sum of money. So for the time being my domestic arrangements didn't need to change, though probably in the medium term the house would need to be sold. It was too big for me, its value was high, the maintenance expenses and property taxes and so on would be difficult for me to come up with, and ET CETERA I DIDN'T CARE. I walked the streets in a blind rage and all at once it was as if all the anger gathering in the air poured into me too, I could feel it, the anger of the unjustly dead, the young men shot for walking in a stairwell while black, the young child shot for playing with a plastic gun in a playground while black, all the daily black death of America, screaming out that they deserved to live, and I could feel, too, the fury of white America at having to put up with a black man in a white house, and the frothing hatred of the homophobes, and the injured wrath of their targets, the blue-collar anger of everyone who had been Fannie Mae'd and Freddie Mac'd by the housing calamity, all the discontent of a furiously divided country, everyone believing they were right, their cause was just, their pain was unique, attention must be paid, attention must finally be paid to them and only them, and I began to wonder if we were moral beings at all or simply savages who defined their private bigotries as necessary ethics, as the only ways to be. I had been brought up by those dear departed Belgians to believe that 'right' and 'wrong' were ideas that came naturally to the human animal, that these concepts were born in us, not made. We believed that there was a 'moral instinct': hard-wired into the DNA in the way that, according to Steven Pinker, the 'language instinct' was. This was our family answer to the religious allegation that persons without religion could not be moral beings, that only the moral structure of a religious system validated by some sort of Supreme Arbiter could give human beings a firm grip on good and evil. My parents' answer to that was 'Hogwash', or alternatively a term they had learned from Australian friends and gleefully adopted as their own: 'Horse puckie'. Morality came before religion and religion was our ancestors' way of responding to that built-in need. And if that was so then it followed that it was perfectly possible to lead a good life, to have a strong sense of right and wrong, without ever letting God and his harpies into the room.

'The problem is,' my mother said, sitting on a bench in the Gardens, 'that while we are programmed to want ethics, the programme doesn't tell us what right and wrong actually are. These categories are empty in the brain and require us to fill them up with what? Thought. Judgement. Stuff of this kind.'

'One of the general principles of human behaviour, I've found,' my father added, walking up and down in front of her, 'is that in almost every situation, everyone believes himself or herself to be right, and any opponent wrong.'

To which my mother rejoined, 'Also we live in a time in which there is almost no agreement on any existential questions, we can't even concur simply on what is the case, and when the nature of the real is so disputed, so must the nature of the good be.'

When they got going like this they were like dancers, or badminton players, their words moving in harmony, their rackets wafting the shuttlecock back and forth, forth and back again. 'So the idea that we have an ethics instinct doesn't carry with it the notion that we know what those ethics should be. If that were true philosophers would be out of a job and we would live in a less contentious world,' my father was pointing at me with a finger now, *you see?, you getting this?,* and I like a schoolboy nodding, yes, Dad, yes, Mom, I get it, we all agree on this, these are things we know.

'Yeah, but did you know there's a word for it?' my father asked me.

A word for what, Dad.

'Definition: The supposed innate ability of the human mind to realise the basic principles of ethics and morals. A technical term of philosophy, signifying the innate principle in the moral consciousness of every man, which directs him to good and restrains him from evil.'

No, Dad, what word would that be.

'*Synderesis,*' my mother said. 'Did you ever hear a better word?'

'There isn't a better word,' my father concurred. 'Remember it, kiddo. The best word in the world.'

These were the voices I would never hear again.

And they were wrong. The human race was savage, not moral. I had lived in an enchanted garden but the savagery, the meaninglessness, the fury had come in over the walls and killed what I loved most.

I had never seen a dead body until I saw my parents' corpses at the Mineola morgue. I had sent over clothes for them, one of Suchitra's interns ran that errand, and had chosen coffins online, selecting, as one does, absurdly expensive boxes for them to be burned in. Our home was full of tenured professors, male and female, helping. I had all the help in the world from the leading experts in Sumerian art, subatomic physics, First Amendment law and Commonwealth literature. But nobody could help me look at the bodies. Suchitra drove me out there in her ageing Jeep and because there was no way we could talk about what we needed to talk about we fell into black comedy, remembering particularly gruesome 'corpses of the week' from the old HBO series *Six Feet Under.* My favourite was the woman on a girls' night out in a rented stretch limo rising through the open sunroof to express her happiness and running face first into the bucket of a cherry-picker truck. After which her flattened face would have been quite a task for the series regulars to fix.

And then an over-lit room with two gurneys and two horizontal beings under sheets, two horizontal beings who once, horizontal on a different, softer surface, had conjoined joyfully – maybe clumsily – maybe not – I was unable to imagine my parents as gymnastic sex fiends, but I also didn't want them to be fumbling incompetents – and the result was this blank unthinking entity standing by the gurneys to confirm that they were no longer capable of the act that brought him into being, or of anything else.

They had done their best at the morgue. I went to my mother first and they had removed the terror from her face as well as whatever shards of glass and metal had pierced her and although she was wearing more make-up than she ever did when alive it was her, I could see it was her, and she looked, or I could persuade myself that she looked, at peace. I turned to my father and Suchitra came up behind me and put her cheek against my back and her arms around my waist. OK, I said, OK, and lifted the sheet. Then finally I wept.

The day after the cremation Nero Golden came across the Gardens to our house – the term 'my house' made no sense; my parents were present in every inch of it – and tapped on the French windows with his cane. It was so unexpected – the king knocking on the orphaned commoner's door – that at first I saw him as an unreal projection of my imagination. In the aftermath of death my grip on the real had loosened. There was an old lady, Mrs Stone, living on the Gardens (in four high-ceilinged rooms on the *piano nobile* of a building divided into floor-through apartments), who spoke often of ghosts. This is somebody I haven't mentioned before, and very likely will leave to her own devices after this guest appearance, a lady whom the Gardens' children called Hat because of her love of wide-brimmed sun hats, a widow for many years, her former husband a rancher in Texas who struck oil on his land and at once gave up beef cattle for the high life and an internationally admired stamp collection. Mrs Stone too had buttonholed me by the jungle gym to speak of loss. A death in the family, as also a newborn baby, gave permission for strangers or near strangers to come up and soliloquise. 'My husband I never saw after his demise,' she confided. 'It seems he was happy to get away. No effort at contact at any time. You live and you learn. But one night on Macdougal Alley I saw a liveried teenage boy – a black kid in a pretty fancy outfit – walking on his knees. Why was he walking on his knees, thought I, there's no religious history here. Then finally I worked it out. He wasn't walking on his knees at all. The street level of the alley had risen over time and he was walking on the old ground level and I could only *see* him down to his knees. A stable boy, possibly, going down the alley to work in the old stables that used to be there in the 1830s, servicing Washington Square North. Or a servant boy, employed perhaps by Gertrude Whitney, who lived there, you know, when she founded her museum. In any case, a ghost, a palpable ghost. And that's not all.' I made my excuses and left. But the neighbourhood's ghost stories seemed to pursue me in those melancholy days. The ghost of Aaron Burr haunting the Village looking for whores. Musical ghosts, dramatic ghosts, wearing their stage costumes and performing in winter on Commerce Street. My old self wasn't interested but my orphaned new self let people tell their tales and at night I tried to hear my parents' laughter echoing in empty rooms. It was in this mood that I saw Nero Golden at the French windows and thought, *an apparition.* But he was flesh and blood.

'You permit that I enter,' he said, entering before I permitted it. And upon entering, having placed his cane against a wall and seated himself in my father's favourite chair: 'I am a direct man, Mister René, plain-spoken, who has never found a bush worth beating about. So I say to you regarding your loss that it is *your* loss. Your parents are gone, don't concern yourself with them, they don't exist any more. Concern yourself with yourself. It is not only that you are wounded and must heal. It is also that now your elders no longer stand between you and the grave. This is manhood. Now you are at the front of the line and the grave yawns for you. Therefore, get wisdom; learn to be a man. If you are agreeable, I will offer my assistance.'

This was an impressive oration. If he intended to shake me out of my sadness by irritating me, he succeeded. But before I could speak he raised a peremptory hand. 'I see your reaction from your face, where a thundercloud has settled, threatening a storm. Dispel it! Your anger is unnecessary. You are young and I am old. I ask you to learn from me. Your country is young. One thinks differently when one has millennia behind one. You have not even two hundred and fifty years. I say also that I am not yet blind so I am aware of your interest in my house. Because I think you are kind of a good guy I forgive this, my alternative being to have you killed, ha ha. I think that – now that you are a man – you can learn from all of us Goldens, good and bad, what to do and not do. From Petya how to fight against what is not your fault, how to play when the cards give you a bad hand. From Apu, maybe, don't be like him. It is possible that he has failed to become profound. From Dionysus, my tormented one, learn about ambiguity and pain.'

'And from you?'

'As to myself, Mister René: maybe you guessed already that I am not always a saint. I am hard and boastful and used to a certain superior position and what I want I take and what I don't want I clear out of my way. But when you are facing me you must ask yourself the following question: Is it possible to be both good and evil? Can a man be a good man when he is a bad man? If you believe Spinoza and agree that everything is determined by necessity, can the necessities that drive a man drive him to wrongdoing as well as right? What is a good man in this deterministic world? Does the adjective even mean anything? When you have the answer, tell me. But before all of this happens, tonight, we go out on the town, and drink.'

Later.

'Death, we deal with it, we accept it, we move on,' Nero Golden said. 'We are the living, so we must live. Guilt, but, that's bad. That remains and does us harm.' We were at the Russian Tea Room – his treat – holding shot glasses of ice-cold vodka. He raised his in salute; he drank, I drank. It was why we were here, and the food – blinis and caviar, dumplings, chicken Kiev – we ate only to allow us to drink more.

'If we go home sober,' Nero Golden told me, 'then we will have failed.

We need to reach a condition in which we will not know how exactly we got home at all.'

I bowed my head gravely. 'Agreed.'

Another shot. 'My late wife, you take her case –' Nero jabbed a finger at me – 'don't pretend you don't know the story, I know the loose tongues in my household. Never mind that. As to her death, a great sadness, but not in fact a tragedy, it didn't rise to the level of tragedy.' Another shot. 'I correct myself. A personal tragedy of course. A tragedy to me and my sons. But great tragedy is universal, is it not?'

'It is.'

'So. My point. The destructive aspect for me, the life-altering destructive aspect, was not the fact of death but the fact of responsibility. Mine. My responsibility, this is the issue. This is what haunts me when at night I walk in the Gardens.'

By this stage of the evening I had begun to see it as my task to comfort him even though the purpose of the outing had been vice versa. 'You had a quarrel,' I said. 'This happens. It does not place upon you the burden of her death. In an ethical universe only the murderer is guilty of the murder. It must be so otherwise the universe would be morally absurd.'

He was silent, drinking, waiters hovering to bring more vodka as needed. 'Let me give a different example,' I said, lofty now, finding myself at the heights of thought, feeling truly my parents' child. 'Suppose that I'm an asshole.'

'A total asshole?'

'Complete and total. And stinky.'

'I imagine it, OK.'

'Suppose that every day I stand in front of your house and I abuse you and your family.'

'Are you using bad language?'

'The worst. I abuse yourself and your loved ones in the coarsest terms.'

'This would be intolerable, naturally.'

'So, you have a gun in the house.'

'How do you know this?'

'I am hypothesising.'

'Ah, a hypothesis. Excellent. Understood. A hypothetical gun.'

'And you take this putative weapon and you know what you do?'

'I shoot you.'

'You shoot me through the heart and I'm dead and guess what that makes you.'

'It makes me happy.'

'It makes you a murderer.'

'It makes me happy and a murderer.'

'You are guilty of murder and in court it is not a defence to say, your honour, he was an asshole.'

'It is not?'

'Even assholes when murdered are not responsible for their deaths. The murderer alone bears the burden of the crime.'

'This is philosophy?'

'I need more vodka. The philosophy is in the bottle.'

'Waiter.'

After another shot he became maudlin. 'You're young,' he said. 'You don't know what responsibility is. You don't know guilt or shame. You know nothing. It is not important. Your parents are dead. This is the matter in hand.'

'Thank you,' I said, and after that I don't remember.

Ends.

'In the beginning,' Suchitra said, sitting by my bedside while I groaned that my head hurt, 'in the beginning there was the official Communist Party of India – CPI. But India has a population problem and its left parties also ignore birth control. So after the CPI there was the CPI(M), the Communist Party of India (Marxist), and the Communist Party of India (Marxist–Leninist) aka CPI(M–L). Enough parties? Babe, the party's only just getting started. Try to keep up. Now there is the Communist Party of India (Marxist–Leninist) Liberation, plus the Communist Party of India (Marxist–Leninist) Naxalbari, and also the Communist Party of India (Marxist–Leninist) Janashakti, and in addition the Communist

Party of India (Marxist–Leninist) Red Star, and let us not forget the Communist Party of India (Marxist–Leninist) Central Team, or neglect to mention the Revolutionary Communist Centre of India (Marxist–Leninist–Maoist), to say nothing of the Communist Party of United States of India or the Communist Party of India (Marxist–Leninist) Red Flag, or the Communist Party of India (Marxist–Leninist) New Democracy, or the Communist Party of India (Marxist–Leninist) New Initiative, or the Communist Party of India (Marxist–Leninist) Somnath, or the Communist Party of India (Marxist–Leninist) Second Central Committee, or the Communist Party of India (Marxist–Leninist) Bolshevik. Kindly continue to pay strict attention. There is proliferation among other groupuscules as well. There was the Maoist Communist Centre which merged with the People's War Group to form the Maoist Communist Centre of India. Or possibly it was that the Maoist Communist Centre of India merged with the Communist Party of India (Marxist–Leninist) People's War and founded the Communist Party of India (Maoist). These distinctions can be hard to make. I tell you all this to explain the decision of my Bengali mother and father, two intrepid capitalistically inclined entrepreneur types trapped in Calcutta among the many-headed Ravanas of the Communist Party of India (Uranium–Plutonium), the nuclear-fission warheads of the left, to run away and settle in the Atlanta suburb of Alpharetta, Georgia, which is where I was born. This would perhaps have been a good idea, and in fact economically speaking it was a good idea because they succeeded in a wide range of enterprises, beauty salons, clothing stores, a real estate agency, psychic-healing services, so you see they also proliferated. But unfortunately around them the political institutions of the Hindu right were also being fruitful and multiplying on fertile American soil, expatriate branches of the Rashtriya Swayamsevak Sangh sprouted up, the Vishwa Hindu Parishad flowered, the Bharatiya Janata Party thrived, as did fund-raising organisations funnelling dollars toward the same. My parents escaped from one whirlpool only to be sucked into another and when they started going to RSS gala dinners and speaking admiringly of the barrel-chested person they called NaMo, I had to love them and leave them and make my escape. So I hightailed it to NYC where I am now working my ass off trying to make you laugh and it would be kind of you at this point at least to crack a smile.'

'And this is your idea,' I said, 'of a hangover cure.'

Regarding working her ass off: Suchitra did that every day, every minute of every day. I never knew anyone who worked half as hard and still had time for pleasure, in which category I was fortunate enough to be included. She woke early, went spinning, ran to her office, gave the workday everything she had, went running by the Hudson or across the Brooklyn Bridge and back, and still turned up fresh as a daisy and twice as stylish at whatever the evening had to offer, a gallery opening, a screening, a birthday party, a karaoke night, a dinner date with me, and had enough energy left for lovemaking after it all. As a lover she was equally energetic, if unoriginal, but I wasn't complaining. I was scarcely a sex god myself and at that moment the love of a good woman was saving me from the black pit. Nero Golden's tough affection and his heavy-drinking vodka nights, together with Suchitra Roy's kindly, super-speed love, brought me through those days. I thought of the story of the paramedics in the ambulance playing good cop, bad cop after Mrs Golden's suicide attempt and realised that this time I was the one being put on suicide watch.

There was Silence in Heaven, or, The Dog in the Bardo

New York City was my mother and father all that summer until I learned to live without parents and accept, as Nero had recommended I accept, my adult place at the head of the queue waiting to see the last picture show. As usual it was a movie that helped me, Ingmar Bergman's *Det sjunde inseglet* (*The Seventh Seal*), which the great film director himself thought 'uneven' but which the rest of us revered. The knight (Max von Sydow, who would go on to play the boring artist Frederick in *Hannah and Her Sisters* and the immortal Ming the Merciless in *Flash Gordon*) on his way home from the Crusades playing chess against black-cowled Death to delay the inevitable, so that he could see his wife once more before he died. Broken knight and cynical squire, Bergman's unfunny Quixote and Sancho, looking for this year's birds in last year's nests. Bergman had religious issues to work out, having come from a deeply religious household, but for me it wasn't necessary to see the film in those terms. The title was from the Book of Revelation. 'And when the Lamb had opened the seventh seal, there was silence in heaven about the space of half an hour' (Revelation 8:1). To me, the silence in heaven, the non-appearance of God, was the truth of the secular vision of the universe, and *half an hour* meant the length of a human life. The opening of the seventh seal revealed that God was nowhere with nothing to say and Man was given the space of his little life to perform, as the knight wished to perform, one meaningful deed. The wife I wanted to see before I died was my dream of being a film-maker. The meaningful deed was the film I was dreaming of making, my film of my Gardens dotted with real and imaginary beings like an Altman ensemble cast and the Goldens in their house at the far end from mine. The 'deed' was the journey and the 'wife' was the goal. I said something of this sort to Suchitra and she nodded gravely. 'It's time to finish your script and start raising the money.'

And in the meanwhile the great metropolis, hugging me to its bosom and trying to teach me the lessons of life. The boat on the pond where Stuart Little sailed reminding me of the beauty of innocence, and the space on Clinton Street where Judith Malina was still just about alive and her Living Theatre was still enjoying getting naked spoke to me of old-school don't-give-a-fuck irreverence. And on Union Square the chess players played and maybe Death was playing there too, fast games of Blitz that grabbed lives like they didn't matter or slow games, off the clock, that allowed the black angel to pretend he respected life while still recruiting his playing partners for his *danse macabre*. Absences spoke to me as well as presences: the shoe stores gone from Eighth Street, the eccentricity gone from the Upper West Side where once Maya Schaper ran Cheese and Antiques and, when asked why, liked to reply, 'Because these are the things I love.' Everywhere I walked the city held me in its arms and whispered comfort in my ear.

On the night of Apu's second opening at the Sottovoce Bowery space a block from the Museum of Identity (these pictures were smart and swift and technically adept and energetic and pop-arty and they failed to move me), Laurie Anderson's large paintings depicting the forty-nine-day experience of her beloved deceased rat terrier Lolabelle in the bardo, the Tibetan Buddhist zone between death and rebirth, were showing across town. Suchitra and I were standing in front of one of the largest images of that sweet-faced dog looking wide-eyed at us from the afterlife when all of a sudden the words *It's all right* formed within me and then I said them aloud. 'It's all right,' I said, and a grin widened across my face. 'It's all right, it's all right, it's all right.' A shadow lifted from me and the future looked possible and happiness seemed conceivable and life began again. It was only much later, when I thought back, that I realised that that had been the forty-ninth day since my parents' death.

I don't believe in the bardo. But there you have it.

'Flash! I Love You! But We Have Only Fourteen Hours to Save the Earth!'

I was in the grip of a kind of euphoria that night, seized by the high of having forgiven my parents for dying and myself for remaining alive. Suchitra and I went home to the Gardens and I knew that it was time to do the forbidden thing. Already high on life, we broke open the long-preserved pack of Afghan Moon and inhaled. At once the third eyes in our pineal glands opened as my father had said they would and we understood the secrets of the world. We saw that the world was neither meaningless nor absurd, that in fact it had profound meaning and form, but that form and meaning had been hidden from us until now, concealed in the hieroglyphs and esoterica of power, because it was in the interests of the masters of the world to hide meaning from all but the illuminated. We understood also that it was up to the two of us to save the planet and that the force that would save the planet was love. With our heads spinning we understood that Max von Sydow as Ming the Merciless, totalitarian, whimsical and badly dressed in his bright red science-fiction comic-book evil-genius cloak, was coming to conquer the human race, and that if sometimes Ming's face blurred and began to look like the face of Nero Golden, then that was unfair because of his kindness to me of late, but could a man be simultaneously bad and good, we asked ourselves, and the Afghan Moon replied that irreconcilable contradiction and the union of opposites was the deepest mystery of all. Tonight was for love, said the Afghan Moon, tonight was for the celebration of living bodies and for saying farewell to the lost bodies of departed loved ones, but after the sun rose in the morning there would be no time to lose.

17

If you owed the bank a buck you were a deadbeat with an overdraught. If you owed a billion you were rich and the bank was working for you. It was difficult to know how wealthy Nero Golden actually was. His name was everywhere in those days, on everything from hot dogs to for-profit universities, it was walking around Lincoln Center thinking about donating a *unit* to refurbish Avery Fisher Hall as long as the old name got dumped and the Golden name was up there in block capitals made of gold. *A unit* was the shorthand term his name used to signify 'one hundred million dollars', one hundred million dollars being the price of entry into the world of the really rich, you really weren't anybody until you had your *unit.* His name was walking that *unit* around town, it kind of wanted to put itself on the Tribeca Film Festival, but that would cost a lot less than a whole *unit,* so finally the Film Festival felt like chicken feed; what his name really, really wanted was to be way up there on Yankee Stadium. That would prove his name had conquered New York. After that they might just as well put it on top of City Hall.

I assumed he had brought serious funds with him when he came west, but there were persistent rumours that all his enterprises were highly leveraged, that the whole mega-business of his name was a flim-flam game and bankruptcy was the shadow that went with his name whenever he took it for a stroll. I thought of him as a citizen not of New

York but of the invisible city of Octavia which Marco Polo described to Kublai Khan in Calvino's book, a spiderweb city hanging in a great net over an abyss between two mountains. 'The life of Octavia's inhabitants is less uncertain than in other cities,' Calvino wrote. 'They know the net will last only so long.' I thought of him too as one of those characters in animated cartoons, Wile E. Coyote perhaps, who are constantly running off the edges of canyons, but who keep going, defying gravity, until they look down, and then they fall. The knowledge of the impossibility of the attempt brings about its calamitous ending. Nero Golden kept going, perhaps, because he never looked down.

For many months I was busy closing up our house, locking up what I wanted to keep in a Manhattan Mini Storage facility on the West Side, the one with the funny billboards on the wall overlooking the Highway, *New York has six professional sports teams, and also the Mets,* and *If you don't like gay marriage, don't get gay married,* and *'In my father's house there are many rooms' – John 14:2 – Clearly Jesus was not a New Yorker,* and *Remember, if you leave the city, you'll have to live in America.* Yeah, ha ha, I got it, but mostly I was in a sour mood again, trying hard not to show it in Suchitra's company, but she knew what I was going through. Then the time came to put the house up for sale and Vasilisa Golden came up to me in the Gardens and put her arm around me and kissed me on the cheek and said, let me do this for you, let's keep it in the family, which was such a nice thing to say that I just nodded dumbly and let her handle the sale.

Again, it was hard for me to be objective about the Goldens that year. On the one hand there was Nero's kindness to me, and now his wife's kindness also. On the other, there seemed little doubt that he was an enthusiastic supporter of the Romney presidential campaign, and his remarks about the president and his wife teetered on the edge of bigotry, *of course he likes the gays, he's married to a man,* that was a mild one. Very often he told his 'funny Republican joke', the one about the older white guy who goes up to a White House sentry at some point after the end of the present administration, several days in a row, and each time asks to meet President Obama. The third or fourth time he shows up, the exasperated officer says, Sir, you keep coming back and I keep telling you, Mr Obama is no longer the president of these United States, and no longer resides at this address. So you know that and still you keep coming back and asking the same question and you get the same answer, so why do you keep asking? And the older white guy says, Oh, I just like to hear it.

This, I put up with, though I feared on Nero's behalf that his dark side would overpower the light. I gave him to read the great short story 'The Shadow' by Hans Christian Andersen about the man whose shadow detaches itself from him, travels the world, becomes more sophisticated than his former 'owner', returns to seduce and marry the princess to whom the man is betrothed, and, together with the (pretty ruthless) princess, condemns the real man to death. I wanted him to understand the danger his soul was in, if a godless person may be permitted to use such a term, but he wasn't a reader of literature, and returned the book containing the story with a dismissive gesture of the hand. 'I don't like fairy tales,' he said.

But then . . . the two of them, husband and wife, summoned me to their presence and announced their decision regarding me. 'What you need to do,' Vasilisa Golden said, 'is to come to live with us in this house. It is a big house with many rooms and two of the three boys are not so much here any more and the third is Petya who hardly comes out of his room. So there is plenty of space for yourself and you will be excellent company for us both.'

'Temporarily,' Nero Golden said.

'With the girl, who knows what happens,' Vasilisa pointed out. 'You want to move in with her, you decide to break up, time will tell. Take the pressure off. You don't need pressure right now.'

'For the moment,' Nero Golden said.

It was an offer of true generosity – admittedly a short-term offer – made in absolute good faith; and I didn't see how I could accept it. I opened my mouth to object and Vasilisa raised an empress's hand. 'There is no question of refusing,' she said. 'Go and pack your bags and we will send people to carry them.'

So in the fall of 2012 I went to live in the Golden house, *temporarily, for the moment*, feeling, on the one hand, deeply grateful, like a serf offered a bedroom in a palace, and, on the other, as if I had done a deal with the Devil. The only way of knowing which it was, would be to unwrap all the mysteries around Nero, his present as well as his past, so that I could truly judge him, and maybe to do that it would be better to be within the walls than outside them. They opened the gates and pulled me into their world and then I was the wooden horse standing inside the gates of Troy. And inside me, Odysseus and the warriors. And standing before me, the Helen of this American Ilium. And before our story was done I would betray them, and the woman I loved, and myself. And the topless towers would burn.

The 'boys', Nero's sons, came to see him every day, and these were unusual encounters, speaking of his immense authority over them, not so much father–son meetings as cap-in-hand obeisances paid by subjects to their master. I understood that any film treatment, fictionalised, of course, would have to deal with this strangely authoritarian relationship. Some of the explanation was undoubtedly financial. Nero was generous with money, so that Apu was able to get himself a place in Montauk and spend weeks at a time painting there, and partying as well. Young D Golden in Chinatown gave every appearance of living on a budget, and was working, these days, as a volunteer at a girls' club on the Lower East Side, which would have obliged him to live on Riya's salary, but the truth was, as Vasilisa was quick to inform me, that he took the money his father gave him. 'He has many expenses right now,' she said, but declined to elaborate further, as was the way in the Golden house, whose members did not discuss significant matters with one another, as if they were secrets, even though they knew that everyone knew everything. But maybe, I thought, the sessions between the father and his sons were also like confessionals, where the 'boys' admitted their 'sins' and were, in some way, to some degree, and in return for unknown penances and expiations, 'forgiven'. That was the way to write it, I thought. Or, a more interesting possibility. Maybe the sons were the parent's priests as well as the other way around. Maybe each possessed the other's secrets, and each gave the other absolution and peace.

It was usually quiet in the big house, which was perfect for me. I had been given a room on the uppermost floor with dormer windows looking down over the Gardens and I was utterly content, and busy. As well as my longer-term movie project I was working with Suchitra on a short-form video series for a cable VOD network, well-known indie-film faces talking about favourite movie moments, the bottom-stamping scene in Jiri Menzel's *Closely Observed Trains* (I preferred the greater formality of the UK title to the American *Closely Watched Trains*), Toshiro Mifune introducing the character of his shabby, itchy samurai warrior in Kurosawa's *Sanjuro,* Michael J. Pollard's first scene in Arthur Penn's *Bonnie and Clyde* ('dirt in the fuel line – just blowed it away'), the winter peacock spreading its tail feathers in Fellini's *Amarcord,* the child who falls out of a window and bounces, unhurt, in Truffaut's *L'argent de poche* (*Pocket Money*), the closing moments of Robert Rossen's *The Hustler* ('Fat Man, you shoot a great game of pool.' – 'So do you, Fast Eddie.'), and my personal favourite, the matchstick game in Alain Resnais's *L'année dernière à Marienbad* (*Last Year at Marienbad*), featuring the granite-faced, Draculaesque Sacha Pitoëff ('It's not a game if you can't lose.' – 'Oh, I can lose, but I never do.') We had already filmed a number of talented young American actors and film-makers (Greta Gerwig, Wes Anderson, Noah Baumbach, Todd Solondz, Parker Posey, Jake Paltrow, Chloë Sevigny) expressing their admiration for these classic films and I was honing my editing skills on my laptop by assembling the material into sharp three-minute pieces to be embedded on a wide range of websites. Suchitra was leaving this work to me while she set up her own first film as writer-director, crossing the line from the production side, and we were both deeply immersed in our work, coming together late at night to tell each other the day's news, eat fast and too late, and either make love quickly or simply fall asleep exhausted in each other's arms, either in my artist's garret or her studio apartment. In the aftermath of tragedy, this was how I found my way back to joy.

In my spare moments I studied the dynamics of the Golden house.

Cleaning services, kitchen help, the handyman Gonzalo came and went, so unobtrusively as to seem *virtual,* phantom children of the age of the post-real. The two dragon ladies were unquestionably actual, arrived each morning buzzing with efficiency, sequestered themselves in a room next to Nero's office, and did not reappear until they buzzed off at night like hornets escaping through an open door. All sounds seemed muffled, as if the laws of science themselves operated within these walls with, so to speak, white gloves on.

Nero himself mostly stayed in his home office, even though the main premises of Golden Enterprises were in Midtown in a tower irritatingly owned by a certain Gary 'Green' Gwynplaine, a vulgarian whose name Nero could not bring himself to speak, and who liked to call himself the Joker on account of having been born with inexplicably lime-green hair. Purple-coated, white-skinned, red-lipped, Gwynplaine made himself the mirror image of the notorious cartoon villain and seemed to revel in the likeness. Nero found his landlord intolerable, and announced to me one evening, apropos of nothing, and without explanation – this was his way, his train of thought emerging occasionally out of the tunnel of his mouth, whoever was in the immediate vicinity becoming the station at which it briefly stopped – 'One world. When they let us in, I'll be the first in the door.' It took me a moment to understand that he wasn't talking about pan-globalism but about One World Trade Center, which wouldn't be ready for occupancy for a couple of years, and announcing his intention to leave the Joker's building and move into the new tower built in the place of tragedy. 'On the upper floors I can get a terrific deal,' he clarified. 'Fifty, sixty floors, OK, they can fill those, but above that? After what happened nobody wants to rent in that airspace. So, a great deal. The best deal in town. All that empty floor space needing occupation, finding nothing. Me, personally, I go where the bargain is. High in the sky? Fine. Lowball the price, I'll take it. It's a bargain. Lightning doesn't strike twice.'

His employees rarely saw him. He allowed his hair to lengthen. I began to wonder about the length of his toenails. After Romney's defeat his mood worsened and he was barely visible even to his wife and household. He took to sleeping on a fold-out cot in the office at the house and ordering pizza late at night. During the night he made phone calls to employees in various countries – at least I guessed they were employees – and in Manhattan too. His rule was that he would call you at any moment of the day or night and expect you to be alert and willing to discuss whatever he pleased, business or women or something in the paper. He would talk for hours to his telephone colleagues and that had to be OK with them. One evening in the Gardens when he was in one of his affable moods I put on my most innocent smile and asked him if he ever thought about Howard Hughes. 'That freak,' he answered. 'You're lucky I have a soft spot for you. Don't ever compare me to that freak.' But at the same time he began to retreat even further from the human gaze. Vasilisa was left to spend many days at the spa or up and down Madison in various stores and lunching with girlfriends at Bergdorf or Sant Ambroeus. Ignore a beautiful woman for too long and there will be trouble. How long is too long? Five minutes. Anything over an hour: catastrophe awaits.

The house had become both the expression of her beauty and of the intensity of her need. On oyster-grey walls she hung large mirrors made up of smaller mirror squares, some at an angle, some tinted close to black, expressing, like the Cubists, the need for many perspectives at the same time. A grand new fireplace was installed in the great room, threatening cold-weather incandescence. New rugs underfoot, silken to the touch, the colour of steel. The house was her language. She spoke to him through its renewal, knowing him to be a man influenced by surroundings, telling him wordlessly that if a king needs a palace, that palace requires, to be suitably palatial, a queen.

And slowly it worked. By Christmas he had recovered from the president's electoral victory and had developed a powerful polemic against the defeated contender, the worst contender ever, he said at mealtimes, jabbing his fork at us to emphasise his point, there had never been a weaker contender in the history of contending, you couldn't even call him a true contender, there had been no contest, it was like the guy surrendered before a punch was thrown, so next time round let's not make the mistake of choosing a *clown,* let's make sure it's a guy with *gravitas,* who looks like he can lead. Next time. For sure.

By the inauguration the weather in the Golden house was much improved. It was not permitted to watch the ceremony on television, but the mood of the king and queen was jovial, and flirtatious. I knew that Nero Golden's interior weather was changeable, and that his sexual vulnerability to his wife's charms only increased as he grew older, and that the bedroom was where she invariably achieved the necessary alterations in his personal meteorology. But I didn't know then what I know now – that he wasn't well. Vasilisa, showing herself to be a master of timing, had sensed her opening and made her play. Before any of us, she saw what afterwards became sadly all too plain to us all: that he was weakening, that the time would soon come when he was no longer who he had been. She smelled the first intimation of that coming weakness as a shark smells a single drop of blood in water, and moved in for the kill.

Everything is a strategy. This is the wisdom of the spider.

Everything is food. This is the wisdom of the shark.

Monologue of the Spider to the Fly, or of the Shark to Its Prey

You see because it was specially made specially with those special crystals that glow in that special way when the flame takes them just so, glowing like diamonds in the Ali Baba cave which I didn't know was in fact called Sesame yes that was the name of the cave did you know that well anyway that's what I read in a magazine so when he says Open Sesame he's addressing the cave by its name and I always thought it was just a magic word, *sesame!,* but never mind it's the fire I'm talking about the fire I had made to represent the fire in your heart the fire in you that I love. You know that. I know you do. So here we are as we have been for some time now, are you happy, your happiness is the great work of my life so I hope you will answer yes, now you must ask if I am happy, and I reply, yes, but. Now you will say how can I say but when I know where I was when you found me and where I am now and I agree you have given me everything you have given me my life but still it is yes but, still yes there is a but. You don't have to ask what is it you must know. I am a young woman. I am ready to be more than a lover although to be your lover is always first for me, you are always first for me, but I wish also to be, you know what I wish, a mother. And I understand yes that this violates the terms of our understanding because I said I would give that up for you and our love would be our child but the body wants what it wants and the heart also, it cannot be gainsaid. So this is where I stand my darling and it is a dilemma and I can see only one way forward although it breaks my heart and so I say to you with my heart breaking as I say it that because of my immense respect for you and my respect also for my own honour which obliges me to honour the terms of our understanding that my darling I must leave you. I love you so much but because of the needs of my young body and my broken heart I must go and find a way to have a child somehow though the idea of not being with you destroys me it is the only answer I can find, and so, my darling, I must say it. Goodbye.

In the game of chess the move known as the Queen's Gambit is almost never used because it gives up the most powerful piece on the board for the sake of a risky positional advantage. Only the true grandmasters would attempt so daring a manoeuvre, being capable of looking many moves down the road, considering every variation, and thus being certain of the sacrifice's success: the laying down of the queen to kill the king. Bobby Fischer, in the much-bruited Game of the Century, playing with the black pieces, devastatingly used the Queen's Gambit against Donald Byrne. During my time in the Golden house I learned that Vasilisa Arsenyeva Golden was an avid student of the 'royal game', and could demonstrate to me the famous twenty-two-move checkmate in which the Russian grandmaster Mikhail Tal used the queen-sacrifice to stymie his opponent, a certain Alexander Koblentz. Vasilisa and I would play chess in the idle afternoons when Suchitra was away shooting, and she would invariably win, but then show me how she had done it, insisting that I raise my standard of play. And so I see, in retrospect, that she was also teaching me the game of life, going so far as to demonstrate the move she was going to make before she made it. When she asked Nero Golden for a divorce I understood the depths of her brilliance. It was the winning move.

Her request shook him, and at first he retreated into crassness, quarrelling with her loudly on the landing outside his office, causing the phantom servitors of the household to scurry for shelter, pointing out brutally that their financial agreement would be terminated by her exit, and that she would leave with nothing except a fancy wardrobe and some baubles. 'See how far that takes you,' he barked, and went into his sanctum and slammed the door. Quietly, without attempting to open the slammed door, she entered her clothes closet and began to pack. I went to see her. 'Where will you go?' I asked. At that moment, when she turned the blazing force of her gaze upon me, I saw for the first time the witch-queen unmasked, and actually took a step backwards and away. She laughed, and it was not her normal pretty-girl laughter but something entirely more savage. 'I will go nowhere,' she snarled. 'He will come crawling to me on his hands and knees and beg me to remain and swear to give me my heart's desire.'

Night fell; night, which increased her power. The house was silent. Petya in his room bathed in blue light lost within himself and beyond his computer screens. Vasilisa in the master bedroom with the door open, seated erect on her side of the bed, fully clothed, an overnight bag packed and ready at her feet, her hands folded in her lap, all the lights off except for one small reading light outlining her trim silhouette. I, the spy, in the doorway of my room, waiting. And in the midnight hour her prophecy came true. The old bastard dragging himself defeated into her presence to acknowledge her majesty, to beg her to stay, and to agree to her terms. Standing before her with bowed head until she reaching up drew him down to her and fell backwards onto her pillow and after that allowed him again the illusion of being master in his own house even though he knew as well as everyone else that she was the one on the throne.

— A child.

— Yes.

— My darling. Come to me.

She switched off the reading light.

18

It had been my plan, upon setting out in life, with the inspiration of my parents' lives as the flag under which I sailed, to do my best to be – I admit publicly here to my previously private use of the word – wonderful. What else was there that was worth being? Rejecting humdrum, pedestrian, monosyllabic, demotic Renés, I had set my face toward polymathic exceptional selfhood, boarding my imaginary *Argo* in search of that golden fleece, without any real sense of where my personal Colchis might lie (except that it was probably somewhere in the vicinity of a movie theatre) or how to navigate in its direction (except that a movie camera might be the closest thing to a steering wheel at my disposal). Then I found myself beloved of a fine woman, and standing on the threshold of the life in film that had become my heart's desire. And in that happy state, I did my very best to destroy what I had made.

The reporter at the battlefront was faced every day with a choice: to participate or not to participate? Which was difficult enough when your nation was a combatant, your people were implicated and so, by extension, were you. But sometimes it wasn't your battle that was being fought. It wasn't even a war, more like a prizefight, and you found yourself by chance with a ringside seat. And then suddenly one of the fighters stretched out an arm like a lover inviting you into a threesome. *Join us.* At this point a sane, or at least a cautious, person would go into reverse gear and get out of there as fast as possible.

I did not. I understand that what this says about me is not entirely admirable. What follows, the account of how I joined the war, is even less admirable. For not only did I betray both my host in his own home, and the woman I loved and who loved me, I betrayed myself as well. And having done so I understood that the questions Nero Golden asked me to consider when thinking about him applied to me also. Is it possible for a man to be a good man when he is also a bad man? Is it possible for evil to coexist with goodness and if so do those terms mean anything any more when they are pushed into such an uncomfortable and perhaps irreconcilable alliance? It may be, I thought, that when good and evil were separated they both became equally destructive; that the saint was as appalling and dangerous a figure as the out-and-out rogue. However, when rightness and wrongness were combined in the right proportions, just so, like whiskey and sweet vermouth, that was what constructed the classic Manhattan cocktail of the human animal (yes, with a splash of bitters and a rub of orange peel, and you can allegorise those elements as you please, and the rocks in the glass as well). But I had never been sure what to make of this yin-and-yang notion. Maybe the union of opposites to form human nature was just what human beings told themselves to rationalise away their imperfections. Maybe it was just too neat, and the truth was that evil deeds trumped good ones. It didn't matter, for example, that Hitler was kind to dogs.

It began in this way: Vasilisa asked me, as she sometimes would while I was a lodger in the Golden house, to accompany her on a shopping expedition to the high-end fashion emporia of Madison Avenue, *because I trust your taste, darling, and Nero, all he wants is sexy, the more exposed the better, but that is wrong, isn't it, we know this, sometimes concealed is more alluring than revealed.* To tell the truth, shopping for clothes was among my least favourite pursuits; I bought my own clothes, when I did, mostly online, and quickly. In a fashionable store my attention span was limited. Suchitra wasn't exactly anti-fashion – she had a number of friends who were in the industry and she wore the clothes they sent her with attitude and flair – but she was definitely anti-dawdling in stores, which was one of the many things that endeared her to me. For Vasilisa, however, the homes of exquisite dresses were her theatre, and it fell to me to be her audience, applauding her entrances, back arched, looking over her shoulder at herself in the mirror, then at the human mirror that I represented, then at herself again, while a small gaggle of attendants applauded and cooed. And it was true, she looked exceptional in whatever she put on, she was one of the two hundred or so women in America for whom these clothes were made, she was like a snake who could slip in and out of many different skins, slithering from this to that, with her little forked tongue licking at the corners of her lips, adapting herself and being adored, dressing, as snakes do, to kill.

That afternoon there was an extra brightness to her beauty, an overdazzle, as if she, who didn't need to try at all in the looks department, was trying much too hard. The assistants in many stores, the Fendivini, the Guccisti, the Pradarlings, responded by being even more adulatory than was their professional wont. This she received as the minimum she was due. And after such adoration, on the seventh floor of Bergdorf Goodman, sweeping into the restaurant, first-naming the staff, ignoring but while ignoring also receiving the admiring attention of thin expensive women of various ages, taking her seat at 'her table' by the window, leaning forward with elbows on the table and both hands clasped beneath her chin, and looking directly into my eyes, she asked the catastrophic question.

'René, I can trust you? Really one hundred per cent trust you? Because I need to trust somebody and I think there's only you.'

This was, as the old Latin grammar books had it, a *nonne* question, one which expected the answer 'yes', these being the only questions Vasilisa Golden asked, yes questions, would you like to go shopping with me, do I look OK, can you zip me up, do you think the house looks beautiful, would you like a game of chess, do you love me. It was impossible to say no, and so, of course, I said yes, but I admit I metaphorically crossed my fingers behind my back. What a young rat I was! Never mind, all writers are thieves, and in those days I was hard at work. 'Of course,' I said, 'what is it.'

She opened her pocketbook and took out a folded letter and passed it across the table to me. 'Shh,' she said. Two sheets of paper, from a medical diagnostic laboratory on the Upper West Side, the results of various tests on both Vasilisa and Nero Golden. She took back the page about herself. 'This isn't important,' she said, 'with me everything is one hundred per cent good.' I looked at the remaining document in my hand. I'm not good at reading these documents and she must have seen the confusion on my face and leaned in close across the table. 'Is a seminogram,' she hissed. 'An examination of the seed.' Oh. I looked at the various measures and comments. The words meant nothing. Motility. Oligozoospermia. NICE vitality. 'What does it say?' I murmured. She sighed an exasperated sigh: were all men this useless even when discussing material so significant to their manhood? She spoke very quietly, mouthing the words exaggeratedly so that I could understand. *It means he is too old to father a child. Ninety-nine per cent for sure.*

Now I understood the strain she was under, which had had the effect of making her turn her volume up too high. She had made her big play and Nero had given in – and then this. 'It's like he did it on purpose,' she said in the same very low voice. 'Except I know he doesn't know. He thinks he's a tiger, a machine, he can make babies just by looking at a woman in the wrong way. This will hit him hard.'

'What will you do?'

'Eat your Caesar,' she said. 'We'll talk after lunch.'

There was snow on the ground in the park and a homeless orator sounding off on the way to the carousel. An old-timer, he was, this gent delirious with words: white man, bushy grey beard, wool hat pulled down to his eyebrows, denim overalls, fingerless gloves, circular-lensed John Lennon rimless glasses, he looked like he should have been playing washboard in a Southern jug band. His voice, however, had not a trace of the South, and the gentleman had a thesis to expound in what was a fairly florid vocabulary. The private lives of men and women in America, he wanted to tell us, were being abolished by the public lives of guns, which had become sentient and were attempting nothing less than the decimation and eventually the conquest of the human race. Three hundred million living guns in America, equal in number to the human population, and trying to create a little *Lebensraum* by disposing of significant quantities of human beings. Weapons had come to life! They had minds of their own now! They wanted to do what was in their nature to do, i.e. and viz. and which was to say, to shoot. Consequently these living guns were enabling gentlemen to shoot off their *pizzles* while they were posing for nude selfies, pow!, and they were encouraging fathers to shoot their children accidentally at *one hundred per cent safe* firing ranges, accidentally?, he didn't think so!, pow!, and they were *enticing* little children to shoot their mothers in the head while they were driving the family SUV, blam!, and he hadn't even gotten around to talking about mass murder yet, rat-a-tat!, college campuses, rat-a-tat-tat!, shopping malls!, rat-a-tat-tat-tat!, fucking *Florida,* rat-a-ta-rat-a-ta-tat! He hadn't even *started* talking about *cops'* guns coming to life and getting the cops to take black lives, or crazy vets' guns getting those crazy vets to shoot down police officers in cold blood. No! He hadn't even *begun* to talk about that. What he was telling us here today in the winter park was that *we were being invaded by killer machines*. The inanimate weapon had become animated, like a toy coming to life in a horror movie, as if your stuffed teddy bear could think now and what was he thinking? He wanted to rip your throat out. How could anyone even think about their little private lives when this shit was going down?

I put a couple of dollars in the can at his feet and we moved on. This was no time for the Second Amendment to enter the conversation. 'I'll tell you what I am going to do,' Vasilisa said. 'I'm going to protect Nero from this information and so by the way are you. Sit down here. We are going to doctor the form.' We were at one of the tables by the carousel. Behind us the carousel itself was shuttered for the winter. She got out her pen and methodically altered the handwritten figures. 'Motility I, Roman numeral,' she said, 'that's bad. That means zero motility, and without motility there is no forward movement, you understand me. But if I put a little V after the I, so now it's Motility IV, that's perfect, that's A-OK. And here, sperm concentration, 5 million per millilitre, very low, but now I put a little 1 before the 5, and 15 million, this is normal according to World Health Organisation, I looked it up. And so on, here, here, here. Improvement, improvement, improvement. You see? Now he's fine. Now he is totally capable of fatherhood.'

She actually clapped her hands. The power of the smile of happiness spreading across her face was such that it could almost convince the person upon whom it was unleashed (me) that fiction was fact, that falsifying a diagnosis would actually alter that diagnosis in the real world. Almost, but not quite. 'That may take care of his ego,' I said, 'but the baby won't arrive by stork, will it?'

'Of course not,' she said.

'What then, you'll pretend to go on trying for a while and then persuade him to adopt?'

'Adoption is out of the question.'

'Then I don't understand.'

'I will find a donor.'

'A sperm donor.'

'Yes.'

'How will you get him to agree to that if he doesn't know his own sperm isn't working?'

'He will never agree to it.'

'You'll get a sperm donor without telling him? How is that even possible? Aren't there documents that have to be signed? Isn't his consent necessary?'

'He will never consent.'

'Then how?'

She reached across the table and took my hands in hers.

'My darling René,' she said, 'that is where you come in.'

Later.

'I don't want a stranger's child,' she said. 'I don't want to be made pregnant by a spatula. I want to do it the real way, with someone I trust, someone who is like family to me, someone who is a lovely handsome guy who could easily, don't be embarrassed that I say this, turn me on. Take it as a compliment, please. I want to do it with you.'

'Vasilisa,' I said. 'This is a terrible idea. This would not only be to deceive Nero, but to do the dirty on Suchitra also.'

'Not to deceive,' she said. 'And it will not be even a little dirty, except for reasons of our personal preference. I have no wish to interfere in your love affair. This is just something you would do privately for me.'

Later.

'Nero, René,' she said a little dreamily, 'it's almost like you have the same name, the same syllables, nearly the same, only the other way around. You see? It's fate.'

It began to snow lightly. *Falling faintly, faintly falling.* Vasilisa turned up her coat collar and without another word thrust her hands deep into her pockets and walked purposefully into the west. Enfolded in whiteness your stunned narrator had what he would later describe as an out-of-body experience. It seemed to him that he heard ghostly music, as if the shuttered carousel were playing 'Lara's Theme' from *Zhivago*. It seemed to him that he was hovering over his right shoulder, watching himself as he followed her helplessly across the park and down to Columbus Circle, his body in that moment surrendering all agency and becoming hers to command, as if she were a Haitian *bokor* and he at lunch at Bergdorf Goodman had been administered the so-called zombie's cucumber which confused his thought processes and made him her slave for life. (I am aware that by drifting into the third person and alleging the failure of my will I am making a bid to be exempted from moral judgement. I am further aware that 'he couldn't help it' is not a strong defence. Allow me this at least: that I am self-aware.)

His – my – Julie Christie fantasy faded and he – I – was thinking instead of the Polanski film *Knife in the Water*. The couple who invite a hitchhiker onto their boat. The woman ends up having sex with this interloper. Obviously I saw myself, uneasily, as the hitchhiker, the third point of a triangle. Maybe the couple in the movie had a bad marriage. The woman was clearly attracted to the hitchhiker and did not object to the sex. The hitchhiker was a blank slate on whom the married couple wrote their story. So also was I, following in Vasilisa's footsteps so that she could write the story of her future in the manner in which she had decided it must be written. Here was West Sixtieth Street, and she swept through the doors of the five-star hotel there. I followed her into the elevator and we rose up to the fifty-third floor, bypassing the thirty-fifth-floor lobby. She already had the room key. Everything had been planned and, still in the grip of that curious languid passivity, I lacked the will to forestall what was to happen.

'Go inside quickly,' she said.

Later.

There's a statement I've always attributed to François Truffaut, although now that I look I can't find any evidence that he said it. So, apocryphally, 'The art of the cinema,' Truffaut allegedly said, 'is to point the camera at a beautiful woman.' As I stared at Vasilisa Golden silhouetted against a window beyond which lay the winter waters of the Hudson she looked to me like one of the goddesses of the screen who had escaped from the movies I loved, stepping off the screen into the movie theatre like Jeff Daniels in *The Purple Rose of Cairo.* I thought of Ornella Muti bewitching Swann in Schlöndorff's film of Proust; of Faye Dunaway as Bonnie Parker with her sensually twisting mouth captivating Warren Beatty's Clyde Barrow; of Monica Vitti in Antonioni shrinking erotically against a corner and murmuring *No lo so*; of Emmanuelle Béart clothed in nothing but beauty in *La belle noiseuse.* I thought of the Godardettes, Seberg in *Breathless* and Karina in *Pierrot le fou* and Bardot in *Le mépris,* and then I tried to rebuke myself, reminding myself of the powerful feminist critiques of new wave cinema, Laura Mulvey's 'male gaze' theory in which she proposed that audiences were obliged to see these films from the point of view of the heterosexual male, with women reduced to the status of objects, etc. And Mailer popped into my head too, the prisoner of sex himself, but I dismissed him almost at once. On the subject of my self-awareness: yes, I'm aware of the fact that I live too much in my head, too deeply immersed in films and books and art, and so the movements of my heart, the treacheries of my true nature, are sometimes obscure to me. In the events I must now describe I was obliged to face directly who I actually was and then rely on female mercy to see me through. And there she was, standing before me: my demon queen, my nemesis, the future mother of my child.

Later.

Her manner at first was no-nonsense, peremptory, verging on the brusque. 'Do you want a drink? Will that help? Don't be such a schoolboy, René. We are both adults here. Get yourself a drink. Get me one also. Vodka. Rocks. The ice bucket is full. So! Let's drink to our enterprise, which is, in a way, majestic. The creation of life. Why else are we put on this earth? The species insists on propagating itself. Let's get this over with.'

Also, after not one but two vodkas: 'Today is just to break the ice. Today it is not the right time for baby-making. After today I will inform you when I am ovulating and you will make yourself available. I always know precisely when it happens, I am on time, like the trains in the Italy of Mussolini. This suite will be available permanently. Here is your key. I will meet you here, three occasions in total during each cycle. At other times our relationship will be as it was. You accept, of course.'

It was the voice she used when speaking to the household staff, and it came close to waking me from my dream. 'No, honey, don't take a bad attitude,' she said in an entirely different voice, low, alluring. 'We are both here, which means we have already made all the important decisions. Now is the time for pleasure, and from now on you are going to have much pleasure, I assure you of that.'

'Yes,' I said, but some note of doubt must have crept into my voice, because now she turned up the sexual volume. 'Darling, of course yes, and so am I, because look at you, a gorgeous boy like you. Let's go into the bedroom now. I can't wait any longer.'

What a gambler she was! How swiftly she had recovered from being dealt an unexpectedly bad hand! For it must have been a dreadful blow to her, to receive the seminogram results, devastating for her plans for the future, yet in spite of the suddenness of the crisis she had moved instantly, intuitively, to conceal the information from her husband. And then, without any hesitation, she had bet the farm on me, backing her confidence in her judgement of my character and in her own powers of attraction (she saw in me both the seriousness which meant I could be trusted to keep her secret, and the weakness which meant I would be unable to resist her considerable charms). This in spite of her knowledge that if her stratagem failed and her husband learned the truth her position would become untenable and she might even be in danger. And so might I; she brought me into her conspiracy without any regard for my safety, my future. But I can't blame her, for I found her irresistible, the offer of her body overwhelming, and I led myself willingly into her trap. And now I was in it: her co-conspirator, as morally compromised as she was, and no longer had any choice but to go through with it, and keep her confidences, which were also mine. I had as much to lose as she.

She drew me down to her on the bed. 'Pleasure makes beautiful babies,' she said. 'But is also pleasurable for its own sake.'

Cut.

19

'I don't like your Goldens,' Suchitra said. 'I've been meaning to say this. You should move out soon.' She offered clarification over our now-customary evening cocktail in the British-style pub near Washington Square: Irish whiskey on the rocks for her, vodka and soda for me. 'Actually, I have no strong negative position on the sons, but the father . . . not for me, and his wife ditto. Mostly it's just that house. It creeps me out. Can't say why but it does. Feels like the Addams Family mansion. Don't you feel it when you're in there? It's like a house of ghosts. These deracinated rich people rejecting their history and culture and name. Getting away with it because of the accident of skin colour which allows them to pass. What kind of people are they, denying their race? I don't care if you live in the land of your fathers or not, I'm not proposing some sort of anti-immigration nativist thing, but to pretend it doesn't exist, that you never existed there, that it's nothing to you and you're nothing to it, that makes me feel they're agreeing to be, in a way, dead. It's like they are living their afterlife while they are still alive. I imagine them lying down in coffins at night. No, of course not really, but you know what I mean.'

Suchitra was an atypical New York woman. 'I have had three rules for all my boyfriends,' she told me when we first became lovers. 'Make your own money, get your own apartment, and don't ask me to marry you.'

She herself lived modestly in a two-room rental in Battery Park City. 'In fact I live in one room,' she pointed out. 'The garments and footwear have the other one.' It was a corner room with large windows so the river was the art on her wall, the fog sweeping in at dawn, the ice slabs of winter followed by the first sails of spring, the freighters, the tugboats, the ferries, the racing boat flying the rainbow flag of the local gay sailing club, her heart filling with love for her city whenever she looked at the view, never the same twice, the wind and light and rain, the dance of the sun and the water, and the apartment in the building across the street with the large brass telescope at the window and the clear view of her bed, rumoured to be a pied-à-terre owned by Brad Pitt which he used to escape from his wife; and the green lady with the torch watching over it all from a little way away, enlightening the world. 'The city is my live-in lover,' she told me right at the start. 'She'd be jealous if a guy moved in.'

This was all fine by me. It was in my nature to prefer a deal of space and silence around me, and I liked an independent woman, so her conditions were easily met. On the question of marriage I had an open mind, but was happy to accept her firm position as consonant with my own. However, I now found myself in the zugzwang eventually faced by all liars, deceivers and cheats: the moment on the chessboard when one must make a move and there is no good move to make. It was early spring, and the property market had begun to move; there was a solid buyer for our old family house, and the deal was near completion, Vasilisa all business when she talked to me about it; no hint of our secret life in her voice or on her face. I had my inheritance and was about to receive a substantial boost to my capital as soon as the sale went through. My instinct for the moment was to stay where I was, eventually to rent, and look around until I found the right place to buy. So Suchitra's encouragement to move out was wholly reasonable, but at odds with my desires. For three overt and one covert reasons, I resisted. I shared the first three with her, of course. 'The house is quiet, (a),' I said. 'It's easy to work in. I have the space I need and I'm left mostly to my own devices. And (b), you know these people are at the heart of the work I'm trying to make. Yeah, there is something off about the old man, but he's beginning to like having me around, I have a feeling he could open up to me at any moment, and that's worth waiting a while for. I think Petya is a heavy burden on him and so his age is hitting him hard, he's suddenly getting to act very old. And then there's (c), which is that the Gardens have been my whole life and when I move out of the Golden house I lose access to them. I don't know if I'm ready to do that, to live without that magic space.'

She didn't argue. 'OK,' she said good-naturedly. 'Just sounding off. You'll let me know when you're ready.'

The traitor fears that his guilt is written on his face. My parents always told me I was incapable of keeping a secret and that when I lied they saw a red light flashing on my forehead. I had begun to wonder if Suchitra had started seeing that light, and if her urgings that I leave the Golden house sprang from her suspicion that my time under that roof was not entirely innocent. My greatest fear was that she would notice some sexual difference in me. I had never believed sex to be primarily an Olympic sport; arousal and attraction were the results of a depth of feeling between the parties, of the strength of the connection. This was also Suchitra's view. She was an impatient lover. (Her schedule was so busy that she didn't have time to dawdle over anything.) Foreplay was minimal between us. At night she'd draw me down and say, 'Just get inside me now, that's what I want,' and afterwards she professed herself satisfied, being the type who came quickly and often. I had chosen not to feel in any way belittled by this, though I could have felt almost irrelevant to the proceedings. She was simply too caring a person intentionally to slight my prowess.

With Vasilisa, however, things went very differently. Ours was always an afternoon assignation, the classic French *cinq-à-sept.* We did not sleep together. We didn't sleep at all. Additionally, our lovemaking was wholly goal-oriented, dedicated to the creation of new life, which both terrified and excited me, even though she reassured me constantly that the baby would not be a burden to me, it would not change my life in the slightest way. This was procreation without responsibility. Strangely, the idea made me feel a little worse rather than a little better. 'I can see,' she said in our park-view hotel eyrie, 'that I'm going to have to do my best to make you feel good about this.' It was her firm conviction that baby-making required extreme excitement and she believed herself a professional in that field. 'Baby,' she said throatily, 'I can be a little bit a naughty girl, so I need you to tell me your secrets and then I can make them come true.' What followed was sex of a sort I'd never had before, more abandoned, more experimental, more extreme, and oddly more trusting. Traitors together, who did we have to trust except each other?

Suchitra: would she, during our less operatic bouts of sex, notice my body beginning to move in different ways, having learned new habits, dumbly asking for different satisfactions? How could she not? For I must be different, everything felt different to me, those three days a month had changed everything for me. And what about my monthly exhaustions after my afternoon romps? How to explain those, the regularity of their recurrence? Surely she suspected. She must suspect. Impossible to hide such alterations from her, my most intimate friend.

She didn't seem to have noticed anything. At night we talked about work and fell asleep. Ours had never been a sex-every-night-or-else affair. We were comfortable with each other, happy just to hold each other and rest. This mostly happened at her apartment. (She was always happy for me to be there as long as there was no question of my moving in.) She didn't much like coming to stay at the Golden house. Consequently we didn't spend every night together; by no means. So as things turned out it wasn't very hard to cover my traces. She continued to bring up the subject of me leaving the Macdougal Street place, however. 'You could always get access to the Gardens through other neighbours,' she argued. 'Your parents were well liked and on friendly terms with many of them.'

'I need more time with Nero,' I said. 'The idea of a man who erases all his reference points, who wants to be connected to nothing in his history, I want to get to the bottom of this. Can such a person even be said to be a man? This free-floating entity without any anchor or ties? It's interesting, right?'

'Yeah,' she said, 'OK,' and turned over and went to sleep.

*

Later.

'What about the courtesan?' Suchitra asked me. 'How much do you see of her?'

'She buys clothes,' I answered, 'and sells penthouses to Russians.'

'I wanted to make a documentary about courtesans once,' she said. 'Madame de Pompadour, Nell Gwynn, Mata Hari, Umrao Jaan. Did a lot of research. Maybe I'll revive the project.'

She was definitely suspicious.

'OK,' I said. 'I'll move out.'

Cut.

When I looked at the world beyond myself I saw my own moral weakness reflected in it. My parents had grown up in fantasyland, the last generation in full employment, the last age of sex without fear, the last moment of politics without religion, but somehow their years in the fairy tale had grounded them, strengthened them, given them the conviction that by their own direct actions they could change and improve their world, and allowed them to eat the apple of Eden, which gave them the knowledge of good and evil, without falling under the spell of the spiralling *Jungle Book* Kaa-eyes of the fatal *trust-in-me* Snake. Whereas now horror was spreading everywhere at high speed and we closed our eyes or appeased it. These words were not mine. In one of the curious small-town moments of life in Manhattan the same ranter I had seen in Central Park was walking down Macdougal Street below my window, speaking today about betrayal, his betrayal by his family, his employers, his friends, his city, his country, the universe, and the horror, spreading, and us, averting our gaze . . . as if my conscience had turned into a crackpot homeless man talking to himself without the excuse of a cellphone headset dangling from his ear. Warm weather; cold words. Was he flesh and blood or had my guilt conjured him up? I closed my eyes and reopened them. He was moving away toward Bleecker Street. Maybe it was a different guy.

I still had moments when my orphaning seemed to spread outward from me and fill the world, or at least that part of it which was in my field of vision. Unhinged moments. I allowed myself to think that it had been in the throes of one such unbalanced event that I agreed to Vasilisa Golden's dangerous scheme. I allowed myself to think that the lament for the planet which increasingly filled my thoughts was born of my own little loss and that the world didn't deserve to be thought of so poorly. If I rescued myself from my moral abyss the world would take care of itself, the hole in the ozone layer would close, the fanatics would retreat back into their dark labyrinths beneath the roots of trees and in the trenches at the bottom of the ocean and the sun would shine again and bright music would fill the air.

Yes, time to move out. But what would moving out solve? I was still addicted to my three afternoons a month on the fifty-third floor. The scheme was taking longer to bear fruit than Vasilisa had expected and she had begun to complain. She accused me of having a bad approach to the enterprise. I was jinxing it somehow. I should focus, concentrate, and above all I should want it. If I didn't want it, it wouldn't happen. The baby, not feeling fully desired, would not show up. 'Don't deny me this,' she said. 'Maybe you just want to fuck me, yes? So you are prolonging matters. So, OK I can undertake to still fuck you afterwards. At least from time to time.' When she spoke like this it made me want to weep, but my tears would only have strengthened her conviction that for some reason I was somehow withholding my most powerful sperm from her, that I was being, in her eyes, biologically dishonourable. I had entered a place of insanity and I wanted it all to be over, I didn't want it to be over, I wanted her to become pregnant, no I didn't, yes I did, no, I did not.

And then it happened. And she turned away from me forever and left me devastated. In love with another woman, yes, but devastated by the loss of our treacherous extraordinary delight.

In the movie I was imagining, the work which would be the ultimate betrayal, at this point the action had to switch away from Vasilisa to her husband. So: She walked out of the fifty-third-floor suite and the door closed and that was that.

— Art requires betrayal, and trumps that betrayal, because the betrayal is transmuted into art. That's right, right? Right?—

Slow dissolve.

⚬

'You know where I come from,' Nero Golden said, narrowing his eyes. 'I know you know. Nobody can keep things sub rosa these days.' Late at night he had brought me into his sanctum, wanting to talk. I was simultaneously excited and afraid. – Afraid, because was he about to confront me with information about what I'd been getting up to with Mrs Golden? Had he had us followed, was there a private eye's folder of photographs on his desk? The thought was profoundly disquieting. – And excited, because this could also be the opening up I'd hoped for, the confessional moment when an ageing man, tiring of the unknown self he had wrapped around himself, wanted, once again, to be known. — 'Yes, sir,' I said. 'Don't say that to me!' he shouted, mostly good-naturedly. 'Just go on pretending you're an ignorant little squirt and act surprised when I tell you something. OK?' 'Works for me,' I said.

During his wife's pregnancy the deterioration in Nero Golden's well-being gradually became apparent to us all. He was not so far from the end of his eighth decade and his mind was beginning its slow treason. He still went out at eight each morning dressed in immaculate tennis whites with a white baseball cap on his head, swishing his racket through the air with his usual I-mean-business air about him, and still returned sweaty and exuding a certain strong-jawed contentment ninety minutes later. But one day, just a few days before my late-night summons, there had been an unfortunate episode. He had been crossing the street when a car, a vintage Corvette, jumped the light at the Bleecker–Macdougal intersection and bumped into him. Just barely bumped into him, just hard enough to knock him over, not hard enough to break any bones. His response was to jump up, immediately forgive the driver, refuse to make any kind of report or complaint, and invite the driver, a careless white individual with a thick head of wavy white hair, *back to the house for a coffee.* This behaviour was so outrageously out of character that everyone began to worry. It was a while, however, before the extent of the problem was diagnosed. 'I'm fine, fine,' Nero said after the Corvette incident. 'Stop making a fuss. I was just taking care of the guy because he was obviously shaken up. It was the right thing to do.'

And now I was alone with him in his lair after dark. What was in store for me now? He offered me a cigar; I refused. A cognac; I refused also. I've never been a brandy drinker. 'Take something,' he commanded, so I accepted a vodka shot. *'Prosit,'* he said, raising his own glass imperiously. 'Bottoms up.' I downed the shot, noting that he only applied his lips to the rim of his cognac balloon in the most perfunctory fashion. 'Another one,' he said. I wondered if he was trying to get me drunk again. 'In a little while,' I said, covering my shot glass with the palm of my left hand. 'Let's not rush things.' He leaned forward, slapped me on the knee and nodded. 'Good, good. A sensible man.'

'Let me tell you a story,' he said. 'Once upon a time in Bombay – you see? I name the old city by its old name, the first time that word passes my lips since I land in America, you should be honoured by my intimacy – there was a man named Don Corleone. No, of course that wasn't his name, but his name will mean nothing to you. Even the name he actually used wasn't his name either. A name is nothing, it's a handle, as they say here, just a way of opening a door. "Don Corleone" gives you an idea of the kind of man he was. It's my way of opening his door. Except this Don never killed a man or fired a gun. I want to tell you about this type. He came originally from the south but like everyone else ended up in the big city. Humble origins. Totally humble. Father ran cycle-repair shop near Crawford Market. Boy helped daddy fix bikes, looked at big cars going past, vroom! Studebaker, vroom! Cadillac, and he thought, one day, one day – like everyone else. He grew up, worked at the docks unloading cargo. Simple porter, seventeen-eighteen years old, but with an eye for opportunity. Pilgrim ships came back from the Mussalman holy places, the pilgrims brought back contraband. Transistor radio, Swiss watch, gold coins. Dutiable items. Heavily dutiable. Don Corleone helped them smuggle the items, in his underwear, his turban, wherever. They rewarded him. He acquired some funds.

'Now a lucky meeting with a fisherman smuggler from Daman. One Mister Bakhia. At that time Daman was Portuguese colony. Slack scrutiny. Bakhia and Don Corleone started smuggling from Dubai and Aden, via Daman, loose borders, into India. Good business. Don Corleone moved up the social register. Made friends with heads of other crime families. V. Mudaliar, K. Lala, et cetera. Then pally with politicos, including one certain Sanjay Gandhi, son of Indira. These are facts. By the 1970s he was a big cheese, top banana. There was a young police officer on his tail who wouldn't be bribed. Honest fellow. Honesty a disadvantage in that job. One Inspector Mastan. Don Corleone had him transferred to nowhere and when the officer was on the plane Don Corleone came aboard just to wave him goodbye. Safe travels, Mastan. Have a good trip. Cheeky. Like that. So confident in those times.

'He lived both well and also abstemiously. The best suits, best ties, best cigarettes, State Express 555, and a Mercedes-Benz. A big house on Warden Road, like a palace, but he lived simply in one room on the terrace upstairs. Fifteen feet by ten feet. No more. Downstairs there were movie stars coming and going, and he put a lot of money into the motion pictures, you know. And at least three films made about his own life, featuring the top talent. Married a starlet also. Her name meant Goldie. But in the mid-seventies he fell. Sanjay Gandhi turned out to be a false friend and Don Corleone had a year and a half of incarceration. Knocked the stuffing out of him. Quit smuggling completely. First became a religious fellow like the smuggling pilgrims who gave him his first break. Afterwards tried politics. In the mid-nineties, after the rise of the top family, Zamzama Alankar's Z-Company, there came the first terrorist attacks in Bombay, people thought he was involved, but he was too scared for that stuff. Innocent, innocent, innocent. Next year, heart attack, dead. Hell of a story.'

'Was it really a natural death?' I asked. 'He must have had enemies?'

'By that time,' said Nero Golden, 'he wasn't worth killing any more.'

A long silence.

'And this was the story you wanted to tell me,' I said finally. 'Can I ask why?'

A long silence.

'No,' he said.

Cut.

It was as if he were deliberately tantalising me. This is the world in which he had grown up, that was clearly a part of the message he was sending; but was he admitting to being a participant in that world or explaining his final rejection of it, by leaving it behind him? Or both? He had participated but now he wanted out and that meant going far away, too far for anyone to come after him. Based on what he had said, there was no way to know for certain. Also, relieved as I was not to be confronted with that feared folder containing evidence of my assignations with his wife, I was happy to receive the Don Corleone story as given, drink one more vodka shot, and withdraw. An old man reminiscing about the past; he wasn't the first such, nor would he be the last. He was beginning to forget the present – little things, where did he put his keys, appointments, birthdays – but he had people to remind him of most of that, and his memory for the past seemed, if anything, to be growing sharper. I suspected – and hoped – there would be more night-time sessions like the one just completed. I wanted all his stories – needed them, so that, in the end, I could make him up.

The news of impending fatherhood appeared if anything to comfort Nero, underlining, as he seemed to need to underline, the continuing force of his masculinity. And in business that strength seemed, for a time, undiminished, as the immense work being undertaken on the West Side of Manhattan proved to us all. The huge Hudson Yards redevelopment had been undertaken by the Related Companies LP and Goldman Sachs in a joint venture with Oxford Properties Group Inc. It proceeded on the basis of a $475 million construction loan obtained by the Related/Oxford joint venture from 'various parties'. I'm pretty close to one hundred per cent sure that Nero Golden, under this or that company name, was one of the lenders alongside the big boys, Barry Sternlicht's Starwood Capital Group and the luxury retailers Coach. His initial investment in the redevelopment of the twenty-six acres had come a number of years earlier, under the EB-5 investment programme which allowed immigrants to the United States to invest capital and in return acquire a green card and eventually citizenship. This finally explained to me how Nero and his sons had been able to decamp to America at such short notice and arrive with full rights of work and residence. Subsequently, in the year of Vasilisa's pregnancy, Golden made a further investment in the form of a mezzanine loan, which was similar to a second mortgage, except that it was secured by the stock of the company that owned the property, as opposed to the real estate. So, theoretically, if the property owner failed to make the interest payments, Nero could have foreclosed on the stock in a matter of a few weeks, and by owning the stock would have gained control of the property. As far as I know, this had not happened. But, leveraged or not leveraged, super-investor or billion-dollar-debtor, he was playing for the highest stakes in the biggest real estate game in town.

The name of the entity making the mezzanine loan was GOVV Holdings. When the Roman emperor Nero died (AD 68), ending the reign of the Julio-Claudian dynasty, there followed (AD 69) the Year of the Four Emperors, in which Nero's immediate successor Galba was overthrown by Otho who in turn was toppled by Vitellius who didn't last long, and was replaced by the man who became the first emperor of the Flavian dynasty: Vespasian. Galba-Otho-Vitellius-Vespasian: G-O-V-V.

When Vasilisa bore Nero a son later that year, he was named Vespasian, as if Nero intuited that the child came from a different bloodline, and would in the end establish a new dynasty of his own.

I said nothing, of course.

Waiting for Vespasian

It was during the pregnancy of his wife, while he awaited the birth of the little emperor Vespasian, that Nero Golden became obsessed by the penis of Napoleon Bonaparte. This should have been enough of an indication of his deteriorating mental state to send up warning signals, but instead was treated indulgently by the family, like an old man's amusing hobbyhorse. When he wasn't preoccupied by business affairs, or by the life burgeoning in Vasilisa's womb, or by the demands of being the father of his sons, Nero embarked on his pursuit of the French imperial member. Regarding which, the following: After the death of Bonaparte on St Helena, an autopsy was carried out, during which various organs, including the unimpressive phallus, were removed for reasons now unknown. The little Napoleon eventually came into the hands (I should rephrase that, perhaps) of an Italian priest, and was then sold on, owned for a time by a London bookseller, and making its way across the Atlantic, first to Philadelphia, and next to New York where it was exhibited in 1927 at the Museum of French Arts and described by one newspaper as a 'shrivelled eel' and by no less an authority than *Time* magazine as 'a maltreated strip of buckskin shoelace'. In 1977 it was bought at auction by the noted urologist John Lattimer as part of his quest to bring dignity to his profession, ownership passing to his daughter after his death along with his other possessions, including Hermann Göring's underpants and the bloodstained shirt collar President Lincoln was wearing at Ford's Theatre. All these memorabilia now resided in Englewood, New Jersey; Napoleon's organ was wrapped in cloth and kept in a little box with a monogrammed *N* on the lid, inside a suitcase, in a storage room, and all of this irked Nero, who wanted it to be given the imperial honour it deserved.

'This is what should happen,' he told me. 'I will buy the item and we will return it to the people of France and you will make the documentary film, you and your girl. I will personally bring the container to Paris and enter the Hôtel des Invalides and approach the sarcophagus of Bonaparte where I will be greeted by high officials of the Republic, maybe even by the president, and I will beg leave to place the container on top of the sarcophagus so that Napoleon can finally be reunited with his lost manhood. I will state in a small oration that I do this as an American, in a kind of repayment for the French gift to America of the Statue of Liberty.'

He wasn't joking. He managed somehow to acquire the home landline number of the house in Englewood and cold-called Mr Lattimer's daughter, who hung up on him. After that he asked his two dragons – Ms Blather and Mistress Fuss – to try, which they did until they were accused of harassment by the person at the other end of the line. Now he was strongly considering a personal trip to New Jersey, chequebook in hand, to try to close the deal. It took all Vasilisa's powers of dissuasion to stop him going. 'The owner does not want to sell, my dear,' she said. 'If you show up she would be within her rights to call the cops.'

'Money talks,' he grumbled. 'You can buy a man's lifelong home in the morning if you offer the right price and get him to move out before lunchtime. You can buy a government if you have sufficient cash. And I can't buy a one-and-a-half-inch johnson?'

'Give it up,' his wife said. 'This isn't what's important right now.'

That year we were all engaged in deflecting the subject. No doubt Nero had ambiguous feelings about the son he had been bullied into having. No question that I, as the actual author of the new storyline, had deeply ambiguous feelings about being, so to speak, the uncredited ghostwriter of the new life. Of Vasilisa's feelings I can say nothing. At times she was as enigmatic as the sphinx. And of the reactions of the existing Golden men, more must now be said. This was the year, for example, that Apu Golden began smashing objects to make his increasingly political art, exhibiting broken things to represent a broken society and the anger of the people at its brokenness. 'People's lives are smashed up,' he said, 'and they are ready to smash everything up because why the fuck not.'

And everywhere I went that year, it seemed, I ran into the ranter from the park. In Vasilisa's second trimester, he walked across the shot on Twenty-Third Street outside the SVA Theatre, where Suchitra and I were filming a street interview with Werner Herzog for my classic-movie-moments video series. At the very moment that I uttered the words *'Aguirre, the Wrath of God,'* the old tramp crossed behind Herzog and myself, looking exactly, *exactly,* like the great wild-eyed madman, the *Zorn Gottes* Klaus Kinski himself, muttering about the accelerating *speed* of evil, about the *growing mountain* of evil right in the *middle of the city,* and who cared? Did anyone in America even *care*? Children were shooting their fathers' dicks off in the bedroom. Did anyone even *notice*? It was like *global warming,* the fires of Hell were melting the great ice sheets of evil and the levels of evil were rising all over the world, no flood barriers could keep them out. Blam!

Blam! he cried, reverting to an earlier theme. The gun monsters are coming to get you, the Decepticons, the Terminators, look out for your children's toys, look out in your squares and malls and palaces, look out on your beaches and churches and schools, they're on the march, blam! blam! – those things can *kill.*

'That guy is fabulous,' Herzog said with genuine admiration. 'We should put him in the movie and maybe I will interview him.'

20

"Here is what I will readily confess to you, you handsome devil,' said Petya Golden, gravely. 'I no longer possess a scrap of brotherly love. What is more, I believe that the widely held view that deep affection between siblings is inborn and inevitable, and that its absence reflects poorly upon the individual who lacks it, is incorrect. It is not genetically driven; rather, it is a form of social blackmail.' It was not often that visitors were invited into Petya's lair but he had made an exception for me, perhaps because I remained, in his unique opinion, the most good-looking man on earth, and so I sat in the blue light of his room among the computers and the Anglepoise lamps, accepted his offer of grilled Double Gloucester cheese on toast, and said as little as possible, understanding that he wanted to talk, and his talk was always worth listening to, even when he was more than usually off-kilter. 'In ancient Rome,' he said, 'in fact in all great empires across the world and in every age, your siblings were people to be feared. At the time of the succession it was usually kill or be killed. Love? Those princes would have laughed at the word if you had brought it up.'

I asked him how he might answer William Penn, what he had to say about the idea enshrined in the name of the city of Philadelphia, which had prospered in its early years because its reputation for tolerance attracted people of many faiths and talents and had led to better than average relationships with the local Native American tribes. 'The idea that all men are brothers is ingrained in much philosophy and most religion,' I ventured.

'Maybe one should seek to love mankind in general,' he retorted in accents that denoted extreme boredom. 'But *in general* is far too general for me. I'm being specific about my dislikes here. Two persons born and one as yet unborn: these are the targets of my hostility, which may be limitless, I don't know. I'm talking about untying the ties of blood here, not un-hugging the whole goddamned species, and do not speak to me, please, of African Eve or LUCA, the three-and-a-half-billion-year-old blob of goo that was our Last Universal Common Ancestor. I am aware of the family tree of the human race and of pre-*Homo sap* life on earth and to insist upon those genealogies now would be wilfully to miss my point. You know what I'm saying to you. It's only my siblings I loathe. This has become clear as I consider the baby we will soon be obliged to greet.'

I could not speak, though I felt a tide of paternal rage rising in my breast. Apparently, while my son – my secret Golden son – was blossoming in his mother's womb, his future brother Petya had already formed a poor opinion of him. I wanted to expostulate, to defend the child and attack his foe, but in this matter silence was my doom. And Petya's talk had already moved on. He wanted me to know that he was making a momentous decision, that he had resolved to cure his fear of the outdoors and then leave the house on Macdougal Street forever, thus becoming the last of the three sons of Nero Golden to strike out on his own. He was the one for whom the difficulties of doing so were greatest, but he now revealed unsuspected reserves of willpower. There was a force driving him, and as he spoke I understood that it was hatred, aimed at Apu Golden in particular: hatred born on the banks of the Hudson River on the night of his brother's seduction of, or perhaps by, the metal-cutting Somali beauty Ubah, nurtured during those long solitudes bathed in blue light, and leading, finally, to action. He would cure himself of agoraphobia and leave home. He indicated the plaque above the door of his lair. *Leave thy home, O youth, and seek out alien shores.* 'I used to think it was about moving to America,' he said, 'but here in this house we are still at home, as if we brought it with us. Now, finally, I'm ready to follow my great namesake's instructions. If not exactly to alien shores, then at least away from here, to an apartment of my own.'

I simply received the information. We both knew that agoraphobia was the lesser of Petya's difficulties. Of the greater difficulty, he did not, on that occasion, choose to speak. But I saw a great resolve in his face. Plainly he had decided to overcome the challenges of that greater difficulty as well.

A new visitor appeared at the Golden house the next day, and after that daily and promptly at three o'clock in the afternoon, a sturdily built person sporting a bouffant blond hairstyle, Converse sneakers, a smile that insisted on its deep sincerity, an Australian accent, and – as Nero Golden pointed out – more than a passing resemblance to the retired Wimbledon champion Pat Cash. This was the individual charged with the task of rescuing Petya from his fear of open spaces: Petya's hypnotherapist. His name was Murray Lett. 'If you call me, it's not a fault,' he liked to say; a tennis joke that only served (ouch) to increase his resemblance to the former Australian star.

It was not easy for Petya to be hypnotised, because he kept wanting to argue with the hypnotist's suggestions and in addition he disliked certain Antipodean notes in the man's voice, and his sense of humour, and so on. The first sessions were difficult. 'I'm not in a trance,' Petya would interrupt Mr Lett. 'I'm feeling relaxed and in a good mood but I'm in full control of my wits.' Or, another day, 'Oh dear, I was so nearly there at last. But a fly just went up my nose.'

Petya noticed too much. It was one of the things that most seriously got in his way. On one of my visits to the room of blue light, when he seemed willing for once to talk about the Asperger's, I mentioned the famous Borges story, 'Funes the Memorious', about a man who was unable to forget anything, and he said, 'Yes, that's me, except it's not just what happened or what people said. That writer of yours, he's too wrapped up in words and deeds. You have to add smells and tastes and sounds and feelings also. And glances and shapes and the patterns of cars in the street and the relative movement of pedestrians and the silences between musical notes and the effects of dog whistles on dogs. All of them all the time running around my brain.' A sort of super-Funes, then, cursed with multiple sensory overload. It was hard to imagine what his interior world was like, how anyone could cope with the crowding in of sensations like riders on the rush-hour subway, the deafening cacophony of sobs, honks, explosions and whispers, the kaleidoscopic blaze of images, the muddled reek of stenches. The Inferno, the carnival of the damned, must be like this. I understood then that to say that Petya lived in a kind of hell was the exact opposite of the reality, which was that a kind of hell lived inside him. This understanding allowed me to recognise, and to be embarrassed that I hadn't recognised it before, the immense strength and courage with which Petronius Golden faced the world every day, and to have a greater compassion for his occasional savage complaints against his life, like the episodes on the windowsill and on the subway to Coney Island. And I also allowed myself to wonder: If that immense force of character were now to be dedicated to his animus against his unborn soon-to-be half-brother (actually, as we know, not his brother at all, but let that thought lie for now), his troubled half-brother and above all his treacherous full-blood brother, of what vengeful deed might he be capable? Should I worry for my own son's safety, or was that instinct proof of my knee-jerk bigotry toward Petya's condition? (Was it wrong to call it a condition? Maybe 'Petya's reality' would be better. How difficult language had become, how full of landmines. Good intentions were no longer a defence.)

Let me turn to the drinking. I'm on firmer ground there. Petya had a drink problem; there was no disguising that. He drank alone and heavily and was a melancholy drunk but it was the way he had found to shut off the inferno within and get some sleep, or, more precisely, to pass out and spend some hours being blessedly unconscious. And in the hour before unconsciousness, on the single occasion that he allowed me to witness his nightly slide into oblivion, at the start of Vasilisa Golden's final trimester when he said he 'needed my support', I heard with growing discomfort and even dislike the extent to which his inability to control the flood of chatter pouring into him or to censor his own linguistic flow resulted, when alcohol was added to that tumult of information, in a stream-of-consciousness soliloquy that revealed the extent to which he had internalised the adversarial fragmentation of American culture and made it a part of his personal damage. To put it plainly, his drunk nocturnal self revealed a lurch toward the extremes of conservative attitudes; the presence of a Foxy, Breitbartian other-self bubbled through his lips, fortified by liquor, enabled by isolation and his wholly justifiable fury at the world: Obamacare, terrible!, Maryland shooting, don't politicise it!, minimum-wage rise, scandalous!, same-sex marriage, unnatural!, religious objections to serving LGBT people in Arizona, in Mississippi, freedom!, police shootings, self-defence!, Donald Sterling, free speech!, shootings on university campus in Seattle shootings in Vegas shootings in Oregon high school, guns don't kill people!, arm the teachers!, the Constitution!, freedom!, ISIS beheading, Jihadi John, disgusting!, we have no plan!, take them all out!, we have no *plan*!, oh, and Ebola! Ebola! Ebola! All this and more in an incoherent torrent mixed up with his hostility toward Apu, if Apu was going left then Petya would go right to counter him, whatever Apu was for he would be against, he would construct a moral universe that inverted his brother's reality, black was white, right was wrong, down was up and in was out. Apu himself got the rough end of Petya's monologues a few times that year and responded gently, not taking the bait.

'Let him say what he wants to say,' he told me. 'You know it's badly wired in there.' He tapped his forehead to indicate Petya's brain.

'He's one of the most intelligent people I know,' I said, meaning it.

Apu grimaced. 'It's a cracked intelligence,' he said. 'So it doesn't count. Out there I'm trying to deal with a cracked *world*.'

'He's trying super hard,' I ventured. 'The hypnotherapy, et cetera.'

Apu dismissed this. 'Call me when he stops sounding like he's at the Tea Party with a mad hat on his head. Call me when he decides to stop being the GOP elephant in the room.'

Even more worrying to me than Petya's voluble hostility to Apu's politics was the drunken revelation of his phobia for the differently gendered. This, too, appeared to have its foundation in family matters. From the violence of his language, which I forbear to repeat here, it was plain that the peace treaty he had made with himself long ago, to forgive D Golden's behaviour toward his mother, no longer held; and the way his anger expressed itself was in his vehement hostility toward his half-brother's growing gender confusion. He began to aim at his half-brother such loaded words as *unnatural*, *perverted* and *sick*. He had somehow found out about the afternoon in Vasilisa's clothes closet, and her complicity in his experiments with otherness led him to extend his verbal violence in her direction. The baby became the location of this part of his anger. Again, I worried for the safety of the unborn child.

The hypnosis finally began to work. The bouffant hypnotherapist Mr Lett acquired a new bounce in his Conversed step. 'How's it going?' I asked him on his way out the door after a session and in his excitement he said a mouthful. 'Virry will, thenks,' he said. 'I had ivry confidince it would. Just took a moment or two. I utilise a mithodology of my own in this type of situation, I call it Personally Progremmed Power, thet's PPP for short. It's a quistion of working with the person stip by stip end slowly increasing silf-confidince, end what I like to call silf-ectualisation. Each stip we take down the PPP road will increase the person's belief in himsilf. We're will along thet road now. Most diffinitely, yis. Things are will sit. It's a quistion of giving your frind some tengible ividence, ividence which he can reproduce time after time, of his ibility to take control of his mintal prociss. To be in charge of his physical end imotional reictions. Once he knows he can do thet, he'll feel confidint to control his ixperience in the outside world. Stip by stip. Thet's the ticket. What I'm giving him is the ibility to choose how he wants to respond to the folks around him, end stuff thet may heppen now or in the future, end whativer situations may prisint thimsilves. I'm virry optimistic. G'day.'

As part of this process of taking control, Petya studied the structures of what he called 'enchanted spaces', the occultist pentagram and the Jewish eruv. If he could accept the private island off Miami as one such space, and, as another, Ubah Tuur's fenced-in property upstate, where the unfortunate episode had occurred, then surely he could construct such enchanted spaces for himself. This was how he came up with the idea of the chalk circle around Manhattan Island. He would walk around the entire island and draw the circle himself. He would do this unaided and to increase the circle's power he would sprinkle garlic as he went. To make it easier for him to surmount his fears he would wear very dark black goggles, and a hoodie. He would also listen to loud music on noise-cancelling headphones, and drink a lot of water. Nobody could do this for him. It was a thing he had to accomplish on his own.

The hypnotherapist Lett both celebrated and backed the plan, offering to go shopping and acquire the sticks of chalk and the garlic cloves. Nero Golden, however, was concerned, and made a few calls.

The appointed day dawned hot and humid under a cloudless sky. Petronius Golden descended from the room of blue light dressed as he had promised, with the grim determination of an Ethiopian marathon runner on his face. Murray Lett waited for him at the front door and before Petya stepped into the street the therapist tried to remind him of how much he had improved, counting off the achievements on his fingers and thumbs. 'Rimimber now. Major edvance in silf-ifficacy! Greatly increased focus end concintration! Huge improvement in autonomy end silf-confidince! Much bitter menagement of striss! Much bitter menagement of enger! Big stips forward in impulse control! You can *do* this.' Petya, in that state of greatly increased focus and concentration to which Lett referred, was listening to Nine Inch Nails on his headphones and didn't hear him. He had a satchel full of chalk sticks slung over one shoulder, and carried a backpack containing coconut-water cartons, fruit, sandwiches, granola bars and roasted chicken drumsticks. Also three extra pairs of socks. Seasoned walkers on the Internet had warned him that sweaty feet in perspiration-drenched socks started to blister, and that made the walk impossible to complete. He held a bag of crushed garlic in one hand. In the other hand he flourished a walking stick to whose end he had taped the initial piece of chalk. His pockets were full of more rolls of tape so that he could change the chalk sticks when necessary. 'Think about your social behaviour,' shouted Murray Lett, understanding at last that he had not been heard. 'Avoid introversion. Make eye contect. Those are good things to keep in mind.' But Petya was in his own world and eye contact did not seem to be in his plans. 'One last thing,' shouted Murray Lett, and now Petya did him the favour of pulling his headphones down and listening. 'I hope your sleep pettern has been good,' said Murray Lett in a lower voice. 'Also, excuse me for asking but, the inuresis issue, we have eliminated thet, correct?' Petya Golden went so far as to roll his eyes, put his headphones back on, seemed satisfied that Axl Rose had replaced Trent Reznor, put his head down, and strode out of the door into the Uber waiting to take him to his chosen starting point, the South Street Seaport; leaving Mr Lett in his wake. 'Good on ya,' the therapist called after him. 'Proud of you. Good work.'

Nero Golden was at the door too, accompanied by Mesdames Blather and Fuss, and me. 'Take your time,' he told his son. 'Don't rush it. Do it comfortably. It isn't a race.' When the car had taken Petya away, Nero spoke into his phone. His people would be in SUVs along the route. There would be eyes on Petya every step of the way.

Thirty-two miles, give or take, is the 'great saunter' around Manhattan Island. Seventy thousand steps. Twelve hours, if you're not super-fast. Twenty parks. I didn't go along, but I understood at once that this moment would be a high point of the film I was dreaming up, my imaginary Golden movie. Loud music on the soundtrack, Lou Reed's *Metal Machine,* Zeppelin, Metallica, and the umlaut gang, Motörhead and Mötley Crüe. The walker walking, and (somehow making itself heard through the heavy-metal noise; I hadn't worked that part out yet) the sound of a tambourine at each footfall. In the parks he passes the figures of his life, watching him; are they phantoms, the ectoplasm of his damaged fantasy? Here, his mother in Nelson A. Rockefeller Park, definitely a ghost or a memory. Here, Apu jogging past him on the East River Promenade. Farther along, D Golden and Riya in Riverside Park, all of them motionless, watching as he walks, staring the stare of ghosts. Around them the haunted, frightened trees. Ubah Tuur standing like a sentinel in Inwood Hill Park by the Shorakkopoch Rock, which marks the spot where once upon a time under the largest tulip tree in Mannahatta Peter Minuit bought the island for sixty guilders, and in Carl Schurz Park near Gracie Mansion the bouffant Lett himself, egging him on. Maybe Lett was the one who was really there. Petya moves on, the tambourine man, far from the twisted reach of crazy sorrow. And as he walks, a transformation. At mile ten, in West Harlem Piers Park, he throws away the chalk, stops drawing the line that has followed him this far, and once he has passed the mayor's residence he throws away the garlic too. Something has changed for him. He doesn't need to mark his territory any more. The walk itself is the mark, and the completion of it will perfect his invisible, indelible eruv.

And by the time he returns, staggering a little, to his starting place the sky has darkened; and watched at last by the schooners *Lettie G. Howard* and *Pioneer* and the freighter *Wavertree* he begins, on his bandaged blistered feet, slowly and without regard for watching eyes, to dance. Beneath the diamond sky with one hand waving free. And he has broken his hoodoo. One of them. And maybe learned something about his strength, his ability to confront and rise above his other challenges too. Look at his face right now: it wears the look of a slave set free.

— What of the hatred?

— Oh, that remained.

21

In the aftermath of Petya Golden's great saunter, we were obliged to accept that the hypnotherapist Murray Lett was a miracle worker in spite of his hairstyle, accent and shoes, and learned the lesson of compassion: that the truth often lies below the surface, and a man may be a great deal more than his most easily caricatured characteristics. For Petya now was like a man exonerated of a crime he had never committed and for which he had been serving a life sentence. His face was illumined by a grave joy, which both recognised the injustice of his suffering and accepted, with a gradually fading disbelief, his release from it. And as he embarked on his new life, Lett was the man on whom he leaned, whom he trusted to guide him into the world whose openness to him felt like an impossible treasure; that same world where all the rest of us so casually and often so thoughtlessly lived, failing to notice its daily carnival of wonderments, which Petya now hugged to his bosom like gifts. He went shopping for groceries with Murray Lett to D'Agostino's, Gristedes and Whole Foods; he sat with Murray Lett on the open-air terraces of cafes in Union Square and Battery Park; he went with Murray Lett to his first outdoor rock concert at Jones Beach, featuring Soundgarden and his beloved Nails; he was at The Stadium with Murray Lett chanting 'Thank you, Derek' during one of Derek Jeter's last moments in the Bronx. And it was with Murray Lett that he picked out his new apartment, a furnished ready-to-move-in twelve-month rental 'and then let's see', he confidently said, 'maybe then it will be time to buy', on the fourth floor of a six-storey, Mondrian-ish glass-and-metal building on the east side of Sullivan Street.

It was only at this point that I discovered, and felt like a fool for not having known it before, that Petya had been making very large sums of money on his own all this time, as the creator and sole owner of a number of highly successful games which the whole world was playing on its smartphones and computers.

This was sensational information. We all knew that he played those games constantly, sometimes for fourteen or fifteen hours a day; how had none of us had any inkling that he was doing so much more than merely idling away his troubled hours doing something which his strange, brilliant mind was naturally good at? How did we not guess that he had taught himself code, becoming rapidly and profoundly versed in its mysteries, and that as well as endlessly playing these games he was creating them? How were we blind to the evidence, and couldn't see that he had revealed himself to himself as a twenty-first-century genius, leaving the rest of us in his wake, floundering in a second-millennium world? It was a sign of how badly we had failed him, abandoning him for most of the hours of each day to his own devices, allowing him to stay locked away, marooned in his room as if he were our version of that old Gothic trope, the Madwoman in the Attic, our own Bertha Antoinetta Mason, the first Mrs Rochester, thought by Jane Eyre to resemble a 'Vampyre'. And all this time! All this time! Frugal, hidden Petya, changing nothing about his life, buying himself nothing, had been rising to the Everests of that secret universe, and, to be frank, outdoing us all. Another lesson to be learned: never underestimate your fellow man. One man's ceiling is another man's floor.

They all had secrets, the Golden men. Except perhaps for Apu, who was an open book.

That was the year of the ugly Gamergate business; the gaming world was at war, men against women, 'gamer identity' against diversity, and only a new-tech Neanderthal like myself could have been unaware of the hullabaloo. Somehow, in ways which I was not able to grasp, Petya had managed to stand apart from the fray, even though, when he finally agreed to talk to me about it, he revealed strong opinions about the way the male gaming community was responding to a series of criticisms by allegedly uppity women – media critics and independent game developers – publishing their addresses and phone numbers and subjecting them to worse menaces too, including large numbers of death threats which had forced some of the female targets to flee their homes. 'The problem is not technological,' he said. 'And there is no technological solution to it. The problem is human, human nature in general, male human nature in particular, and the permission that anonymity gives people to unleash the worst sides of that nature. Me, I just make entertainment for the kids. I'm neutral space. I'm Switzerland. Nobody bothers me. They just come visit and ski down my slopes.'

High-functioning autism had helped to make him a game-making marvel and I started digging into the possible rewards. The leading 'baller apps' – apps through which you could connect to friends and play together – were earning eleven, twelve million dollars a month. The old stalwart *Candy Crush Saga*, which even I had heard of, was still taking in five and a half million. War games that made almost all their money by in-app purchases, less than ten per cent of their income from advertising, might be making two, two and a half million. Monthly. I read off the top fifty iOS and Android titles to Petya. 'Are any of those yours?' I asked. A wide grin spread across his face. 'I cannot tell a lie,' he said, pointing to the number-one-ranked game. 'I did it with my little hatchet.'

So, over one hundred million dollars a year from that title alone. 'You know what,' I said to him, 'I just stopped worrying about you.'

There were studies that showed that autism could be 'outgrown', that some fortunate patients could enter the OO (or Optimal Outcome) group whose members no longer showed any of the symptoms of autistic disorder, and that a higher IQ was more likely to lead to this. Inevitably, the research was disputed, but many families offered anecdotal evidence in its support. The Petya case was different. Neither did he achieve, nor did he actually want, entry into the OO group. His HFA and his achievements were closely linked. However, in the aftermath of the breakthrough walk around Manhattan, he seemed increasingly able to manage his symptoms, to be less depressed, less likely to tailspin into crisis, less worried about living alone. He had his buddy in Murray Lett, and his father took care to visit him every day, and he still took his prescribed medication, and he was . . . functional. As to his new release from fear of the outdoors, nobody could say how permanent it might be, or how far from 'home base' he might be willing to roam. But, on the whole, he was in the best shape he'd been in for a long time. Not worrying about him had become a possibility.

He still drank too heavily. Somehow, perhaps because this was a much more familiar problem, it concerned all of us less than it should have.

For a time after that I worried about myself instead. The baby was due soon, and to tell the truth I couldn't stand the situation in which I found myself, so I scrambled to do as Suchitra wanted and moved out of the Golden house. And yes, my parents had had many close relationships with their neighbours on the Gardens, and to my great delight their diplomat friend from Myanmar, whom in these pages, in order to make him up more easily, I have renamed U Lnu Fnu – the sad-faced sunken-eyed bespectacled widower who had narrowly failed in his quest to follow U Thant as the second Burmese UN Secretary General – welcomed me into his home. 'It will be a pleasure for me,' he said. 'It is a large apartment and to be alone in it feels like being a fly buzzing inside a bell. I hear the echo of myself and it is not a sound I love.'

As a matter of fact, my timing was perfect, because he had had a tenant in his spare room for a while, and when I asked him about possibly renting that room this tenant was on the point of vacating it. The exiting character was an airline pilot, Jack Bonney, who liked to say that he flew 'for the biggest airline you've never heard of', Hercules Air, which historically had carried cargo but now also accepted soldiers and other clients. 'One time recently,' he said, 'we had the British prime minister on board with his security detail, and I was like, should he be on your Air Force One? And the security guys said, we don't have a plane like that. And I airlifted mercenaries into Iraq, that was something. But the biggest thing I ever flew? From London to Venezuela, two hundred million dollars' worth of Venezuelan currency, which the Brits printed for them, who knew, right. Here's the weird thing. At Heathrow, they're loading the pallets, and there's no security, I'm looking around, but there's just the regular airport personnel, no armed escort, nothing. Then we get to Caracas and wow, just a huge military operation. Bazookas, tanks, terrifying guys in body armour with guns sticking out of them in every direction. But in London, nothing. That freaked me out.'

When he was gone and I was comfortably ensconced U Lnu Fnu visited me in my room and said in his delicate, careful voice, 'I was glad of his company but glad also that you are quieter by nature. Mr Bonney is a good man but he should be careful about his loose-tongued chitchat. Walls have ears, my dear René. Walls have ears.'

He was solicitous of my well-being, spoke once, shyly, after asking permission, about his respect for my parents and his understanding of my pain at their loss. He himself, he shyly mentioned, had suffered the pain of loss as well. Suchitra was happy about my new location but, noticing my continuing low spirits, took a different tack. 'You look like a sad sack since you moved out of the Addams Family mansion. You sure you're not hankering for a little taste of sweet Russian pastry?' Her tone was light, but it was clear she really wanted to know the answer.

I reassured her; she was a trusting soul and soon laughed it off. 'I'm glad you managed to stay on in your beloved Gardens,' she said. 'I can only imagine how long your face would've gotten if that hadn't worked out.'

But my son, my son. Impossible to be far away from him, impossible also to be close. Vasilisa Golden, heavily pregnant, on the point of delivering, walked in the Gardens every day with her headscarfed babushka of a mother, a cliché flown in to be of service in a melodrama, and I thought: my son is in the grip of people who don't even speak English as a first language. This was an unworthy thought, but in my frenzy of frustrated fatherhood I had no thoughts except unworthy ones. Should I spill the beans? Should I remain silent? What would be best for the boy? Well, of course what would be best for him would be to know who his true father was. But I was also, I admit, more than a little afraid of Nero Golden, the fear of the young artist just starting out for the fully evolved and puissant man of the world, even in his present, slowly deteriorating state. What would he do? How might he react? Would the child be in danger? Would Vasilisa? Would I? – Well, I certainly would, I thought. I had repaid his kindness after my orphaning by impregnating his wife. At her request, it's true, but he would not accept that as an excuse, and I feared his fists; his fists at the very least. But how could I remain silent for a lifetime? I had no answers, but the questions bombarded me night and day, and there was no bomb shelter to be found.

I felt like a fool – worse than a fool, like an errant child, guilty of a great naughtiness and fearing adult retribution – and there was nobody to talk to. For the first time in my life I felt some appreciation for the Catholic device of the confessional and the forgiveness of God that followed it. If I could have found a priest at that moment, and if a string of *mea maxima culpas* would have silenced the incessant interrogation taking place within me, I would gladly have gone that route. But none was available. I had no connection to that churchy world. And my parents were gone and my new landlord, U Lnu Fnu, while undoubtedly a calm and calming presence and a seasoned diplomat, had already been unhappy at his previous tenant's talkativeness, and would certainly recoil from the radioactively emotive material I needed to unload. Suchitra was obviously out of the question. I knew, by the way, that if I could not calm myself soon she would smell a rat and that would be the worst of all possible ways for the truth to come out. No, the truth must not come out. The truth would ruin too many lives. I had to find a way of silencing the possessive voice, the voice of fatherly love that wanted its secret to be known, shouting in my ear. A therapist, then? That was the secular confessor-figure of our times. I had always loathed the idea of going to a stranger for help in examining one's life. I myself was the would-be storyteller; I hated the idea of someone else understanding my own story better than I. The unexamined life is not worth living, Socrates said and drank the hemlock, but that examination, I had always thought, should be an examination of the self by the self; autonomous, as a true individual should be, leaning on no man for explanations or absolution, free. Therein lay the Renaissance humanist idea of the self expressed in, for example, Pico della Mirandola's *De hominis dignitate – The Dignity of Man*. Well! That high-mindedness had flown out of the window when Vasilisa announced she was with child. Ever since then, the wild storm had raged within me, beyond my power to assuage. Time, perhaps, to swallow one's pride and find professional help? For a moment I thought of turning to Murray Lett, but saw at once that that was a stupid idea. There were excellent therapists among my parents' circle of friends. Maybe I should turn to one of them. Maybe I needed someone to take the weight of my knowledge from me and put it in a safe and neutral place; a psychological sapper to defuse the bomb of the truth. So I wrestled with my demons; but after much inner wrangling I chose, rightly or wrongly, not to seek a stranger's help after all, but elected to confront those demons alone.

Meanwhile the folk of the Gardens were fully absorbed in the drama unfolding at the Tagliabue place across from the Golden house, where the greatly put-upon wife Blanca Tagliabue, tired of being left at home to mind the kids while her husband Vito went out on the town, and bored of his (truthful, I believe) protestations of absolute fidelity, had begun an affair with the neighbourhood's wealthy Argentine resident, Carlos Hurlingham, whom I had dubbed 'Mr Arribista' in one of my treatments, had left the children in the care of nannies, and had flown off in Señor Hurlingham's 'PJ' to take a look at the famous Iguazu Falls on the Argentine–Brazilian border and no doubt to indulge in various south-of-the-border activities while she was there. Vito was beside himself with rage and grief and stormed around the Gardens raging and griefing, giving immense pleasure to all his neighbours. If I had not been so preoccupied with my own difficulties I would have found some pleasure in the fact that all the disparate characters in my Gardens narrative were beginning to link and combine to form a coherent shape. But at that moment I cared only for my own sadness and so failed to keep up with the Tagliabue–Hurlingham *telenovela* as it unfolded.

That wasn't very important. They were at best minor characters and might not make it past the cutting-room floor. What was much worse was that in my distress I took my eye off Petya Golden. I'm not saying I could have prevented what followed if I had been more vigilant. Maybe Murray Lett should have intuited it. Maybe nobody could have done anything. But I regret my negligence nonetheless.

The Sottovoce galleries, two generous spaces all the way west on Twenty-First and Twenty-Fourth Streets, had both been taken over by one of the season's big shows, of new work by Ubah Tuur. The large-scale pieces, reminiscent of Richard Serra's metal monsters, but slashed and transformed by knives of flame into exquisite lacy patterns, so that they also seemed to be giant curved rusted-metal versions of the latticework stone *jalis* of India, stood illumined by spotlights like more playful, fanciful relatives of the stark alien 'sentinels' in Kubrick's *2001.* In the Twenty-First Street location I ran into the ebullient Frankie Sottovoce, pink-cheeked with wind-blown white hair, waving his arms and giggling with delight. 'It's a big hit. Only the most major collectors and museums. She's a star.'

I looked around for the artist but she wasn't there. 'You just missed her,' Sottovoce said. 'She was here with Apu Golden. You should come again. They are here all the time. Most mornings. You know her from the party in the Gardens. She's great. So incredibly smart. And beautiful, my God.' He shook a hand loosely as if it were recovering from being scorched by her beauty's flame. 'She's a force,' he concluded, and skipped away to seduce someone more important.

'Oh,' he paused, turning back to me, his love of gossip briefly overpowering his business instinct. 'The other Golden came too, the older brother, you know.' He tapped his temple to indicate *the crazy one.* 'He saw her here with Apu and I don't think it made him so happy. Took off like a bat out of hell. Maybe a little rivalry thing? Hmm hmm?' He laughed his silly high giggling laugh and was gone.

That's when I should have guessed. That's when I should have seen in my mind's eye the red tide rising in Petya's face, as he understood that after all this time the woman he loved remained in his brother's arms, the woman his brother stole from him, ruining his best chance of happiness. That treacherous night under Ubah's roof long ago, reborn in all its power in his thoughts, as if it had happened right at that moment. The rage reborn too, and with it a lust for vengeance. That one glimpse of Ubah and Apu hand in hand was all it took, and what followed, followed with the horrifying inevitability of a gunshot after a trigger is pulled. I should have known there would be trouble. But I was thinking of other things.

In New York City, FDNY dispatchers send out 44 units and 198 firefighters for a five-alarm fire. The probability of two such blazes happening within three blocks of each other on the same night is extremely remote. The likelihood of these fires being accidents is . . . negligible.

Security was taken seriously at the Sottovoce galleries. During opening hours there was manpower, and cameras, and an emergency lockdown procedure that could seal all the entrances in twenty seconds. This was 'Situation A'. Situation B, from closing time until reopening time, was handled by laser beams which, if broken, would trigger alarms, by surveillance cameras relaying information to the security company's command centre which had eyes on the screens twenty-four hours a day, and by titanium grilles as well as roll-down steel doors, each of them worked by a double digital lock and key system: two slots for ID cards with keypads below them, and no single executive knew all the PIN codes. To open the gates, two senior Sottovoce personnel had to be present, each using his or her card and keying in their individual code. To hack the system, Frankie Sottovoce liked to say, you would need to be a genius. 'The place is a fortress,' he boasted. 'Even I can't get in there if I'm passing by at night and need to take a leak.'

What exactly happened? In the night's dead time, around 3.20 a.m., a dark-windowed Chevrolet Suburban with no plates drew up outside the Twenty-Fourth Street gallery. The driver must have visited the gallery previously and used what the NYPD's public statement described as 'very sophisticated skimming equipment' to clone the ID cards and discover the PINs. The steel doors rolled up and the titanium gates opened and then plastic jerrycans filled with gasoline were uncorked, thrown into the gallery, and set alight, perhaps by the same sort of blowtorch used to create the sculptures on display. The SUV left as the fire billowed outward, and a similar procedure was followed on Twenty-First Street. There was one witness, an unreliable wino, who described the Suburban's driver as a man in a black hoodie and dark goggles. 'He looked like the Fly,' the witness said. 'Yeah. Come to think of it I remember he totally had hairy Fly arms sticking out the ends of his sleeves.' As this testimony plunged deeper into science fiction, the witness was thanked and allowed to leave. No other witnesses emerged. The investigation's best hope was to identify the car, but it was not immediately found. And by the time the fires were extinguished the sculptures were irreparably ruined.

INTERIOR. NIGHT. PETYA GOLDEN'S APARTMENT. BEDROOM.

Sitting up in bed, still wearing his black hoodie and goggles, PETYA, with the sheets pulled up under his chin. He is sobbing uncontrollably. He pulls off the goggles and throws them across the room. Bottles of liquor open on bedside table.

INTERIOR. NIGHT. PETYA GOLDEN'S APARTMENT. LIVING ROOM.

Still weeping, almost screaming with grief, PETYA has started to smash up his new home. He throws a lamp across the room, it hits a wall and shatters. He picks up a chair and throws it after the lamp. Then he squats down on the floor with his head in his hands.

INTERIOR. DAY. PETYA'S APARTMENT. LIVING ROOM.

Mix through to the next morning, PETYA in the same position.

The DOORBELL rings. Repeatedly. He does not move.

Cut.

EXTERIOR. DAY. OUTSIDE THE 'MONDRIAN BUILDING'.

NERO GOLDEN is ringing the doorbell. Cut into CLOSE-UP of his face as he speaks directly into the camera. Under the VO we can hear the ding-dong of the bell as he continues to ring it.

NERO

Of course I understand at once that it is him. They show the drawing on television and when I see it I know. This is not the Fly. This is Petronius. Also the car. He has taken the plates off but it is my car. I myself gave him the key when he moved into the apartment. He is a good driver, a safe driver. What father would expect such a thing from his son? We keep it in the parking garage under 100 Bleecker, the NYU high-rise, we sublet the space from a journalism professor living on the twentieth floor. I know the car, I know my son, I know the woman. Naturally. That is the woman that his brother took from him. This is revenge. A terrible thing, but after all he is a man.

Cut.

INTERIOR. NIGHT. PETYA'S APARTMENT.

The apartment is in disarray, but PETYA has allowed MURRAY LETT to enter. He, PETYA, is still hunched over, squatting on the floor, at rear of shot. LETT is down with him, his arms on PETYA's shoulders. PETYA is talking non-stop. We don't hear his monologue.

RENÉ (V/O)

He bought the blowtorch online. That was easy. After taking the plates off the Suburban he drove to a convenience store in Queens and picked up the plastic gas jerrycans. Then he drove to a different, drive-through C-store in Nassau County and filled those gas cans up. As for breaking through the security systems at the galleries, he just said it was really easy. Maybe he hadn't expected the wave of guilt that hit him immediately after the attacks. He very nearly drowned in it. The meltdown was very severe. He became anxious, hysterical, depressed, drunk. The therapist wanted him put on suicide watch. His father hired round-the-clock nursing staff to sit with him.

Cut to PETYA, talking furiously, but we still hear only RENÉ'S narration. At times PETYA is speaking in lip sync with RENÉ.

RENÉ

His rage attack was aimed mostly at himself, full of guilt and shame. However, he also talked a lot about how much he hated his brother. His feelings for Apu had curdled into lumps of hatred so thick that they could only be dissolved by his brother's lifeblood, he said, and maybe even that would not be enough, maybe he would subsequently also need at frequent intervals to shit on Apu's rancid grave. In the crime pages of the cheap newspapers, he read about men who had kept women prisoner for years and he said, maybe I could do that, I could shackle and gag him and keep him in the basement near the boiler and hot-water cylinder and torture him whenever I wanted. In those days after the arson attack Petya was drinking very heavily. He was also completely out of his mind.

Cut.

EXTERIOR. DAY. NERO'S STUDY. THE GOLDEN HOUSE.

NERO GOLDEN with a thunderous expression stands with his back to the window and his two DRAGON LADIES await his instructions.

NERO

I want the best criminal defence lawyer in America. Get him today and get him here.

The door opens and VASILISA GOLDEN stands there, her hands on her womb. NERO turns to her, angry at the interruption, but the look on her face silences him.

VASILISA

It's time.

Cut.

22

Spring, the last of the ice gone from the Hudson, and happy sails breaking out across the weekend water. Drought in California, Oscars for *Birdman,* but no superheroes available in Gotham. The Joker was on TV, announcing a run for president, along with the rest of the Suicide Squad. There was still more than a year and a half of the current president's term to run but I was missing him already and nostalgic for the present, for these his good old days, the legalisation of gay marriage, a new ferry service to Cuba, and the Yankees winning seven games in a row. Unable to watch the green-haired cackler make his improbable declaration, I turned to the crime pages and read about killings. A gunman shot a doctor in El Paso and then killed himself. A man shot his neighbours, a Muslim family in North Carolina, because of a parking dispute. A couple in Detroit, Michigan, pleaded guilty to torturing their son in their cellar. (Technically not a killing, this one, but a good story, so it counted.) In Tyrone, Missouri, a gunman killed seven people and then made himself his eighth victim. Also in Missouri, a certain Jeffery L. Williams shot two policemen in front of the Ferguson city police headquarters. A police officer named Michael Slager shot and killed Walter Scott, an unarmed black man, in North Charleston, South Carolina. In the absence of the Batman, Mrs Clinton and Senator Sanders offered themselves up as the alternatives to the Suicide Squad. In a Twin Peaks restaurant in Waco, Texas – 'Eats! Drinks! Scenic Views!' – nine people died in a biker war and eighteen others went to the hospital. There were floods and tornadoes across Texas and Arkansas, seventeen dead, forty missing. And it was only May.

'Dostoevsky got all his plots by reading the crime pages of the newspapers,' Suchitra mused. 'STUDENT MURDERS LANDLADY. Whatever the Russian for that is. And bingo! *Crime and Punishment.*'

We were having breakfast – home-brewed macchiato coffee and the cronuts we had waited in line to buy on Spring Street at 5.30 a.m. – sitting at the table in the glass-window corner that looked south toward the harbour and west across the river. It occurred to me that I was happy, that I had found the person who could bring me joy, or she had allowed me to find her. Which also probably meant that I could never tell her the truth about the baby; which in turn meant that Vasilisa Golden had a hold over me which I could never break. It's true that by revealing her secret Vasilisa would undo her own strategy as well as destroying my best chance of a good life. But maybe she was so sure of herself that it didn't matter. She had overcome the drama of her dalliance with Masha the fitness trainer, had she not. And Nero was older every day and more and more anxious not to live and die alone. . . . I pushed such thoughts away, understanding that I was succumbing to paranoia. Vasilisa would not tell. And meanwhile, eating my cronut and looking at the movie reviews in the Sunday *Times,* I was content, happy to let Suchitra think aloud, as she liked to do during these rare moments of calm in her nonstop schedule. From these Sunday brainstorms – just letting her mind freewheel, free-associate from thing to thing, she often came up with projects she wanted to pursue.

'Is that true?' I asked. 'About Dostoevsky?'

That was all she needed. She nodded earnestly, waved her cronut at me while she chewed the piece in her mouth, swallowed, and was off. '*True* is such a twentieth-century concept. The question is, can I get you to believe it, can I get it repeated enough times to make it as good as true. The question is, can I lie better than the truth. You know what

Abraham Lincoln said? "There's a lot of made-up quotes on the Internet." Maybe we should forget about making documentaries. Maybe mix up the genres, be a little *genrequeer.* Maybe the mockumentary is the art form of the day. I blame Orson Welles.'

'Mercury Theatre on the Air,' I said, joining in the fun. '*War of the Worlds.* Radio. That's a long way back. People still believed in the truth back then.'

'Suckers,' she said. 'They believed Orson. Everything starts somewhere.'

'And now seventy-two per cent of all Republicans think the president's a Muslim.'

'Now if a dead gorilla from the Cincinnati zoo runs for president he'll get at least ten per cent of the vote.'

'Now so many people in Australia state their religion as "Jedi" in the census that it's an official thing.'

'Now the only person you think is lying to you is the expert who actually knows something. He's the one not to believe because he's the elite and the elites are against the people, they will do the people down. To know the truth is to be elite. If you say you saw God's face in a watermelon, more people will believe you than if you find the Missing Link, because if you're a scientist then you're elite. Reality TV is fake but it's not elite so you buy it. The news: that's elite.'

'I don't want to be elite. Am I elite?'

'You need to work on it. You need to become post-factual.'

'Is that the same as fictional?'

'Fiction's elite. Nobody believes it. Post-factual is mass market, information age, troll generated. It's what people want.'

'I blame truthiness. I blame Stephen Colbert.'

This was our Sunday banter, but on this occasion I was the one who had a light-bulb moment. My big project, based around the Goldens, should be written and shot in documentary fashion, but scripted, played by actors. The moment I had that thought the script appeared in my head, and within a few weeks it was in draft form, and by the end of the year it would be selected for the Sundance Screenwriters Lab, and the year after that . . . but I'm running ahead of myself in my excitement.

Rewind to that Sunday in the spring. Because later the same day I had an appointment with my son.

Yes, I was playing with fire, but the human programme is powerful, and it wants what it wants. The idea of having no contact with my own flesh and blood was appalling to me, and so, once I had left the Golden house, I shamelessly ingratiated myself with Nero Golden, for whom the newborn child, his first in a long time, was also an obsession. Telling him I wanted to make sure we stayed in touch after all his kindness, after he had been as generous to me as if he were my own family, so that now he felt like family to me (I warned you that I was shameless), I suggested that we continue our new practice of meeting for a meal – tea, perhaps? – at the Russian Tea Room. 'Oh, and it would be great if you bring the baby along,' I innocently added. The old man fell for it, and so I was able to watch my little fellow grow, and play with him, and hold him in my arms. Nero came to the Tea Room with the baby and his nanny, and the nanny handed the kid to me without any argument, and receded into a corner of the restaurant. 'It's amazing how good you are with the boy,' Nero Golden told me. 'I get the feeling you're getting a little broody yourself. That girl of yours is terrific. Maybe you should knock her up.'

I held my son close. 'It's OK,' I said. 'This little guy is more than enough for now.'

The child's mother was not happy about my strategy. 'I prefer it that you make yourself scarce,' Vasilisa called me to say. 'The boy has excellent parents who can provide him with everything he requires and then some, which you naturally cannot. I don't know what is your motive, but I'm guessing maybe it is financial. This is my mistake, it should have been discussed ahead of time. So, OK, if you have a figure in mind, say what it is, and let's see how it corresponds with the figure in my mind.'

'I don't want your money,' I said. 'I just want sometimes to have tea with my son.'

This caused a silence, in which I could hear both her incredulity and relief. Then, finally, 'Fine,' she said with considerable irritation. 'However, he is not your son.'

Suchitra, that Sunday, was also a little puzzled by my interest in the boy. 'Is this some kind of hint?' she asked me in her straight-out shoot-from-the-hip way. 'Because let me say I have a whole career developing here and stopping in my tracks to be somebody's baby mama is not in my plans at the present time.'

'What can I tell you, I just like babies,' I said. 'And the great thing about somebody else's baby is, when you're done playing, you get to hand it back.'

They had kept Petya out of jail. The absence of persons from the building, and the consequential lack of damage to human beings, meant that the crime was classified as arson in the third degree, a class C felony. New York law stated that the minimum punishment for a C felony was one to three years in jail, and the maximum punishment was five to fifteen. However, if extenuating circumstances could be demonstrated, judges were allowed to impose alternative sentences involving much less jail time, or even none at all. The 'best criminal defence lawyers in America' successfully argued that Petya's HFA be taken into consideration. The *crime passionnel* argument, which might have been effective in, for example, France, was not used. Petya was ordered to undergo psychiatric evaluation followed by treatment, and to be placed under community supervision and to pay the fees required, as well as making full restitution for the damage he had caused. Nero hired Murray Lett on a full-time basis and the therapist dropped his other clients and moved into Petya's apartment to protect him from self-harm and to work on his many issues. Lett's role was accepted by the court, which made things easier. That took care of the criminal aspect, and Petya duly reported as required to his supervising officers, submitted to random drug testing, agreed to electronic monitoring by a bracelet locked around his ankle, acquiesced in strict probation conditions, and performed his hours of community service silently and without complaint, working on the maintenance and upkeep of public buildings, permitted to work indoors because of his recrudescent agoraphobia, painting, plastering, hammering, wordlessly, uncomplainingly, passively; detached from his body, or so it appeared, allowing his limbs to do what was required of them while his thoughts went elsewhere, or nowhere.

The question of financial restitution was more complex. A civil suit for damages had been brought by Frankie Sottovoce, naming Nero as well as Petya, and that was ongoing. Ubah Tuur was not involved. It turned out that Sottovoce had bought the pieces from her outright before the opening, so that at the time of the fires they belonged to him. She already had her money. The gallery was insured, but there was a sizeable gap, the Sottovoce lawyers argued, between what the insurance company would pay and what the Tuur pieces would be worth if placed on the open market. Also the buildings required gut renovations and there would be much income lost from shows that could not be put on while that happened. So, a multimillion-dollar case, remaining unsettled – though the bottom line was that Petya's earnings from his baller apps were amply sufficient to settle the suit in full – with the Golden lawyers using all the delays of the law in the hope of finally bringing Sottovoce to the negotiating table to make a more easily bearable deal, and using, too, all the concomitant legal loopholes or (perhaps a better term) flexibilities to keep Petya out of prison while the financial matters were being settled.

It was Apu Golden who first intuited that, whatever the outcome of the civil suit, Petya's fire had badly damaged the house of Golden as well as the two Sottovoce galleries. (It had also ended his own relationship with Frankie Sottovoce, who had unceremoniously suggested he should find a new artistic home.) I visited him in the Union Square studio and he offered me some Chinese green tea from Hangzhou and a plate piled with chunks of hard Italian cheese. 'I want to speak to you like a brother,' he said. 'Like an honorary brother, because at this point you are that. Look at our family. You know what I'm saying? Look at it. We are, I'm sorry to put it bluntly, a wreck. It's the beginning of the fall of the Usher place. I wouldn't be surprised if the Macdougal Street house cracks in half and falls into the street, you know what I mean? Yeah. I have intimations of doom.'

I remained silent. He was just getting into his stride. 'Romulus and

Remus,' he said. 'That's how D thought of us. He was so busy feeling left out of our games that he never saw how tough it was for me to be Petya's brother, how much work I put in to give him a good childhood, or as good as possible, considering his situation. I played with train sets and Scalextric cars into adulthood because he enjoyed those things. We all did. My father too. And now it feels like we all failed, after he crashed and burned. He crashed, the galleries burned. He's in pieces over there with the Australian, who knows if he can be put back together. And D, who knows what's going on with him. Or is it *with her* now? I don't know. Does even he know? Or she? Crazy. Did you know you're not supposed to say "crazy" any more, by the way? Also you're not supposed to say "insane" or, I guess, "nuts." These words are insulting to the mentally ill. There's now a bad word for these bad words, did you know that? Nor did I. Even if you're just saying, this shit is insane, you're not even thinking about mentally ill people, for God's sake, you're still insulting them anyway, apparently. Who comes up with this stuff? They should try living with the situation for a while and see if they don't need to let off some steam. See if they don't need to say, yes, I'm sorry, but sane is a thing and therefore so is insane. Not crazy is a thing and so it follows that crazy also exists. If it exists we use the word. That's language. Is that OK? Or am I a bad person? Am I nuts?'

The subject had changed suddenly. In the last days of the protest in Zuccotti Park, Apu had fallen out with a lot of the Occupy people, partly because of his frustration at their leaderless anarchic rudderlessness, partly because, he said, 'they are more interested in the posture than the results. This language thing is part of that. Excuse me: if you clean up the language too much you kill it. Dirt is freedom. You have to leave a little dirt. Cleansing? I don't like the sound of that.' (At a later point in my research, I met a few of the protesters, most of whom had no memory of Apu. The one who did said, 'Oh, yeah, the rich painter who used to come down here to get himself some street cred. Never liked the guy.')

I guessed that Apu's tirade had its origins in something personal, because fundamentally he wasn't driven by ideas. *Cherchez la femme,* I thought, and she spilled out of his mouth a moment later. 'Ubah,' he said, 'she's totally into all of this. You know. Watch your mouth. Be careful what you say. Walk on eggshells. Every footstep could land on a land mine. Boom! Boom! Your tongue is in danger every time you open your mouth. So exhausting, I have to tell you.'

'So, are you guys not seeing each other any more?'

'Don't be stupid,' he said. 'Can I say that without offending less intelligent persons? Well, I say it. Of course I'm seeing her. She's so extraordinary I can't stop. If she wants me to watch my mouth, whatever, OK, I watch it, at least when she's around – and then unfortunately you get the fallout because I have to let rip when she's out of the way. But it took some doing, holding on to her after my goddamn brother destroyed her whole show. I mean her *whole* show. Just scrap metal now. You know how long those pieces take to make? I mean, months. Of course she was mad, and he's my brother, for God's sake. For a while she couldn't speak to me. But it's better now. She calmed down. She's basically a calm person and a good person. She knows it's not my fault. This is what I mean, we were never Romulus and Remus, Petya and I. I was just trying to hold it together, my family life, my boyhood, and now those days are gone, it's all a wreck.'

He shook his head, remembering his original subject. 'Oh, yeah. Excuse me. I just went off down a little fury road. I'll come back now. What I wanted to say, at the beginning, the whole reason I sat down here with you and the tea and the cheese, is, my whole family is a wreck, and you, my brother who is not my brother, you are the only family member with whom I can discuss this. One brother is an arsonist, the other one doesn't know if he's my half-brother or my half-sister. And my father, apart from getting older and maybe beginning to lose it mentally, I mean, he totally lost it with this woman, his *wife,* I mean it's hard even to say the word, and now this baby, I can't even think of it as my brother. My half-brother. My half-Russian half-brother baby. I sort of blame the baby for everything. It shows up and the world falls apart. It's like a curse. I mean, it's driving me mad, and I'm the sane one. But this is all just me being grouchy which as everyone knows is normal. This is not what I invited you over to tell you. I know you don't go for this stuff, but still, listen to me. I've started seeing ghosts.'

It was the end of Apu's political period. I almost laughed out loud. For the first time that day I allowed my gaze to fall on the new work he was making, and was happy to see that he had shaken off the overly strong influence of contemporary agitprop artists – Dyke Action Machine!, Otabenga Jones, Coco Fusco – and that his earlier, much richer and livelier iconography drawn from world mystical traditions had returned. One large, landscape-format painting in bright oranges and greens struck me in particular, a life-size triple portrait of his favourite witch, the *mãe-de-santo* of Greenpoint, flanked by her preferred deities Orisha and Oludumaré. Mysticism and psychotropic drugs were never far apart in Apu's practice, which probably explained the advent of visions. 'Are you doing ayahuasca now, is that it?' I asked. Apu recoiled in faux-shock. 'Are you kidding? I would never cheat on my *mãe* and her guys.' (The use of ayahuasca in shamanistic practice was connected to the religion of Santo Daime in Brazil, and some people called the drug *daime* in honour of that saint.) 'Anyway, it's not visions of God I've been seeing.'

It was sometimes hard to know if he was speaking literally or figuratively. 'Come and look,' he said. At the far end of the gallery there was a large canvas covered in a paint-spattered sheet. When he pulled the sheet away I saw an extraordinary scene: a vast and detailed Manhattan cityscape from which all vehicles and pedestrians had been removed, an empty city populated only by translucent figures, the male figures dressed in white, the females in saffron: green-skinned, some floating close to the ground, some up in the air. So, yes, ghosts, but whose ghosts? Ghosts of what?

Apu closed his eyes and breathed. Then, exhaling, he gave a little smile and opened the floodgates of the past.

'For a long time,' Apu said, 'he controlled us with money, the money he gave us to live on, the money he promised us as our share, and we did as he asked. But also with something much more powerful than money. This was the idea of the family. He was the head and we were the limbs and the body does what the head instructs it to do. We were brought up that way: in the old-school concepts. Absolute loyalty, absolute obedience, no arguments. It wore off eventually, but it worked for a long time, long into our adult lives. We are not children but for so long we jumped when he jumped, we sat when he said sit, we laughed and cried when he said cry or laugh. When we moved here, it was fundamentally because he said, now we move. But we all had our own reasons for going along with the plan. Petya of course needs a lot of support. For D, even if he didn't know it, America was his road to this metamorphosis that he wants, or he doesn't want, I don't know, or he doesn't know, but at least here he can explore it. For me, there were people to get away from. Entanglements. Not financial, though for a period I had gambling debts. I got past that time. But there were romantic difficulties. There was a woman who broke my heart, another woman who was a little crazy, good crazy most of the time but not all of it, and maybe dangerous for me, not physically but again in the heart, and a third who loved me but who stuck to me so close I had no room to breathe. I broke up with them all or they broke up with me, it doesn't matter, but then they didn't go away. Nobody ever goes away. They circled me like helicopters shining bright floodlights down on me and I was caught in their crossed beams like a fugitive on the run. Then a friend of mine, a writer, a good writer, said something that scared the pants off me. He said, think of life as a novel, let's say a novel of four hundred pages, and then imagine how many pages in the book your story has already covered. And remember that after a certain point, it's not a good idea to introduce a new major character. After a certain point you are stuck with the characters you have. So maybe you need to think of a way of introducing that new character before it's too late, because everyone gets older, even you. He said this to me, just before my father decided we had to move. And so when my father made his decision I thought, you know, this is great. Even better than trying to introduce a new character here, where the exes are circling with their floodlights. This way I get to throw away the whole book and start writing a new story. That old book wasn't that good anyway. So I did it, and here I am, and now I am seeing ghosts, because the trouble with trying to escape yourself is that you bring yourself along for the ride.'

In the painting, now, I picked out the figures of the hovering helicopter women, and saw the small black silhouette of a cowering man below them, the only shadow-figure in that work without shadows. The haunted man and the ghosts of the lost past, haunting him. And the present, I now perceived, was unstable, the buildings crooked and distorted, as if seen through a pane of old, uneven glass. The look of the cityscape reminded me of *The Cabinet of Dr Caligari.* And that at once brought back my early image of Nero Golden as the master criminal Dr Mabuse. I didn't bring that up, but asked about German Expressionism. He shook his head. 'No, the distortion is not referential. It's actual.' He had developed a problem of the retina, macular degeneration, 'luckily the wet kind, because for the dry kind, there's no treatment, you lose your sight and that's that. Also, luckily, only in the left eye. If I close the left eye everything looks normal. But if I close the right eye the world turns into this.' He jerked a thumb at the painting. 'Actually I think it's the left eye that sees the truth,' he added. 'It sees everything distorted and deformed. Which in fact everything is. The right eye is the one that sees the fiction of normality. So I have truth and lies, one eye for each. It's good.'

In spite of his customary sardonic manner I could see he was agitated. 'The ghosts are real,' he said, gathering his strength. 'For some reason I feel better saying this to an anti-spiritual being like yourself.' (I had once told him that I thought the word *spiritual*, which was now applied to everything from religion to exercise regimes and fruit juice, needed to be given a rest, for perhaps a hundred years or so.) 'And it's not a drug thing. I swear. They just appear, in the middle of the night but also in the middle of the day, in my bedroom or in the street. They are never solid. I can see through them. Sometimes they are sort of buzzy, crackling, broken up like a defective video image. Sometimes they are well defined and clear. I don't understand. I'm just telling you what I'm seeing. I have the feeling I'm losing my mind.'

'Tell me exactly how it happens,' I said.

'Sometimes I don't see anything,' he said. 'Sometimes I just hear things. Words that are hard to make out, or, also, perfectly clear. Sometimes also the images show up. What is strange is that it's not necessarily that they are talking to me. The circling exes, yes, for sure, but otherwise it's like they are just getting on with their lives but I am excluded from those lives, because I have excluded myself, and there is a deep feeling of having done something wrong. All of them are from back home, you understand? All.' The smile had gone from his face now. He looked very upset. 'I have studied the seeing of visions,' he said. 'Joan of Arc, Saint John the Divine. There are similarities. Sometimes it's painful. Sometimes it seems to come from within, from the region of the navel, being extruded from the body. At other times it feels purely external. Afterwards often one passes out. It's exhausting. This is what I have to tell you. Tell me what you think.'

'It doesn't matter what I think,' I said. 'Tell me why you think it's happening.'

'I think I left in a bad way,' he said. 'I was in bad shape. I left without making my peace. This is where you will find it hard to go along with me. The familiar spirits are angry with us, the deities of the place. There is a right way and a wrong way to do these things and I, we, all of us, we just ripped ourselves away, just tore off the corner of the page where we were standing, and that was a kind of violence. It's necessary to put the past at rest. I have the strong sense right now of not being able to see my way forward. It feels like there isn't a way forward. Or that for there to be a way forward, first there must be a journey backwards. That's what I believe.'

'What are you talking about?' I asked. 'I mean, can you make offerings to propitiate whatever is doing this? This is deep water for me. I can't feel the bottom.'

'I have to go back,' he said. 'Anyway, Ubah wants to make a visit. So, think of it as a combination of a tourist trip and a cure for homesickness. Think of it as my need to find out if there's a *there* there for me. Then you don't have to endanger your rationalist world view.' This, almost angrily. But then a grin to excuse and compensate for the harshness of his tone.

'What do you think would happen if you didn't go?'

'If I didn't go,' he said, 'then I think a dark force out of the past would fly across the world and probably destroy us all.'

'Oh.'

'Maybe it's too late. Maybe the dark force has made up its mind anyway. But I'm going to try. And in the meanwhile Ubah can stroll on Marine Drive in the evening and see the hanging gardens on Malabar Hill and visit a movie studio, and maybe we'll take a side trip to look at the tomb of Taj Bibi in Agra, why not.'

'You'll go soon?'

'Tonight,' he said. 'Before it's too late.'

23

Every time I heard something about the family's past, I became aware of the gaps in the Golden family narrative. There were things that were not being told and it was hard to know how to get beyond the veil that fell across the story. Apu seemed frightened of something, but whatever it was, it wasn't a ghost. Skeletons in the cupboard seemed likelier. I found myself thinking, not for the first or last time, about the story Nero Golden told me in the Russian Tea Room on our first visit there together, the story of 'Don Corleone'.

I said to Suchitra later that day, 'I wish I was going along with them on their trip. It might be an important part of the story.'

'If it's a mockumentary you're making now,' she said, 'then make it up.'

I was a little shocked. 'Just make it up?'

'You have an imagination,' she said. 'Imagine it.'

A *golden story,* I remembered. For the Romans, a tall tale, a wild conceit. A lie.

It so happened, and it did not so happen, that the great sitarist Ravi Shankar in all his life only ever played on four sitars, and on one of those four he taught the Beatle George Harrison something about the instrument, and those lessons took place in a suite at the grand hotel by the harbour, and now Ravi Shankar was gone but the sitar remained in a glass case, benevolently watching the suite's guests come and go. The grand hotel had been beautifully restored after the terrorist atrocity, the strength of the old stone building had enabled it to stand firm, and the interior looked better than ever, but half the rooms were empty. Outside the grand hotel there were barriers and metal detectors and all the mournful apparatus of security, and the defences were a reminder of horror and the opposite of an invitation. Inside the hotel the many celebrated stores in the shopping arcades reported a decrease in sales of fifty per cent or more. The consequence of terror was fear and though many people spoke of their determination to support the grand hotel by the harbour in its period of rebirth the tough language of the numbers said, *not enough did.* Courting couples and ladies of quality no longer splashed out on tea and snacks at the Sea Lounge and many foreigners too went elsewhere. You could repair the fabric of the building but the damage to its magic remained.

What am I here for? the man who now called himself Apuleius Golden said to Ubah Tuur while the sitar of Ravi Shankar listened in. This is the building where my mother died. This is the city I stopped loving. Am I really so crazy that I believe in ghosts and fly across the world for what? Some sort of exorcism? It's stupid. It's like I'm waiting for something to happen. What can happen? Nothing. Let's be tourists and go home. Let's go to Leopold for coffee and for art to Bhau Daji Lad Museum and also Prince of Wales Museum which I refuse to call Chhatrapati Shivaji Museum because he didn't give a damn about artworks. Let's eat street food on Chowpatty Beach and get a stomach upset like real foreigners. Let's buy some silver bracelets in Chor Bazaar and look at Kipling's father's friezes and eat garlic crabs in Kala Ghoda and feel sad that Rhythm House has closed and mourn Cafe Samovar also. Let's go to Blue Frog for the music and Aer for the high-rise view and Aurus for the sea and Tryst for the lights and Trilogy for the girls and Hype for the hype. Fuck it. Here we are. Let's do it.

Calm down, she said. You sound hysterical.

Something's going to happen, he said. I was pulled across the world for a reason.

In the lobby a glamorous woman flung herself upon him. Groucho! she cried. You're back! Then she saw the tall Somali beauty watching her. Oh, excuse I, she said. I've known this one since he was a boy. We called his older brother Harpo, you know. She tapped her temple. Poor boy. And this one Groucho because he was always grouchy and he chased women.

Tell me about it, said Ubah Tuur.

We have to throw a party! said the glamorous woman. Call me, darling! Call me! I'll round up everybody. She rushed off, talking into her phone.

Ubah Tuur's eyebrow interrogated Apu.

I don't remember her name, he said. It's like I never saw her before in my life.

Groucho, said Ubah Tuur, amused.

Yes, he replied. And D got called Chico. We were the fucking Marx brothers. Get your tutsi-frutsi ice cream here. I don't want to belong to any club that will accept me as a member. That's in every contract, that's what they call a sanity clause. Ha ha ha . . . you can't fool me. There ain't no Santy Claus. How much would you charge to run into an open manhole? Just the cover charge. I've had a great evening, but this wasn't it. I'd kill you for money. Ha ha ha. No, you're my friend. I'd kill you for nothing. That was worth running halfway around the world to get away from.

It's already worth the trip here, she said. I'm learning things about you I never knew before, and we haven't even left the hotel.

I've been looking for a girl like you, he said, groucholy. Not you, but a girl like you.

Cut.

They had not walked more than a few steps along Apollo Bunder in the direction of the Gateway before Ubah stopped and drew Apu's attention to the quartet of almost comically visible men perspiring in black hats and suits, white shirts with narrow black ties, and sunglasses, two walking behind them and two across the street.

Looks like we have some reservoir dogs for company, she said. Or blues brothers, whichever.

When confronted the quartet responded respectfully. Sirji, we are associates of some business associates of your great father, said the one who looked most like Quentin Tarantino as 'Mr Brown'. We are tasked precisely with your personal security and instructed to proceed with maximum subtlety and discretion.

Tasked by whom? Apu asked, annoyed, suspicious, still grouchy.

Sirji, by your esteemed fatherji, via channels. Your esteemed father was unaware of your decision to return and having learned that you have returned he is concerned for your well-being and wishes all to be well.

Then please inform my esteemed father, via those same channels, that I am not in need of babysitting, and once that is done you gentlemen can kindly take your leave.

Mr Brown looked more mournful than ever. It is not for us to instruct, he said. It is for us only to obey.

This was an impasse. Finally Apu shrugged and turned away. Just stay back, he said. Keep your distance. I don't want you in my field of vision. If I turn my head, jump back. Stay out of my eyeline. The same goes for my lady friend. Jump back.

Mr Brown bowed his head with a kind of gentle grief. OK, sirji, he said. We will make our effort.

They stood and looked at the boats in the harbour. It's ridiculous, Apu said. I understand that he had Petya followed on his long walk, because that's Petya, but he needs to start treating me like an adult.

Ubah began in her unflappable manner to giggle. On the way here, she said, I thought, India, I'm going to be shocked by the poverty, it's maybe even worse than back home, or as bad but different, anyway it's going to take an adjustment. I didn't realise we would be walking into a Bollywood movie the moment we hit town.

Cut.

When they got back to the hotel after dinner there was a gentleman waiting for them in the lobby, silver-haired, aquiline of profile, dressed in a cream suit and cricket club tie, holding a Borsalino hat in his hands. He spoke the English of the English gentleman class though he was not an Englishman.

Excuse me, I'm so sorry. Would you mind awfully if I, I hope you will not think it an intrusion if I make so bold as to request a very few minutes of your time?

What is this about?

Might we, could we possibly, in a more discreet setting, could I make so bold as to request, perhaps? Away from eyes and ears?

Ubah Tuur actually applauded. I think you set all this up, she said to Apu. To entertain me and fool me into thinking that it's like this all the time. Of course, sir, she said to the man in the cream suit. It will be our pleasure to welcome you into our suite.

Wipe.

In the suite. The man stood awkwardly next to the glass case containing Ravi Shankar's sitar, fiddling with the brim of his hat and refusing offers to be seated.

I am sure you will not recognise my name, he said. Mastan. I am Mr Mastan.

No, sorry, don't know that name, Apu said.

I am not a young man, Mr Mastan replied. God has granted me over seventy years. But almost half a century ago when I was a young police officer in the CID, I had one might say a relationship with an associate of your father's.

Another associate of an associate, Apu said. Quite a day for them.

Forgive me for asking, said Mr Mastan. Did your esteemed father ever tell you about his associate, the man he referred to jokingly as Don Corleone?

Now Apu was very silent, so profoundly silent that the silence was a form of speech. Mr Mastan nodded deferentially. I have often wondered, he said, how much your father's sons knew about their father's business dealings.

I'm an artist, said the artist. I did not concern myself with finances.

Of course, of course. This is only natural. The artist lives on a higher plane and is unimpressed by filthy lucre. I myself have always admired the bohemian spirit though, alas, it is not in my nature.

Ubah noticed that, having digested the words 'police officer' and 'Don Corleone', Apu was listening very intently.

May I tell you about my own connection to your father's associate, the don? Mr Mastan asked.

Please.

In a phrase, sir, he ruined my life. I was pursuing him, sir, for his various serious crimes and misdemeanours. If I may say so, I was hot on his trail. Also, being young, I had not yet acquired the wisdom of the city. I was unbribable, sir, and incorruptible. No doubt many great men would have described me as a hindrance, an obstacle preventing the wheels of society from being well oiled and running smoothly. And perhaps that is so, but that then is who I was. Incorruptible, unbribable, an obstacle. Your father's associate spoke to less intransigent persons in the upper echelons and I was removed from the case and banished. You are familiar with the poet Ovid, sir? He displeased Augustus Caesar and was exiled to the Black Sea and never returned to Rome. This also was my fate, to languish for years without hope of preferment in a small town in the mountains, in Himachal Pradesh, known for the mass production of mushrooms and of red gold, which is tomatoes, and for the fact that in mythological times it was the exile place of the Pandavas. I too was a little Pandava in my mushroom and tomato exile. After many years my luck turned. As fate would have it a local gentleman whose name I will not introduce here saw in me an honest man and so I left the police force and began to oversee the mushroom and tomato crop to prevent loss through smuggling. In time, sir, I departed the mountains and became successful in the field of security and investigation. I give thanks to God that I did well. Now I am a retired individual, with sons working in my stead, but I keep my ear to the ground, sir, that I do.

Why have you come here to tell me this story, Apu asked.

No, no, sir, you are mistaken, and it is I who am to blame because I have spoken too much and prolonged what should have been a briefer encounter. I came to tell you two things. The first thing is that although I am no longer a policeman and Don Corleone who ruined my life is no more, I am still one who quests for justice.

What does this have to do with me?

Regarding your great father, sir. He is high, so much higher than I could ever dream of being, but even in my old age, with God's help and the force of the law I will bring him down. He was the associate of my nemesis the don and complicit in his actions and he is the one who remains and therefore.

You came to threaten me and my family. I think you have outstayed your welcome.

No, sir, again I have said too much and strayed from the point. I did not come to threaten. I came to warn.

Of what?

A family that has been too much involved with the dons, Mr Mastan said, and then without so much as a word of farewell it ups sticks and departs. Such a family may have left behind, in this town, persons with hurt feelings. With hurt feelings and business that is incomplete. With, perhaps, thoughts of having been left in a bad place owing in part to your esteemed parent's actions. These persons with hurt feelings are not big men like your father. Or perhaps a little big in their own area but, in the world at large, small. They are not without some force in the locality but it is a local force. He is maybe beyond them now. But you, innocently or foolishly or arrogantly or foolhardily, you have returned.

I think you should go, Ubah Tuur said. And once Mr Mastan had bowed and taken his leave, she said to Apu, I think we should go too. As soon as we can.

It's garbage, he said. He's just a bitter man trying to get his own back. It's an empty threat. No content.

I want to go anyway. The movie's over.

And all of a sudden he stopped arguing. Yes, he said. Agreed. Let's go.

Cut.

George Harrison played sitar on 'Within You Without You', 'Tomorrow Never Knows', 'Norwegian Wood', and 'Love You To'. The flights all left in the middle of the night so when they were packed and ready it was dark and they sat in the darkness and imagined George and Ravi Shankar sitting where they were sitting, making music. For a while they didn't speak to each other but then they did.

I'll tell you something my father told me when I was a young man, Apu said. My son, he said, the greatest force in the life of this country is not government or religion or the entrepreneurial instinct. It is briberyandcorruption. He said it like one word, like electromagnetism. Without briberyandcorruption nothing would happen. It is briberyandcorruption that oils the wheels of the nation, and it is also the solution to our nation's problems. If there is terrorism? Sit down across the table with the terrorist boss and sign a blank cheque and push it across the table and say, put as many zeros as you like. Once he has pocketed the cheque the problem is over because in our country we understand that there is honour in briberyandcorruption. Once a man has been bought, he stays bought. My father was a realist. When one works at his level then some don or other will inevitably knock on your door, either offering a bribe or requesting one. There is no way of keeping your hands clean. In America it's not so different, my father told me after the move across the oceans. Here also we have our Chicken Little, our Little Archie, our Crazy Fred, our Fat Frankie. They also believe in honour. So maybe the worlds are less different than we pretend.

He talked to you about this.

Not often, Apu said. But once or twice he made his briberyandcorruption speech. We all heard it a few times and knew it well. Beyond that I did not interfere.

How do you feel now that we're leaving, so quickly. We met, what, two people. You never showed me where you went to school. We haven't bought a pirate video. We haven't been here yet.

I feel relieved.

Why relieved?

I don't need to be here any more.

And how do you feel about feeling relieved? That you're pleased to be leaving? Isn't that a strange feeling?

Not really.

Why?

Because I've come to believe in the total mutability of the self. That under the pressures of one's life one can simply cease to be who one was and be just the person that one has become.

I don't agree.

Our whole bodies change all the time. Our hair, our skin, everything. During the course of seven-year cycles every cell that makes us up is replaced by another cell. Every seven years we are one hundred per cent not who we were. Why should this not also be the case with the self? It's pretty much seven years since I left this place. I'm different now.

I'm not sure about the science on that.

I'm not talking about science. I'm talking about the soul. The soul that is not made of cells. The ghost in the machine. I'm saying that in time the old ghost moves out and a new ghost moves in.

So seven years from now I won't know who you are.

And I won't know who you are. Maybe we have to start over. Maybe we are inconstant. That's just how it is.

Maybe.

Cut.

The night was humid. Even the crows were asleep. Sad-faced Mr Brown and the other reservoir dogs were waiting out front, wearing shades in spite of the darkness.

We dismissed your taxi, Mr Brown said. It is our duty to bring you to Chhatrapati Shivaji International Airport, formerly Sahar.

That is annoying of you, Apu said. We don't need you.

It will be our honour, Mr Brown said. See, three Mercedes-Benz sedans are waiting. Lead car, your car and backup car. Please. Only the best for you, sirji. S-class Maybach, like a private jet for the road. This is written in the literature. I myself will accompany you in this primo vehicle.

The night city concealed its nature from him as he left it, turned its back on him as he had turned his back on it. The faces of the buildings were grim and closed. They crossed Mahim Bay on the Sea Link but then left the Western Express Highway too early, before the airport exit.

Why are you going this way? Apu Golden asked and then Mr Brown turned around and took off his sunglasses and no answer was necessary.

It is a business matter, Mr Brown said. It is not personal. It is a question of one client outbidding another. One client from whom there is no work since a long time versus another, regular customer. Sir, it is to send a message to your esteemed fatherji. He will understand the message, I am certain of it.

I don't understand, Ubah cried. What message?

Mr Brown replied gravely: The message says, your actions, sir, made things difficult for us, after we warned you not to act. But after you acted you put continents and oceans between us and we did not have the means or will to follow. But now you have unwisely allowed your son to come. That approximately is the communication. I offer my apologies, madam, you are an innocent bystander, isn't it, you are collateral damage. It is my great regret.

The cars drove along an unimportant bridge across the Mithi River near the edges of the great Dharavi slum, and in the glistening silver Maybach the music was turned up very loud. Rich people enjoying themselves. What else. Why not. No question of any gunshots being heard. Anyway, the silencer was on.

24

Funerals happen quickly in the tropics, but murder investigations inevitably force delays. I was at the Golden house every day after the news broke and it seemed that the calamity had stopped time. Nothing and nobody seemed to move except in the room where Ms Blather and Ms Fuss were making arrangements for the return of the bodies and even their office seemed to be draped in a cloth of silence. Petya had come home to be near his father, but was mostly closeted with the Australian therapist in the room of blue light. D Golden spent most days in the house too, lost in a corner dressed in black with Riya holding his hand. Nobody spoke. Outside the house, for a moment, the story roared. Frankie Sottovoce was everywhere mourning the death of his star sculptor. The dead woman's family, tall and graceful, carrying themselves as nobly as royal sentinels, stood behind Sottovoce on television in dry-eyed sorrow. Nero Golden did not appear in public but it was plain to those of us inside the house that something had broken in him, that the message he had received was not one from which he would easily recover. On the other side of the world also there was both noise and silence. There were policemen and autopsies and journalists and all the siren sounds that follow a violent death but those who had known the family before its departure for New York remained invisible, no word from any of them, as if the silence had fallen over the Goldens' lost world too, like a shroud. The unidentified woman who had greeted Apu in the hotel lobby with cries of 'Groucho!' – she was not to be seen. The other women he had spoken of, his three former loves, the circling exes, did not appear to mourn him. It seemed that the city had turned its back on the departed, both the expatriates and the deceased. If Mr Brown and his associates were arrested we did not hear of it. The news fell out of the headlines. Groucho was dead. Life went on.

The two dragon ladies at the Golden house, as expected, proved more than equal to the task of bringing the bodies home speedily once they had been released by the Mumbai authorities. A reputable firm, cumbersomely named IFSPFP – International Funeral Shipping Program Funeral Providers – was engaged and quickly made all the correct preparations for transportation, including sealer caskets and USA-approved shipping containers. They did the paperwork, acquiring certified English translations of the death certificates and written authorisation from the local authorities to remove the bodies, and found an early shipping window so that Apu and Ubah could return to New York City as promptly as possible. On the tarmac of JFK a sad parting occurred. Frankie Sottovoce and the Somali artist's family took possession of Ubah's body and carried it away to be buried according to their practice. Apu came back to Macdougal Street.

It was a strange and broken farewell. The sealer casket was not opened. The body had not been embalmed and so state law did not permit open-casket viewing. When Nero refused to permit any form of religious ceremony to be carried out and specified cremation rather than burial, the IFSPFP funeral director bowed his head and suggested he leave the family for an hour and then return. Later he would bring back the cremains. Or he would dispose of them if that was what was preferred. 'No,' Nero said. 'Bring him back.' The funeral director inclined his head once more. 'If I may,' he said softly. 'There is no law in this state that says where you may keep or scatter ashes. You may keep them in a crypt, niche, grave, or in a container at home, as you think best. If you choose to scatter them, do so as you please, but refrain from placing them where they are obvious to others. Cremation renders ashes harmless, so there is no public health risk involved. Scattering on private land requires the landowner's consent, and it is wise to check local ordinance zoning if you wish to scatter on public lands. If you wish to scatter off the coast or out of New York Harbor you need to bear in mind Environmental Protection Agency regulations regarding burial at sea – '

'Stop,' said Nero Golden. 'Stop at once, and go away immediately.'

During the hour that followed no word was spoken. Vasilisa took the child Vespasian upstairs and the rest of us stood or sat in the company of the casket, each of us alone with our own thoughts. During this awful hour I realised that Apu in death had finally persuaded me of something which I had resisted through our friendship: that the human ineffable invariably coexisted with the properly knowable, and that there were mysteries in men which explanations could not explain. No matter how I tried I could not understand the ease with which he, of all the Goldens, had agreed to shed his Indian skin and head west from his city to the Village. The old man had enough dark doings in his past, and Petya had enough real and present damage, and Dionysus enough secret longings for his future, to explain their choices, but Apu had been deeply involved in the life of his home town, loving and being loved, and heartbreak seemed an insufficient explanation for his willingness to go. The voice of reason in me proposed that of all Nero's sons he had seen most clearly into his father's shadows and had been scared by what he saw there, and maybe that was a part of the truth. Maybe what he said, about being raised in the old ways, so that his father's decision was simply the law which had to be followed, had something to do with it also. But another voice, the voice he had instilled in me and which I had resisted, now conjured up a different scene, in which he sat, cross-legged perhaps and meditating on the wide marble terrace of the old family house on the hill, his eyes closed, looking inward or wherever he looked for guidance, and heard another voice, not the voice that was murmuring to me, or maybe it was the same voice, or maybe it was his own voice or a voice he made up, or maybe, as he would put it, he tapped into the thing he always believed was there, the universe-sound, the wisdom of all that there was, the voice he trusted; and that voice said *Go.* And so, like Joan of Arc, like Saint John the Divine, like the 'Apu Golden' he invented, on whom his old self's ghosts came calling in New York – like the mystic he was, listening to his voices, or *on impulse* as we sceptics might say, he went.

The mystical experience existed. I understood that. When my rational self reasserted itself it would say, yes, agreed, but it was an interior experience, not an exterior one; subjective, not objective. If I had stood beside Apu in his Union Square studio I would not have seen his ghosts. If I had knelt beside him on that Walkeshwar terrace seven and a half years ago the Force would not have spoken to me. Not everyone can become a Jedi knight. Many Australians say they can, that's true. And Apu, perhaps, learned how to trust and use what he once called the spirit level. But no, no, not I.

For forty days and nights after Apu's return, the Golden house was in mourning, off-limits, its curtains drawn at noon as well as midnight, its shutters shuttered, and if anyone came and went they did so as ethereally as ghosts. Nero vanished from view. It was my guess that Petya had moved back in and maybe Lett the therapist was there also, but that was just speculation. Petya Golden did not visit his brother's coffin while it stood in the great room of the Golden house, did not forgive him, never spoke his name again, and never asked what happened to Ubah's body, was there a grave he could visit, he never asked. Some wounds do not heal. The folk in the Gardens got on with their lives and respected the withdrawal of the wounded house from their little world. I didn't go there though my desire to see the little fellow Vespasian was as strong as ever. Once I thought about contacting Vasilisa to plead for some time with him but I knew the blunt response I would get, and held my tongue. It was a busy time for me anyway; Suchitra and I had our hands full. In that political season we were drawn into the world of political videos, for women's groups in particular, defending Planned Parenthood, attacking the Republican insensitivity to women's issues. We were becoming famous; that year our videos swept the Pollie awards for political ads, in particular for a piece in which a child victim of sex trafficking told her story. Suchitra – her professional name shortened to Suchi Roy for ease of pronunciation – was becoming a bit of a media star, and I was happy to be her helpmate. So I turned away from death and toward life. But life had become noisy and even alarming that year. Beyond the closed world of the Gardens, things were getting very strange.

To step outside that enchanted – and now tragic – cocoon was to discover that America had left reality behind and entered the comic-book universe; DC, Suchitra said, was under attack by DC. It was the year of the Joker in Gotham and beyond. The Caped Crusader was nowhere to be seen – it was not an age of heroes – but his arch-rival in the purple frock coat and striped pantaloons was ubiquitous, clearly delighted to have the stage to himself and hogging the limelight with evident delight. He had seen off the Suicide Squad, his feeble competition, but he permitted a few of his inferiors to think of themselves as future members of a Joker administration. The Penguin, the Riddler, Two-Face and Poison Ivy lined up behind the Joker in packed arenas, swaying like doo-wop backing singers while their leader spoke of the unrivalled beauty of white skin and red lips to adoring audiences wearing green fright wigs and chanting in unison, *Ha! Ha! Ha!*

The origins of the Joker were disputed, the man himself seemed to enjoy allowing contradictory versions to fight for airspace, but on one fact everyone, passionate supporters and bitter antagonists, was agreed: he was utterly and certifiably insane. What was astonishing, what made this an election year like no other, was that people backed him *because* he was insane, not in spite of it. What would have disqualified any other candidate made him his followers' hero. Sikh taxi drivers and rodeo cowboys, rabid alt-right blondes and black brain surgeons agreed, we love his craziness, no milquetoast euphemisms from him, he shoots straight from the hip, says whatever he fucking wants to say, robs whatever bank he's in the mood to rob, kills whoever he feels like killing, he's our guy. The black bat-knight has flown! It's a new day, and it's going to be a scream! All hail the United States of Joker! USJ! USJ! USJ!

It was a year of two bubbles. In one of those bubbles, the Joker shrieked and the laugh-track crowds laughed right on cue. In that bubble the climate was not changing and the end of the Arctic ice cap was just a new real estate opportunity. In that bubble, gun murderers were exercising their constitutional rights but the parents of murdered children were un-American. In that bubble, if its inhabitants were victorious, the president of the neighbouring country to the south which was sending rapists and killers to America would be forced to pay for a wall dividing the two nations to keep the killers and rapists south of the border where they belonged; and crime would end; and the country's enemies would be defeated instantly and overwhelmingly; and mass deportations would be a good thing; and women reporters would be seen to be unreliable because they had blood coming out of their whatevers; and the parents of dead war heroes would be revealed to be working for radical Islam; and international treaties would not have to be honoured; and Russia would be a friend and that would have nothing whatsoever to do with the Russian oligarchs propping up the Joker's shady enterprises; and the meanings of things would change; multiple bankruptcies would be understood to prove great business expertise; and three and a half thousand lawsuits against you would be understood to prove business acumen; and stiffing your contractors would prove your tough-guy business attitude; and a crooked university would prove your commitment to education; and while the Second Amendment would be sacred the First would not be; so those who criticised the leader would suffer consequences; and African Americans would go along with it all because what the hell did they have to lose. In that bubble knowledge was ignorance, up was down, and the right person to hold the nuclear codes in his hand was the green-haired white-skinned red-slash-mouthed giggler who asked a military briefing team four times why using nuclear weapons was so bad. In that bubble, razor-tipped playing cards were funny, and lapel flowers that sprayed acid into people's faces were funny, and wishing you could have sex with your daughter was funny, and sarcasm was funny even when what was called sarcasm was not sarcastic, and lying was funny, and hatred was funny, and bigotry was funny, and bullying was funny, and the date was, or almost was, or might soon be, if the jokes worked out as they should, nineteen eighty-four.

In the other bubble – as my parents had taught me long ago – was the city of New York. In New York, for the moment, at least, a kind of reality still persevered, and New Yorkers could identify a con man when they saw one. In Gotham we knew who the Joker was, and wanted nothing to do with him, or the daughter he lusted after, or the daughter he never mentioned, or the sons who murdered elephants and leopards for sport. 'I'll take Manhattan!' the Joker screeched, hanging from the top of a skyscraper, but we laughed at him and not at his bombastic jokery, and he had to take his act on the road to places where people hadn't gotten his number yet, or, worse, knew very well what he was and loved him for it: the segment of the country that was as crazy as he. His people. Too many of them for comfort.

It was the year of the great battle between deranged fantasy and grey reality, between, on the one hand, *la chose en soi*, the possibly unknowable but probably existing thing in itself, the world as it was independently of what was said about it or how it was seen, the *Ding an sich,* to use the Kantian term – and, on the other, this cartoon character who had crossed the line between the page and the stage – a sort of illegal immigrant, I thought – whose plan was to turn the whole country, faux-hilariously, into a lurid graphic novel, the modern kind, full of black crime and renegade Jews and cocksuckers and cunts, which were words he liked to use sometimes just to give the liberal elite conniptions; a comic book in which elections were rigged and the media were crooked and everything you hated was a conspiracy against you, but in the end! Yay! You won, the fright wig turned into a crown, and the Joker became the King.

It remained to be seen if, come November, the country would turn out to be in a New York state of mind, or if it would prefer to put on the green fright wigs and laugh. *Ha! Ha! Ha!*

25

As the drama of the tragedy of the Golden house moves into its later acts, I return my attention – now! But I was derelict in my duty then! – to the increasingly painful life of Dionysus Golden. It was hard to be in any kind of regular contact with [him]. (I still used the male pronouns when I thought about [him], though that increasingly felt wrong, and so as a gesture toward [his] ambiguity I put them in square brackets. In the absence of clear guidance from [him] – 'I don't yet know what my pronouns are,' [he] told me with a kind of embarrassment – this was my interim solution.) The world around D, the world in which D felt any kind of a sense of safety, had diminished to two and a half places: the Two Bridges Girls Club on Market Street near three playgrounds in the angle of the Manhattan Bridge and the FDR, where [he] volunteered four days a week, and the Chinatown apartment where [he] lived with Riya Z. Sometimes they went to the nightspot on Orchard Street where fire-haired Ivy Manuel sang – this was the half-place in [his] comfort zone – but then there was the question of how to dress, and who might approach, saying what, and D's growing and crippling shyness. At 2-Bridge the problem of attire was solved by the club's unisex staff uniform, a white collared shirt worn over and outside loose black Chinese pants, and black sneakers on the feet, but everywhere else D was at a loss to know how to present [himself]. After [his] adventure in Vasilisa's clothes closet [he] had admitted to [himself] [his] pleasure in women's clothing and had found the courage to tell Riya what had occurred and Ivy also and they had talked about it. 'Good,' Riya said. 'It's a first step. Think of this as the beginning of the next three years or so. Think of transition as slow magic. Your private one thousand and one nights, in which you stop being the frog you don't want to be and you become, maybe, the princess.' And Ivy added, 'But you don't have to go further than you want to. Maybe you're just a frog who wants to look pretty in pink.'

[He] was getting professional help but it didn't really help. [He] kept wanting to argue with the Professional. [He] refused to tell me who the Professional was; instead, [he] used me to vent the frustrations [he] kept to [himself] around Riya, whose thing was identity, who had dedicated herself to the idea of the transmorphic fluidity of the self, and who sometimes seemed just a little too eager for D's MTF transition to occur, and to be a complete metamorphosis. I should have been able to help [him]. Maybe I could have prevented what happened. Maybe we all could. Or maybe D Golden was just unsuitable for life on earth.

I imagine the following conversation taking place in a bare, black-and-white, cell-like room, with the speaker sitting expressionless on an upright metal chair, and [his] interrogator, the Professional, as a highly sophisticated android, a sort of combination of Alicia Vikander in Ex Machina *and the supercomputer Alpha Soixante in Godard's* Alphaville. *We do not hear either of the figures in the room speaking. There is no sync sound. We hear only the Monologue; although, as the Monologue quotes direct speech, the lip movements of the figures in the room sometimes – not always – match what is being narrated. There is something about the scene that is like an encounter between a prisoner and [his] attorney on visiting day in jail. It would not be surprising if the speaker were wearing an orange jumpsuit (if the scene were in colour), or shackles on [his] wrists and ankles. There is also something about the scene which, if properly filmed, might be funny.*

Monologue of D Golden Regarding [His] Own Sexuality & Its Examination by the Professional

Chapter One. She asks me, right at the beginning, the Professional, comes right out with it, first question, when you were a child, did you prefer the colour pink or the colour blue?

I am frankly amazed by the enquiry. Is this a question to be asked at this date in the history of the world, I say: blue or pink?

Indulge me, she says, humour me, as if she's the patient and I'm the shrink.

I reply, because I'm in that kind of obstinate mood now, Diana Vreeland, editor of *Vogue,* once said that pink is the navy blue of India, so I guess pink and blue in India are the same thing.

Why do you find this question so irritating, she asks, it's just a choice between two colours. I might also ask, did you prefer train sets or dolls. Would you rather answer that question instead.

I should say now in parenthesis that I have never been a Marxist but her line of attack provoked in me strong anti-capitalist sentiments. I thought, I replied, that we had moved beyond the materialist categories imposed by the market, pink for a girl, blue for a boy, trains and guns for boys, dolls and frocks for girls. Why are you trying to push me back into this antique, exploded discourse?

You are responding with considerable hostility, she said. Have I touched on something that triggers this display of emotion?

OK, I said, the truth is that my favorite colour was yellow and remains yellow. For a time I tried to swear in yellow like Stephen Dedalus's friend, *damn your yellow stick,* but I couldn't hang on to the habit.

Good, she said, this is progress, yellow on the spectrum is halfway between the blue and the pink. I thought that was very stupid, Neanderthal stupid, Cro-Magnon stupid, but I swallowed that back and didn't say it. Maybe this isn't for me, I thought.

As to the other question, I told her, I never had a train set. My brothers had one and I watched them play, though they were too old for toys. Also Scalextric cars, it was embarrassing, I mean, grow up. I was the much younger half-brother, you see. Me, I had a pair of sandalwood animals to put in the bath because water released their perfume. A sandalwood elephant and a camel. I made up adventures for my sandalwood friends and each night there was a different bath-time story. What the elephant hid in his trunk, why the camel hated the desert, and so on. Maybe I should have written them down. I don't remember most of them now. So, in answer to your questions, I suppose, if the choice is dolls or trains, well then, sandalwood animal dolls. I never dressed them up, however. I only told them stories and got them wet.

So we went on, she pushing, I pushing back. At a certain point I told her the story of my stepmother and the keys to the house. I admit it: the worst thing I ever did. I told the Professional so. I told her my regret. She wasn't interested in regret, she went down the same road Riya was on when we had our fight and I got out of the car. Hatred was not enough to explain why I did that, she said. In the end we got to it. Suppose I suggest, she said, that you wanted to be the lady of the house. Suppose that I suggest that that was at the bottom of it. What's your immediate reaction to that. So my immediate reaction was, boom!, I'm out of here, this isn't going to work, and when I'm almost at the door she asks, quietly, what are you going to do instead, and I stop, my outstretched hand falls away from the doorknob, and I come back and sit down and I say, I guess maybe you're right. So what does that make me. Who am I.

That is what we're here to find out, the Professional said.

Chapter Two. I ask some more about the toys and colours. Once upon a time, I say, if a boy liked pink and dolls his parents would be afraid he was homosexual and try to interest him in boy stuff. I'm saying they might have doubts about his orientation but it wouldn't occur to them to question his gender. Now it seems you go to the other extreme. Instead of saying the kid's a pansy you start trying to persuade him he's a girl.

OK, she said, then are you gay? Are you physically attracted to other guys? No, I said. This is maybe the only thing I know I am not. Good, she said. So let us stop trying to untangle the motivations of imaginary parents and focus on the task in hand, which is you. If you are not a male homosexual are you a female homosexual?

What, I said.

Are you a lesbian, the Professional asked.

I'm not yet in transition and I am living with a heterosexual woman, I said.

In the first place we are not discussing your lover's sexuality which may also be complex and which you may be simplifying to make it serve you better, but this is not the subject. And in the second place the question does not have to do with what you are doing but with who you are. It's the difference between saying, I work as a pizza chef, and I'm a person who loves good food.

You're weird, I told the Professional.

I am not the subject, the Professional said.

How can I be a lesbian, I protested, it's physically impossible.

Why.

For obvious reasons.

So, two questions. The first question: have you ever felt attracted to a lesbian woman? To a woman who prefers to make love with other women?

There have been occasions, I said. One or two. I did not pursue them.

Why.

For obvious reasons. They would not have wished to sleep with me.

Why.

Oh come on.

Very well. Second question. What is a woman?

This is a mystifying question that suddenly makes me feel extremely foreign. I cannot imagine it being asked in most of the countries of the world. Is this something Americans have become confused about? Are you going to ask me about toilet facilities? Are you going to recall the banning of *The Vagina Monologues* at Mount Holyoke College?

Is this something *you* are confused about.

I know what a woman is. I just don't know if I am one. Or if I want to be one. Or if I have the courage to become one. I am very much afraid I do not have the courage. In general, I am very much afraid.

Of what are you afraid.

The nakedness of the change. Its drama, the extremeness of the alteration, its appalling visibility. The gaze of others. The judgement of others. The injections. The surgery. The surgery above all else. This is natural, correct?

I don't know the meaning of that word, *natural.* It is a word that has been misused for so long that it is better not to use it. Another such word is the word *sex.*

I live with someone who would agree with you.

Allow me to propose a sentence to you. 'There is no such thing as a woman's body.'

By which you obviously do not mean to say that there is no such thing as a woman's body. Because there are women, that can't be denied, and there are bodies, this is also objectively true, and the one is contained within the other. *Ergo* . . .

You have grasped my point, even as you argued with it. We exist and so do our bodies and we inhabit our bodies but we are neither defined by them nor confined by them.

And so we arrive at the mind–body problem. You propose that we should reject the idea that there exists one unifying reality, substance or essence, and so the separation of mind and body is impossible. This is monism and you don't like it? You prefer Descartes and his duality. But is *woman,* then, or even *female,* a category of the mind alone? Is there no physicality to it? And is this non-corporeal gender, this disembodied non-physical thing, incapable of change, even though by reason of being non-physical it ought to be as mutable as smoke, as the breeze? Or are we in religious, or perhaps Aristotelian, territory, and gender, like mind, is a quality of the soul? I have been doing my reading. But this is hard for me to grasp.

I will put it simply. To be born with female genitalia and reproductive organs does not make you a woman. To be born with male genitalia does not make you a man. Unless you so choose. This is the proposition to which I am asking you to respond. That there is nothing definingly female about a vagina. Nor are you excluded from the female if you possess a male member. A trans woman with a penis is still a woman. Can you agree with this or not?

You mean I might not need to have the surgery.

The castration.

Even the word hurts.

Not unless that is what you choose.

So we're back at this *choosing*.

I could propose you call it freedom. I could say, this is your right.

I know something about choosing. I am from a family that chose to transform itself. I chose the name by which you call me. I chose to leave the world that made me to come to a world in which maybe I could make myself. I'm in favour of choosing. I have already been transformed once by this choice I made. But.

But.

If I say I'm a woman but I keep my male organ and then I'm among lesbian women and I want to have sex but they don't want to have sex with a person with a male organ then how am I a woman if my choosing to be a woman is not acceptable to women.

If a person reacts to you in that way then that person would be a TERF.

TERF.

Trans exclusionary radical feminist.

And that's a bad thing to be.

In the conversation we are having, that is a bad thing to be, yes.

So you take these women with vaginas who won't have sex with women who have penises and you call them by a bad name and say they are bad people and how does that help me.

It helps you stand by your choice.

Because I am right and they are wrong.

There is a women's private festival in Michigan and it's forty years old, a place for women to come together and make music and cook and talk and simply be together, and these are some of the women who made the women's movement, cis women, older women, mostly, revolutionaries in their own time. But they will not allow trans women with male organs to be a part of the event and so there is a dispute that is on the edge of being a physical fight. Trans activists camp outside the festival with weapons, and they plan protests and disruptions and sometimes carry them out, graffiti, cut water lines, slashed tyres and flyers of their penises. I am proposing that in this dispute the women with vaginas are wrong because they cannot adapt to a different time in which a woman with a vagina is just one kind of woman and other kinds of women are as much women as they are. If you choose to be an American and become a citizen you don't have to give up everything about who you were before. You yourself became an American but when you are challenged you say that you feel foreign so you have kept your foreign part in some way intact. If you choose to be a woman the same liberty exists. And if somebody tries to exclude you from your gender choice it is your right to protest.

But what if I can't see that these choices are choices. What if I learned from the male gay community that homosexuality was inborn, that it was a human way to be, it couldn't be chosen or unchosen, and what if I hated the reactionary idea that you could re-educate a gay person to make a different choice and give up his gayness. What if I can't see how these choices you are proposing, these multiple-possibility gender nuances, are not part of that same reactionary ideology, because what is chosen can be unchosen, and it's a lady's right to change her mind. What if I propose that my identity is just difficult, and painful, and confusing, and I don't know how to choose or what to choose or even if choosing is what has to happen, what if I just need to stagger blindly toward finding out what I am and not who I choose to be. What if I believe there is an *I am* and I need to find that. What if this is about discovery not choice, about finding out who I've always been, not about picking a flavour from the gender ice-cream display. What if I think that if a woman's *I am* means she can't have sex with a woman with a male organ then that needs to be respected. What if I worry that there could be a civil war on this side of the gender divide and what if I think that's the wrong war. What if we are all separate kinds of women and not all the same, and if separations, including sexual separations, are OK and not bigoted or bad. What if we're a federation of different states of being and we need to respect those states' rights as well as the union. I'm losing my mind trying to work all this out and I don't even know the words, I'm using the words I know but they feel like the wrong words all the time, what if I'm trying to live in a dangerous country whose language I haven't learned. What then.

Then I would say, we have work to do to break the cotton ceiling in your head.

Which is.

Underwear is made of cotton. The contents of a trans woman's underwear act as an axis to oppress and marginalise her. Quote unquote.

Somebody told my girlfriend a joke about becoming a transbillionaire. I identify as a billionaire and so now I'm rich, she said. How would you respond to that?

That isn't funny.

[He] reached the threshold but [he] never entered the room. Trapped between the fear and the language, [he] found [himself] unable to move, but [he] couldn't stay where [he] was, either. The warning signs were plain enough. Riya got a call from the 2-Bridge girls' club telling her, not unkindly, that they had had to ask [him] to stop coming in, because [he] had begun to importune the girls with intensely personal questions and they were no longer comfortable with having [him] around. The atmosphere at 2-Bridge was at once relaxed and committed, the girls felt at ease and worked hard in social justice or environmental education programmes, or learning digital and audio arts, or doing introductory STEM courses, or helping to run the building's astonishing planetarium (a gift from a wealthy benefactor), or studying dance or nutrition. I visited [him] there in the early days of [his] volunteer work, before the downward spiral began, and [he] seemed happy around their happiness, and their relaxed attitude to gender diversity seemed to help [him]. Gay or straight, cis or trans, asterisk or no asterisk, genderqueer or agender, none of this was a problem. At first this was encouraging, even exciting, but as [he] confronted [his] own roadblocks to transition, [his] physical and social fears and [his] difficulty with the new language, it didn't help [him] to think that [he] might be suffering from generational problems, by which the generation following [him] was untroubled. I thought of the early Neanderthals in Golding's *The Inheritors* looking with anger and uncomprehending envy upon the new, more sophisticated, fire-owning human race, *Homo sapiens*, when it showed up for the first time and doomed them, the forerunners, to extinction. So [he] began to see [himself] as a primitive entity, and the girls at 2-Bridge as the new people who were better than [he] was but who were also [his] replacements, able to go where [he] could not, able to enter the promised land which was barred to [him] by the limitations of [his] perceptions. So [he] began to harry them, to corner them in the canteen or at the doors of their classrooms or at play on the nearby softball field or hockey rink, to ask for answers they did not have and advice they did not know how to give, and, becoming aggressive, to upset them. [His] dismissal was inevitable. [He] accepted it without demur.

We took our eyes off [him]. No question of that. We should have seen [his] growing fragility and maybe we did but we all chose to look elsewhere. After Apu's murder Nero Golden withdrew from all society into a darkness whose apparent cause was obvious but whose more occult meaning would only later become clear. He kept the urn containing his son's ashes on his desk and, it was said, talked to him continually, every day. The two dragon ladies had access to him, and he made time for Petya, always made time for his most obviously troubled child, was constantly forgiving and supportive as Petya slowly made his way back from arson to his better self; but for his rudderless and crashing no-longer-youngest son he had next to nothing. What he did have was young Vespasian and a wife who found many ways of insisting on the infant's special claims on his father's affections. Little Vespa, they called him, as if he were a motor scooter they could both ride back to happiness. In little Vespa's company Nero's face was sometimes softened by a smile. Vasilisa treated her husband with the same motherly care she lavished on her young pride and joy, in part, I'm sure, because she saw and wanted to lessen his grief, but also, I have no doubt, for selfish reasons. Of all of us she was the one who saw most clearly the dwindling of this bullish and ferocious man. She saw the advance of his forgetfulness, the loosening of his grip on the chariot reins, and understood that in time he would be her baby too, and all this she was willing to accept because the prize at the end of her project was very great. (My thoughts regarding Vasilisa had soured considerably since the birth of my son and the wall she subsequently erected between the boy and me.) Vasilisa's mother was in the house too but Nero had taken against her and Vasilisa kept her headscarfed babushka away, essentially using her as little Vespa's nurse. In their relationship, it was clear, the mother had no power. She did as she was told. And she too was biding her time. She too knew the nature of the game that was being played. She stayed in the background and sang Russian songs to the boy and told him Russian stories, including perhaps the story of Baba Yaga, the witch, so that he could grow up knowing the score. If she had been able to read children's books in the English language she might have said that Vespasian was the golden snitch.

26

I took my eyes off D Golden too. All that summer and fall Suchitra and I were busy with the Batwoman. In that electorally surreal year our sudden elevation by the video awards system to the status of political-ad stars had attracted the attention of progressive advocacy groups and big-money super-PACs supporting the Joker's formidable, eminently qualified but unpopular opponent. The animated cartoon we made for one such advocacy group, with the help of some of the best artists ever to draw the Joker, went viral, the grinning villain in midtown New York screeching out lines his political incarnation had actually used, sneering at his own party, *The fools! I could shoot someone dead in Times Square and I wouldn't lose any votes!* until a female superheroine in bat-gear swooped down to put him in a straitjacket and hand him over to the white-coated men from the funny farm. Political Batwoman was born and the candidate, or her people, reposted our ad on the official social media of the campaign, and it got three million hits in the first twenty-four hours, and in the end we made three follow-ups that all did just about as well. The election became a contest between the Batwoman and the Joker–Batwoman, who owned her dark side, but used it to fight for good, justice, and the American way, a leader who could save the country from becoming a calamitous Joke. We defined the struggle; it became what we said it was.

The Batwoman idea was Suchitra's, though a lot of the scripting was done by me, or by the two of us together. We were a good team, but I kept wondering what she saw in me; we were so unequal, her non-stop creative brilliance so much brighter than my own little light, that there were times when I felt like her pet. Late one night when we were done with work I had enough to drink and asked her, and she laughed and laughed. 'What a pair we are,' she said, 'both of us so insecure and neither of us aware at all of the other's insecurity.' Didn't I see? I was the one with the education, I was the intellectual, I was the one who saw connections and references and echoes and arguments and shapes, she just knew how to point the camera and do a lot of other tech stuff. And that was absurdly undervaluing herself, but now it was her insecurity speaking. I reminded her of just one of the beautiful things she had taught me. An image has a shape and so does sound and so does montage and so does drama. The film sense is that art which ensures that the four shapes are the same. This was her adaptation of the theories of Sergei Eisenstein, director of *Alexander Nevsky* and *The Battleship Potemkin*. 'OK,' she conceded with a grin when I reminded her. 'Yeah, OK, that was pretty good.'

Those confessions – my sense of creative inferiority, her feeling of intellectual lessness – brought us much closer. This is how we are: we fall in love with each other's strengths, but love deepens toward permanence when we fall in love with each other's weaknesses. We fell into the love that had been lying beneath our love like water below ice, and understood that while we had been having a lot of fun together we had been only skating on the surface, and now we were in as deep as we could go. I had never had a feeling like it, and nor had she, she said, and we stared at each other in a kind of happy disbelief. So this was where my attention was. As the Golden family plummeted, I soared. We soared, my honey lamb and I, and like the hawk in *Oklahoma!*, we made lazy circles in the sky.

'Oh, incidentally,' she said, somewhere in the middle of the bliss, 'you know those three rules that I may have mentioned?'

'"Make your own money, get your own apartment, and don't ask me to marry you." Yes?'

'I think they may be negotiable.'

'Oh.'

'"Oh"? Really? That's all you've got?'

'I was just wondering,' I said, 'how to break the news to my landlord, U Lnu Fnu.'

'For catfish,' said U Lnu Fnu, 'I go sometimes to the Whole Foods on Union Square, but they don't always have. Otherwise to Chinatown. Also necessary, vermicelli noodles, fish sauce, fish paste, ginger, banana stem, lemongrass, onions, garlic, chickpea flour. Sit and be patient, please. This is traditional breakfast of my country: mohinga. Sit down, please.'

'Mr U,' I began. He stopped me with a gentle raised arm. 'Now at the end I must correct you,' he said. 'You know, this "U" is not a name, but a title of respect given to older men holding senior positions. Also to monks. So "Mr U" is like saying, "Mr Sir". Lnu was my father's name which I also took. You should address me as Fnu. That is best.'

'Mr Fnu . . .'

'Fnu. Now we are friends. Eat your mohinga.'

'Fnu.'

'I know what you want to say. You want to go and live with your girl, so you are giving notice, but because you love the Gardens you want to ask if it is possible to keep the access key. And because you are polite and you know I am living in solitude you will say, you have come to be very fond of me, you want often to pay a visit, and yada yada yada.'

'You watched *Seinfeld*?'

'Every episode, also now reruns.'

'How did you know?'

'Your girl, she called me, because she knows you become tongue-tied when you have to ask for something. Which it is my pleasure to give. Keep the key. I will rent your room to someone else, naturally, but you are always welcome to pass by.'

'The Gardens are so beautiful at this time of year.'

'I will never go home,' the old diplomat said. 'Not even to the changing

Myanmar of Daw Aung San Suu Kyi. There is a point on the journey at which the traveller sits down by the river and knows it's the end of the road. There is a day when he accepts that the idea of return is an illusion.'

'I'm sorry,' I said, not finding any better words.

'Also the Goldens are so interesting, aren't they?' said U Lnu Fnu, cheering up, actually clapping his hands, and revealing a hitherto unsuspected catty side to his character. 'They are falling apart as one watches, and nowadays I have a lot of time to watch.'

What sort of man was I, breakfasting on fish and noodles with an elderly lonely Burmese (Myanmaran) gentleman and pretending my love for the Gardens was merely horticultural and nostalgic. What sort of man, planning to live with the woman who loved him, preserved his ability to enter the secret space where his secret child was to be found, daily, in a stroller, guarded by a fierce Russian matriarch; and yet kept his fatherhood secret, even from his true love. What sort of man, raised in that very space by people of principle, raised to be honourable and true, would succumb as readily as he had to a siren's call. Perhaps all men were traitors. Perhaps good men were just traitors who had not yet reached the fork in their road. Or perhaps my desire to generalise from my own behaviour was just a way of excusing myself for what I had too easily done.

And Suchitra making the call to my landlord: was that loving, or was that a little strange? Did she know more than I thought? And if so, what did her behaviour mean? – But of course she knew nothing about the boy. Thus guilty secrets make paranoids of us all.

Even as my personal happiness increased, so did my unspoken self-criticism, and yet, and yet, in spite of everything, here in the Gardens was my son. How could I turn my back on him and walk away – even into a life rich with love? Often now, very often, I rued the day when I allowed myself – when I chose! – to be drawn into the orbit of the Golden house, displaying such poor foresight that I believed that they were and would be my subjects and my passports to my cinematic future, that I would be the one with power over the narrative, and I failed to see that I was the subject, not any Golden man, and that the way the story worked out would tell me more about myself than about anyone else. Like many young men I was in many ways a secret from myself and from those who loved me, and before all was done those secrets would have to be revealed.

After Hubris comes Nemesis: *Adrasteia*, the inescapable. A good man may be a bad man, and a bad woman may be good. To be untrue to thyself, youth!, that is the highest treason. Even the strongest fortresses can be taken by a siege. And the sky that we look upon may tumble and fall, and a mountain may crumble to the sea. And in the end your rough magic, O Prospero!, will eat you away unless, like Ariel, you set it free. Unless you break your staff.

The magic baby in Aeschylus' *The Net Fishers* turned out to be the superhero Perseus. The magic baby in Sophocles' *The Trackers* turned out to be the god Hermes. Now there was Vespasian, named for an emperor, the magic baby in the Gardens and in my heart. To survive, did I have to let him go? Did I have to set him free?

The Clinton Oaks Correctional Facility in Jefferson Heights, Minnesota, was the only maximum-security prison in the state. After the escape of two inmates, however, investigators found that guards there had routinely failed to perform security rounds, and made false entries into prison logbooks to say they had, when they hadn't. As many as nineteen officers were subsequently disciplined for such failures. However, the negligence of the guards was not the primary factor in the prisoners' escape. Love – or sex and desire, anyway – turned out to be the key. The inmates, the convicted murderers Carl Zachariassen and Peter Coit, who shared a prison cell and were serving life sentences with no possibility of remission, worked in the tailor shop at the facility, and became friendly with a prison worker, Mrs Francine Otis, married, and a mother of two boys. The friendship deepened, let us not use stronger language than that, and Otis, as she afterwards confessed, had relations with both men in a storage closet leading off the long, narrow main work area of the tailor shop. Subsequently Otis brought the men the tools they needed, including metal-cutting equipment, and they proceeded with their plan. They cut rectangular holes in the steel at the backs of their cells, beneath the bunk beds, and put dummies made from sweatshirts in their beds to fool the guards when they made their rounds. (Though, as was afterwards established, the guards made no rounds that night.) Outside the hole in the cell wall was an unused catwalk which had not been patrolled for many years. They went down it five floors to a steam pipe which was off, because the weather was warm at that time of year, and cut a hole into it and crawled along to a manhole four hundred feet beyond the prison walls, where, using the tools provided by Francine Otis, they cut away the steel lock and chain with which the manhole was secured, and so made their escape.

The manhunt lasted three weeks, and involved over eight hundred officers as well as helicopters and search dogs. Zachariassen and Coit, as Otis afterwards confessed, had originally planned to meet her at a location on Route 35, where she had promised to have clothes, money and guns waiting for them, and, sadly, delusionally, was expecting them to take her with them so that they could begin a new life of love and sex in Canada; but in the event they decided not to meet her, which was just as well for her, as their original scheme had been to take what she brought them and then murder her. During the next three weeks they were sighted a few times, their scent was picked up by dogs, DNA traces were found in a forest cabin, and in the end they were cornered in the Kabetogama State Forest not far from the Canadian border. Coit was captured alive, but Zachariassen was killed resisting arrest, receiving three shots in the head. The manhunt was widely reported on the national news.

We took our eyes off D Golden because we believed that Riya Z was with [him] every day, that her eyes would see everything that needed to be seen. But for three weeks, after her father escaped from Clinton Oaks, every minute of every day and night until he was shot dead in the Kabetogama Forest, Riya was out of her mind. And this, too, was the moment when D was asked to withdraw from the 2-Bridge club. It was the perfect storm; D needing her most at the moment when her attention was elsewhere.

They're saying on the news he's trying to get to Canada but that's crap, she said, irrationally. He's trying to get to me.

This was a Riya D had never seen, frightened, uncertain, a weak electricity crackling at her edges. The one thing [he] had believed in was her. In her, [he] had found [his] miracle rock. Then she crumbled and [he] couldn't bear it.

Why would he come here to the city. It's so far, the risk is too great, and in the city he would surely be seen and caught.

The city is where you go to hide, she said. In the country, in small towns or in the fields or forests, everybody sees you and everyone knows your business. In the city you are invisible because nobody cares.

But this is halfway across the country. He won't come.

He promised me he would come. He will come.

Zachariassen didn't come. He was running for the border in a northern forest. But in spite of the reports of sightings far from New York she remained convinced he was on his way, and so she got out the pearl-handled Colt revolver and loaded it and put it in her pocketbook and even after that she was like a cat on a hot tin roof. At the Museum of Identity her colleagues noted the wild-eyed frazzle in her, the uncalm, shocking in one usually so self-possessed, and everyone had a solution, maybe she needed a vacation, maybe she was unhappy in her relationship, maybe she should start taking kava kava which was one hundred per cent organic and herbal and would really help her relax.

At night she hardly slept and sat instead by the bedroom window expecting that her murderous parent might at any moment climb up onto the flat roof outside, and on more than one occasion she came close to shooting a cat. Also more than once she did something she had never done before, which was to consult the drag queen Madame George downstairs at the Tarot Crystal Ball Horoscope Tell Ur Future salon, and when Madame George assured her that her future was long and bright she said, that's wrong, deal the cards again, and even though the fortune teller added, your boyfriend, bring him down here, he's the one I'm worried about, she didn't do as she was asked, because she thought she knew D's problems and didn't need a drag queen's help to understand him, and right now just for once it wasn't all about him it was about her and her evil bastard of a father coming after her in the night. She went to see the termagant owner of the pink-and-yellow building and started telling Mrs Run too loudly, much too loudly, that it was about time the building got a proper security system, with a video entry phone and an alarm and better locks on the exterior and interior, much better locks, anybody could get in, it was a tough and dangerous town, and she stopped only when Mrs Run told her, 'You come to me ask for light bulb in hall, I think about it. You come to me like a hopping vampire *jiangshi* creature with screaming in your mouth and in one minute time I say to you, get outa my house right away. So you choose now.' Riya stopped dead, and stood silent and panting in the hallway while Mrs Run snapped her fingers under her nose and turned her back and walked off into the Run Run Trading store to glare angrily at the hanging ducks. And Riya, perspiring and breathing heavily, didn't even then understand that she was out of her mind with fear, but D Golden, watching her with great alarm from the top of the first flight of stairs, understood all right and it knocked [him] off balance as well.

Three weeks of Riya's craziness intensifying [his] inner turmoil. [His] days alone in the apartment, [his] nights crowded by her claustrophobia-inducing fear. [His] own fear, [his] fear of [himself], magnified by her fear of the shadow of her father. And in the end the shadows were too strong, they took possession of [his] mind and spirit. And none of us there to see it, or to help.

I did go to see [him] one last time, although I didn't know it was the last time. While Riya was at work trying to hold down her job in spite of her near-hysterical terror of the imagined proximity of Zachariassen-on-the-run, I took [him] for a walk through Chinatown. On a bench in Kimlau Square at the confluence of eight streets, below the proud benign gaze of the statue of the war hero Lieutenant Benjamin Ralph Kimlau of the 380th Bombardment Group of the Fifth Air Force, lost in aerial combat against Japan in 1944, D Golden confessed [his] failure to reconcile the warring elements within [himself]. That day [he] was wearing a check shirt, cargo pants and aviator shades, the faintest trace of lipstick, and a pink baseball cap over [his] long hair, which now reached below shoulder level. 'Look at me,' [he] wailed. 'Miserable in men's clothes, too scared to go public in a dress, and this painted mouth and pink hat, what a sad little gesture.' I repeated what everyone told [him], step by step, transition was a magic journey of a thousand and one nights, and [he] just shook his head. 'No open-sesame moment for me. No immortal storyteller to tell my pathetic story.' I just waited for the more that I could see was coming. 'I have dreams now in which every night I see the hijra of my childhood, dressed up as Michael Jackson, doing pencil turns in the street, banging on my car window, shrieking *dance with me.* When I wake up I'm sweating cold sweat. Truth is, I know what the hijra is saying, he she, insisting it would have to be all or nothing. If you're going to do it you have to go all the way. Operation, everything, like a real hijra. Anything less feels dishonest, like dressing up as Michael when you're just a sex worker at Chowpatty Beach. But, oh God. Truth is, I'm too weak, too scared, too fucking terrified,' [he] said. 'Maybe Apu is the lucky one.'

[He] looked around. 'Where are we?' [he] asked. 'I'm lost.'

I took [him] back to [his] apartment. And this is how I remember [him] now, marooned on a bench amid eight roads of traffic, knowing [he] couldn't be a hero in [his] private war, the cars flowing toward [him] and away, and [he] unable to pick a direction, not knowing which way was home.

They killed Zachariassen and that was on the evening news and Riya calmed down, at once, as if a switch had been thrown, she just let out a great sigh and breathed out all her craziness and there she was again, restored to her old self, 'real' Riya rescued from the counterfeit of her fear, apologising to everyone for her temporary insanity, normal service had been resumed, she assured everyone, don't worry about me. And soon enough, sure enough, we didn't. And so all of us, except D Golden, forgot about the gun.

❁

[He] arrived at the Golden house in splendour, emerging from the back of a Daimler limousine deliberately chosen to echo the vehicle in which all the Goldens had arrived on Macdougal Street to take possession of their new home. A liveried chauffeur held the door open and lowered a little flight of steps so that D's feet in their curvy-heeled Walter Steiger shoes could find their way down to street level without a misstep. [He] – no! – Now it had become appropriate to change her pronouns and say simply she, her, herself! – very well then, *she* was wearing a long scarlet Alaïa evening dress, over which *her* cascade of hair shone alluringly in the sun, and *she* carried a small jewel-encrusted Mouawad bag. So, dressed to kill, handing her key to the chauffeur so that he might open the front door for her, D Golden for the last time entered her father's house – for the first time, perhaps, as herself – her true self, the self she had always feared she might be, and whom she had had such difficulty in setting free.

Nero stood on the landing at the head of the stairs, flanked by Mss Blather and Fuss, with a fire in his eye. 'The children of kings are born to kill their fathers,' he said. 'Also, those garments are the possessions of my wife.'

Vasilisa Golden emerged to stand beside her husband. 'Then this is the thief I've been searching for,' she said.

D neither looked up nor replied. She moved gracefully through the house to the French windows, and out into the Gardens. Well, what a fluttering of curtains at windows then ensued! Seemed everyone living on the Gardens wanted a look. D, she paid no attention to any of that, she walked over to the bench where once, years earlier, her brother Petya had sat and made children laugh with his stories. There she sat down with the stolen pocketbook in her lap and her hands folded over it – Riya's pocketbook! – and she closed her eyes. There were children playing up and down the Gardens and their shrieks and laughter were the soundtrack of her silence. She wasn't in a rush. She waited.

Vito Tagliabue, the abandoned and cuckolded husband, came out to offer her his solidarity, saluting her courage and congratulating her on her fashion sense and then not knowing what else to say. She inclined her head graciously, accepting both salute and congratulations, and indicating that he was now dismissed. The Baron of Selinunte backed away, as if in the presence of royalty, as if turning his back on her would be a breach of protocol, and when he fell over a toddler's abandoned and multicoloured plastic tricycle it introduced a happy note of slapstick into the otherwise sober moment. D's lips twitched in a small but definite smile and then, calm, unhurried, she resumed her meditation.

In the film I would intercut her stillness with a scene of rapid movement, Riya coming home, finding her clothes closet open and untidy and the pocketbook containing the weapon missing, and a note left on her dressing table, a single sheet of paper folded in half; and then Riya sprinting into the street, hailing a cab, there isn't one, then there's one that doesn't stop, and then finally she gets one.

Once the children had gone indoors to eat or rest or whatever children did these days in front of whichever screens, D Golden in the Gardens opened his eyes and rose to his feet, and began to walk.

And Riya in the taxi, urging the driver to hurry, and he arguing back, sit still, lady, you're the passenger and I'm the driver, let me drive my cab. She slumps back into her seat and closes her eyes (intercut, in the Gardens, a reprise of D opening her eyes) and on the soundtrack we hear D's voice reading the suicide note.

D GOLDEN (V/O)

It isn't because of the difficulties of my own life that I do this. It's because there's something wrong with the world which makes it unbearable to me. I can't put my finger on it, but the world of human beings doesn't function well. The indifference of people to one another. The unkindness of people. It is disenchanting. I am a passionate human being but I don't know how to reach out to anyone any more. I don't know how to touch you, Riya, though you are the kindest person I know. In the Old Testament God destroyed the city of Sodom but I am not God and can't destroy Sodom. I can only remove myself from its precincts. If Adam and Eve came into the world in the Garden of Eden then it's appropriate that I, who am both Eve and Adam, take my leave from the world in a Garden too.

I think of Maurice Ronet in Louis Malle's *Le feu follet* (1963), also moving around his city, Paris, carrying a gun, saddened by the human race, and closing in on suicide.

She walked the length of the Gardens, slowly, formally, one end to the other end, and then, at the far end from Nero's property, her former home, and outside what had been my own family's home, she turned, and her grandeur was that of a queen. Then she walked back, halfway back, and stopped, and opened her purse.

And because it's a movie, at this point it's necessary for Riya to burst through the French windows of the Golden house and cry out.

RIYA

Don't.

Now there were faces at every window. The residents of the Gardens, abandoning all discretion, stood behind glass transfixed by the approaching horror. After Riya Z's cry, nobody spoke, and Riya, too, ran out of words to say. There was something of the gladiator about D Golden at this moment, she had the air of a warrior waiting for the verdict of the emperor's thumb. But she was her own emperor now, and had already delivered her verdict. Slowly, deliberately, wrapped in the solitude of her decision, and with the peacefulness of her ultimate clarity, she took the pearl-handled Colt out of the jewel-encrusted handbag, placed the tip of the barrel against her right temple, and fired.

27

The Greek fleet had to set sail for Troy to retrieve the faithless Helen, and so the angry goddess Artemis had to be appeased so that she would allow a fair wind to blow, and so Iphigenia daughter of Agamemnon had to be sacrificed, and so her grieving mother Clytemnestra, Helen's sister, would wait until her husband returned from the war and would then murder him, and so their son Orestes would avenge his father's death by murdering his mother, and so the Furies would pursue Orestes, and so on. Tragedy was the arrival in human affairs of the inexorable, which might be external (a family curse) or internal (a character flaw) but in either case events would take their inescapable course. But it was at least a part of human nature to contest the idea of the inexorable, even though other words for tragedy's superforce, destiny, kismet, karma, fate, were so powerful in every tongue. It was at least a part of human nature to insist on human agency and will, and to believe that the irruption into human affairs of chance was a better explanation for the failures of that agency and will than a predestined and irresistible pattern inherent in the narrative. The antic clothing of the absurd, the idea of the meaninglessness of life, was a more attractive philosophical garment to many of us than the tragedian's sombre robes, which, when worn, became both the evidence and the agents of doom. But it was also an aspect of human nature – just as powerful a characteristic of the contradictory human animal as its opposite – fatalistically to accept that there was indeed a natural order of things, and uncomplainingly to play the cards you were dealt.

Two urns of human ash on Nero Golden's desk: was this tragic inexorability at work, or a dreadful, doubly random misfortune? And the demented Joker out there, swinging from the Empire State Building with his greedy eye on the White House: was he the consequence of an extraordinary concatenation of unpredictable mischances, or the product of eight years and more of public shamelessness of which he was the embodiment and apogee? Tragedy or chance? And were there escape routes for the family and the country, or was it wiser to sit back and accept one's fate?

Nero Golden spent hours each day alone at his desk gazing upon the ashes of his sons, interrogating them for answers. To lessen his sadness Vasilisa brought him news of little Vespasian's development, his first words, his first steps, but the old man was inconsolable. 'I look at him, I look at Petya, I wonder, which of them is next,' he said. Vasilisa responded to this strongly. 'As for my son, he is safe,' she said. 'I will protect him with my life and he will grow up to be a strong and excellent man.' He looked up at her from his seat with a certain milky disapproval, but also vulnerability, even weakness in his gaze. 'And my Petya,' he said. 'Will you not protect him too?' She came to put a hand on his shoulder. 'I think Petya's crisis is already past,' she said. 'The worst has happened and he is still with us and he will be better again, as he was before.'

'For the sons to die before the father,' he said. 'It is as if the night falls when the sun is still in the sky.'

'Your house has a new sun shining upon it, a fine young prince,' she told him, 'so the day ahead is bright.'

The summer was over. The weeks of heat wave declined toward cloudy humidity. The city buzzed with the usual September magic, its annual fall reincarnation, but Suchitra and I were in Telluride for the film festival; our series of interviews about classic movie moments had added up to a pretty good documentary, *The Best Bits*, featuring some impressive talking heads discussing the film scenes they loved most – not only Werner Herzog but also Emir Kusturica, Michael Haneke, Jane Campion, Kathryn Bigelow, Doris Dörrie, David Cronenberg, and, in his last interview, the sadly departed Abbas Kiarostami – and we had been selected to bring it to the prestigious Labor Day weekend feast of cinema in the Colorado mountains, in the town where Butch Cassidy and the Sundance Kid held up their first bank, and the benign (and not so benign) spirits of Chuck Jones and his dwatted wabbit and his daffy duck watched over us all. Even there, in that cinéaste Eden, the talk occasionally turned to the dead, in that year when the Starman, the Purple One, the Deer Hunter, Young Frankenstein ('that's 'Fraankensteen'!'), R2D2, the Bird on the Wire and the Greatest had all taken their leave. But we had the movies – *La La Land*, *Arrival*, *Manchester by the Sea* – to occupy our minds and eyes, so death took a back seat at least while the festival was running, because real life, as we all well understood, was immortal, real life was the deathless stuff shining in the darkness up there on the silver screen.

Back in the city, in a state of considerable elation because of the good reception of our film at Telluride, I went to offer my respects to Nero, thinking also to invite him to the Russian Tea Room for vodka and blinis, to repay him for his boozy solicitude after my orphaning. I confess I was altogether too cheerfully high on our triumph in the Rockies, and may not have tried hard enough to adopt an appropriately mournful demeanour in that house of multiple calamities, but when I entered the Golden residence to find the great Nero in the living room taking tea, served on the best household china, with the ranting apocalyptic hobo who had reminded me of Klaus Kinski, and apparently taking the fellow's babbling seriously, I failed, I admit it, to suppress a laugh, because this cut-price Fitzcarraldo, who had put on a battered top hat for the occasion and who was slurping his tea noisily from a rare Meissen porcelain cup, now also bore a striking resemblance to the Mad Hatter, and Nero, leaning intently toward him, made an adequate March Hare.

My laugh caused Kinski to draw himself up in what I understood from my long familiarity with the works of P. G. Wodehouse to be high dudgeon. 'I amuse you?' he enquired as severely as one of Bertie Wooster's formidable aunts. I waved my hands, no, no, not at all, and controlled myself.

'There is nothing humorous in what I am here to say,' Kinski boomed, returning his attention to his host. 'I come to sit upon the ground and tell sad stories of the death of kings.' The words of Shakespeare's Richard II sat strangely in the mouth of an American tramp seated on a Louis XV chair drinking Lapsang from a Meissen cup, but never mind. 'Sit down, René,' said Nero, beckoning me toward him and patting a place on the settee. 'Have some tea and listen to this fellow. He's damn good.' There was a new sweetness in Nero's manner that was unsettling. He smiled, but it was more like a baring of the teeth than a sign of pleasure. His voice was soft, but it was a velvet glove concealing the painful rawness of his thought.

'It's going to go badly,' Kinski said suddenly, the teacup shaking in his hand. 'The mountain of evil is taller than the tallest building and the guns are all alive. I hear America cry out, where is God? But God is full of wrath because you stepped away from his path. You, America!' – here, oddly, he pointed directly at Nero – 'you spurned God and now he punishes you.' 'I spurned God and now he punishes me,' Nero repeated, and when I cast a glance in his direction I saw there were real tears in his eyes. The openly godless man, plunged into crisis, had invited this whiskey-breath malarkey merchant into his home and was actually being affected by his unhinged eschatology. I go away for five days, I thought, and when I come home the world has shifted on its axis. 'Nero,' I began to say, 'this man . . .' – but he waved me down. 'I want to hear it,' he insisted. 'I want to hear it all.'

So we had moved from Rome to Greece, and the man who had taken for himself the name of the last of the twelve Caesars was now trapped in a New York version of *Oedipus the King*, desperate for answers, with his version of blind Tiresias prophesying calamity. Kinski was hollering on but I had heard his shtick enough times to be bored by it, and switched off. Then Vasilisa was standing in the doorway and ended it. 'Enough,' she commanded, and her finger, pointing at Kinski, silenced and demolished him. I imagined a science-fiction, Darth Sidious bolt of power emanating from that finger. The teacup trembled dangerously in the tramp's hands but he set it down intact and jumped nervously to his feet. 'How about a coupla dollars?' he retained the chutzpah to ask, 'What about my fee?' 'Leave,' she said, 'or we'll call the cops and they can see about your fee.'

When he was gone she turned on Nero and spoke to him with the same Nurse Ratched note of authority in her voice that she had used on Kinski.

'Don't do that again,' she said.

Oh, I thought. We're in the cuckoo's nest.

My story has not, thus far, followed Nero Golden on his regular journeys to the apartment on York Avenue where he met his preferred prostitute, Mlle Loulou. I myself have never in my life seen the inside of a brothel, never paid anyone for sex, a fact which speaks, perhaps, of moral probity – but also, contrariwise, of a naïf innocence, of some deficiency in the story of my manhood. My inexperience in the field made it difficult for my imagination to follow Nero on these excursions up whatever narrow stairway lit by red light bulbs into whatever cushioned and perfumed boudoir; I knew that they had always been a part of his adult life and that, before he met his present wife, he would sometimes speak bawdily of his exploits to the most louche members of his poker circle, the pair of silver foxes named, perhaps, Karlheinz and Giambologna, or perhaps Karl-Otto and Giambattista, I forget – German and Italian playboys, anyway, politically ultra-conservative, the Axis powers at the card table in their tan leather jackets and bright cravats, whose rich wives had died in puzzling circumstances and left them all their money. Regarding the practicality of associations with the call-girl tribe they thought as one: you could fit them in between meetings and you didn't have to remember their birthdays, and you could use the same nickname for them all, Mlle Gigi, Mlle Nastygal, Mlle Babycakes, or Mlle Loulou. The names the girls themselves gave you were fakes anyway. And – this, in marketing diction, was their USP, their unique selling proposition – for a price, they would do anything you wanted, and keep their mouths shut afterwards. On poker nights Nero and the playboys, Karl-Friedrich and Giansilvio, had boasted of the sexual feats they had persuaded their ladies of easy virtue to perform, and complimented the athletic strength, the gymnastic grace, the contortionist flexibility of their chosen whores. Nero alone spoke of his tart's intelligence. 'She is a philosopher,' he said. 'I go to her for wisdom.' This brought forth braying laughter from Karl-Theodor and Giambenito. 'And fucking!' they bellowed in unison. 'Yes, also fucking,' Nero Golden agreed. 'But the philosophy is a plus.' Tell us, they cried, share with us the wisdom of your whore. 'For example,' Nero Golden answered, 'she says, I allow you to buy my body because I see you have not sold your soul.' 'That is not wisdom,' said Gianluca. 'That is flattery.' 'She speaks also of the world,' Nero went on, 'and believes that a great catastrophe is coming, and only from the total collapse of everything will the new order be born.' 'That is not wisdom,' said Karl-Ingo. 'That is Leninism.' Then they all laughed uproariously and shouted, 'Play cards!'

Now, in the time of his decline – his admittedly slow mental deterioration – Nero went uptown to his chosen lady less often. But from time to time he did go, perhaps wanting to listen to her hard-won truths in much the same way as he had been willing to listen to Kinski the tramp. In the aftermath of his double loss he was lost in a fog of meaninglessness and was looking everywhere to find a way of making the world make sense once again. He was still able to function fairly well as long as he was among people he knew. He had forged a relationship with a Haitian limo driver androgynously named Claude-Marie whom he now kept on retainer, knowing him to be both competent and discreet, and as a result could travel from Macdougal Street to York Avenue, do what he had to do there, and return without any trouble. On the particular day of which I must now speak, however, Claude-Marie was in a court of law embroiled in a bitter divorce, and sent along his Auntie Mercedes-Benz instead. Auntie Benz's real name was something Creole-French and unknown; the automobile name by which she now went was an honorific bestowed upon her by admiring relatives. In her day she had been a fine and skilful chauffeuse but in her white-haired years she had grown eccentric. Her driving was unsteady, and so Nero arrived at Mlle Loulou's door somewhat shaken up.

'Hello, little fool,' he said. It was his name of love for her. 'Your big fool is here.'

'You are sad,' she said, in the false French accent he liked her to adopt. 'Maybe I punish you a little and you punish me a little and you feel better *comme toujours*?'

'I need to sit for a minute,' he said. 'A strange driver. I felt, yes, I felt afraid.'

'You have death on your mind, *chéri*,' she said. 'It's completely understandable. A twice-broken heart will not soon mend.'

He did not know who she was outside this room with the red sofa and the gold bedspread and he didn't care. The person she was inside this room was sufficient for his needs. Confessors and philosophers were what he sought. The sex, which anyway, these days, was difficult, was almost beside the point. Some light had turned off inside him and arousal seemed like a nostalgic city in a country he had left behind. 'Why have these things happened,' he asked her, 'and what do they mean?'

'Life is cheap,' she said. 'You said so yourself, you told me, to Mr Gorbachev.'

'I said the Russians said so. But I am old and so inevitably life becomes precious, no?'

'A boy is killed for selling cigarettes on the street, *paf!* A girl is killed for playing with a toy plastic gun in a playground, *bof!* Sixty people shot in Chicago on the Fourth of July, *pow-pow-pow!* A rich boy kills his father for cutting his monthly allowance, *zap!* A girl in a crowd dancing to music asks a stranger to stop grinding against her ass and he shoots her in the face, *take that, bitch, die*. And I haven't even reached the West Coast yet. *Tu comprends?*'

'Violence exists. I know this. The question of value remains.'

'You mean, in the case of yourself and your loved ones, you make an exception. In this case they must be in a charmed circle and the horror of the world cannot touch them and when it does it is a fault in reality.'

'Now you are just unpleasant. What do you know.'

'I am closer every day to death than you, old man, and you are very old,' she said, affectionately, embracing him. 'And I am your fool, so I can tell you the truth.'

'Believe me,' he said, 'I know more about death than you. It's life that I can't grasp.'

'Permit me to grasp this,' she said, and the subject changed.

After their session things got worse because Auntie Mercedes-Benz was nowhere to be seen. It later transpired that she had parked around the block and fallen asleep, and the earplug of the audio cord connected to her phone had fallen out, so she didn't hear it ringing. Nero rang Mlle Loulou's door in a panic, utterly flustered, unable to handle the situation, and Loulou had to come down and hail a yellow cab and get into it with him and bring him home. When they got back to Macdougal Street he was still quivering and so with a sigh she got out of the car, helped him out of it, and rang the doorbell. Mlle Loulou was a tall, striking woman from the place she insisted on calling 'L'Indochine' and she maintained her composure when Vasilisa Golden herself answered the door. 'Ma'am,' she said, 'your husband is not himself.'

After a silence, Vasilisa answered coarsely. 'Tell me,' she said, 'can he still get it up?'

'If you don't know that, lady,' Mlle Loulou replied, turning to leave, 'I'm surely not going to be the individual to fill you in.'

28

Death speaks, in Somerset Maugham's play *Sheppey* (1933): 'There was a merchant in Baghdad who sent his servant to market to buy provisions and in a little while the servant came back, white and trembling, and said, Master, just now when I was in the market-place I was jostled by a woman in the crowd and when I turned I saw it was Death that jostled me. She looked at me and made a threatening gesture; now, lend me your horse, and I will ride away from this city and avoid my fate. I will go to Samarra and there Death will not find me. The merchant lent him his horse, and the servant mounted it, and he dug his spurs in its flanks and as fast as the horse could gallop he went. Then the merchant went down to the market-place and he saw me standing in the crowd and he came to me and said, Why did you make a threatening gesture to my servant when you saw him this morning? That was not a threatening gesture, I said, it was only a start of surprise. I was astonished to see him in Baghdad, for I had an appointment with him tonight in Samarra.'

I believe we all felt there would be another death. In those last weeks I didn't often see Petya, perhaps nobody did except for the Australian, but it's my conviction that he knew it too, that he saw Death threatening him in the marketplace and became desperate to avoid it, to mount a borrowed horse and gallop toward Samarra, believing he was escaping from what he was in fact riding to meet. The last of the three Golden men who had come with their father to America exuding such princely grandeur, such powerful strangeness, found in his brothers' deaths the motivation he needed to survive, and he made an immense effort to pull his life back onto something like a proper course, to turn his back upon Death and reach out to life.

The cat was Nero's idea. He had heard somehow, had received a message from somewhere out there in the non-stop jibberjabber of the information multiverse, that the company of cats could be helpful to autistic adults; and became convinced that a feline pet might be Petya's salvation. Fuss and Blather duly showed Nero photographs online of immediately available pusses and when he saw the white alpine lynx he clapped his hands and said, 'That's the one.' Blather and Fuss tried to persuade him that an alpine lynx was closer to a wild beast than a pet, wouldn't Petya be happier with a nice fat lazy long-haired chocolate or blue Persian, they suggested, but he was adamant in his new vague way and they gave up and went uptown to the cat shop and brought the monster home. It turned out that Nero knew his son. Petya immediately fell in love, named the cat Leo though she was female, and took her to his bosom, vanishing with her into the room of blue light. This was a cat who could leap up and catch a bird in flight, whose purr was like a roar, and who somehow, with a wild animal's instinct, knew the way through the jungle of Petya's inner torment to the good place in his heart. At night when the house was still and only the ghosts of the dead walked its corridors the cat sang softly in Petya's ear and gave him back what he had lost, the blessed gift of sleep.

The world outside the haunted house had begun to feel like a lie. Outside the house it was the Joker's world, the world of what reality had begun to mean in America, which was to say, a kind of radical untruth: phoniness, garishness, bigotry, vulgarity, violence, paranoia, and looking down upon it all from his dark tower, a creature with white skin and green hair and bright, bright red lips. Inside the Golden house the subject was the fragility of life, the easy suddenness of death, and the slow fatal resurrection of the past. Sometimes at night Nero Golden could be seen standing in the dark outside the room of his firstborn child, head bowed, hands folded, in a posture of what might have been thought – if he weren't so widely known as an unbeliever – to be prayer. What might have been thought to be a father pleading with his son, *not you too, live, live.*

We didn't know where death would come from. We didn't guess that it had already, at least once, been inside the house.

After he turned away from his son's closed door, Nero Golden would go back to his study, take the Guadagnini violin out of its case, and play his Bach Chaconne. On the other side of that closed door, Petya was cared for by his lynx, and the drinking was somewhat – but only somewhat – reduced. And he no longer cried out in anguish while he slept.

The Sottovoce lawsuit was settled suddenly, at twenty-five per cent of the original claim. Frankie Sottovoce wasn't well. There was a heart condition, an irregularity, and beneath the medical aspect a sickness also of the soul. The twinkle in his eye had dimmed and the familiar flamboyance of his waving arms had diminished into a languid flapping. Ubah's death had hit him hard. It was clear that he had been carrying a secret torch for her but, seeing her deeply embroiled with Apu, had held back from declaring his feelings. Strangely for someone who spent his days in the hothoused, networking world of art, exuding extrovert bonhomie, the gallerist had led a secretive, often solitary private life, briefly married, childless, long divorced, living in a pricey suite at the Mercer Hotel and ordering room service whenever his presence was not required at an art function. A friendly man, he had few friends, and once in the Gardens he had spoken to Vito Tagliabue about Vito's father Biaggio's long incarceration in the Grand Hotel et Des Palmes in Palermo. 'Your poor parent passed away alone and his body was discovered not by those who loved him but by a member of the hotel staff,' he said. 'This will also be my fate. They will bring up a burger and a glass of red wine and find that they are too late to grant me my last supper.' His hidden feelings for Ubah had overwhelmed him after she died. Now, as the vengeful tide ebbed, he accepted that the destroyed work had been adequately insured and that his multimillion-dollar action against the Goldens had been born of the turbulence of his emotions. 'I don't care any more,' he told his lawyers. 'Let's close it out.' I saw him just once in those days, at the Matthew Barney opening at Gladstone, and was shocked by the change in him, the paleness, the lassitude. 'Good to see you, young man,' he greeted me, flapping a hand. 'Good to see that there are still people who are full of gas and roaring ahead one hundred miles per hour.' I understood that he was telling me about himself, that his gas tank was dry, that he was running on empty. I tried to address the subject he would not raise. 'She was an extraordinary woman,' I said. He looked angry in his new exhausted way. 'So what?' he said. 'Dead is not extraordinary, everybody does it. Art is extraordinary, almost nobody can do it. Dead is just dead.'

After the end of the lawsuit came the end of community service. Petya, off that hook as well, very determinedly revived. He came out of his room with Lett the therapist, cradling his cat in the crook of his left arm, and, finding his father standing there in pitiful love, placed his right hand on Nero's shoulder, looked his father forcefully in the eye, and said, 'We're all going to be fine.' He repeated this sentence thirty-seven times, as if he were retweeting himself. To make it true by the force of repetition. To chase the Shadow away by unquenchably asserting and reasserting the Light. I was there that day, because after a hiatus Petya had texted me to ask me to come over. He wanted witnesses and that, I knew, was my place in the Golden story. Or it had been, until in Vasilisa's bed I crossed the line that divides the reporter from the participant. Like a journalist throwing a grenade from the trenches, I was a soldier now; and therefore, like all soldiers, a legitimate target.

'Hi, gorgeous,' he said when he saw me. 'Still the most handsome man in the world.'

Something about the Petya tableau that day resembled to my mind a grand oil painting, a *Night Watch,* maybe; we stood in Rembrandt's golden light and luminous shadows and felt, or maybe I only imagine that we felt, like guardians of an embattled world. Petya with his alpine lynx and his solicitous Australian and his furrowed-brow father and his large crooked smile. And servitors at angles in the corners of the frame. Was I the only person in the Golden house that day who heard the beating of fatal wings, the proleptic sighs of the guilty undertaker, the slow falling of the curtain at the end of the play? I'm writing against time now, my words following not so long after the people in them, writing double, because I'm also finally finishing up my Golden screenplay, my fiction about these men who made fictions of themselves, and the two are blurring into each other until I'm not sure any more what's real and what I made up. In what I call *real* I don't believe in ghosts and death angels but they keep pouring into what I invent like a ticketless crowd bursting through the gates at a big game. I'm sitting on the fault line between my outer world and the world within, astride the crack in everything, hoping some light gets in.

Inside the house it felt that month like a frozen time, a waiting time, the characters trapped in oil on canvas, striking attitudes, and unable to move. And outside in the street there was a plague of jokers, crazy slash-mouthed clowns frightening the children, or their phantoms were, anyway. Very few people in the city claimed actually to have seen a creepy clown that fall but reports of them were everywhere, the reports put on fright wigs, the rumours stalked the streets giggling and making witchy fingers with both hands and screeching about the end time, the last of days. Ghost clowns in an unreal reality. Eschatological insanity coming to the polls, and the Joker himself screaming into a mirror, the molester screaming about molestation, the propagandist accusing the whole world of propaganda, the bully whining about being ganged up on, the crook pointing a crooked finger at his rival and calling her crooked, a child's game become the national ugliness, I-know-I-am-but-what-are-you, and the days ticking away, America's sanity at war with its dementedness, and people like me, who didn't believe in superstitions, walking around with their hands in their pockets and their fingers crossed.

And then finally there was, after all, a scary clown.

After a long period of estrangement, Vasilisa wanted to talk. She took me into the Gardens and made sure we were out of range of interested ears. The new note of power in her voice told me she was still inhabiting her Big Nurse persona, still making it clear that from now on she was the one in the catbird seat. 'He's not the same man,' she said. 'I am having to accustom myself to that. But he is the father of my child.' – This, to my face, looking me right in the eye! The daring of it was breathtaking. I felt the red mist rising. 'If you contradict me,' she said, raising a hand before I had said a word, 'I will have you killed. Be in no doubt that I know who to call.'

I turned to leave. 'Stop,' she said. 'This is not how I want our conversation to go. I want to say, I need your help with him.'

I laughed out loud at that. 'You really are an extraordinary human being,' I said. 'If in fact you are a human being. That these two remarks can come out of your mouth consecutively is awe-inspiring. But not really indicative of your membership of the human race.'

'I understand that there is a trouble between us,' she said. 'But Nero is innocent of that and it is for Nero that I ask. The grief in him as well as the decline of his mind. Which is slow, the medication helps, but it is also inevitable. The progression. I fear for him. He wanders off. I need someone to go with him. Even if he goes to that woman I want you to go there as well. He is looking for answers. Life has become an agony and he wants a solution to its mystery. I don't want him to find it in her arms.'

'I can't do it,' I told her. 'I'm preparing a feature film. It's a busy time.'

'You won't do it,' she said. 'That is what you're saying. You have become a selfish man.'

'You have many resources,' I said. 'People at your disposal. Use them. I'm not your employee.' I spoke sharply. I didn't feel in the mood to be ordered around by her.

She was wearing a long white dress, tight in the bodice, loose below the waist, with a high lacy ruff of a collar. She leaned against a tree and I thought all at once about Elvira Madigan, eponymous heroine of Bo Widerberg's beautiful film, the doomed lover walking a tightrope in a wood. She closed her eyes and spoke in a voice like a sigh. 'It's all such a charade,' she said. 'The family name is not the name. Mlle Loulou is not Loulou. Maybe I am not me and that lady playing the part of my mother is just somebody I hired to play the part. You know what I mean? Nothing is real.' These were scattered thoughts and I saw that beneath her self-control she was in a torment of her own. 'Only my child is real,' she said. 'And through him I will come into a real place in the end.' She shook her head. 'Until then everyone is a kind of performance,' she said. 'Maybe even you. You have become like a priest confessor to this family but you are no priest, who are you really, what do you want, maybe I should be suspicious, maybe you are the Judas.' Then she laughed. 'I'm sorry,' she said, briskly, beginning to move away. 'We are all on edge. Things will improve one day. And yes, go, be with your girl, who knows nothing of anything, and it's better that way.'

That was another of her threats, of course, I thought, watching her as she retreated. She would not 'have me killed' but she would, if necessary, destroy my happiness by telling Suchitra what I had done. I knew then that I had to be the first to tell Suchitra, whatever the cost. I had to find the courage for the truth and hope our love was strong enough to survive it.

And Elvira Madigan, I thought, another pseudonym. That was not the ill-fated Danish tightrope walker's real identity. Hedvig Jensen; that's who she really was. Bearer of the commonest of names.

Yes: I had been drawn into the Golden world of make-believe, and only the truth could set me free.

Leo the cat was to Petya what the magic feather had been to Dumbo. With the lynx in his arms he became again the brilliantly strange man we first met, walking in the Gardens, talking loudly to anyone who'd listen, and making the children laugh. It was a mild fall, beautiful weather in a crazy time, so his greatcoat remained in its closet, but there was a rainbow-striped scarf flung carelessly around his neck, and his gallery of outrageous suits was on parade, the broad-lapel cream suit in which he had first appeared among us, a leprechaun-green three-piece when he wanted to channel Oscar Wilde, a double-breasted chocolate outfit, dark chocolate with a broad milk-chocolate check. The cocktail mixer was in one hand, and the martini glass in the other, and the olive jar sat on the bench as before. But now, beside the jar of olives there was an iPad and to this the children gravitated like planets around a sun, while Petya showed them, and encouraged them to play, the beta versions of his latest games. The games were his stories now, and the children plunged in eagerly, voyaging to the worlds inside his head. For a few beautiful days, thoughts of death were pushed aside, and the bright book of life stood open at a new page.

'You realise,' Suchitra said, 'that this has become a movie about you, and all these Golden boys are aspects of your own nature.'

'No they're not,' I protested.

'In a good way,' she said. 'It makes the film a more personal testament. All the characters are the auteur. It's like Flaubert. *Madame Bovary, c'est moi.*'

'But I'm not an artist,' I said, 'not sexually conflicted, not autistic, not a Russian gold digger, not a powerful old man in decline.' I did not add, 'not a baby', because of course the baby was partly me. Fifty per cent. A big part. A big part that was being kept out of my reach. A guilty secret to which I still had not found the courage to confess.

We were in the editing suite at DAW on West Twenty-Ninth Street and Batwoman, freeze-framed, was watching us from the Avid screen. Our fourth and last Bat-video was in its final stages. The Joker was trying to foment an insurrection that would destroy US democracy. At a packed MetLife Stadium mobs of crazy clowns howled hatred at the sky. How much could one fierce female Bat do? Well, that depended on you. *Vote for the first Bat president of the United States. Because this election is no joke.*

'You carry their questions with you wherever you go. The question of Apu's life, remember what his father said to you? Is it necessary to be profound, or can you remain permanently on the surface? You need to answer this question also. D Golden, as his father also said, was all about ambiguity and pain. I feel it in you also, some ambiguity. I feel that you are in pain. As for Petya, he's hemmed in by himself, he can't escape his nature, though he so much wants to be free. And maybe his games, the games he invents, are his freedom. That's the place where he isn't afraid. Maybe that's a place you also need to find. You've been standing on the threshold for so long, maybe it's time you finally went in through the door. And the old man . . .'

'You're going to tell me I'm like him too? He's kind of a monster, even in his fallen state . . .'

'He is enfolded in tragedy, and so are you. He has lost sons, you lost parents. Your grief defines you and shuts you off from other people. That's what I think.'

'Are we having a fight?' I asked. Her words had packed quite a punch.

'No,' she said, wide-eyed, meaning it. 'Why do you think that? I'm just saying what I see.'

'You're being pretty hard on me.'

'I just see who you can be and I want you to see it too. Be profound. Own your tragedy. Find your freedom. Resolve your ambiguity, whatever it is. Maybe it's about me.'

I have to tell her about the baby, I thought. *That's what's shutting me off.*

'No,' I said. 'About you, I'm certain. Profoundly certain. Not ambiguous at all.'

'OK,' she said, closing the subject, breaking into a big, wide smile. 'Good. Let's finish Batwoman.'

Zap! Pow! Bof! – Take that, you giggling loon! – Ow! Unfair! Why is everyone against me? Owww! It's a fix! Everybody's a liar! Only the clown tells the truth! – Blam! – *Ow.*

29

One night not long after D Golden's suicide in the Gardens, an event that put a dark hole in Paradise for us all, Riya Zachariassen, known as Riya Z, woke up from a dream of horror to find that she had lost her grip on her picture of the world. She couldn't remember the whole dream but she was almost sure she had been carrying a very valuable painting in a great museum and then she dropped it and the frame broke and the glass shattered and she somehow managed to put a foot through the canvas itself, but maybe that was just something she remembered from a movie, dreams were slippery as eels. As she came awake the dream itself stopped being important but she understood that the picture was the one containing everything she thought about the way things were, it was her reality, and now it was broken and somebody would come looking for her in a minute and blame her for breaking it and then she would be fired.

It is hard for a person of no faith like myself to comprehend the moment when faith dies in the human heart. The kneeling believer who suddenly understands that there is no reason to pray because nobody's listening. Or simply the slow erosion of certainty until doubt becomes more powerful than hope: you keep walking by the river as a drought dries it up until one day there's a dry riverbed and no water to nourish you in time of thirst. I can picture it but I can't feel it, except perhaps as the end of love. You wake up one morning and look at the person sleeping in the bed beside you, softly snoring his familiar and until now well-loved snore, and you think, I don't love you or your snore any more. The scales that fall from Saul's eyes in the Acts of the Apostles – or the things like scales, 'there fell from his eyes as it had been scales', the King James Bible says – were the scales of unbelief, after which he saw clearly and was immediately baptised. But the image also works the other way around. The somethings-like-scales fell from Riya's eyes and she saw clearly that her reality had been an illusion, that it had been false. That's as close as I can get.

She lay very still next to the empty space where her lover had been. She had always hated the Birkenstocks in which, in spite of her protests, D insisted on sheathing [his] feet when they were at home; but now she couldn't move the sandals from their place on that side of the bed. They were old-fashioned enough to have, still, a landline phone, a phone that never rang. It was D's voice on the voicemail – 'It's Riya and D, and now over to thee' – and she couldn't bring herself to delete it. If she stayed very still and did not think, she could almost believe he would walk in from the bathroom and climb back into the bed. But she couldn't stop thinking, so she knew that wouldn't happen. What had happened was that she no longer thought what she had thought she thought. So she had no idea what to think.

In the gravity of her mourning solemn Riya reminded me somehow of Winona Ryder, not the wacky teenage goth Winona of *Beetlejuice*, dancing in the air to a fine Belafonte calypso, shaking her body line, but rather *Age of Innocence* Winona, tightly controlled and less innocent than she looked. In the Scorsese movie – I confess I haven't read the Edith Wharton novel – it's Michelle Pfeiffer who is the unconventional one, the one who embraces a new, modern way of being and suffers terribly for it and is finally defeated by Winona Ryder's serene conservative manoeuvring. But suppose the Winona character had been the one in the grip of the new, and that one day she lost her hold on her sense of how things were and should be. That Winona could have been in this movie. That was Riya; my rewritten Winona, more lost and devastated than the original ever was, at sea without a life belt.

It is hard for new ideas to come into the world. The new ideas about men and women and how many human beings were somewhere in between those two words and needed new vocabularies to describe them and give them the feeling of being seen, of being possible and permissible, were ideas that many good people had developed and put out there for the best of reasons. And other fine people, brilliant people like Riya Z, had embraced the new thinking and made it their own and worked hard to put it into practice and make it part of a new way for the world to work.

But then one night Riya opened her eyes and realised that she had changed her mind.

Draft Letters of Resignation From Riya Zachariassen to the Museum of Identity (Unsent)

Dear insert name of employer, This is to inform you that in accordance with and whereas and inasmuch and as per my contractual obligations and in full discharge of my responsibilities and regarding a final date and after unused days of allocated vacation time have been deducted. And loose ends and efficient handover and with gratitude for and in appreciation of and in the hope that and so on. Owing to a radical re-evaluation of and evolution of thought leading to the incompatibility of my present position with the values of. Therefore the interests of the Museum are better served by my departure. Yours sincerely, the end.

Or,

When I was a young girl in Minnesota and beginning to be concerned with living an ethical life, I thought about India, such an important part of my own heritage, and I asked myself, who in India suffers the most injustice, and the answer I came up with, aged eight, was, goats. Cows were sacred but goats got slaughtered for meat and nobody cared. I decided I would dedicate my life to the care and protection of those unloved bleating creatures. Then I grew up and changed my mind of course but it has remained my way to find the thing that needs my passion and then to dedicate myself to it without holding back. After goats there were other early obsessions: birth control, autoimmune diseases, eating disorders, water scarcity. My adulthood coincided with the dawning of the Age of Identity, and the discussions and issues and innovations in and around this subject convinced me that I had found my calling, and when the opportunity to work at the Museum offered itself it was like a dream come true and so it has seemed every day until now. I confess to you, however, a weakness of the passionate-obsessive cast of mind. It can happen that one day one wakes up to find that, you know what, I don't care so much about this any more. This is no longer for me. Previously adored goats, condoms, bulimia, water, you're just not my thing any longer. So it is now with me and identity. I'm over it. Goodbye.

Or,

I need to think and the city is full of noise.

Or,

I acknowledge that I am a plural entity. I am the daughter of my deceased psychotic father. I am also the mourner of my dead love. I am, alternatively, one of the tribe of skinny people. I am, additionally or contrariwise, a scholar. I am, equally, dark-haired. I have these views and not those views. I can define myself in many different ways. This is what I am not: I am not one thing. I contain multitudes. Do I contradict myself? Very well, I contradict myself. To be plural, to be multiform, is a singular thing, rich, unusual, and myself. To be forced into narrow definitions is a falsehood. To be told, if you are not one thing then you are nothing, is to be told a lie.

The Museum of Identity is too engaged with that lie. I can't work in it any more.

Or,

I suspect that identity in the modern sense – national, racial, sexual, politicised, embattled – has become a series of systems of thought some of which helped drive D Golden to his/her death. The truth is that our identities are unclear to us and maybe it's better that they remain that way, that the self goes on being a jumble and a mess, contradictory and irreconcilable. Maybe after all D was just a man with some female feelings and [he] should have been allowed to remain in that place and not pushed toward transition by people like me. Not pushed into a femaleness [he] could neither wholly reject nor, ultimately, bear. Pushed toward [his] death by people like me, who allowed a new idea of the real to be stronger than the oldest idea of all: our love.

D told me a story about a hijra in Bombay who dressed as a man at home and in fact was a man for his/her mother and father and then changed her clothes and became a woman when she left the house. That should be all right. Flexibility should be all right. Love should dominate, not dogmas of the self.

I was ready to go with D through all [his] changes and stay with [him] when they were done. I was [his] lover when [he] was a man and I was ready to remain her lover through transition and into her new self. What does this tell me about me, about human beings, about the reality that is beyond dogma? It tells me that love is stronger than gender, stronger than definitions, stronger than the self. This is what I have learned. Identity – specifically, gender identity theory – is a narrowing of humanity, and love shows us how broad we can be. To honour my dead lover I reject the politics of identity and embrace the politics of love.

This was what the philosopher Bertrand Russell replied when asked what advice he would pass on to future generations. He said: 'Love is wise.' But I understand that these are contentious times. If battle there must be, let it commence.

ACTUAL LETTER

Dear Orlando,

As I told you just now in your office, I have to resign my position. It's hard for me to explain why and it is a tough decision and I'm ready to sit down with you and talk it through some more if you so desire. Maybe, as you say, I'm suffering an extreme grief reaction and my thoughts are therefore confused and I will think better of it when I've had time to mourn and process what has happened, and it was kind of you to suggest counselling and a leave of absence, but I think it's better I just go. Thanks for everything. All the best.

Riya

The storm blew up on her social media at once. (To someone as out of step as myself with his generation and the one immediately following, the thought can't help but occur: Why put this stuff out there in the first place? Why tell a crowd of strangers that you are going through a painful and deeply personal re-evaluation of your thinking? But I understand that this is no longer even a question.) From every side the invisible army of the electronic universe laid into her. Anonymous individuals with pure hearts and no sense of the hypocritical defended their certainties about identity while cloaking themselves in the disguises of false names. 'So how'd you feel now about white women dressing up as Pocahontas on Halloween? What's your position on blackface? Are those OK with you?' 'Are you a SWERF now as well as a TERF? Maybe you aren't even an RF any more. What are you? Are you anyone?' And much bad language. And, repeatedly, *Delete your account.* The disapproval came from friends as well as strangers, it came from the highly assertive gender-political circles in which she had moved so comfortably for so long and which now accused her of betrayal, but also from the indie-fashionista world in which she had been something of a rising star, and from several of her erstwhile colleagues at the Museum of Identity, *the thing about your new position isn't so much that it's wrong, or that it's so regressive, it's that it's so poorly thought out. It's so stupid. And we thought you were the smart one.*

Across the Atlantic, in another theatre of the identity wars, the British prime minister was narrowing the definition of Britishness to exclude multiplicity, internationalism, the world as the location of the self. Only little England would do to define the English. In that distant argument about the identity of the nation there were loud voices pushing back against the prime minister's grunting narrowness. But here in America, in the language of gender, the only words that didn't exist, Riya thought, the only unspeakable words, were 'I'm not sure about any of this. I'm having second thoughts.' That kind of talk could get you de-platformed.

Ivy understood, Ivy Manuel who had always resisted being pigeon-holed. 'Fuck 'em if they don't get it,' she said. 'Come on over and let's go for a fucking run by the river and let's have a fucking drink and let's sing a fucking improper song together. "My Boy Lollipop" or some shit like that.'

One more encounter with the hobo Kinski before his big scene, which I will get to in due order, should have warned me that he was gearing up for something. But such is our desire to believe in the ordinariness of ordinary life, the normality of our dailiness, that I didn't get it. He was skulking about outside the Red Fish, the music place on Bleecker, inside which a Faroese singer was scheduled to perform a suite of confessional songs inspired by YouTube videos – in English, not Faroese, luckily for the audience. What was Kinski's interest in any of this, YouTube, the Faroe Islands, music? But there he was, skulking. Hey, anybody got a spare ticket, a ticket you don't need and could maybe donate to a good cause? Him being the good cause he had in mind. I was there because the Faroese singer's American collaborator was a friend, and Kinski, seeing a familiar face, lit up and became high energy.

'You can do this for me,' he said. 'Never mind everything else. This is important. This guy. *Poetry & Aeroplanes,* ever heard that? Beautiful. Did you know he recorded an album in the house where Ingmar Bergman died? Did you hear his TED talk? Whoa.'

These were the most articulate words (except perhaps for his Shakespeare quote at tea in the Golden house) and the only non-apocalyptic thoughts I'd ever heard coming out of his mouth. 'And you know all this, how?' I asked.

His face darkened and, to keep it company, his vocabulary deteriorated. 'Fuck off,' he said. 'Never mind how.'

I was curious now and, as it happened, I did have an extra ticket in my pocket, because Suchitra, of course, was working late. 'If you want to get in,' I said, 'I need the story.' He looked down at the sidewalk and shuffled his feet. 'My buddy turned me on to him,' he muttered. 'Bagram Air Base. Back in the day.'

'You're a vet,' I said, genuinely surprised.

'You want proof?' he snarled. 'Give me a blindfold and a disassembled AR-15. I'll give you fucking proof.'

This was when, if I'd had my warning radar switched on, I should have understood that all was not well, that this was a man near an edge. But I was guilty about my ignorance of his service, and then compounded my mistake by asking him a question about his 'buddy', and getting the response I should have known I'd get. 'Didn't make it. Ambush in Pakhtunkhwa. Now can I get the fucking ticket.'

I watched him during the concert. The songs were witty, even funny, but there were tears pouring down his face.

At some point soon after this unexpected musical run-in – maybe two days later, maybe three – Kinski got his hands on an automatic rifle, just as he had rhetorically requested outside the Fish. According to the deposition he later made at Mount Sinai Beth Israel – the deathbed confession, I should more accurately say – he neither bought nor stole it. He was kidnapped in the park, he said, and his kidnappers gave him the gun and turned him loose. It was an improbable story, even an absurd one, told in fractured mumbles and gasps, and in my view it wouldn't have been worth taking seriously for a moment except for two things: first, it was a deathbed confession, and that had to be given its proper and solemn weight; and second, it was coming out of Kinski's mouth, and given the crazy things that had always come out of that mouth, this was no crazier than the rest of it, so there was a tiny, crazy chance that it might be true.

The following, more or less, was Kinski's version. When he was melancholy, he said, he went uptown to wander the relatively empty spaces to be found in the northern latitudes of the park. He got caught in a downpour and took shelter under a tree, huddling there until the heavens relented. (Note: On the particular day in question there had indeed been a change in the weather, a few days of unseasonal warmth and blue skies had given way to chilly rain.) – At this point, owing to his rapidly deteriorating physical condition, the account became fragmented and unclear. – He was approached by (two? three? more?) individuals dressed as clowns – or Jokers – he used both words – who overpowered him and put a sack over his head and bound him. – Or they didn't bind him but just led him forward on foot. – Or not a sack but some sort of blindfold. – He couldn't see where he was going because of the sack. – Or blindfold. – Then he was in the back of a van and the blindfold was removed and a new man, also disguised as a clown – or Joker – was talking to him about – what? – *recruitment.* – There was stuff about the presidential election. Its illegitimacy. It was being stolen. It was a coup orchestrated by the media – by powerful corporate interests – by China – and Americans had to take their country back. – It was hard to tell if these were Kinski's own sentiments or if he was repeating what the supposed boss Joker in the van had told him. – Then at one point the words 'We can learn from Muslim terrorists. From their self-sacrifice.' – After which, much incoherence, a mingling of self-pity, despair, and his old prophecies of imminent doom. – 'Nothing to live for.' – 'America.' – That was about it. The medical team intervened and stopped the deposition. Emergency procedures followed. He didn't speak again, and didn't last very much longer. All of which is my best effort at piecing together a coherent story from what was reported in the press and what, with some difficulty, I was able to dig out for myself.

His friend had died – who knows how many friends? – and he had returned from military service mentally ill. He had lost contact with those who might have cared for him and declined in every way and ended up as a bum ranting about guns. Over the years during which his path crossed mine his rant changed. In the beginning he sounded anti-gun, fearing the proliferation of weapons in America, coming up with the idea that guns were alive; then, with the addition of religious fervour, he amped up his end-of-days rhetoric; and finally, clowns or no clowns, Jokers or no Jokers, abduction or no abduction, he became a servant of the gun himself, the warm gun that brought happiness, and did its bidding, *bang bang shoot shoot,* and so people died, and so did he.

For what is an undeniable fact is that Kinski attacked the Halloween parade, and the fusillade of shots he unleashed resulted in a tally of seven people dead, nineteen wounded, before a police officer gunned him down. He was wearing a Joker mask and a Kevlar vest – a remnant, perhaps, of his days in Afghanistan – so his injuries were not immediately fatal. He was taken to the MSBI emergency room and lived long enough to make the statement above, or something like it, but it must be said that in the opinion of the hospital staff the balance of his mind was disturbed and nothing he said could be considered reliable.

On the list of the dead, two names stood out: Mr Murray Lett and Mr Petronius Golden, both of Manhattan, NY.

On Halloween the residents of the Gardens traditionally had a private celebration, stringing the old trees with lights, putting a DJ's booth outside the house of the fashion magazine editor, allowing the local children to run wild playing trick or treat. Many of the adults, too, dressed up. It was a way of enjoying the festival without venturing into the great crowds that gathered on Sixth Avenue nearby to witness or participate in the parade itself.

Petya might have been happy in the Gardens but Leo the cat wanted to go to the parade, Petya told Murray Lett, and what Leo wanted, Leo was going to get. He was feeling good!, he said, really very good!, he felt he had really emerged from his time of crisis, he could put it behind him, he wanted to embrace life, and life was out there on All Hallows' Eve on Monday, marching down Sixth Avenue dressed up as skeletons, zombies and whores. 'Even with the Gardens party, this house feels so funereal,' he cried. 'Let's find ourselves some kick-ass costumes and kick some parade ass!' His fear of open spaces had ebbed, he said, and besides when the Village was this crowded it didn't feel like an open space anyway. Murray Lett the Australian had never fully embraced the over-the-topness of the American Halloween. Once he had been invited to a party on the Upper West Side and had gone as *Mars Attacks!* in a huge Tim Burton Martian head that was hot inside and meant he couldn't eat or drink. Another year he had been Darth Vader, wearing overly bulky plastic armour that made sitting down difficult, and a black helmet with a voice-changer box, which gave him the same problems as the *Mars Attacks!* head regarding heat, food and liquid intake. Nowadays he tended to stay in his apartment and hope no trick-or-treating kids rang the doorbell. But Petya would not be denied. 'We will be Romans!' he cried. 'I of course, being Petronius, will be Trimalchio, host of the *Satyricon* feast, and you – you can be a reveller of some sort. Our costumes will be inspired by Fellini. There will be togas! And laurel wreaths upon our brows, and flagons of wine in our hands. Marvellous! We will run toward life and drink deeply at its watering holes and we will be drunk on life by the morning.' When I heard the plan I thought of *Gatsby*, of course, *Gatsby* which Fitzgerald came close to calling *Trimalchio in West Egg*, and that was a sad thought for it brought back to my mind my nights of laughter with my parents, and so also inevitably the dreadful manner of their ending, and I succumbed briefly to renewed sadness; but then Petya's glee was infectious and I thought, yes, why not, some gaiety after everything, good idea, and if Petya wished to be, for one night, life's high-bouncing lover, then yes! Let him wear his toga and bounce.

Costumes at short notice were a tall order, but that was what Fuss and

Blather were for, and anyway a toga was just a bedsheet with big ideas. Roman sandals were found, and laurel, and a bundle of birch twigs tied with red ribbon – the Roman fasces – which Petya would hold as a symbol of his consular authority. A completely anachronistic fool's cap and bells were found and offered to Murray Lett and I very much wanted him to choose to wear them so that he could channel Danny Kaye in *The Court Jester* and practise his tongue-twisters, *The pellet with the poison's in the vessel with the pestle; the chalice from the palace has the brew that is true!* But he went for a toga to be like Petya and if Petya was going to hold the fasces then Lett would carry the cat.

So it was; and so imperially attired they went away from the Gardens, away from that house weighed down by death into the parade that celebrated life; and so, running toward life and away from death, they found death waiting for them, as the old story had prophesied, in Samarra, which was to say, on Sixth Avenue between Fourth Street and Washington Place. Death in a Joker costume carrying an AR-15. The gun's soft chatter inaudible beneath the cacophony of the crowds, the honking of horns, the megaphoned messages, the bands. Then people began to fall and harsh uncostumed reality ruined the party. There was no reason to believe that Petya or Murray Lett had been specifically targeted. Guns were alive in America, and death was their random gift.

And the cat, the alpine lynx. Here, in close-up, the outstretched arm of the dead Roman, the fasces fallen from his grasp. (A deliberate echo, in the framing, of the inert arm of the fallen Kong at the end of the original 1933 movie.) And Leo snarling hatred at anyone who dared come near. And when all of it was done, when the screaming had subsided, when the crowd running, falling, had calmed and been dispersed and those dead and wounded by the bullets and those crushed underfoot by fear had all been taken to their necessary places, when the avenue was empty except for wind-blown trash and police cars, when it was really over, the cat was gone, and nobody ever saw Leo the lynx again.

And the King, alone in the golden house, saw all his gold in all his pockets all his stacks all his sacks all his buckets begin to glow more and more brightly until it caught fire, and burned.

PART III

30

In truth, I had hoped for a gentler life. Even while I dreamed about arriving, at some wonderful point in the future, at a place of true distinction, I hoped for more kindness while I was making my way along the road. I did not understand then that Scylla and Charybdis, the two mythical monsters between whom Odysseus' ship had to sail in the Strait of Messina – the one 'rationalised' as giant rocks, the other as a ferocious whirlpool – are symbolic, on the one hand, of other people (the rocks on which we break ourselves and founder), and on the other, of the darkness circling within ourselves (which sucks us down, and we drown). Now that my film *The Golden House* is finally finished and about to make its debut on the festival circuit – almost a decade in the making, and after the upheavals in my private life near the end of that period, finishing it feels like a miracle – I should try to set down what I learned in the process. About the movie business I learned, for one thing, that when a person with money says to you, 'I love this project. I *love* it. So creative, so original, there is nothing like it out there. I am going to back you one thousand per cent, to the fullest of my ability, total support, one thousand and *one* per cent, this is *genius,*' what he is saying, translated into English, is 'hello'. And I learned to admire anyone who actually got his or her movie to the finish line and into theatres, whatever it was, *Citizen Kane* or *Porky's XXII* or *Dumb Fucks XIX*, never mind, you made a movie, dudes, respect. About life outside the movie business I learned this: that honesty is the best policy. Except when it's not.

We are icebergs. I don't mean that we are cold, only that we are mostly under the surface, and the part of us that is hidden can sink the *Titanic*.

In those days after the Halloween shootings I spent much of my time in the Gardens, making myself available to the Goldens for whatever services might be required. With Suchitra's agreement I spent several nights a week bedding down in Mr U Lnu Fnu's apartment. He had not rented out my old room and said he was glad of the company in an 'awful time, awful time'. As for Suchitra in these last hours before the country voted, she was working something like twenty-hour shifts at the DAW editing facilities, cutting together footage which the Democrat presidential campaign wanted to use, in her capacity as a leading member of a Women in Media group which had volunteered its professional services to the team. She confessed to feeling exhausted and overwhelmed and a little low in spirits, and maybe I should have understood that much of that had to do with me. But I was in the Gardens not only for altruistic but also for almost predatory reasons, because of my strong instinct that the story I had set out to tell was about to give me the denouement it presently lacked, and that if I lay in wait for it, hiding in the Gardens shrubbery like a hungry lion in the long grasses at the foot of an acacia tree on the African plain, my prey would come trotting by. It had not occurred to me, crowded by deaths as my narrative already was, that there might also be a murder story unfolding. It was Vito Tagliabue who first alerted me to the possibility that Nero Golden was not in fact, or not only, the victim of slowly advancing senile dementia; that the truth was that he was slowly being poisoned by his wife.

Life in the Gardens had always been somewhat reminiscent of *Rear Window*. Everyone looked out and across at everyone else, all of us brightly illuminated in our windows, which were like miniature movie screens within the larger screen, playing out our dramas for our neighbours' pleasure; as if the actors in movies could watch other movies while those other movies also watched them. In *Rear Window* James Stewart lived not far away, at the fictional '125 West Ninth Street', which would, in the real world, be 125 Christopher Street – that is, Ninth Street west of Sixth Avenue – but the Gardens would have worked just as well. It was my plan to introduce, in my filmed version, a few residents who would be deliberate *hommages* to the characters in Hitchcock's great film, Miss Torso the extrovert dancer, Miss Lonelyhearts the older single woman, and so on. Maybe even a travelling jewellery salesman, cast as a Raymond Burr lookalike. It had not been any part of my plan to develop the storyline to include an attempted murder, but this is what stories will do to you, they take off in unexpected directions and you have to hang on by their coat-tails. And so it was that I was crossing the Gardens from Mr U Lnu Fnu's building to the Golden house when Vito Tagliabue stuck his handsome head, its hair slicked back and glistening, out of his back door and actually said, to my immense surprise, 'Pssst!'

It stopped me in my tracks and my brow, I admit, furrowed. 'Excuse me,' I said, to clarify things, 'did you just now say "Pssst?"'

'*Si,*' he hissed, beckoning me to him. 'Is it a problem?'

'No,' I answered, approaching. 'It's just that I never heard anyone say "pssst" before.'

He pulled me into his kitchen and shut the garden door. 'What do they say, then?' He had an agitated air. 'It is not an American word?'

'Oh, I guess they might say, "Hey!" or "Excuse me?" or "Got a minute?"'

'It's not the same,' Vito Tagliabue pronounced.

'Anyway,' I said.

'Anyway,' he agreed.

'There was something you wanted?'

'Yes. Yes. It is important. But it is hard to say. I speak in total confidence of course. I am certain of your integrity, that you will not say you heard this from me.'

'What is it, Vito?'

'It is a hunch. You say hunch? Yes, a hunch.'

I gestured with my hands, continue, please.

'This Vasilisa. This wife of Signor Nero. She is a hard case. She is ruthless. Like all . . .' He paused. I thought he was going to speak from personal bitterness, *like all wives*, or *all women*. '. . . like all Russians.'

'What are you saying, Vito?'

'I am saying, she will kill him. She precisely at the moment is killing him. I see his face when he walks here. This is not his old-age decline. This is something else.'

His ex-wife Bianca Tagliabue had moved into the house of her new lover, Carlos Hurlingham, my 'Mr Arribista', across the way. Every day the new lovers flaunted themselves in the Gardens, humiliating Vito, rubbing his nose in their love. If anyone had murder on his mind, I thought, it was probably Vito himself. However, I humoured him a little longer.

'How is she doing this?' I asked.

He shrugged operatically. 'I don't know. I have not the details. I just see him looking sick. Sick in the wrong way. Maybe something with his medications. He has to take many medications. So, is easy. Yes, something with the medications, I am sure. Almost sure.'

'Why would she do this?' I pressed him. Again, a shrug and a wave of the arms. 'It is obvious,' he said. 'All the other heirs, they are gone now. Only her baby remains. And if by chance Nero also' – here he drew a finger across his throat – 'then who inherits? In Latin it is the phrase, *cui bono?* – who benefits? – you see? It is perfectly clear.'

At the heart of the matter was my child. My son aged two and a half who barely knew me, who kept forgetting my name, to whom I could not send gifts, with whom I could not play in the Gardens or beyond them, my son the heir to another man's fortune, his mother's passport to the future. My son in whose little face I so clearly saw my own. I was surprised that no one else seemed to notice the strong likeness, that in fact people said he looked just like his father who was not his father, a victory of the ostensible over the actual. People see what they are supposed to see.

Vespasian, what kind of a name was Vespasian, anyway? It irritated me more and more. 'Little Vespa', indeed. A little Vespa was what Audrey Hepburn drove so recklessly around the Eternal City on her *Roman Holiday,* with Gregory Peck panicky on the pillion. My son deserved a better handle than those movie stars' handlebars. He deserved at the very least the name of one of the grand masters of the cinema, Luis or Kenji or Akira or Sergei, Ingmar or Andrzej or Luchino or Michelangelo, François or Jean-Luc or Jean or Jacques. Or Orson or Stanley or Billy or even, prosaically, Clint. I had begun to dream only-half-unseriously of a kidnapping, or running away with my Federico or Alfred and escaping into the world of cinema itself, plunging into the movies in the opposite direction to Jeff Daniels in the Woody Allen movie, breaking the fourth wall to dive into the movies rather than out of them into the world. Who needed the world when you could run across the desert behind Peter O'Toole's camel or, with Kubrick's astronaut Keir Dullea, murder the mad computer HAL 9000 while it sang 'Daisy, Daisy, give me your answer, do'? What was the point of reality if you could skip with a lion and a scarecrow down the Yellow Brick Road, or descend a grand staircase beside Gloria Swanson, ready for Mr DeMille to shoot your close-up? Yes, my son and I, hand in hand, would marvel at the gigantic buttocks and breasts of the whores in *Fellini's Roma* and sit in despair on a Roman sidewalk mourning a stolen bicycle and jump into Doc Brown's DeLorean and fly back to the future and be free.

But it couldn't happen. We were all trapped in Vasilisa's charade, the child most of all, the child was her winning move. For a moment I wondered exactly how ruthless Vasilisa might be; had she somehow engineered the deaths of two of the three Golden boys at least, and might she also have put a hit out on the third if he hadn't taken his own life? But I had seen too many movies, and was succumbing to the same melodrama as lovelorn, angry Vito Tagliabue. I shook my head to clear it. No, she was probably not a murderer or a commissioner of murders. She was just – 'just!' – a conniving and manipulative creature who was close to winning her war.

✲

The new closeness that grew up between Nero and Riya after the three deaths put a Siberian scowl on the second Mrs Golden's beautiful (if slightly frozen) face, but came as no surprise to me. The three-times-unfathered father had nobody with whom to mourn Apu or Petya but her grief about D's death was equal to his own. There was no noun in any language they knew that named the parent whose child had died, no equivalent of *widower* or *orphan,* and no verb to describe the loss. *Bereavement* wasn't exact but it would have to do. They sat together in Nero's study in the silence of their loss, their silence like a conversation in which everything that needed to be said was said, like James Joyce and Samuel Beckett silently suffused by sadness both for the world and for themselves. He was frail, complaining sometimes of dizziness, at others of nausea, and he would doze off and wake up again several times in an evening. There were failures of memory. Sometimes he didn't remember she was there. But at other times he was once again his old sharp self. His decline wasn't a straight-line graph. There were ups and downs, though the trend was inescapably downward.

One night she took him uptown to the Park Avenue Armory where in a semicircle of eleven tall concrete towers professional mourners from around the world performed the myriad sounds of that most silent of silences, death. A blind accordionist from Ecuador played *yaravíes* in one tower, and three Cambodian mourners who had escaped the efforts of the Khmer Rouge to eradicate their kind performed the ceremony called *kantomming,* playing a flute and large and small gongs. The performances were not long, maybe fifteen or twenty minutes, but their resonances echoed within Riya and Nero long after they left the space. Nero said only, 'The bird was useful.' Alone in one of the towers a giant and non-specific bird, something like a rooster, was seated on a concrete shelf, a mourner from Burkina Faso completely hidden inside his bird suit with a bird head sitting on his own, and bells on his ankles that jingled softly when he moved his feet. The bird mourner made no sound apart from that occasional faint jingle, and sat very still except for the occasional very slight shudder, and his grave and kindly presence was powerful enough to heal just a little of Riya's and Nero's pain. 'Do you want to go again?' Riya asked Nero when they were out on the sidewalk again. 'No,' he said. 'Enough is enough.'

One night after many nights of wordlessness Nero did speak. The study was in darkness. They needed no light.

'You shouldn't quit your job, daughter,' he said. He had started calling her that.

The statement, made without any preamble or shadow of a doubt, caught her off guard.

'You know what, thank you, but this is stuff you don't understand,' she said, too harshly. 'This is my stuff, or it was for a long time.'

'You are right,' he said. 'This question of gender is beyond my comprehension. Man, woman, OK. Homosexual, all right, I know it exists. This other world, men with surgically constructed organs, women without women's parts, you lost me. You're right. I'm a dinosaur, and my mind is not one hundred per cent. But you? You know this inside out. You are right. This is your stuff.'

She didn't reply. They had grown comfortable in their silences; there was no need to answer him.

'It's about him, I know,' he said. 'You blame yourself and so you abandon your field.'

'My field,' she said. 'It should be a soft safe place for understanding. Instead it's a war zone. I choose peace.'

'You're not at peace,' he said. 'So much of this identity subject you have no problem with. Black, Latino, women, this is all fine. It's this in-between sex area that you call the war zone. If you want peace there, maybe be the peacemaker. Don't run away from the fight.'

He heard a question in her silence. 'Why, you think I can't inform myself a little?' he said. 'You think because my brain is slowly weakening, shrinking like a cheap shirt, that it's all gone? Not yet dead, young woman. Not dead yet.'

'OK,' she said.

'Take the leave of absence. Think things through. Don't quit.'

'OK,' she said.

'Me,' he said, 'I shifted my identity too.'

*

Later, after Riya has left, the old man is alone in the darkened room. The landline telephone rings. He decides whether or not to answer, reaches out, pulls his hand back, reaches out again, answers.

Yes.

Golden sahib.

Who is this.

I do not think so you will remember my name. I was a small fry in a very big frying pan.

What is your name.

Mastan. Formerly Inspector, Mumbai CID, subsequently Himachal Pradesh. Afterwards, private sector. Presently retired.

Pause.

Mastan. I remember.

That is honour for me. That such a big big *seth* should recall. What a memory, sir. Your own son could not recall, a much younger man.

You met one of my sons.

Sir, in Mumbai, sir. Goes now by name Apu. Which is to say, went by said name. Apologies for my clumsy English. Condolences on your loss.

How did you get this number.

Sir, I was police officer, subsequently private security. These things are possible.

Pause.

What do you want.

Only to talk, sir. I have no authority, no power, I am retired, this is USA, no jurisdiction, nothing, cold case, and you are a so so powerful man and I, nobody. Only to clarify certain things. To satisfy myself before reaching my end. For my own satisfaction only.

And I should see you, why.

In case you want to know identity of persons who killed your son. I am supposing only that this is of interest.

Long pause.

Tomorrow morning. Nine a.m.

Sharp, sahib. On the dot. Thanking you in advance.

*

Still later, Riya is asleep, and is woken by her cellphone. To her very great surprise, the caller is Nero Golden.

Can you come?

Now? It's the middle of the night.

I need to talk, and now I have the words, and maybe tomorrow I won't have them.

Give me a moment.

Daughter, I need you now.

31

He was about to be eighty years old and had started forgetting very recent events but the past glowed more and more brightly in his memory like gold at the bottom of the Rhine. The river of his thought was no longer clear, its water an opaque and muddied flow, and within it his consciousness was slowly losing its grip on chronology, on what was then, what now, what was waking truth and what had been born in the fairyland of dreams. The library of time was disordered, its categories jumbled, its indexes scrambled or destroyed. There were good days and bad days but with every passing day it was his faraway yesterdays that shone more clearly than last week. Then the past called him on the phone in the dark of night and all he had buried rose from its grave all at once and swarmed around him and he made a phone call of his own. In what followed I hear an echo of another Hitchcock movie. We were no longer in *Rear Window*. We were entering the world of *I Confess*.

(You remember I Confess*? A murderer confesses his crime to a Catholic priest who is bound by the rules of the confessional to keep the killer's secret. Hitchcock hated Montgomery Clift's Method-acting techniques, and some people hated the film's total humourlessness, but Éric Rohmer and Claude Chabrol praised the film for its 'majesty' in* Cahiers du Cinéma*, pointing out that as the priest is silenced, the film is dependent*

on the actor's expressions. 'Only these looks give us access to the mysteries of his thought. They are the most worthy and faithful messengers of the soul.' Riya Zachariassen, hurrying across Manhattan at dead of night, was no priestess, but she was about to receive a confession. Would she keep the secret? If so, how would her looks and glances communicate what she knew? And: would possession of the secret endanger her life?)

The past, his abandoned past on the storied hill. The hill had always been a magical place ever since Ram's brother Lakshman shot an arrow into the earth and brought the faraway Ganges here to quench their thirst. An underground spring burst through the ground and they drank. There was still fresh water in the Banganga Tank. *Baan,* an arrow in Sanskrit, and *Ganga* of course the mother river. They lived among the living stories of the gods.

And after the gods, the British, and in particular the Hon. Mountstuart Elphinstone, governor of the city between 1819 and 1827, who built the first bungalow on the hill and all the city's grandees followed his example. Nero remembered the hill of his childhood, a place of many trees and some low elegant mansions with their red-tiled roofs visible among the foliage. He walked in memory through the Hanging Gardens and watched his sons play in the Old Woman's Shoe in Kamala Nehru Park. The first tower block was built on the hill in the 1950s and people laughed at it. Matchbox House they called it because it looked like a giant matchbox standing on its end. Who would want to live there, people jeered, look, how ugly. But the *machis* buildings went up and the bungalows came down. That was progress. But this was not the story he wanted to tell. He wanted to finish the story he began to tell me that day in the Russian Tea Room.

(He let Riya in himself. They went to his darkened study and sat in darkness. She said nothing, or almost nothing. He had a long story to tell.)

He first met the man he started calling Don Corleone around the same time as the theatrical release of *The Godfather,* back when he was getting his feet wet for the first time in the world of film production. At that time everyone else called the don Sultan Ameer. His crime family was S-Company, '*S* for Sultan, Super and Style', as the don liked to boast. He was a big-time criminal, master smuggler, but people loved him because he allowed nobody to be killed and he was a sort of social worker at heart. Helped the poor in the slums and the petty shopkeepers also. Prostitution he did, it's true; brothels in Kamathipura, yes, he ran them. Bank robberies, also. Nobody's perfect. So, yes, on the whole, give or take, a Robin Hood type, you could say. Not true, not really, operating on that mega scale is not to be compared to a bunch of small-operator bow-and-arrow bandits in Sherwood Forest, UK, but people thought him a good guy, more good than rotten. He was the first celebrity gangster. Knew everybody, was seen everywhere. Police, judges, politicians, all in his pocket. Walked the city freely, without fear. And without gangsters like him half the movies people loved would not have been made. Major investors, the mafia dons. You could ask any big filmmaker. Sooner or later the mafia came to call, with bags of money in its hands.

He trained the next generation, all local boys nurtured by him. What did Zamzama Alankar know about smuggling that Sultan Ameer didn't teach him? He trained Zamzama (aka. KG, for 'Kim's Gun,' or just the Cannon), he trained Little Feet, he trained Short Fingers, he trained Big Head, all the top guys. They, all five of them, loved movies, and Sultan Ameer had a film-star lover – this was the girl called Goldie, he poured money into dud movies trying to make her an icon – so naturally they went into the motion picture business. Nobody called it Bollywood then, that was a much later invention. Bombay film industry. Bombay talkies. It was just called that.

(Bombay Talkie, *if I may briefly interject, was and remains my favourite Merchant–Ivory movie, especially the song-and-dance number 'Typewriter Tip Tip Tip' in which dancers pirouette on the keys of the giant 'fate machine', and the director explains, 'As we human beings dance on them we press down the keys and the story that is written is the story of our fate.' Yes, we are all dancing out our stories on the Typewriter of Life.)*

So. Don Corleone in the Bombay talkies helped some falling stars regain their footing, Parveen Babi for example, also Helen. He was friends with Raj Kapoor and Dilip Kumar. His smugglers smuggled and his thieves thieved and his whores whored and his judges and politicos and cops did as they were told but up there on the silver screen at Maratha Mandir his movie *Kuch Nahin Kahin Nahin Kabhi Nahin Koi Nahin* (*Nothing Nowhere Never Nobody*), held the record for most consecutive weeks screened until of course that other bloody movie, *The Bride Stripped Bare by Her Bachelors, Even*, came on and broke every damn record in sight. But *KN4*, as people called his biggest hit, Sultan Ameer/Don Corleone was proud of that, his proudest achievement, he used to say, and he had his own name for it, 'Everything Everywhere Everytime Everyone', or 'E4All', because that's what it was, all things to all people. And it was true his beloved Goldie never made it to the top, was never above-the-title as Hollywood types say, but she was happy, he bought her a big house in Juhu next door to the great Dev Anand and she could invite that living god over for samosas and cups of tea.

And Nero: he was just a businessman, putting most of his energy into the construction business, going up in the world like his buildings, and also like everyone else in that starry-eyed city obsessed with the movies. He met the don at so-and-so's beach house in Juhu, or maybe such-and-such's, it wasn't important. One of the two or three great hostesses who dominated the city's glittering nightlife, let's say that. They hit it off immediately and at the end of the night Sultan Ameer said, 'Tomorrow I'm going to see Smita to narrate my new picture, why not come along?' With those words he seduced Nero forever and the businessman's life started to move down a new path.

Superstars – ultrastars! – didn't read scripts. One went to them and narrated the picture, told its story, and made sure in the telling that the superstar's role came across as the indispensable central element of the project. Smita was one of the most beloved actresses of her time, not just a beauty or a sex symbol but a wonderful, powerful actor. She led an outrageous life by local standards, carrying on openly with a famous star who was also a married man. In the end puritanism and vilification would drive her out of the business and she became a wounded recluse, but that was later, right now she was the highest of the high, on the pinnacle of Mount Kailash, a goddess of goddesses, the top. For Nero his meeting with her was one of the great events of his life, even though the narration didn't go well, because the part required Smita to age, during the course of the film, from seventeen to maybe fifty-five. 'You see,' the immortal personage said to the don, 'I am so grateful you came to me with this, because most parts are not *stretching*, isn't it, and what I want to do as an artist is to *stretch*, to *expand*, so this picture, I *love* it. I just love it. There are just one-two things, OK, I want to put them right out in the open, right on the table, because everything should be hundred per cent agreed before we start shooting, isn't it, when we are on set we should all be hundred per cent pulling in the same direction, so can I say?' Of course, Sultan Ameer replied, this is why we are here, please. She frowned and looked in Nero's direction. 'And he is who?' she wanted to know. Sultan Ameer clucked his tongue and made a dismissive gesture. 'Not to mind him,' he said. 'He is just like that.' This diminished the frown. Then the celestial entity turned back to the don and said, 'You see, as you narrated, the character becomes the mother of a nineteen-year-old girl. Now I have never – never in my *life*! – played the mother of a teenage child. This is my difficulty. You understand that the choices I make, the pictures I choose, seriously affect the annual box- office performance of our whole beloved industry, so I must be careful, isn't it? I hear a voice speaking, from the public that loves me! – from the star that I am! – and the voice is saying –' Sultan Ameer interrupted her. 'Storyline can be changed,' he said. 'Tell your voice to stop speaking.' – But it was too late. '"No," the voice is saying. "You owe it to the world."'

Nero, who sat silently in the corner, Nero who was just like that, was entranced. When they left the divine presence he said, 'I'm sorry she didn't like it.' Sultan Ameer snapped his fingers. 'She will like it. Story is easy to shift. And maybe a Mercedes and if there is a suitcase in the dickey containing black money then, fataakh! Done deal.' He clapped his hands. Nero had just begun to nod to express understanding when the don added, 'This can be your investment in the project.'

'The Mercedes?'

'And the suitcase. The suitcase is very important.'

That was how it began. In the next few years Nero established a profitable sideline as the don's money launderer and bagman. How did that happen? He just slid into it, driven by his obsession with the movie world. Stardust in his eyes, filmi glamour turning his head, and the money everyone made was crazy. Or, more accurately, there had always been a lawless side to him, the construction business was scarcely law-abiding, after all, it was crooked as corkscrews, as W. H. Auden might have put it. In those days the construction boom had begun and tall buildings, 'matchbox houses', were rising all around the city and Nero was at the heart of the transformation. In the new high-rise grab for the sky, how many laws were flouted or broken, how many pockets were lined to make troubles go away! The buildings went up and kept on going up beyond the number of floors authorised by the municipal corporation. Afterwards the electricity or water or gas authorities might threaten to cut off supply to the floors that should not exist but there were ways of smoothing those ruffled feathers. The movie star's suitcase was by no means Nero's first. It also happened that many of the new buildings were straightforwardly illegal, built without properly sanctioned plans, not conforming to the proper codes. Nero was guilty of such work also, but so was everybody, nobody was innocent, and like the other big builders he had friends in the other type of high places, so like everyone else he got away with everything he did. 'The builder is the law,' he liked to say. 'And the law is, keep on building.' Ethics? Transparency? Those were foreign words, words for people who didn't understand the city's culture or its people's way of life.

That was who he was. He knew it, his sons knew it, that was the way of the world. His friendship with Don Corleone aka Sultan Ameer unlocked the door to the dungeon in which the deeper lawlessness was lurking, waiting to be set free. Now there were starlets at his parties and cocaine in the bathrooms and he had moved from being a straight, suited-and-booted, ditchwater-dull high-rise builder with a blueprint and a briefcase to becoming a figure in the city in his own right. And with status came more business, and with business came more status, and so on, around and around. During these years he developed the frankly vulgar self-promotional manner which still hung around him like a flashy fur coat in his New York years. He moved his family into the luxury Walkeshwar home. He bought a yacht. He had affairs. His name glittered in the night sky from Andheri to Nariman Point. Life was good.

There were many different ways in which money could be cleaned. For smaller sums there was smurfing, a way of breaking up dirty money into small amounts and using it to buy things like money orders or bankers' drafts, which would later be redeposited in different banks, still in smallish amounts, and then withdrawn as laundered cash. Nero used this method for things like the money suitcases. But for larger projects, a larger-scale method was required, and the real estate business was the ideal vehicle. Nero became, to those in the know, the unacknowledged master of 'flipping one' and 'flipping two'. 'Flipping one' was purchasing high-end, big-ticket real estate with black money and then quickly reselling it, usually for a profit, as prices were rocketing. The money from the sale was white money, clean as a whistle. 'Flipping two' was buying property – with the seller's agreement – for less than the market value, paying him the balance under the table in black money, and then proceeding to 'flipping one'. Nero ran the largest real estate brokerage firm in the city and in underground parlance it became known as 'Flipistan', the country to which dirty money went for a vacation, to get cleaned up and come back with a nice honest tan. For a price, of course. Nero used Flipistan for his own black-money deals, but whenever members of S-Company asked for his services, he made a generous percentage on the deal.

Then the sky fell in on Don Corleone. The prime minister's son Sanjay Gandhi, formerly his drinking buddy, went after Sultan Ameer during his mother's years of authoritarian Emergency rule and the S-Company godfather was convicted in courts controlled by Sanjay, not by him, and he was sent down for a year and a half. Curiously, just as the Emergency ended and Sanjay fell from grace, the don was freed. But he was a changed man, had lost his nerve in prison and found God instead.

Even though they were both of the same religious persuasion Nero was a Muslim in name only and this new devout Corleone was not to his liking. The don gave up gangsterism and tried, unsuccessfully, to enter politics; the two men drifted apart. In the 1980s Sultan Ameer was withered and all but forgotten, beginning his long struggle against the cancer that eventually claimed him, and Nero was a big wheel. But an even bigger wheel had begun to turn.

Before he was notorious, Zamzama Alankar was known for his moustache, a growth so thick and ominous that it seemed to be a parasitic organism originating somewhere deep inside his head, perhaps even in his brain, and growing down his nose until it reached the outside world, like an alien emerging onto his upper lip and bringing with it news of its host's immense and dangerous power. It was a moustache that won a moustache competition back home in the coastal village of Bankot, but Zamzama was after far bigger game. He had been born the son of a policeman in that remote township on the shore of the Arabian Sea near an old sea fort, but, perhaps because his relationship with his stern father soured during childhood, he never had much time for the law or the officers who enforced it, whether on the water or on solid ground. He first rose to prominence because of his central role in the hawala system by which money was transferred from place to place by word of mouth and without paperwork – handed to a hawala broker in place A, who then, for a small commission, communicated receipt to a broker in place B, who paid an equal sum of money to the designated recipient as long as the recipient knew the password. Thus money 'moved without moving', in the words of the hawala, and there could be many more links in the chain if required. The system was popular because the commission paid by the client was far lower than in the normal banking system, and, in addition, the procedure could bypass problems such as variable exchange rates; the hawala chain fixed its own exchange rate and everyone adhered to it. The whole network relied on the honour of hawala brokers around the country and indeed the world. (Though if a hawala broker acted dishonourably, it would have been unwise to bet on his living to a ripe old age.) The system was illegal in India because, like smurfing and flipping, it was an effective means of money laundering, but Zamzama continued to operate it on a large scale, not only in the Indian subcontinent but also throughout the Middle East, the Horn of Africa and even certain parts of the United States. Hawala wasn't enough for him, however. He wanted to sit in the *kursi*, that is, on the throne of the underworld, and with Sultan Ameer out of the way in jail, he made his bid for power, assisted by his lieutenants Big Head, Short Fingers and Little Feet. He faced competition from the associates of a rival boss named Javed Greasy but he soon brushed the challenge aside, using a technique that came as a profound shock to all the members of Sultan Ameer's relatively non-violent crime family. The name of this technique was murder. The bodies of Javed Greasy and his family, laid out like fish on a slab on Juhu beach at low tide, not only resolved the leadership issue; they also sent a message to the whole city, overworld as well as underworld. It was a new day, the corpses said. There was a new player in town, and there were new rules. S-Company was Z-Company now.

His brother Salloo, known as Salloo Boot, had helped Zamzama establish his first foothold in the city by targeting the don of the Dongri district, Daddy Jyoti, and taking a bunch of his men to surround Daddy and his men and beating them severely with empty glass bottles of soda water, Campa-Cola and Limca. That got rid of Daddy, who was never seen again in the city, but a more serious gang war followed, against the Pashto gang from Afghanistan, who started in the money-lending business with offices in the ideally named Readymoney Lane, but moved rapidly into small-scale extortion, obliging little shopkeepers and small businesses to pay protection money, in the city's slums as well as its markets. The prices at tailors' shops, watch-repair services, hairdressers and vendors of leather goods rose to cover the requirements of the racketeers. Prostitutes on Falkland Road had to charge their marks more as well. The costs of extortion could not be absorbed by businesses with such tight margins, so they were passed on to the consumer. In this way much of the city found itself paying, so to speak, an extra, gangland tax. But what to do? There was no option but to cough up.

The Pashtos also decided to eliminate Boot and Cannon – that is, Zamzama – and hired Manny, a top *dacoit* or bandit from Madhya Pradesh, to do the job. Now it so happened that Salloo Boot had a dancer girlfriend, Charu, and one night in the early 1980s he picked her up from her home in Bombay Central and drove her in a Fiat toward a love nest in Bandra. But Manny and the Pashtos were on his tail, and surrounded the Fiat at a gas station where Salloo Boot had stopped en route. With genuine gallantry Manny and the Pashtos asked Charu to get out of the car and buzz off. After that they shot Boot five times and left him dead. They went as fast as possible to Zamzama's base at Pakmodia Street to catch him off guard before news of his brother's death reached him, but the building was heavily guarded and a major gun battle ensued. Zamzama was unhurt. Soon afterwards the Pashto leaders were arrested and charged with Boot's murder. When they were standing trial a Z-Company shootist, a Christian killer called Derek, burst into the courtroom and shot them dead with a machine gun.

During the 1980s at least fifty mobsters from Z-Company and the Pashtos were killed in the continuing gang war. But in the end the Afghan mob was eliminated and godfather Zamzama had his throne.

After his older brother's death Zamzama took the decision to dispense with a personal life. 'Girlfriend is weakness,' Nero heard him say. 'Family is weakness. This in others is valuable. But in the boss it cannot be permitted. I am the cat that walks alone.' Alone, that was to say, except for a twenty-four-hour bodyguard detail of twelve persons – that is, thirty-six persons working twelve at a time in eight-hour shifts. Plus a team of twelve trained countersurveillance drivers behind the wheels of armoured Mercedes stretches, experts in the arts of dry cleaning, which was to say, making sure the motorcade was not being tailed. (Again, four drivers at a time, three shifts.) And the front door of his house was solid steel and the windows also were bulletproofed and boasted thick metal shutters, and there were heavily armed men on the roof at all times. The city was governed by a man living in a cage he had built for himself. Making himself invulnerable, he made the vulnerabilities of people's persons, families and capital assets the foundations of his wealth and power.

(I am not an expert in the industry now known as Bollywood, but it loves its gangster movies as much as its gangsters. The film buff entering this universe might well start with Raj Gopal Varma's Company, *Apoorva Lakhia's* Shootout at Lokhandwala, *Sanjay Gupta's* Shootout at Wadala, *or Milan Luthria's* Once upon a Time in Mumbaai *and* Once upon a Time in Mumbaai 2. *The extra* a *in* Mumbaai *is an example of a new numerological fad. People add or subtract vowels to make their names, or in this case the names of their movies, luckier and more successful:* Shobhaa De, Ajay Devgn, Mumbaai. *I am unable to comment on the efficacy or otherwise of such alterations.)*

It was *Aibak*, the film about Qutbuddin Aibak the first of the Slave Kings and the building of the Qutb Minar, that showed the industry that the new godfather meant business. The high-budget historical drama had been a lifetime pet project of one of the grandees of Bollywood, the producer A. Kareem, and it featured three of the 'six boys and four girls' who, according to common parlance, were the ultrastars of the time. Two weeks before the commencement of principal photography Kareem received a note informing him, a Muslim himself, that the proposed film was insulting to Islam because it referred to the new ruler as a slave, and demanding that the project be cancelled, or, alternatively, that a 'permission slash apology fee' of one crore of rupees in used, non-sequential banknotes be paid to the representative of Z-Company who would present himself in due course. Kareem immediately called a press conference and publicly jeered at Zamzama Alankar and his gang. 'These philistines think they can phuck with me?' Kareem cried, pronouncing both *ph*'s as powerfully plosive sounds. 'So ignorant they do not know that the names by which this dynasty is known, Mamluk or Ghulam, both mean "slave". We are making a banner production here, a landmark picturisation of our history. No bunch of goons can stop us.' Four days later, a small heavily armed group of men led by Zamzama's lieutenants Big Head and Short Fingers invaded the secure lot in Mehrauli near the real Qutb Minar where the extremely elaborate set for the movie had been built, and set it on fire. The film was never made.

A. Kareem complained of intense chest pains soon after the destruction of the movie set and died literally of a broken heart. Doctors examining the body said that the organ had literally burst apart inside him. Nobody ever jeered at Zamzama Alankar again.

Nero continued to invite Zamzama to parties at his home, and the movie industry's A-list continued to attend. Zamzama himself began to throw the most lavish affairs anyone had ever seen, flying planeloads of guests to Dubai, and everyone went. This was how it must have been in the heyday of Al Capone, the dark glamour, the seduction of danger, the heady cocktail of fear and desire. The Zamzama parties were reported in all the papers, the stars glittering in their nocturnal finery. The police sat on their hands. And sometimes on the morning after a great fireworks of a celebration, there would be a knock on the door of a producer sleeping off his overindulgences in a stateroom on a Z-Company yacht, perhaps in the company of a starlet who was too stupid to know that this was never, ever the way to the top; and there would be Big Head or Little Feet with a contract for the producer to sign, giving away all the overseas rights of his latest film at highly disadvantageous terms, and there would be a large weapon pointing at his head to help persuade him, and the days of gallantry were gone, nobody told the naked starlet in the bed to make herself decent and run. Party in the front, business in the back, that was the Z-Company way. Many of Bollywood's leading lights had to ask for, and receive, police protection, and they were never sure if it would be enough, or if the men in uniform would turn out to be beholden to Zamzama, and the guns intended to protect would point inward at the principal rather than outward toward the dangerous inscrutable city. And the law? The law turned a nearly blind eye. Small fry were sometimes thrown in jail as a sop to public opinion. The big fish swam freely in that sea.

Daughter, daughter, Nero said. I was among the worst of them, because they never tried to extort me. I willingly did their money work, and they were good to me financially, and I accepted it all, it was the way of the world, I thought, and maybe it was, but the world is a bad place, you should look for a better world than the one we have made.

He was not a victim of the extortion racket but he didn't have to be. The threats and assassination attempts and actual killings of those years had him scared stupid. He had a lot to lose. He had expensive property, he had buildings going up all over town, he had a wife, and he had sons. He had all the weaknesses Zamzama looked for and needed. It was not necessary for the Z-Company people even to mention these weaknesses to him. They were the unspoken bond between the mob and Nero. Who was he to them? They had the dirty washing and he did their laundry. He was their dhobi. They actually called him that, Big Head the dwarf and Short Fingers with the orange hair and Little Feet who had the biggest feet anyone had ever seen. 'Hey, dhobi!' they said on the phone. 'Got some washing for you. Come and take it to the *ghat.*' When he saw them they would snap their fingers. 'Get it cleaned up,' they would command. 'Chop chop.' Zamzama himself was more respectful, always using terms of respect along with Nero's real name. *Sahib, ji, janab.* The respect was a way of expressing contempt. The meaning of the respect was, 'I own you, motherfucker, and do not forget it.' Nero didn't need reminding. He was not a hero. He didn't want to lose his family or his toes. There was no chance that he would forget.

The villains were spilling off the movie screens, jumping down into the cinemas larger than life, movie-sized, and charging down the aisles and out into the streets, guns blazing, and he had the guilty feeling that the industry was responsible, it had created these monsters and made them glamorous and sexy and now they were taking over the town. *Bombay meri jaan,* he thought, humming the song, Bombay my life, my darling, where have you gone, the girls on Marine Drive in the cool of the evening with wreaths of jasmine in their hair, the Sunday-morning jazz jam sessions on Colaba Causeway or Churchgate, listening to Chic Chocolate, to Chris Perry's saxophone and Lorna Cordeiro's voice; Juhu beach before people like him surrounded it with buildings; Chinese food; the beautiful city, the best city in the world. But no, that was wrong, the song which was to the city what 'New York, New York' was to another metropolis had always warned that it was a tough town, difficult to live in, and it was that song's fault, too, the gamblers and the cut-throats and the thieves and the corrupt businessmen it sang about had poured out of the lyrics like the actors leaping out of the movies, and here they were now, terrifying decent folk, folk like the naive girl in the song who defended the great city, *oh heart it's easy to live in this town,* but even she warned, *look out, you will reap what you sow. You will reap just what you sow.*

(Yes, it was the movies' fault, it was the song's fault. Yes, blame art, Nero, blame entertainment. So much easier than blaming human beings, the actual actors in the drama. So much more pleasant than blaming yourself.)

He went on doing it, the suitcases, the smurfing, the flipping. He even agreed to become one end of a big-money hawala chain, when 'asked nicely' by Zamzama Alankar himself – with a little cascade of *sahibs, janabs and jis* – one evening during a pool party at the Willingdon Club. *They never tried to extort me.* They didn't have to. He was Zamzama's willing pawn. He thought himself a king in the city but he was only a humble foot soldier. Zamzama Alankar was the king.

And he wasn't completely telling the truth about the extortion. He admitted it. The truth was that they never tried to extort cash money from him. What they extorted was much, much worse.

Zamzama, the Cannon, was not a sentimental man. Once, according to his legend – he was a man who paid a lot of attention to the nurturing of his legendary aspects – Little Feet had kidnapped a mob pimp named Moosa Mouse who had been interfering with certain company girls, and had him sealed in a metal container at the docks, and had then hired a vessel to take the container out to the farthest reaches of the harbour where it was dispatched to the bottom of the sea. Two days later Mouse's mother was on TV crying her eyes out. Zamzama said, 'Get me her cell number now,' and a minute later, *while she was still being interviewed on live television,* he called her up. Bewildered, she answered the phone, and there was Zamzama's voice in her ear saying, 'Bitch, your mouse is now a fish, and if you don't stop that noise you will shortly be *keema* yourself. Kaboom!' *Keema* was mincemeat. 'Kaboom' was Zamzama's favoured sign-off and whoever heard that in his or her ear knew exactly who was speaking. The woman's crying stopped, boom, like that, and she never spoke to any journalist ever again.

He also had no time for the kind of *Bombay-meri-jaan* romanticisation of the past to which Nero was prone. 'That city of dreams is long gone,' he told Nero unceremoniously. 'You yourself have built over and around it and crushed the old under the new. In Bombay of your dreams everything was love and peace and secular thinking and no communalism, Hindu-Muslim *bhai bhai,* all men were brothers, isn't it? Such bullshit, you're a man of the world, you should know better. Men are men and their gods are their gods and these things do not change and the hostility between their tribes also is always there. Just a question of what's on the surface and how far beneath is the hate. In this city Mumbai we have won the gang war but a bigger war lies ahead. Only two gangs in Mumbai now. The *gang* gang, the mafia, that is me. Z-Company, we only are that. And what are we, ninety-five per cent? Musalman people. People of the book. But there are also the political gangs, and they are Hindu. Hindu politics is running the municipal corporation and Hindu politicos have their Hindu gangs. Raman Fielding, you know the name? Aka Mainduck the Frog? You understand? Then understand the following: First we were just battling it out for territory. That battle is over. Now there comes holy war. Kaboom.'

Sultan Ameer 'got religion' in later life but his was of the mystical, Sufistic kind. Zamzama Alankar by the beginning of the 1990s had become an adherent of a much more fiery version of their common faith. The person credited with making this profound change in Zamzama's world view and range of interests was a demagogic preacher named Rahman, founder and secretary of a militant organisation based in the city and calling itself the Azhar Academy, dedicated to promoting the thought of a nineteenth-century Indian firebrand, Imam Azhar of Bareilly, the town which gave its name to the Barelvi sect of which the preacher Rahman was the leading light. The Academy had made itself known in the city by demonstrating against the ruling party, demonstrations that the ruling party described as 'riots', but which demonstrated, at the very least, that the Academy could put a substantial crowd on the street at short notice and then turn that crowd loose. To Nero's great dismay Zamzama started parroting the demagogue Rahman's words, often almost verbatim. The immorality and decadence of. The evil hostility and degeneracy of. Needs to be confronted head-on by. The pure and pristine teachings of. The correct perspective of. The true glory and splendour of. Our responsibility to save our society from. The benefit of the genius teaching of. Our resolve is greater than. Ours is a scientific mode of living in the world and in the hereafter. This world is nothing, only a gateway to the grandeur beyond. This life is nothing, only a clearing of the throat before the immortal song beyond. If it is required of us to sacrifice life we sacrifice nothing, only a clearing of the throat. If it is required of us that we rise up we will rise up with the flame of justice in our hand. We will raise the just hand of God and they will feel its tight slap on their face.

'Damn it, Zamzama,' Nero said to him when they met aboard the *Kipling*, Zamzama's sailboat in the harbour, which was the Cannon's preferred location for confidential discussions. 'What's got into you? You always struck me as a party man, not a praying mantis.'

'The time for loose talk is over,' the don replied, with a new note in his voice which Nero found menacing. 'Now the time for hard deeds approaches. And also, dhobi, do not use blasphemous language in my presence ever again.' It was the first time Nero had been reduced from *sahib* to *dhobi*. He didn't like the sound of that at all.

There were no more parties in Dubai. In the house behind the steel door, there was now a lot of praying. To a man of Nero's temperament, it was bizarre. Perhaps the time had come, he thought, to detach somewhat from Z-Company. Complete separation would be impossible because of the mafia's influence over the construction unions and even more over the non-unionised 'immigrant' labour force converging on the city from all over the country without papers or legal standing. But perhaps he had worked on the money side long enough. Enough, perhaps, of smurfing, flipping and hawala. He was by now a legitimate tycoon and should divest himself of these shadier portfolios.

To Zamzama he said, 'I think I'm getting too old and tired for the money work. Maybe I could train a successor to take my place.'

Zamzama was silent for a full minute. The *Kipling*, at anchor, its mainsail lowered and flaked, rocked gently on the water. The sun had set and the lights of the Back Bay glittered around them, an arc of beauty which Nero had never ceased to cherish. Then the mafia boss spoke. 'Do you like classic American rock and roll band, Eagles?' he asked. 'Glenn Frey, Don Henley, et cetera, et cetera, et cetera?' And, without waiting for an answer, he went on, 'Welcome to the Hotel California.' Upon which, to Nero's consternation, the don began – loudly, tunelessly, in a manner that struck fear into Nero's heart – to sing.

'You can check out any time you like, but you can never leave.'

This was the beginning of the great darkness, Nero said in the darkness of his study in the Golden house. After this discussion I was in hell. Or, I had been in hell for a long time, but now I felt the fire burning the soles of my feet.

But also, you know the funny thing about that song, about the hotel? It wasn't even true. Because leaving, when, where, how, that became his subject as well as mine.

You are shocked by me, he said. You are horrified by me and you haven't even heard the bad part yet. You are frightened by what I have told you and there is only one question in your mind. You loved my child. My poor confused child. You loved my child and you are asking, without words you are asking, I see in your eyes in the dark that you're asking. How much did my children know.

As for your beloved, in everything I have told so far he is free of all guilt. He was not born, or a little boy. As for the others, they grew up in a certain social stratum, the stratum of big city big business, and they knew what it took. Without greasing the palms, nothing got done. They knew about my Don Corleone, yes. But he was a well-liked guy. For them all this was normal as it was for everyone else. They liked the movie world also. The movie stars at our home. The ease of being with

A-list women. As if they also had stepped up onto the silver screen. This was pleasurable and if the dons were there too, so what, it was a known thing. Nobody cared. In the time of Sultan Ameer nobody judged. But when Alankar took over, then I shielded them from my involvement. The less they knew the better for everyone. This was a different type of individual and I kept my family away. My business was my business, I accept there are criticisms to be made, I neither justify nor defend my choices and actions, I only state. Your boy was seven years old in 1993 and twenty-two in 2008 when we came to New York. I must say that of all three of them he was always the most self-absorbed. His war was within himself, I see it clearly now. His cannons trained on himself from then until. Until. So to keep things from him was simple. The things I needed to keep from him, I don't think he knew. Also the oldest boy, my damaged boy, Harpo they called him, it could be a cruel town, yes; for him too the great question of his life lay in his head, a question with no answer. Him also I absolve. There remains the question of Apu. Apu who was Groucho then. Apu, to be frank: I think he knew. He knew but he didn't want to know and so, the drink the drugs, to deafen himself and blind himself and make himself unconscious. I never spoke to him about the dark side. He didn't ask. 'If my father was a dentist,' he said to me once, 'would I care how many fillings or root canals he did today, on whom? So, I think of you like that. You're the dentist when you go to work but at home you are the father. That is what your family needs from you. Not fillings but fatherly love.'

I told him very little. Only the surface things which everyone knew. Bribery, corruption. Small potatoes. But I think he guessed the big potatoes. I think this was why the debauchery, the drink, the women, the drugs.

Back home he was not that much of an artist. He had the lifestyle of the artist but not the work ethic. He was a bohemian but in Bohemia they make beautiful glass. He made very little of anything except making love and let me say though you will find it vulgar, excuse me, the drugs do not make one a better lover except in one's own estimation. So probably he was ineffective also in that department. When he came to

America he cleaned up his act. (*A snap of the fingers.*) Just like that. By this I was impressed, he was a new man, and so everything began to work for him. His talent came out and everyone saw it. I saw it for the first time. I never suspected he had so much talent.

All three of them shared this ability: to close the book of the past and to live in the present. This is a fortunate gift. I myself am closing the book of the present and living mostly in the past.

But there remains the matter of the buzzing in Apu's ears, the voices, sometimes the visions. He had a long history with hallucinogens. You could say if this is how you understand things that they made him more sensitive to what is unseen, that they revealed to him the pathway to the visionary world, opening, what are they? The doors of perception. Or you could say that that is all nonsense. You could say alternatively that he suffered damage. That he too was damaged in the brain, in the heart of himself. Three sons and all with damage in the brain, in the heart of themselves! This is not an equitable fate for a father. This is not just. Nevertheless it has been my fate. Apu saw visions and heard voices. So he was crazy too.

So I think he knew what I did but also he arranged with himself to un-know. This is why he went back with his woman and did not think about it first. He went back home and died. I think when he died he would have known what killed him and why. He would have known it was the consequence of my actions. This I also understand. The message was sent and I have received it. The darkness is gathering. There is not long before the end. This is why I speak tonight. So that everything can be said.

There are two things to talk about and they happened fifteen years apart. 1993, 2008. These are the dates.

In December 1992 Nero was on the *Kipling* with Zamzama Alankar again. The mosque built by the first Mughal emperor Babar in the northern city of Ayodhya had just been destroyed by Hindu activists who claimed that it stood on the mythological site of the birthplace of Lord Ram, the seventh avatar or incarnation of Vishnu. There were riots in Mumbai. First

Muslims rioted then the party faithful of the Hindu extremist Shiv Sena attacked them in return and the police, Zamzama said, were openly partisan, openly pro-Sena and 'anti-us'. These riots were in the process of dying down but Zamzama's rage was volcanic and knew no bounds.

Last straw, he shouted at Nero. Camel's back is broken and now the camel must be shot.

It is not wise to get involved in this matter. Focus on your strong points. Business is good.

It is not a question of wisdom. It is a question of necessity. And to destroy a holy mosque because of the rumoured location there of the origin point of an imaginary being, this is what is *unwise.*

They do not think he is fictional.

They are incorrect.

Alankar had had contact with concerned persons from a neighbouring country. The neighbours felt strongly that action must be taken.

A plan has been formulated, Alankar said. A major consignment of arms, ammunition and RDX explosive will be sent by the neighbours, by sea to the Konkan Coast in the first week of January. The landing place is Dighi. It will be necessary for you to arrange the suitcases for the coastguard so that a gap will be left in the water through which the consignment will come on speedboats.

For me, Zamzama? This is not my kind of business. Politics? No, no, no. You must not ask this of me.

Yes, yes, yes. Your house is so well fortified, isn't it? I have seen it, the motorised heavy metal gates, the alarm systems, the security guards. Your family must feel safe there. Do they feel safe? They must. Do they sometimes go out of doors? Of course, they are Mumbaikars, they lead a full life. A happy family. Congrats.

We are old associates, you and I. This is not a way to talk to me.

You have become so successful, so wealthy, well done. How unfortunate if your workers down tools. How tragic if by chance, a fire.

So there is no choice but to do it. Very well, it will be done.

Also there will be a second consignment some weeks later, at Shekhadi. Same drill.

The neighbours' plan required a precise sequence of actions. First there would be killings. In Dongri, the previous fiefdom of Daddy Jyoti who had been driven out of town by his soda-bottle beating, there lived a community of what were called *mathadi* workers, that is, labourers who carried loads on their heads. These were street sleepers so they were easy to acquire. A number of these head-load workers would be acquired and the dispatching would be done with small knives to the throat to give the appearance of a ritual religious rite. Dongri was an area of high communal sensitivity and the neighbour was confident that the ritual killings would cause the opposition to rise up in force. The opposition was highly organised and had police support but they would face heavily armed resistance. Weapons would be pre-stocked in flash-point zones. And there would be grenades and there would be bombs. And then the bombs would incite more opposition crowds and those crowds would be met by automatic rifles and more explosives. And a fire would be lit that would spread across the country and the neighbours would be glad because the bastards would have been taught a lesson.

God willing, Zamzama said, we will give the bastards one hell of a bloody nose.

It was the last time Nero ever set foot aboard the *Kipling*. It was almost time to go ashore but the Z-Company chief had one more thing to say. You and I, he said, maybe we will never meet again. It will not be possible for me to remain in this country after the events that will occur. For you the position is easier. I have always been thoughtful regarding you and there is as you are aware a long chain of intermediaries between us and you have one hundred per cent deniability, so I think it will be OK for you to stay put with your wife, family. But maybe just in case you also should construct an exit strategy.

Zamzama was right. The two men in fact never met again. And he was right about the exit strategy too.

The events of March 12, 1993, were widely reported and it will not be necessary to go into details. Car bombs and scooter bombs. Bomb in the basement of the Stock Exchange. Three bazaars, three hotels, airport, cinema, passport office, bank, kaboom, kaboom, kaboom. Even Mahim fishermen's colony, kaboom. Taxi-bomb at the Gateway to India, big fucking kaboom.

The neighbours must have been disappointed, however. There was considerable loss of life but the hoped-for civil war did not occur. The city and the nation kept their nerve. There were arrests, things calmed down, peace returned. Zamzama Alankar was gone along with his lieutenant Short Fingers, and these two were named Public Enemies #1 and #2. It was widely believed they eventually settled down as guests of the neighbours, and Zamzama continued to run Z-Company by remote control. The neighbours, however, claimed to have no knowledge of the fugitives' whereabouts.

In the following years there was a major rift in the underworld. After the attacks the police assault on Z-Company was unprecedented, all the arrangements and understandings fell apart, and the whole edifice came this close to disintegrating. The satphones and online secure communications systems went on working so Zamzama was able to send instructions and rule the roost, but wasn't it just a little too grand of him and Short Fingers to issue orders from a distance, they weren't the ones taking the heat. Gradually the distance between the two absentee leaders and the two in situ, Big Head and Little Feet – who had to face gangsterism and terror charges, and the not-proven verdict that allowed them to walk free took five years to engineer, that was five years of life under the hammer of the law – it caused resentment. At the end of five years Z-Company was still Z-Company, the loyalty of the cadres was still there, but everyone knew there was a Splinter-Z, a group that owed primary loyalty to the dwarf and the guy with the huge shoe size, and though a kind of truce held between those two and the two staying with the neighbours there was, increasingly, little love lost there.

Nero was invited in for a meeting with Head and Feet. This did not take place on a luxury yacht in the harbour but in a *basti* deep inside the Dharavi slum, to which he was taken by men who didn't speak to him and didn't look like they wanted a chat. Inside the slum dwelling Head nodded at him and Feet pointed a toe at a brick. Sit, Feet said.

So here's what we know about you, said Head.

You're the dhobi, said Feet.

What is dirty, you clean.

Therefore, hard to believe you knew nothing. *We* knew nothing. That is a matter for us to resolve with the boss. But you? You knew nothing? That stretches our credulity.

That puzzles our *dimaags*.

However. Our *brains* also know the following, (a) and (b). (A), you don't like politics.

And (b), you don't get involved in religion.

So, there's a balance. On the one hand, on the other hand.

It has been decided to give you benefit of doubt.

The following is our position. This operation has damaged the Company. From now on it is our intention to disengage from such operations.

We have put this to the boss and Fingers.

They are in agreement.

A fresh start. Return to basics. Not straying from our area of maximum expertise.

However, in Company business, there are many issues of trust. And our trust in you is, how to say it.

Compromised.

Shaken.

Shot.

An untrustable trust is untrustworthy.

It is a distrust.

However, we have given you benefit of doubt.

See above.

Therefore we simply disengage from you. You continue with your life, we with ours.

But if at any time any single information leaks from you regarding ourselves.

We will cut off your penis.

And your sons' penises.

And we will put them in your wife's mouth.

And I will fuck her from behind.
While I slit her throat from the front.
You are a free man. You may go.
Go fast.
Before we change our mind.
That penis thing sounds like a good idea.
No, no. He is joking only. Goodbye, dhobi.
Goodbye.

Fifteen years passed. Fifteen years: a long time, long enough to forget what one wants to leave behind. His sons grew up, his wealth grew too, and the shadow of the underworld, the shadow that rises from below, no longer lay upon his house. Human life continued with its ups and downs. He had his exit strategy in place but there was no need to use it, no need to leave home, no need to tear his world in half and throw half of it away. Fifteen years. Long enough to relax.

Then it was 2008. And in August 2008, at the airport, as he stood in the immigration line after a business trip to New York, Nero saw a ghost. The ghost was standing in the passport control line next to his own, and its trademark orange hair was gone. Now it was black like everyone else's. But other than the hair it was obviously him. Public Enemy #2. Nero looked at Short Fingers in wonderment. Surely he would be seized at any instant, gunned down if he tried to resist? His eyes met Fingers', and he frowned his puzzlement across to the Z-Company megaboss. Fingers just gave him a big thumbs-up sign (with, it must be said, a very small thumb) and turned away. They approached the passport control windows. Uniformed officers carefully scrutinised documents in the super-bureaucratic manner perfected by all minor Indian functionaries. And when Short Fingers was second in line, there was an extraordinary chance occurrence. All the computers in the immigration hall went down, boom! Like that. All the screens black. There followed several moments of consternation as immigration officers tried to reboot their machines, and other officers ran hither and yon. The computer crash was as total as it was mysterious. The waiting lines grew restive. Finally, there was a signal from a senior immigration officer, and the lines began to move, everyone was waved through, manual check only, and Fingers was cleared and gone, and two minutes later, as Nero approached his window, boom!, the computers all came back on. Z-Company had not lost its touch.

Why had Short Fingers taken the great risk of returning? Why had Zamzama sent him? These thoughts preoccupied Nero deep into the night and at two o'clock in the morning he had his answer because for the first time in a decade and a half his cell rang in the coded sequence that spelled trouble. Three rings, off, one ring, off, two rings, off, answer the fourth time. Yes, he said. The voice of Short Fingers in his ear like the claws of the Devil sucking him down into the abyss. One more time, Fingers said. One last time.

The Western Region of the Indian Coast Guard was divided into five DHQs. DHQ-2 was the Mumbai department and boasted three stations along the coastline, at Murud Janjira, Ratnagiri and Dahanu. Each station had at its disposal a number of offshore patrol vessels, inshore patrol vessels, fast and extra-fast patrol vessels, and smaller, even faster patrol and interceptor boats. Also helicopters and surveillance aircraft. But the sea was a large place and with proper organisation it was possible to leave a specified zone unwatched. The number of suitcases required for such an operation was large.

What is it this time.

Don't ask. Just make the arrangements.

And if I refuse.

Don't refuse. The don is in poor health. The neighbours are not the best of hosts. His personal situation is restricted, his finances are running low. He thinks he has little time left. He wants this one last great deed. He has no choice. The neighbours insist. There is a threat of eviction.

It has been fifteen years. I've been out of the game a long time.

Welcome to the Hotel California.

I'm not going to do it.

Don't refuse. I'm asking nicely. I'm saying please. Please: don't refuse.

I see.

*

On November 23, 2008, ten gunmen armed with automatic weapons and hand grenades left by boat from the hostile neighbouring country. In their backpacks they carried ammunition and strong narcotics: cocaine, steroids, LSD and syringes. On their journey they hijacked a fishing boat, abandoned their original vessel, brought two dinghies aboard the fishing boat and told the captain where to go. When they were near the shore they killed the captain and got into the dinghies. Afterwards many people wondered why the coastguard had not seen them or tried to intercept them. The coast was supposed to be well guarded but on this night there had been a failure of some sort. When the dinghies landed, on November 26, the gunmen split up into small groups and made their way to their chosen targets, a railway station, a hospital, a movie theatre, a Jewish centre, a popular cafe and two five-star hotels. One of these was the Taj Mahal Palace and Tower Hotel, where Nero's wife, in the aftermath of a quarrel with her husband, was in the Sea Lounge eating cucumber sandwiches and complaining about her marriage to her friends.

I can't speak, Riya said.

Don't speak.

You helped the gunmen enter the city, the ones who killed your wife.

There is no need to speak.

And then you fled. You and all your sons.

There is a little more to say. After what happened the body of the gangster Short Fingers was found dumped on a street in Dongri. He had been killed with short knife cuts to the throat. His former associates Big Head and Little Feet were angry at the attack, which placed the Company and its operations in jeopardy once again. This was their message to Zamzama Alankar. Later, Apu also was the victim of their rage. They were sending me a message. The message said, we know you helped, and this is our reply. These are the names the man Mastan is coming to give me. These names I already know.

So you are responsible for your son's death as well as his mother's.

What I did, I did to save their lives. I compromised myself to protect them. I am the king of my house but I became a servant. The laundryman. The dhobi. But you are correct. I failed. You accuse me and I am guilty of it and fate has punished me by taking my children. One child dead at the hands of my enemies, one by his own hand, one at the hand of a madman, but all three are my punishment and my burden to bear forever, yes, and their mothers too. I have been taught the lesson and I have learned it. The dead bodies of my children and their mothers weigh on my shoulders and their weight pushes me down. You see me crushed, daughter, like a cockroach beneath destiny's heel. You see me crushed. And now you know everything.

And what do I do now, now that I know everything?

It will not be necessary for you to act. Tomorrow morning at 9 a.m. sharp the angel of death is coming to take tea.

32

What would it mean if the Joker became the King and the she-bat went to jail. Outside the Gardens the giggles were becoming louder, sounding more like shrieks, and I didn't know if they were screams of rage or joy. I was simultaneously exhausted and scared. Maybe I was wrong about my country. Maybe a life lived in the bubble had made me believe things that were not so, or not enough so to carry the day. What did anything mean if the worst happened, if brightness fell from the air, if the lies, the slanders, the ugliness, the ugliness, became the face of America. What would my story mean, my life, my work, the stories of Americans old and new, *Mayflower* families and Americans proudly sworn in just in time to share in the unmasking – the unmaking – of America? Why even try to understand the human condition if humanity revealed itself as grotesque, dark, *not worth it*? What was the point of poetry, cinema, art? Let goodness wither on the vine. Let Paradise be lost. The America I loved, gone with the wind.

I didn't sleep well that last weekend before the vote because my mind ran on thoughts like these. Riya called me at 5 a.m. and I was wide-eyed and staring at the ceiling. You have to come, she said. Something's going to happen and I don't know what it is but I can't be here alone. The old man had fallen asleep at his desk, slumped forward in his chair with his forehead against the wood. Her night had been as sleepless as mine. But she was not a Catholic priest in a Hitchcock movie and she needed to share with somebody the burden of what she had been told, of the secrets that were now also hers. I went to meet her and we sat in the Gardens before dawn and she talked. What should I do? she said. What is there to do? I replied. But I already knew the answer because I was bursting with creative excitement; the story had rescued me from the depths of my nocturnal despair. It was the missing piece I'd needed, and it gave me the dark heart of my movie, the big reveal, the point of it. Art is what it is and artists are thieves and whores but we know when the juices are flowing, when the unknown muse is whispering in our ear, talking fast, get this down, I'm only going to say it once; and then we know the answer to all the doubting whys that plague us in our night terrors. I thought of Joseph Fiennes as the young Bard in *Shakespeare in Love,* jumping up from the desk at which he's writing – what? *Romeo and Juliet*? – and doing a little private pirouette and telling himself without vanity or shame, 'God, I'm good.'

(This raises an interesting question: did Shakespeare know he was Shakespeare? But that's for another day.)

(There is no muse of cinema, nor of fiction, neither. In this case the muses-most-likely would probably be Calliope – if what I was doing could be considered an epic – or Thalia, if comedy, or Melpomene, if I could rise to the heights required for tragedy. Not very important. Never mind.)

Let it play out, I said. Let's see what the retired policeman has to say.

Drama has a way of bushwhacking the dramatist. Something's going to happen and I don't know what it is, Riya said, and called on me for support, but what neither of us guessed was that the something that was going to happen was me.

We made our way back into the Golden house and found ourselves, in the large family room that gave onto the Gardens, confronted by Vasilisa holding her young son – my young son – my son! – in one hand and a gun in the other. Small, pearl-handled, golden barrel. The girl with the golden gun. She looked like an Italian movie star in her pinkish silk nightgown over which there floated a floor-length lace peignoir – Monica Vitti, or Virna Lisi, I wasn't sure which. The gun, however, was definitely a Godard touch. I thought of his murderer heroine in *Pierrot* leaving the dwarf dead with her scissors through his neck. I had no desire to become a version of that dwarf. I actually raised my hands. Play the scene, I thought. Riya looked at me as if I was mad.

Good morning, Vasilisa, Riya said in a normal, non-filmic voice. Put that thing down, please.

What are you people doing in my house? Vasilisa said, not lowering the weapon. (She, at least, was sticking to the script.)

Nero called me, Riya said. He wanted to talk.

He wanted to talk to *you*?

He talked for a long time. There's a man coming to see him soon.

Who is coming? Why have I not been informed?

I came because Riya is worried, I said. About the man.

We will all meet this man, said Vasilisa. This mystery will be solved. She put the pistol back in her pocketbook, where it lived.

Cut. Then a sequence of quick shots, bridging the passage of time, intended to show Nero's poor condition. He is unsteady on his feet and in his voice and gestures.

When she woke up her husband Nero was not in good shape. The lucidity of the long night's oratory had vanished. He was fuzzy and indistinct, as if the effort of remembering had worn him out. Vasilisa helped him into the bedroom and said, 'Shower.' After he had showered she said, 'Dress.' After he had dressed she said, 'Shoes.' He looked piteous. 'I can't tie the laces,' he said. 'They are loafers,' she told him. 'Shoes.' After the shoes were on his feet she held out a handful of pills. 'Swallow,' she said. After he had swallowed she commanded, 'Tell me.' He shook his head. 'A man from yesterday,' he said.

The only reason I know anything about Borsalino hats is that my parents used to argue in their friendly way, enjoying the argument more than the outcome, about whether the celebrated fedoras should be included in their collection of famous Belgians. The Borsalino hat company is not located within Belgian borders. It is to be found in the city of Alessandria, in Piedmont, Italy, which sits on the alluvial plain between the Tanaro and Bormida rivers, about fifty-six miles from Torino. I know three things about Borsalino hats: that they are very popular among Orthodox Jews; that they became cool when Alain Delon and Jean-Paul Belmondo wore them in the 1970 French gangster movie named after them; and that they are felt hats, and the felt is made from Belgian (aha!) rabbit fur.

The man Mastan, the retired police officer, sat on the same upright chair in the living room of the Golden house formerly occupied by the murderer Kinski, looking a little alarmed to be confronted by a grim-faced Vasilisa and Riya and myself as well as Nero. It was the weekend, so many of the household staff were away. No Blather, no Fuss. The handyman Gonzalo was absent, as well as the major-domo Michael McNally and Sandro 'Cookie' Cucchi the chef. I answered the door myself and showed the inspector in. A handsome man! Silver-haired, a septuagenarian like Nero, maybe not quite as far through his seventies, he looked in profile like he could have been the model for the Crazy Horse Memorial in South Dakota. Except that his cream suit was straight out of a Peter O'Toole movie and his tie with its slanting red-and-gold stripes was a tie any British gentleman would have been proud to wear. (I only found out later, with the help of research, just how proud. The tie of the Marylebone Cricket Club was a thing greatly desired in cricket-playing circles.) He sat very straight, very upright, but very ill at ease, playing with the Borsalino hat upon his knee. There was a moment of awkward silence. Then he spoke.

I came to the United States for three reasons, he said. In the first place, to visit my sister in Philadelphia. Her husband is successful in the recycling of plastic bottles. This is how one makes one's fortune in America. Get one good idea and stick to it. Professor Einstein used to say he only had one good idea. But in his case it was the nature of the universe.

Nero was at his goofiest, unfocused, his eyes wandering, humming a little private tune.

The second reason was to visit the grave of P. G. Wodehouse, he said.

(That got my attention. Wodehouse, so beloved of my parents and myself. Wodehouse, who had also come to mind when Kinski sat in that chair.) Mr Wodehouse is very popular back home, Mastan said. His tombstone is a marble book engraved with the names of his characters. My favourite is not there, however. Miss Madeline Bassett who thought the stars were God's daisy chain. But she is a minor character. I, also, myself. The same. Mine has always been a strictly supporting role.

My husband is not well, Vasilisa stiffly said. If there is a point to this visit, please arrive at it promptly.

Oh, the point, madam, yes. Bear with me. There is the point ostensible and the point actual. The point ostensible is what I have said to him telephonically. A word of warning. But the gentleman has been a worldly man. Perhaps it is not necessary to warn him of what he already knows. The community of our people in America has grown, madam, it boasts now recyclers of plastic bottles, madam, also new technology geniuses, garlanded actors, campaigning attorneys, politicians across the spectrum, fashion designers, and also, madam, criminal gangs. I'm sorry to say. In America the word *mafia* has specific Italian connotations so it is better to avoid it and call our people's gangs by other names. Let us concede that they are still small, there are only the beginnings of what the Italians call families and what our people call *gharaney*, households, or, nowadays, *companies,* a term presently popular in the mother country. However there is much enthusiasm among these American companies, these new households, much potential for rapid growth. There is also a degree of outreach to the mother country, an interest in globalisation, in shared activities. Our people in the USA are willing to help the people in the mother country, to facilitate actions here, in return for parallel facilitations back home. Things change, madam. Time passes. Things formerly impossible become possible. I wished to discuss these matters with the gentleman but now that I am face-to-face with him I find it redundant to do so. He may be aware, he may not. It may be a concern to him, or not. His intelligence may retain the capacity for analysis of threat and risk, or it may have lost that capacity. It is not my business. I see this now.

So we come to the point actual, madam, thanking you for your patience. The point actual was to take a look at the gentleman and to see what taking such a look inspired in myself. It is a man who has escaped judgement for many wrongs. For his part in desperate deeds, madam. It is a man who has expertly covered his tracks, who has used tradecraft and money to erase all links between himself and many things that are beyond words. I promised to tell him the names of his son's murderers but of course he knows them already, he dealt with them for years on cordial terms, until they turned against him. It is possible the security forces of this great country would have been interested in these matters and perhaps I could have interested them, but I fear that without evidence I would look to them like a fond and foolish man even though I was once their colleague in a distant land. It is possible that having taken a look at this man I would have wished to take matters into my own hands although we are both old men. It is possible I would have wished to hit this man in the face, absurd as a fistfight between two old duffers would be. It is not beyond the bounds of possibility that I would have wished to shoot him dead. I am still a crack shot, madam, and a weapon in America is easily acquired. But now that I look upon this man, a man whom I have hated for the larger part of my life, this man who was a strong man, I see that I have found him in his time of weakness, and he is not worthy of my bullet. Let him face his God. Let him receive judgement when he is standing before the judgement seat. Let hell receive him and let him burn in hellfire for all eternity. Thus my point is made and I will take my leave.

Riya's hand was on Vasilisa's shoulder, warning her, leave your pistol where it is.

Mr Mastan rose and bowed his head. Then as he turned for the door Nero hauled himself up from the depths of the sofa where he sat and shockingly, awfully, shouted at the very top of his voice.

You come into my house and speak like this to me in front of my wife?

The retired policeman stopped in his tracks, his back to Nero, his hat still in his hand.

Bastard! Nero screamed. Run! It is you who are a dead man now.

33

When the detective arrives on the scene, the movie audience instinctively relaxes, expecting crime to be followed by justice, for right to triumph. But it is not inevitable that the just will gain the victory over the unjust. In another Hitchcock movie, *Psycho,* the horror arises from the fact that the wrong people die. Janet Leigh is the biggest star in the movie but, not even halfway through the running time, aah!, she's dead in the shower. Then the detective, Martin Balsam, arrives, nice, comfortable, safe Martin Balsam, so professional, so reassuring, and our tension eases. Things will be all right now. And then, aah! He's dead too. Note to self: it's extra scary when the wrong people die.

The retired detective, Inspector Mastan formerly of the Bombay CID. Must we expect something terrible to happen to him?

One last thing about Mr Hitchcock. Yes, he liked to make cameo appearances in his films, he said it made people watch the movies more closely to see when and how it would happen, but also, very often, he got the cameo out of the way early so that the search for it didn't become a distraction. I say this because I now have to record, as the auteur of the present work in progress (to put it much too grandly, considering that this is very much a rookie project), that as I watched – participated wordlessly in – the scene I have just described, something uncontrollable welled up inside me. In that time of spilling secrets, I let my own secret spill.

Yes: characteristically, I hide my feelings. I lock them away or I sublimate them into movie references. Even at this crucial moment in my narrative, when I step out of the shadows into the centre-stage spotlight, I'm trying (and failing) to resist talking about Akira Kurosawa's late masterpiece *Ran,* in which, so to speak, King Lear was married to Lady Macbeth. The thought was triggered by something Inspector Mastan said. He called himself *fond and foolish* and whether he knew it or not was almost quoting Shakespeare's broken king. Pray, do not mock me, Lear pleads. I am a very foolish fond old man . . . And to deal plainly, I fear I am not in my perfect mind. There he sat upon his sofa, his last throne, screaming senile hatred. The Ancient of Days, who had disrupted the lives of his three sons and was destroyed not as Lear was, by their hostility, but by their destruction. And here before him, as monstrous in my eyes as the Lady Kaede in *Ran,* Kurosawa's Lady Macbeth, stood Vasilisa Golden, mother of his fourth and only surviving – and only supposed – child, with a pistol in her pocketbook and fire blazing from her eyes. And I, the fool, beginning my soliloquy which would reveal the truth. As if I didn't understand that mine was a supporting role. As if, like Inspector Mastan, I could be, at least for this one scene, the star.

I had come to despise the second Mrs Golden for her airs, for the way she discarded me like a used tissue once I had served her purpose, for the gun in her handbag, for her sanctimonious worship of an imitation icon, for her fake babushka mother, for the undeniable truth that everything she did, every gesture, every inflection of her voice, every kiss, every embrace, was motivated not by true feeling but by cold-blooded calculation. The wisdom of the spider, the wisdom of the shark. She was loathsome. I loathed her and wanted to do her harm.

In the retired police inspector's British-Indian delivery, in his rigid self-control, in his voice that was never raised even when cursing Nero Golden to eternal damnation, I recognised something of myself. Maybe Suchitra had been right when she said that everyone in my story was an aspect of my own nature. Certainly I heard myself not only in

Mr Mastan's suppression of feeling but also, at this moment, in Nero's impotent dotard's shriek. I was no dotard, not yet, but I knew something about powerlessness. Even now as I chose to cast away the shackles placed by Vasilisa on my tongue I understood that the truth would hurt me most of all. Yet I would tell it. When Riya called me summoning me to the Golden house, *something's going to happen,* Riya in her own state of distress and confusion, in which mourning was now mingled with dreadful knowledge, provoked in me a flood of feeling I didn't immediately understand but whose meaning had now, abruptly, become clear.

The election was upon us and Suchitra in her usual indefatigable way had volunteered to work the phones and then on Tuesday do the legwork and get out the vote. She should have been the one with whom I first sat down, calmly, to confess, to explain, to express my love and beg forgiveness. I owed her that at the very least and instead here I was up on my hind legs in the Golden living room with my mouth open and the fateful words trembling on my lips.

No, there's no need to set down the words themselves.

Near the end of Satyajit Ray's sublime *Pather Panchali* can be found what I consider to be the greatest single scene in the history of the cinema. Harihar the father of little Apu and his older sister Durga, who left them in their village with their mother Sarbajaya while he went to the city to try to earn some money, returns – having done well – with gifts for his children, not knowing that in his absence young Durga has fallen ill and died. He finds Sarbajaya sitting on the *pyol*, the porch of their home, silenced by tragedy, unable to welcome him home or respond to what he tells her. Not understanding, he begins to show her the children's gifts. Then in an extraordinary moment we see his face change when Sarbajaya, whose back is to the camera, tells him the news about Durga. At this moment, understanding the inadequacy of dialogue, Ray allows music to surge up and fill the soundtrack, the high piercing music of the *tar-shehnai* crying out the parents' grief more eloquently than their words ever could.

I have no music to offer. I offer only silence instead.

When I had said what there was to say, Riya walked across the room to stand in front of me. Then, raising her right hand, she hit me as hard as she could on the left side of my face. That is for Suchitra, she said. Then with the back of her hand she hit me even harder on the right side, and told me, That is for you. I stood still and did not move.

What did he say? Nero, in the confusion of the morning, wanted to know. What is he talking about?

I went over to where he sat, got down on my haunches, and looked him in the eye, and said it again.

I am the father of your son. Little Vespa. Your only surviving child is not yours. He is mine.

Vasilisa descended upon me in Byronic fury, came down like the wolf on the fold, but before she reached me I saw a light come on in the old man's eyes and then there he was, present again, alert, the man of power returning from his cloudy wandering exile and re-entering his skin.

Bring the boy, he commanded his wife. She shook her head. He shouldn't be a part of this, she said.

Bring him at once.

And when Little Vespa was brought – Vasilisa holding him, the babushka mother beside her, the two women's bodies half turned away from the man of the house, shielding the child between them – Nero looked keenly at the boy, as if for the first time, then at me, then back at him, and back at me again, and so on, many times; until the child, unprovoked but perceiving the crisis as children can, burst into noisy tears. Vasilisa gestured to the older woman, *enough*. The boy was removed from his father's presence. He did not look in my direction even once.

Yes, Nero said. I see. He said no more but I seemed to see, hanging in the air above his head, the terrible words once thought by Emma Bovary about her daughter Berthe. *It's strange how ugly this child is.*

You see nothing, said Vasilisa, moving toward him.

Nero Golden raised his hand to stop her in her tracks. Then, lowering the hand, he spat on the back of it.

Tell me everything, he said to me.

I told him.

*

I don't have to listen to this, Riya said, and left the house. I refuse to listen to this, said Vasilisa, and stayed in the room, listening.

When I had finished he thought for a long time. Then he said, his voice strong and low, Now my wife and I must speak alone.

I turned to go, but before I left the room he said a strange thing.

If some harm should befall us both, I appoint you the boy's guardian. I will have the lawyers draw up the paperwork today.

No harm will befall us both, Vasilisa said. Also, it's the weekend.

We will speak privately now, Nero answered her. Please show René out.

As I walked away down Macdougal toward Houston, the adrenaline drained from my body and I was seized by fear for the future. I knew what had to be done, what I could not avoid doing. I tried to call Suchitra. Voicemail. I texted her, *we need to speak.* I wandered in the city making my way home down Sixth Avenue and over into Tribeca, blind to the streets. On the corner of North Moore and Greenwich I got her reply. *Home late what.* There was no way to answer. *No prob see you whenever.* I turned right on Chambers and walked past Stuyvesant High School. I expected the worst. What else could happen? What could she think of me, of what I had to tell her? Only the worst.

But if human nature were not a mystery, we'd have no need of poets.

34

Later. Let's say, quite a while later. Some wise man once suggested that Manhattan below 14th Street at 3 a.m. on November 28 was Batman's Gotham City; Manhattan between 14th and 110th Streets on the brightest and sunniest day in July was Superman's Metropolis. And Spider-Man, that Johnny-come-lately, hung upside down in Queens thinking about power and responsibility. All these cities, the invisible imaginary cities lying over and around and interwoven with the real one: all still intact, even though after the election the Joker – his hair green and luminous with triumph, his skin white as a Klansman's hood, his lips dripping anonymous blood – now ruled them all. The Joker had indeed become a king and lived in a golden house in the sky. The citizens reached for clichés and reminded themselves that there were still birds in the trees and the sky hadn't fallen and it was, often, still blue. The city still stood. And on the radio and on the music apps playing in the Bluetooth headphones of the careless young the beat went on. The Yankees still worrying about their pitching rotation, the Mets still underperforming, and the Knicks still doomed by the curse of being the Knicks. The Internet was still full of lies and the business of the truth was broken. The best had lost all conviction and the worst were filled with passionate intensity and the weakness of the just was revealed by the wrath of the unjust. But the

Republic remained more or less intact. Let me just set that down because it was a statement often made to comfort those of us who were not easily to be comforted. It's a fiction in a way, but I repeat it. I know that after the storm, another storm, and then another. I know that stormy weather is the forecast forever and happy days aren't here again and intolerance is the new black and the system really is rigged only not in the way the evil clown has tried to make us believe. Sometimes the bad guys win and what does one do when the world one believes in turns out to be a paper moon and a dark planet rises and says, No, I am the world. How does one live among one's fellow countrymen and countrywomen when you don't know which of them is numbered among the sixty-million-plus who brought the horror to power, when you can't tell who should be counted among the ninety-million-plus who shrugged and stayed home, or when your fellow Americans tell you that knowing things is elitist and they hate elites, and all you have ever had is your mind and you were brought up to believe in the loveliness of knowledge, not that knowledge-is-power nonsense but *knowledge is beauty*, and then all of that, education, art, music, film, becomes a reason for being loathed, and the creature out of Spiritus Mundi rises up and slouches toward Washington DC, to be born. What I did was to retreat into private life – to hold on to life as I had known it, its dailiness and strength, and to insist on the ability of the moral universe of the Gardens to survive even the fiercest assault. And now therefore let my little story have its final moments in the midst of whatever macro garbage is around as you read this, whatever *manufactroversy*, whatever horror or stupidity or ugliness or disgrace. Let me invite the giant victorious green-haired cartoon king and his billion-dollar movie franchise to take a back seat and let real people drive the bus. Our little lives are perhaps as much as we are able to comprehend.

I remember telling Apu Golden how I wept on election night in November 2008. Those were good tears. The equal and opposite tears of 2016 washed the goodness away.

In the world of the real I had learned hard lessons. Lies can cause tragedies, both on the personal and the national scale. Lies can defeat the truth. But the truth is dangerous too. Not only can the truth teller be vulgar and offensive, as I was in the Golden house that day. Telling the truth can also cost you what you love.

There wasn't much discussion after I told Suchitra about Vasilisa Golden's child. She heard me out in silence and then excused herself and went into the bedroom and shut the door. Ten minutes later she re-emerged, dry-eyed, in perfect command of her emotions. 'I think you should move out, don't you?' she said. 'And you should do it now.' I moved back into my old room at the home of Mr U Lnu Fnu. As to our working relationship she said she was willing to continue to support my feature film plan, which after so many years was close to being green-lit, but that apart from that we should work separately in future, which was more than fair. Also, and to my surprise and great discomfiture, she immediately launched into a series of brief but apparently passionate love affairs with high-profile men and all of these were extensively shared on social media and knocked me, I admit, for a loop. How deeply could she have cared for me if she could dive so swiftly into the next things? How real had it been? Such thoughts plagued me, though I knew, in my deepest heart, that this was me trying to shift the blame, and the blame could not be shifted, it rested firmly on my shoulders. – So this was not a good time for me but, yes, I got my film *The Golden House* made, my almost-decade-long obsession-project – in the end a drama, a fully fledged fiction, not a mockumentary, the screenplay completely rewritten since my time at the Sundance Screenwriters Lab – and, yes, the people I needed to like it seemed to like it, and, yes, with the help of an Italian-American producer friend in Los Angeles, North American distribution rights were acquired by Inertia Pictures. There it was in the trades, *a release in the theatres and on demand in the first quarter,* Variety *has learned exclusively,* so it had to be true. *Pic is Unterlinden's feature film writer-directorial debut.* In a tough time for indie movies this was an outstanding agreement. Strangely, when the good news came through, I felt nothing at all. What was there to feel? It was just work. The main benefit was that I could now afford to rent an apartment of my own.

But to get that apartment would be to lose my access to the Gardens, and the Gardens were where my son played every day, even if it was impossible to approach him. Also, I had become fond of Mr U Lnu Fnu, who tried in his gentle way to comfort me for my loss of Suchitra's love. He asked me on what day of the week I had been born, and Suchitra too. I didn't know, but there were websites now where you could enter the date and be told the day, and so I discovered that it was Sunday (for me) and Wednesday (for her). I told Mr U Lnu Fnu and at once he clucked his tongue and shook his head. 'You see, you see,' he said. 'In Myanmar, this is known to be unlucky combination.' Saturday and Thursday, Friday and Monday, Sunday and Wednesday, Wednesday evening and Tuesday: these were the hexed pairings. 'Better find someone with complementary day,' he said. 'For you, Sunday child, every other day is good. Not Wednesday! Why pick the one day that has jinx? How to guarantee unhappy life!' Oddly, this superstition from across the globe did in fact offer some comfort. But then in those days when I had lost both my lover and my child, I was drowning, and clutching at straws.

Your work goes well when your life's going terribly. Is that a rule? Loneliness and Heartbreak: these are the names of the gates of Eden?

My story has now gone beyond my film and the divergences are sharp. In the movie, the retired Indian police inspector comes to see the old bastard with murderous intent, and in fact pulls out a gun and shoots him dead, and is then shot dead by the pistol waiting in the pocketbook of the old man's Russian wife.

In what I have to call real life, Mr Mastan was dead within twenty-four hours of leaving the house on Macdougal Street, pushed off a subway platform into the path of a train when he was on his way to Penn Station to return to his sister's home in Philadelphia. The attacker was a thirty-year-old Queens woman of South Asian ethnicity, who was taken into custody almost immediately and charged with second-degree murder. On being detained she said, 'That was an old meddler. He interfered in a household matter.' The *Times* report said this: 'The police described her as emotionally disturbed and said that she had made up a story just one month earlier about pushing someone onto the tracks.'

That earlier statement had been quickly found to be a lie. This time, however, she had really done it. In spite of her statement, no relationship between her and the dead man could be established, and the investigating officers concluded that none existed. An emotionally disturbed female had pushed a man to his death. No further investigation seemed to be required.

Even that little life of mine had begun to feel less comprehensible by the day. I understood nothing. I had become what I always hoped I might be but without love it was all ashes. I thought every day about reaching out to Suchitra but there she was on Instagram telling the world about new liaisons that were knives in my heart. And my crime, my only son, was right outside my window growing up before my eyes, learning words, developing a character, and I helpless to be a part of it. Vasilisa had made it clear to me that if I came within fifteen feet of him she would go to court and get a restraining order. So I hung back at my Burmese mentor's window and gazed in misery upon my forbidden flesh and blood as he approached his third birthday. Maybe it would be better for me to leave the Gardens and start a new life somewhere else, Greenpoint, for example, or Madagascar or Sichuan or Nizhny Novgorod or Timbuktu. I dreamed, sometimes, of being flayed, and walking naked and skinless through an unknown city that didn't give a damn about my dreams. I dreamed of walking up a staircase in a familiar house and realising suddenly that in the room I was about to enter at the head of the stairs a man was waiting for me with a hangman's noose and my life was about to end. All this when I was, after more than a decade, an overnight success, and there were lucrative offers to direct hip-hop videos and motor car commercials and episodes of hit sixty-minute television drama series and even a second feature film. None of it made sense. I had lost my bearings and there I was sitting in my tin can whirling in the void.

Can you hear me. Can you hear me. Can you hear me.

It was Riya – Riya who had hit me so hard that my ears rang for days – who helped me take my first unsteady steps down the road to functioning adulthood. We began to meet perhaps once a week, always in the same bar-restaurant on the Bowery near the Museum of Identity, and she would talk to me about her decision to go back to her job, which her boss Orlando Wolf had with considerable sensitivity kept open for her. She described it as a relationship in which love had died but enough common ground remained to make it worth working on. Maybe with enough good effort something like love might be reborn.

This was also how she recommended I approach my own broken love. Give Suchitra time, she said. Let her go through what she's doing now, all these second-rate boldface men. That's her anger in charge. Give her time and I think she'll come back to you to see what can be worked out.

I found that hard to believe but it made me feel better. I liked seeing Riya's recovery too. The election result seemed to have energised her, to have given her back much of her old strength of spirit and incisiveness of mind. She stayed away from gender politics because, in her own words, she was still 'broken' in that area, but worked on new rooms chronicling and displaying the rise of the new 'identitarian' far right, the arrival in America of the European ultraist movement whose birthplace was the French youth movement, the Nouvelle Droite Génération Identitaire, and programming events around racial and national identity, a series she called *Identity Crisis,* dealing in general with racial and religious issues, but focusing, above all, on the schismatic convulsion that had gripped America following the triumph of the cackling cartoon narcissist, America torn in half, its defining myth of city-on-a-hill exceptionalism lying trampled in the gutters of bigotry and racial and male supremacism, Americans' masks ripped off to reveal the Joker faces beneath. Sixty million. Sixty million. And ninety million more too uncaring to vote.

Once the French sent us the statue in the harbour, she said, now they send us this.

Identity was a neo-fascist rallying cry now and the Museum was obliged to change and Riya made herself the standard-bearer of that change. We became lazy, she said. For eight years we persuaded ourselves that the progressive, tolerant, adult America embodied by the president was what America had become, that it would just go on being like that. And that America is still there but the dark side was still there too, and it roared out of its cage and swallowed us. America's secret identity wasn't a superhero. Turns out it was a supervillain. We're in the Bizarro universe and we have to engage with Bizarro-America to grasp its nature and to learn how to destroy it all over again. We have to learn how to trick Mr Mxyztplk into saying his name backwards so that he disappears back into the fifth dimension and the world feels sane again. And we have to engage with ourselves and understand how we became so fucking weak and apathetic and how to retool and dive back into the battle. Who are we now? Who the fuck even knows.

OK, OK, I thought, losing patience (though only inwardly) with her rant. Good for you. I'm glad you're up and running again, and you do that, all of it, go for it. All I wanted to do was put my fingers in my ears and shout la la la la la. All I wanted was for there to be no news on the television and for the Internet to collapse forever and for my friends to be my friends and to have good dinners and go listen to good music and for love to conquer all and for Suchitra somehow by magic to come back to me.

Then one night alone in my aching bed I remembered what Nero Golden said to me after my parents died. Get wisdom. Learn to be a man.

The next afternoon I presented myself at the editing suite where Suchitra was hard at work. When she saw me, she stiffened. I'm really busy, she said. I'll wait, I said. I'll be working really late, she said. Is it OK if I wait? I asked. She thought about it. You can wait if you want, she said. I will, then, I said. She turned away and did not look at me again for five hours and forty-three minutes and I stood still and silent in the corner and did not interrupt. When she finally began to shut down work for the day it was a quarter to eleven at night. She swivelled her chair around to face me.

You waited very patiently, she said, not unkindly. It must be important.

I love you, I said to her, and I saw her defensive barricades go up. She said nothing in reply. The computer monitor dinged and showed a dialogue box telling her that one of her open programs had cancelled the shutdown. She gave a sigh of tired irritation and quit the program and restarted the shutdown. This time it worked.

Sometimes in extremis human beings receive from – depending on your belief system – either some inner or some higher power the gift of tongues, the right words to say at the right time, the language that will unlock and heal a bruised and guarded heart. So it was in that late hour amid the darkened computer screens. Not only the language but the nakedness behind the words. And behind the nakedness the music. The first words that fell from my lips were not mine. And what made them work was that I, who could never carry a tune, actually tried to sing, awkwardly at first and then with unasked-for tears running down my face: 'Bird on the Wire', swearing my traitor's fidelity in the words of the song and promising to make profound amends. Before I had finished she had begun to laugh at me and then we were laughing together, crying and laughing, and it was all right, it was going to be all right, in our two cracked voices we were drunks in our own midnight choir, and we would try in our way to be free.

At some later point when we were in bed together I added more prosaic thoughts to the magic of the song. It had been more than a year since the Joker's conquest of America and we were all still in shock and going through the stages of grief but now we needed to come together and set love and beauty and solidarity and friendship against the monstrous forces that faced us. Humanity was the only answer to the cartoon. I had no plan except love. I hoped another plan might emerge in time but for now there was only holding each other tightly and passing strength to each other, body to body, mouth to mouth, spirit to spirit, me to you. There was only the holding of hands and slowly learning not to be afraid of the dark.

Shut up, she said, and drew me toward her.

Sunday and Wednesday birthdays, I told her. My information from Myanmar is that we are jinxed by that combo.

I'll tell you a secret, she said. Burmese jinxes are not permitted to enter the United States. There's a list of countries whose jinxes aren't allowed in. Most of them are Islamic of course but Myanmar is on there too.

So as long as we're in the US we're safe?

We'll have to work something out about taking vacations abroad, she said.

35

Fire is licking around the edges of my story as it comes to a close, and fire is hot and inexorable and will have its day.

The Golden house in those last months was like a besieged fortress. The besieging forces were invisible but everyone in the house could feel them, the unseen angels or demons of impending doom. And one by one the help began to leave.

The film echoed here is maybe the greatest masterpiece of the great Luis Buñuel. Its original title, *The Outcasts of Providence Street,* is not explicitly religious – 'providence' is not necessarily divine, it might be no more than a metaphor, as also its colleagues karma, kismet and fate – so the characters cast out by destiny might be no more than unlucky losers of life's lottery – but by the time the movie arrived on cinema screens as *The Exterminating Angel* Buñuel had clarified its meaning beyond any doubt. When I first saw the film at the IFC Center I was perhaps too young to understand it. There is a large feast in a lavish mansion and while it's taking place all the household staff find flimsy pretexts and desert their posts and duties and leave the building, leaving only the butler and the guests to face whatever is coming. I understood this simply as surrealist social comedy. That was before I learned that there are people who can sense impending calamity, like cattle predicting earthquakes, and that self-preservation is the explanation for their apparently irrational acts.

There was no feast in the Golden house and the staff did not desert on one single evening. Life does not imitate art as slavishly as that. But gradually, over a period of weeks, and to the increasing consternation of the lady of the house, people began to quit. The handyman Gonzalo left first, simply not showing up for work one Monday and then never being seen again. In a big house there was always something that needed fixing, a blocked toilet, a chandelier with dead light bulbs, a door or window that needed easing. Vasilisa reacted to Gonzalo's disappearance with petulant annoyance and a few remarks about the unreliability of Mexicans that were not well received below stairs. McNally the butler/major-domo was able to handle most of Gonzalo's odd jobs and knew who to call in for things he couldn't fix by himself, so the absence did not cause the master or mistress of the house any serious discomfort. But the subsequent departures were more disruptive of the building's daily routine. Vasilisa had always been rough on maids, often reducing them to tears with her savage critiques of their usually diligent work, and there had been a high turnover of cleaning and bed-making staff during her incumbency, so it was no surprise that the latest young Boston Irish girl should flee saying no, she didn't want a raise, she just wanted to get away. In the kitchen there was a firing. Cucchi the chef sacked his assistant Gilberto because of an epidemic of petty pilfering. When the good kitchen knives started vanishing Cucchi confronted the young Argentinian who denied everything and flounced out. You can't quit, Cucchi yelled after him, because I'm firing you first. McNally tried to cover the gaps by calling temporary work agencies and asking his professional colleagues in other grand homes to lend him people if they had some spare capacity and so the household limped along. But the rats kept on leaving the ship.

A part of me had been grudgingly impressed by Vasilisa's swift and effective damage control in the days following my spilling of secrets in her living room. Nero Golden had been publicly humiliated and he was not a man who took kindly to humiliation. But not only did Vasilisa rescue her marriage, she also convinced Nero to continue to recognise Little Vespa as his son and heir. Those, I said to myself, were some fancy moves. Those were moves that placed her among the all-time pantheon of designing women. She knew how to hold on to her man.

It is not for me to speculate on what may or may not have happened between them behind the bedroom door. I will avoid such salaciousness, tempting as it is to conjure up the spectacle of Vasilisa at work. Desperate times, desperate measures, but in the absence of a sex tape there's no more to be said. And to be honest it's unclear that the bedroom was the basis of her defence. Much more plausibly one might say that she exploited Nero's mental decline. This was an old and increasingly sick man, more and more forgetful, his mind very often a meandering trickle now, offering only short glimpses of its previous, formidable flow. Vasilisa took the duty of nursing him upon herself, dismissing the day- and night-nurses who had been hired previously to relieve her of the difficulty of the work. So, a further exit of household staff, and Vasilisa uncomplainingly performing the duties of primary caregiver. She and she alone was in charge of his medication now. Fuss and Blather were pushed further and further away from the presence of their boss until one day Vasilisa with feral sweetness told them, I am familiar with all his business practices, and am fully able to be his close personal assistant, so, thank you for your service and let us discuss severance pay. The large house began to echo with absences. Vasilisa was playing all her trumps.

The ace of trumps was Little Vespa himself. Not only was my son growing up to be the most charming of fellows as he approached his fourth birthday, he was also in Nero's milky eyes the sole survivor of a calamity. A man who has lost three sons will not easily give away the fourth, and as Nero's decline accelerated and his memory flickered and faded and the child sat on his knee and called him Papa it was easy for the old man to forget the details and hold tightly to his only living child as if he were the reincarnation of his dead brothers as well as being himself, as if he were a treasure chest which contained all that his father had lost.

Who was left? The babushka mother who might or might not have been from Central Casting, Siberia. McNally the butler and Cucchi the chef. Cleaning teams from professional housecleaning services that came and went and charged five hundred dollars a visit. No visitors. And Nero, invisible, not seen by any of his neighbours. I began to believe in Vito Tagliabue's theory. She must have known he didn't have long. And if she was tampering with his medication then the fewer eyes the better. She must have known this was a short-term state of affairs. What were his doctors saying to her? Was there a terminal condition that was not made public? Or was Vasilisa herself that condition. I see her in my mind's eye kneeling each day in the living room of the Golden house, the 'great room', as she called it, in front of her copy of Tsarina Alexandra Romanova's Feodorovskaya icon of the Mother of God, praying. Let it be today. Let it come now.

Baba Yaga, kill your husband, but please don't eat my child.

The chef and the butler had been getting on each other's nerves and it was 'Cookie' who cracked. The chef's default setting was complaint anyway, he was the maestro of the moan, endlessly undervalued and misunderstood, longing to serve up banquets cooked in his beloved extremist style, derived from the work of the grandmasters Adrià and Redzepi, food as performance art, plates billowing with seas of foam, and pieces of toast upon which black ants, still living, had been baked into lean strips of rare wagyu beef. Instead he was asked to make kids' food for Little Vespa, burgers and more burgers, and vegan rabbit food for Vasilisa. Nero Golden himself didn't care what he ate as long as it contained plenty of meat. 'Cookie' Cucchi's laments fell upon deaf ears. He had threatened to quit almost every week but had stayed for the money. Now, in the short-staffed house, tempers were frayed and finally McNally ordered the would-be gastronome to shut up and cook. The chef tore off his white hat and apron and waved a meat cleaver in the major-domo's direction. Then with a grand thump he buried the blade of the cleaver in a wooden chopping board, leaving it there like Excalibur in the stone, and stormed out of the house.

Nero was drowsy and distracted. (This description is a version of the testimony afterwards given by Michael McNally to the police.) Mostly he stayed in his room, half asleep, but sometimes he was to be found wandering downstairs like a sleepwalker. But he could spark into sudden, shocking life. On one occasion he grasped McNally by both shoulders and shouted into his face, *Don't you know who I am, you asshole? I have built cities. I have conquered kingdoms. I am one of the rulers of the world.* I don't know who he imagined he was talking to, McNally said. It wasn't me. He was looking into my eyes but who knows who he saw. Maybe he saw himself in those days as the emperor whose name he bore. Maybe he thought he was in Rome. I couldn't honestly say, McNally confessed. I don't have that level of education.

He's being poisoned, Vito Tagliabue called me to repeat. No question in my mind.

There was a strange occurrence two days before the fire. The Golden house awoke to find that an enormous gunnysack of dirty laundry had been left on the Macdougal Street doorstep. There was no note. When the sack was opened it was found to be full of what McNally described as *foreign clothes.* Could he be more specific? From his attempts to describe them I understood them to be Indian clothing. Kurtas, pyjamas, lehngas, veshtis, sari blouses, petticoats. There were no instructions and the sender was unknown. Vasilisa, annoyed at the mistake, ordered them to be left out with the trash. There was no need for the master of the house to be informed. The house was not a laundry. Some ignorant foreigner had made an ignorant foreigner's mistake.

There were construction workers digging up the street. Something to do with vital repairs to the neighbourhood's infrastructure. When McNally was sent out by Vasilisa to ask how long the disruption would last he was told, three months, maybe, shrug. Which could mean six, nine or twelve. It meant nothing except that the workers were settling in for a substantial period of time. Construction work was the city's new brutalist art form, erecting its installations wherever you looked. Tall buildings fell and construction sites rose. Pipes and cables rose from and descended into the hidden depths. Telephone landlines ceased to work and water and power and gas services were randomly suspended. Construction work was the art of making the city become aware of itself as a fragile organism at the mercy of forces against which there was no appeal. Construction work was the mighty metropolis being taught the lessons of vulnerability and helplessness. Construction workers were the grand conceptual artists of our time and their installations, their savage holes in the ground, inspired not only hatred – because most people disliked modern art – but also awe. The hard hats, the orange jackets, the buttocks, the wolf whistles, the strength. Truly this was the trans-avant-garde at work.

Parking was suspended and the song of the jackhammers filled the air, radical, atonal, the kind of urban percussion Walt Whitman would have loved, driven by the potent sweat of large uncaring men.

From the cinder-strew'd threshold I follow their movements,
The lithe sheer of their waists plays even with their massive arms,
Overhand the hammers swing, overhand so slow, overhand so sure,
They do not hasten, each man hits in his place.

So it was for the two days after the incident of the laundry.

Then came the explosion.

Something to do with a gas main. The blame shifting between agencies, this safety check not carried out, that human error, a leak, a spark, kaboom. Or it might have been a cynical landlord illegally connecting pipes underground, a leak, a spark. A possible crime, an illegal gas line concealed from ConEd inspectors, possible manslaughter charges, the landlord not answering calls and unavailable at his registered address. Who sparked the spark? Unknown. Investigations will be made and a report issued in due course. Terrorism instantly ruled out. No workers injured, mercifully. The blast smashed windows and shook walls and a fireball billowed and one house, owned by Mr Nero Golden, caught fire. Four adults and one child in the building at the time: the owner and his wife, her mother, their young son, and an employee, Mr Michael McNally. It appeared that the building had not been correctly maintained, the indoor sprinkler system had not been serviced for a considerable time and failed to function. Mr McNally was in the kitchen heating olive oil in a pan, preparing to cook lunch for the family. According to his initial statement the blast blew out the kitchen windows and knocked him off balance and dazed him. He believes he lost consciousness, then recovered, and scrambled for the door into the Gardens between Macdougal and Sullivan Streets. There he lost consciousness again. When he came to his senses the kitchen was on fire and the flames were spilling out of the burning frying pan and spreading rapidly across the entire first floor. The other residents were upstairs. They had no way of getting out. The fire department responded with its usual alacrity. There were some access problems resulting from the construction work. But the fire was rapidly contained, limited to one single residence. All other properties in the neighbourhood were unharmed.

In the age of the smartphone, it was natural that many photographs were taken and videos made. Many of these were afterwards submitted to the proper NYPD authority to be studied in detail for any further illumination they might provide.

But at the Golden house that day there were people trapped by the fire. The high drama of the event played itself out, and ended in a triple tragedy and one miracle.

Unconfirmed reports mentioned that several individuals heard the sound of someone in the upper reaches of the mansion playing a violin.

As I see in my mind's eye the flames rising higher until they seemed to be licking at the sky itself, hellfire flames like something out of Hieronymus Bosch, it is hard to hold on to that belief in the good to which I dedicated myself, hard not to feel the heat of despair. They, the flames, seem to me to be burning away the whole world I had known, to be consuming in their orange heat all the things I had cared for, had been brought up to defend and fight for and love. Civilisation itself seemed to be burning in the fire, my hopes, the hopes of women, our hopes for our planet, and for peace. I thought of all those thinkers burned at the stake, all those who stood up against the forces and orthodoxies of their time, and I felt myself and my whole disenfranchised kind bound now by strong chains and engulfed by the awful blaze, the West itself on fire,

Rome burning, the barbarians not at the gates but within, our own barbarians, nurtured by ourselves, coddled and glorified by ourselves, enabled by ourselves, as much our own as our children, rising like savage children to burn the world that made them, claiming to save it even as they set it ablaze. It was the fire of our doom and it would take half a century or more to rebuild what it destroyed.

Yes, I suffer from hyperbole, it is the previously existing condition for which I need health care, but just sometimes a paranoid man is really being pursued, just sometimes the world is more heightened, more exaggerated, more hyperbolically infernal than even a hyperbolist-infernalist could ever, at his wildest, have dreamed.

So I saw the dark flames, the black flames of the inferno, licking at the sacred space of my childhood, the one place in the whole world in which I had always felt safe, always comforted, never threatened, the enchanted Gardens, and I learned the final lesson, the learning of which separates us from innocence. That there was no safe space, that the monster was always at the gates, and a little of the monster was within us too, we were the monsters we had always feared, and no matter what beauty enfolded us, no matter how lucky we were in life or money or family or talent or love, at the end of the road the fire was burning, and it would consume us all.

In *The Exterminating Angel* the revellers at the feast in Mexico found themselves trapped in the salon of the grand mansion of their host Señor Edmundo Nóbile by an invisible force. Surrealism permitted its followers the indirections and strangenesses of poetry. Real life in the Gardens was much more prosaic. Nero, Vasilisa, her babushka and my son were all imprisoned in the Golden house by the banality, the lethal conventionality, the deadly realism of a fire.

If life were a movie I would have heard about the fire, run toward it like a superhero on speed, pushed aside the hands grasping at me and plunged into the flames, returning as burning beams fell around me with my child shielded safely in my arms. If life were a movie he would have buried his head in my shoulder and murmured, Papa, I knew you'd come. If life were a movie it would conclude with a wide-angle shot of the Village with the ashes of the Golden house smouldering in the centre of the frame as I walked away with the child and a famous song welled up on the soundtrack, 'Beautiful Boy' by John Lennon, perhaps, and the credits began to roll.

That didn't happen.

By the time Suchitra and I reached Macdougal Street it was all over. Michael McNally was being treated at Mount Sinai Beth Israel and would subsequently be questioned by NYPD detectives who absolved him from responsibility for the fire. The other adults were dead before a ladder crew could get to them, Nero and the babushka quickly overpowered by the smoke, losing consciousness, never waking up again. There had been one moment of operatic emotion. The beautiful Mrs Golden, Vasilisa, had appeared at an upstairs window holding her almost-four-year-old child, screaming 'God, please save my son', and before anyone could reach her she had thrown the child out of the window away from the fire. One of the firemen at the scene, Mariano 'Mo' Vasquez, thirty-nine, who happened to be the catcher for his local baseball team on Staten Island, lunged forward and caught the soot-covered child just in time, 'like a football', he told the TV cameras later, and then blew air into the boy's lungs and got his breathing going again. 'He gave some coughs and then started yelling and crying. It was beautiful, man. Just a miracle, man, a miracle, and now I find out it's the boy's fourth birthday tomorrow, that kid had a guardian angel looking out for him for sure. It's a fine and beautiful thing and I give thanks to Almighty God that I could be in the right place at the right time.'

After that Vasilisa fell backwards away from the window and all her hopes all her ambitions all her strategies fell away with her, nobody deserved such an ending no matter what they had been in life, and a few instants after she dropped from sight the fire roared out through the open window and there was no possibility of saving her. And later of course the fire was extinguished, and charred bodies, etc., no need to go into any of that. The building would have to be demolished and a new structure would be raised in its place. No other houses were damaged by the fire.

So ended the story of the Golden house. They thought they were Romans but that was just a fantasy. Their Roman games which begat their Roman names: just games. They thought of themselves as a king and his princes but they were no Caesars. A Caesar had indeed risen in America, his reign was under way, beware, Caesar, I thought, the people raise you up and carry your throne through the ecstatic glorifying streets and then they turn on you and rend your garment and push you down upon your sword. Hail Caesar. Beware the Ides of March. Hail Caesar. Beware SPQR, *senatus populusque Romanus,* the Senate and the people of Rome. Hail Caesar. Remember Nero the last of his line fleeing at the end to Phaon's villa outside the city and ordering a grave to be dug for him, Nero then too cowardly to drive the sword into his own body and forcing his private secretary to do it at the last. Epaphroditos, slayer of the king. There were indeed once Caesars in the world and now in America a new incarnation on the throne. But Nero Golden was no king nor did he have a fallen Caesar's end. Just a fire, just some random meaningless flame. What was it his underworld pals had called him in Bombay? The laundryman, yes. The *dhobi.* Here's the dirty laundry, *dhobi.* Clean it up. No king on a throne. He was just the laundryman.

The laundryman.

The dirty laundry on the doorstep. The gunnysack full of Indian clothes.

I began feverishly to search the media for photographs of the fire scene, iPhone videos, everything, wherever I could find them, whatever had been shot professionally or posted by the public at large. The rubbernecking crowd behind the safety barriers. Faces seen through smoke and water. Nothing. Nothing again. And then something.

Two South Asian men in a photograph, watching the fire burn, one of them a dwarf. It was impossible to see the feet of his companion but I guessed that they would be unusually big.

Time passes. Big men dwindle, small men grow. This man shrinks into old age, those men's reach grows longer. They can stretch out their arms and touch places and people they couldn't reach before. There are companies here to lend assistance to companies there, to facilitate journeys, to execute strategies. Clowns become kings, old crowns lie in the gutter. Things change. It is the way of the world.

The news reports the next day were unanimous. The crooked landlord charged with manslaughter in the second degree. A tragedy. And a wonder that the young boy survived. Case closed.

And another story, not of interest to the American media, which I found by chance on my computer. The death in a distant country of a once-feared South Asian mafia don. Mr Zamzama Alankar, formerly the godfather of the powerful Z-Company crime family, had gone to stand before the last judgement seat. An unconfirmed report.

36

There is a dawn mist on the river and crossing the harbour a Chinese junk with her brown sails set fair and the sun low and silver and the sunlight skipping over the water like a stone. At the glass-topped table in the glass corner where two windows met we sit with glass tears in our eyes not knowing where to look or how to see. Below us running through the whiteness a woman with wild red hair and a tiara on her head like a queen escaping a kidnap and running for her life. Suchitra and I sit facing each other and the steam rising from the coffee cups and the smoke from her cigarette make three wandering columns in the air.

Imagine a cube of air, maybe twelve inches by twelve inches by twelve, moving through the vast open spaces of the world. This or something like it I once heard the Canadian film-maker David Cronenberg say. The cube is what the camera sees and the way the cube moves is the meaning of it. That is what it is to make a film, to move that cube through the world and see what it captures, what it makes beautiful, and what it makes sense of. That is the art of the cinema.

See us facing each other, both in profile, in wide-screen format and desaturated colour. See the camera move between us, to the midpoint between us, and then turn on its axis, in full circles, slowly, many times, so that our faces slide by one by one and in between our faces the river of the city and the fog slowly lifting and the light rising on the day. In her hand a sheet of paper. This is the subject. This is the meaning of the scene.

Scenes that did not make the final cut of this text: me at the police station trying to find out what happened to Little Vespa, who is he with, where was he taken, who is caring for him. Me wandering disconsolately down Fourth Street, kicking at a pebble, my hands jammed deep into my pockets, my head down. And finally, me in a lawyer's office in Midtown while he reads me a document, then hands the document to me, and I nod, I'll let you know, and leave. Too much exposition. The scene that matters is this one, the two of us and the piece of paper in the day's first light.

I never thought he'd do it, I say. And if he did, she would have challenged it, saying he was no longer of sound mind.

The mother.

Yes. The mother, his wife. But now there are no next of kin. There's just this document. If some harm should befall us both, I appoint as the boy's guardian Mr René Unterlinden.

You know what you are asking, she says.

Yes.

First she persuaded him to accept another man's child as his own. Now you want me to accept the same child, another woman's child, as mine. And you know that children were not a part of my plan.

Down below us the runner with the red hair and the tiara has paused. She stands, hands on hips, breathing deeply, her head tilted up. As if she too is waiting for an answer. But of course she doesn't see Suchitra and me and knows nothing. We're up on the twenty-first floor.

Will you think about it, I say as the camera moves past my face.

She closes her eyes and the camera stops, and waits, and goes in closer. Then she opens her eyes and there are only her eyes, filling the screen.

I think we can do this, she says.

Then a jump-cut. Now a different pair of eyes fills the screen. Very slowly the camera pulls back to reveal that they are the eyes of Little

Vespa. He stares at the camera without any expression at all. On the soundtrack we hear the lawyer's voice-over. The estate is being examined by lawyers from both countries and there are many irregularities. But in the end it is a very large estate and there are no other heirs and he is only four years old.

Now there are the three of us, Little Vespa, Suchitra and myself, in an unspecified room, a room in the Brooklyn home of the foster-family to whom he was brought for temporary safe keeping. The camera moves to the midpoint of the triangle and begins, very slowly, to rotate upon its axis, so that each of our faces passes by in turn. All our faces are expressionless. The camera begins to turn faster, then faster still. Our faces blur into one another and then the camera is spinning so fast that all the faces disappear and there is only the blur, the speed lines, the motion. The people – the man, the woman, the child – are secondary. There is only the whirling movement of life.